UNIVERSE 2

EDITED BY
R O B E R T
SILVERBERG
AND
K A R E N
H A B E R

SPECTRA

BANTAM
BOOKS

NEW YORK
LONDON TORONTO
SYDNEY AUCKLAND

UNIVERSE 2
A Bantam Book / March 1992

Published simultaneously in hardcover and trade paperback

ISBN 0-553-08038-5
ISBN 0-553-35123-0 (trade paperback)
LC 91-643458
Published simultaneously in the United States and Canada

Bantam Books are published by Bantam Books, a division of Bantam
Doubleday Dell Publishing Group, Inc. Its trademark, consisting of
the words "Bantam Books" and the portrayal of a rooster, is Registered
in U. S. Patent and Trademark Office and in other countries.
Marca Registrada. Bantam Books, 666 Fifth Avenue, New York,
New York 10103.

PRINTED IN THE UNITED STATES OF AMERICA
FFG   0 9 8 7 6 5 4 3 2 1

FOR
PAT LO BRUTTO

CONTENTS

UNIVERSE 2

This is the second in a new series of anthologies of previously unpublished science fiction stories, carrying on the name and spirit of the distinguished *Universe* series that the late Terry Carr produced between 1971 and 1987. And that would really be all that needs to be said by way of introduction, if we were trying to be exceedingly concise. But this is a big book. There's room for a little amplification of that one-sentence statement of this volume's existential condition. And so I offer some amplification herewith:

This is the second in a new series

The *Universe* anthologies that Terry Carr edited bore the designation *Universe 1, Universe 2,* and so on up to *Universe 17,* the last one he edited. When my wife Karen Haber and I undertook the task of continuing *Universe* under our own editorship in 1988, we debated the wisdom of beginning with *Universe 18* or of calling the book *Universe —Second Series, Number One,* and decided against both, rejecting the first because it struck us as odd to begin over, under new auspices and in considerably different format, with the eighteenth volume in a series, and rejecting the second simply because it seemed cumbersome. It's our intention that our *Universe* be an appropriate successor to Terry's, maintaining and carrying forward his ideas of excellence in science fiction; but that doesn't mean that we are attempting to produce an exact replica of Terry's book under author auspices. Certainly we're trying to publish the sort of stories that Terry would have published had he lived, because we share his belief that the *Universe*/Carr kind of science fiction is a good kind of science fiction. But though the Silverberg-Haber *Universe* is similar in tone to the Terry Carr *Universe*, it isn't and can't be identical to it, and it would be folly to pretend otherwise. We have made a new beginning in Terry's name, using the name of his famous anthology. But the new series of *Universe* collections is not, much as we would like it to be, Terry Carr's *Universe*. It's Robert Silverberg and Karen Haber's *Universe*, published in honor of Terry Carr's memory. And so we've begun the numbering over from *Universe 1*.

of anthologies of previously unpublished

Well, that's actually a bit of a fib—this time only. One of the stories in this number of *Universe* actually was published earlier elsewhere, under a different title and in a somewhat different version. But it appeared only in a semiprofessional magazine of very limited circulation. It seemed to us too good to let it remain unknown to the general science fiction audience, and so we have included it (in its revised version) here. To protect the privacy of all involved in this bit of blatant chicanery, we don't propose to tell you which story it is, but the initials of its author are Brian W. Aldiss. And we advise potential contributors to *Universe 3*, for their own benefit, that we don't intend to use any such previously published material again, no matter how limited the edition of its first appearance, so please don't send us tear sheets of your stories from last year's issues of *Ectoplasm Journal* and *Galactic Gazette* in the hope that we'll snap them up. We want *Universe* to be an anthology of original fiction only. We made an exception for the Aldiss simply because we felt like making an exception, and because he's a friend of ours of many years' standing, and if you can't publish your friends' stories if you feel like it, regardless of existing policies and dogmas, what's the use of having your own anthology? So there. Besides, we liked it a lot. But we won't do it again. (Unless we do.)

science fiction stories

Here's a tough one. Terry Carr's *Universe* published science fiction, not fantasy (or horror stories, which nobody much was writing in those days anyway). Terry liked fantasy and even edited several anthologies of it, but he tried to keep it out of *Universe*, on the sensible grounds that *Universe* was a science fiction book and should publish only science fiction, if only for the sake of truth in packaging. Now and then he would publish a fantasy anyway, such as Fritz Leiber's "A

Rite of Spring" in *Universe* 7. When he did, though, it was for such reasons as the story's being irresistibly charming (as Leiber's was), or because the author was one he liked very much (he revered Leiber), or because he was able to make out a case of sorts, however slender, for the story's being science fiction instead of fantasy (Leiber's story was based on the "science" of numerology).

We feel pretty much as Terry did about these things. Karen and I read fantasy now and then and occasionally even write some. Each of us has written some horror stories also and (rather less frequently) has read some by other people. But we don't want to publish fantasy or horror fiction in *Universe*, since it's ostensibly a *science fiction* publication. So all those stories about nice families in Kansas who are terrorized by giant cockroaches emerging from their basements go back with rejection slips attached, and we don't care if the cockroaches are time-traveling mutant cockroaches or invaders from Betelgeuse IX; we say it's a horror story, and we say to hell with it.

But fantasy presents a more difficult problem, because it's not all that easy to distinguish it from science fiction, and we can easily run into all sorts of muddled problems of definition if we try to take a purist position. I have an easier time of it than Karen, because the boundaries between the two genres were very firmly drawn by some very ferocious editors during my formative years, and because I'm a fairly dogmatic and rigid sort: I "know" what fantasy is, I "know" what science fiction is, and I'm sure that I can tell the difference, except when I can't. A story about a killer virus is probably science fiction; a story about a virus that will grant you three wishes is fantasy, though it might be good fun, and we might even publish it if the biological end of the story was handled with enough ingenuity. (What would a story about the ghost of a robot be? Fantasy? Science fiction? How about the adventures of King Arthur in the twenty-third century? Once again, depends on the handling, I'd have to say: submit them to us and we'll let you know.) At any rate, we try to keep *Universe* free of elves, wizards, sorcerers, quests, and dragons. They're all entertaining notions in their place, as anyone old enough to remember John Campbell's legendary magazine *Unknown Worlds* will attest. But this isn't their place.

carrying on the name and spirit

I've already dealt with this part in the previous paragraphs. But one more recap won't hurt. *Universe*/Silverberg-Haber is intended to continue *Universe*/Carr in a way that the editor of the original series would admire. I have a pretty good idea of what he would admire: I knew him for close to thirty years, and we were neighbors and close friends for fifteen of those years. We argued endlessly but amicably about science fiction and we published many of each other's stories. (I had five in his *Universe* books, four in the first four numbers; he wrote three for me, I think, in the ten-year life of my *New Dimensions* anthology.) There will probably be half a dozen stories in each issue of the new *Universe* that Terry wouldn't remotely have considered publishing. (And I can very clearly see him grinning and saying, in his quiet, low-key way, "That's just the sort of stuff I'd have expected you to put in there, too.") But there will, I hope, be twice as many stories per volume that he'd have jumped on immediately in delight.

of the distinguished Universe *series*
I don't think anyone will give me any serious argument there. The seventeen Carr-edited issues of *Universe* published stories by Ursula K. Le Guin, Gene Wolfe, George Alec Effinger, Harlan Ellison, Gregory Benford, Brian W. Aldiss, Greg Bear, Michael Bishop, Edgar Pangborn, Joanna Russ, Bob Shaw, Jack Vance, John Varley, James Tiptree, Jr., and a lot of other splendid writers. A couple of those stories won Nebulas; a couple won Hugos. Terry won two Hugos himself—one of them posthumous—in the Best Editor category. Everyone respected *Universe* when it was in his hands; everyone read it to keep in touch with the best in new s-f; anyone who was everyone wrote for it, though publishing conditions in those days forced Terry to pay a laughably modest amount for the stories he ran. (Laughably? Not if you were trying to pay the rent with one of those checks . . .) "Distinguished" is the only word that applies. It's our plan—our hope, at least—to live up to the reputation of our illustrious predecessor.

that the late Terry Carr produced between 1971 and 1987.
For those who came in late, one last, sad bit of amplification:
Terry Carr was a lanky, genial, soft-spoken guy who was born in Oregon, grew up in San Francisco, went to New York in 1961 to take up an editing career, and returned to the San Francisco area a decade later to continue editing there. He began reading science fiction when he was about twelve, loved it passionately all his life, and both wrote and edited it with the deepest devotion. It was never just a job for him. Every word he produced (and he produced them slowly and with much

anguish) was a statement of true love. Young writers looked up to him with awe; established ones valued his advice and insight; everyone who had anything to do with science fiction over a thirty-year span admired him. I don't know anyone who disliked him; I find it hard to imagine how anyone could.

Early in the 1980s his health began to give way, and he weakened slowly but inexorably until he was barely able to leave the house. He died in April of 1987, a couple of months after his fiftieth birthday. The last time I saw him, it was at a science fiction convention; the last time I spoke with him, a week or so before his death, it was about a science fiction anthology he was editing (and which I had to complete on his behalf). Science fiction was by no means his whole life—far from it—but it certainly was central to his existence, and, in time, he became central to its. It was my unhappy task to notify the science fiction community that Terry had died; and in the next few days a startling outpouring of shock, disbelief, and expressions of love for him came back from all around the world.

The new series of *Universe* anthologies is, I suppose, his monument now. His name is no longer on the cover as editor, and more's the pity for that; but his imprint is on every page.

—Robert Silverberg
Oakland, California
November, 1990

This powerful, coolly told story of future warfare conducted by surrogate soldiers is the work of a professional photographer from St. Louis who took up writing science fiction a couple of years ago after spending a season at the Clarion Writers' Conference. He says this is the fourth story he's sold—but if the present work is any evidence of future performance, he's destined before long to reach that enviable level of accomplishment where he won't be able to give you such statistics, because he's too busy writing stories and selling them to keep an up-to-date score.

LIFE ON THE ARTIFICIAL HEART

MARK W. TIEDEMANN

The lid on the coffin closed over Gish. He wondered, briefly, if this would be the One, the time he would die. For the first time. Adrenaline rushed through him on the wake of anticipation. The socket linked to the base of his skull, his mind emptied into another place.

He emerged inside the skin of the sleek armored mongrel machine stationed at the base in the mountains of Sichuan Province. His body lay inert in its coffin in San Diego while his mind stretched his new limbs.

The others strutted around the staging area. Killer surrogates, war machines, they danced and capered like mad demons gaining control of new bodies. Then the word came down and Gish fell into formation with his mates. He was one of the sappers this time. He felt proud and pleased to be chosen. It was quite a responsibility, especially for the youngest member of the squad. They filed onto the launch area and took off. It was night, and moon had yet to rise.

Below was broken terrain, destroyed and poisoned. The squad skimmed the surface until they reached the Tongtian River. The squad leader, Coramel, ordered them into the water. Gish submerged into the river and powered the surrogate along through the murk and pollution. The entire region was rotting under the Sload terraforming, turning into something human flesh could not survive.

They encountered the first Sload outpost five hundred meters short of their objective. Underwater sensors swept through the grimy waters. Three machines broke off, left the water, and took the blister out. Coramel ordered the assault then.

The factory was snug against the bank

of the Qumar River near its junction with the Tongtian. Gish left the water and, in the grays and greens of his laser optics and radar scans, saw the collection of columns, spheres, cones, and boxes, red and yellow heat signatures identifying work-intensive areas, and reddish-orange smoke vomiting from the stacks.

Through his telemetry Gish pinpointed the strike areas and prepared his arsenal of small missiles, particle beams, lasers, and heavy-caliber slugs. Bright blue points glowed all over the factory.

Sload infantry fell out in their combat suits, large, distorted figures that moved with insectlike precision. Clouds of vapor provided them with cover, limiting the squad's ability to select individual targets. Coramel signaled the attack.

Gish poured fire into the clouds. He fended off attacks by missile and beam, keeping in mind that only sloppy troops got hit. Old Tarby had taught him to never lose his control, get lax. Gish walked through the defense perimeters, wishing for death even while he kept it at bay. He cut a path through them and drove for the factory and his assigned targets. Beams from the parapets began licking out at the squad. Shields went up, and from that point on it was all tenacity.

A bright flash in his telemetry indicated a squad mate gone. Sloppy, he reminded himself, envious of the death. He had not died yet, not passed that test. Not today, though. It would have to wait. He filled in the gap and pounded toward the factory.

Then they reached the walls. Beams sliced openings in the walls, missiles followed. The innards of the alien installation bellowed outward, burst. Explosions began to multiply upon each other.

He reached his primary objective and began drilling a hole through the thick wall. Another surrogate joined him. Cover was provided by four others. The hole punched through and he extruded a hose into the structure. This was the environmental blister for the Sloads, their home, where they did not need environmental suits. Gish began pumping pure oxygen into it. Oxygen was poison to them, deadly and corrosive. He wondered for a moment what kept them on Earth. But they were trying to alter Earth for themselves, so the question carried with it its own answer. He pumped oxygen.

The factory died. The Sload infantry was slaughtered, and the guts of the facility were strewn along the banks of the river. Gish imagined he could sense the aliens dying in the air he fed them.

They withdrew and returned to their base. Elated, they pranced on the staging area, charged from victory. Then it was over. Gish was pulled out of the link. He resisted leaving the surrogate, unwilling to surrender the power in the machine. But his senses faded until there was nothing left but the red the sun makes through closed eyelids. . . .

Gish walked alongside his squad mates into the Heartland. It was an enclosed mall that stretched between the military sector and San Diego proper, where military and civilian mingled freely and every entertainment that could be purchased was available. Coramel, Randall, Lacy, Van Hallis, and Tarby walked with him. They were all older, and they let their age show in their faces. But despite his youth, Gish felt one of them tonight. The raid had been successful, and he had done his part well.

Crisp neon and brittle lasers split up the damp-looking pavement, glassy geometries, and furry shadows of the bars, shops, and flops. It was always nighttime here. The shiny material of their blue uniforms caught the lights and darknesses.

They passed a flop, and the women and men in the windows beckoned them with smiles and gestures.

Van Hallis pointed and laughed. "Which ones are real, which are fake? Take your pick." He looked at the others and chuckled at Lacy's sour scowl. "Hard to tell, ain't it? Even our Newborn here"—he pointed at Gish—"could be a fake from the look of him. Young, smooth-faced. You expect to smell mother's milk on him."

Tarby stopped and put a hand to Van Hallis's chest. "You gonna start already?"

"Me? No! I'm just here to celebrate Apollo Squad's victory! Hell, I want to have a good time—"

"Then no more cracks about Gish."

Gish looked away, embarrassed. So much for my pride, he thought. He spotted a small clinic across the way where a person could have cosmetic surgery done to add years to the face. Gish sucked in his lips and walked on. Fake is fake, he thought, whether flesh or surrogate. He could not wait to grow older, though.

Lacy caught up to him and squeezed his neck. "Don't let him get to you. Van Hallis is cracked, you know."

Gish nodded, not trusting his voice.

They stopped outside of Samsey's and huddled. Van Hallis glared at Tarby, who ignored him.

"You children have fun," Van Hallis said, running his hand over

3

his bald head. "I got other plans. There's a vendor I want to check out."

"Souvenirs?" Lacy asked, her lips curling in disgust. "When are you going to stop buying those things? They're all fake, you know. No way is FEA going to let real Sload parts into the country except for the labs."

"The Federal Environmental Agency don't control everybody," Van Hallis said. He laughed.

"Go on," Tarby said. "Rest of us can celebrate, have a good time."

"Doin' what?" Van Hallis asked. "Getting drunk and making motions with one of Andrew's fakes?"

Coramel poked Van Hallis in the chest. "If we want. Go on. Just don't get busted. See you back at the barracks."

Van Hallis laughed and walked away.

Coramel shook his head. "I'm going to transfer him."

"Promises, promises," Randall said.

"Van Hallis is a candidate for rehab," Lacy said. "You ought to just ground him."

Coramel glared at her. "My decision, right?"

Lacy spread her hands.

"We're all candidates for rehab," Randall said, turning toward Samsey's. "So let's indulge in some."

Within, tables surrounded a sunken dance floor. Bodies writhed to the ominous insistence of pulse music; Gish wondered how many of the dancers were real, how many surrogates. Some of them seemed capable of moving in impossible ways. Among them were flickering holograms: naked bodies, body parts, geometric patterns, shifting clouds, strings of words forming slogans and platitudes worming between them. Harsh light filtered through the pall of smoke gathered above the spectators and burned Gish's eyes.

They skirted the dance floor to the left and headed for an archway at the rear. They entered a quieter room. Large booths and tables clustered before a long, brightly polished bar. The light was even and warm; bodysuited men and women waited tables under the watchful gaze of Andrew, the owner-bartender of Samsey's, who nodded to them as they entered.

Above the mirror behind the bar was a large tactical map. China, the Southeast Asia Peninsula, the Bay of Bengal, and India were all outlined in white. The Sload Reserve was a huge heelprint in the center of the Asian Continent, its southern and western boundaries defined by the curve of the Himalayas and the Karakoram Mountains. Blue Xs marked the most recent offensives. Beside each X was the squad logo and a paragraph detailing casualties and accomplishments. Apollo Squad's logo—stylized balances superimposed over the profile of a human brain—glowed prominently beside the X at the junction of the Qumar and Tongtian Rivers.

Mostly troops were present. Several looked up at them and raised their glasses in salute.

Lacy pointed at a tall, curly-haired waiter, and said to Randall, "I still say that one's real."

Randall shook his head. "Surrogate."

Tarby glanced at them. "Pity house rules don't let you just ask them."

Three troops from Deimos Squad sat at the table Gish and his mates stopped at. They looked up as Randall rested his knuckles on the edge of the table and leaned toward them, smiling. "This one's reserved for Apollo."

The oldest Deimos looked at the tactical display, nodded, and finished his drink. The others stood with him.

"Buy you a drink?" Coramel offered.

"No, thanks."

As they sat down, Lacy said, "Deimos hasn't done shit in months." She looked back at the waiter. "If he's fake, he's damn good."

"Why don't you just take him upstairs and find out that way?" Randall grinned. "That's what you want to do anyway."

Lacy scowled. "Nobody can tell that way." She chuckled sarcastically. "Maybe we could have Van Hallis check him out."

"Not amusing," Coramel said.

Lacy shrugged. "Maybe I'll take him upstairs later anyway. He's pretty."

A waitress stopped at the table. Gish stared at her breasts, cloudy and indistinct beneath the gauzy fabric of the bodysuit. With a start, he realized she was waiting for his order.

"Oh, uh . . . vodka."

She smiled and hurried off.

"I think she likes you," Randall said.

Gish blinked. "You think she's real?"

"Only one way to find out. Right, Lacy?"

The others chuckled. Tarby fingered the medallion that hung

from his neck. Gish eyed it admiringly. The Medal of Valor. Tarby's dark skin was like well-worn leather. He looked more like a grandfather than a soldier, but that medal testified to the steel capacity within him. Gish wanted to be like Tarby someday: old, respected, competent. Absently, he ran his fingers over the smooth skin of his own face. No lines, no roughness, nothing to give him age, dignity. For all anyone knew he was an expensive surrogate for some wealthy ancient in a private coffin somewhere. The only thing that set him apart was the uniform.

Drinks arrived. As the waitress walked away, Randall said, "Surrogate."

Tarby sighed. "I don't mind Van Hallis not being here, but I wish Lorenz, Ogilvie, and Mason had made it."

"Couple days in rehab, they'll be fine," Lacy said.

"True, but that won't matter. They'll miss my announcement." Tarby swallowed some beer. "I'm retiring. This was my last run."

Gish stared at Tarby, his heart slamming his ribs. Tarby looked at him evenly.

"You're sure about this?" Coramel asked. "You've been a troop longer than any of us. You've earned retirement, but . . ."

Tarby arched his eyebrows questioningly.

Randall said, "But what are you going to do with yourself?"

Tarby smiled. "You mean life as a civ isn't livable for a troop?" He grunted. "I've been a soldier for twenty-two years. I'm bored with it. I'm going to retire and do something else."

"But what else *is* there?" Gish blurted.

"Maybe I'll buy one of those expensive surrogates and be young again." He laughed at the shocked looks around him. "Funny. We operate surrogates in combat and that's okay, that's honorable. But people who use them privately are somehow . . . soiled."

"There's no delusion in what we do," Lacy said. "Our surrogates aren't remotely human. We don't lie to ourselves."

"We don't, huh? Well, maybe not. It's a fine point." Tarby shook his head. "I've died six times in a surrogate. I don't like the idea that the next one will be my breakdown. Besides, I'm sick of Van Hallis and his type. Military's full of them. He ought to be in a rubber room, and I don't want to end up like him."

"But you're an artist," Gish said. "You work a surrogate like nobody else."

"You haven't seen that many. The man who taught me ended up

carrying on a three-way conversation between himself, Jesus, and his ex-wife, all inside a cell that provided every physical need. He soiled himself, the room cleaned him up. He hurt himself, the room fixed him. He tried to starve himself, the room fed him. He finally figured out how to just turn himself off and die. After seven years. The room couldn't fix that."

Gish laughed nervously. "That won't happen to you."

Tarby nodded. "True. I'm retiring before it does. I used to think *he* was the best. But he'd only been killed five times before he lost it. Others I knew were luckier. They came out of their surrogates catatonic and stayed in coma till they died. Others, though, end up twisted like Van Hallis. Not me. I'm out."

Coramel raised his glass. "I wish you good luck."

Gish joined the toast, thinking, he won't quit, not really, he can't, it's all he knows, all I know.

Randall made jokes and they all laughed and some semblance of their earlier mood returned. Gish felt emptied of something vital, though. He looked around at all the troops and tried to imagine not being one. The attempt formed a thin membrane separating him from the laughter around him. He felt apart, lost, and he hated Tarby now. That would pass, he knew, but it ruined everything for the time being. He did not want to be there.

He pushed away from the table and stood. "I think I'm going upstairs before I'm too drunk to appreciate it."

"Hey," Lacy said, "they got shit for that. Two little pills, sober you up in a minute."

Tarby looked at him sympathetically. "Gish—"

"Not now," he said. "Maybe later."

"Hey, Apollo!" A tall, thin troop wearing the stylized armature against a black background patch of Zeus Squad tumbled into an empty chair and grinned at them. Her eyes were large and unfocused.

"That chair's reserved," Randall said.

She waved a hand. "Sure, sure. I won't be here long. Just wanted to sit with you all for a minute, soak up some of the glory. Chatter says you did a righteous one on the Sloads yesterday. If it's okay, Zeus would like to buy you all a round of whatever."

"Thanks," Randall said, "but—"

"That'd be fine," Coramel cut in. "We'd appreciate that."

Zeus smiled broadly. "Hey! Righteous! Be right back." She stood uncertainly, wavered, and almost fell. Gish caught her, and she grasped his shoulder. She blinked at him for a few seconds. "Hey, surrogates are great, aren't they?"

Gish tensed, prepared to shove her away, but saw Coramel's warning look. He drew a deep breath. "You're wasted, Zeus. I'm Apollo Squad."

Zeus looked puzzled, then glanced at his uniform. "Sure, sure, sorry." She laughed then. "Newborns all look like surrogates." Laughing louder, she staggered away across the room to her own table.

"Don't let it get to you, son," Tarby said.

"I said later," Gish snapped, and strode to the bar.

Andrew came over to him. The look in the big bartender's eyes told Gish he had witnessed everything. Gish blushed and looked down at his hands.

"A girl," he said, and, as Andrew reached below the bar, added, "Someone with time in her face."

Andrew slid a black disk across the bar. Gish pressed his thumb to it, imprinting it, and headed to a curtained doorway.

He pushed through the curtains and stood in a small space with four exits. Behind him was the bar; to the right led to rest rooms; the left led upstairs. The one straight ahead led to a restaurant Gish had never been in.

As he prepared to mount the stairs to the left, three people—two women and a man—came from the restaurant and went through the curtain into the bar. All were well-dressed. The woman in the lead wore a cream blouse with broad shoulders that came to points and a neckline that plunged to her waist, with ballooning pants to match. She was very young and beautiful.

Surrogate, Gish thought with distaste. Rich folks in robot bodies, too afraid to taste life directly.

The man wore a light-blue tunic that vaguely resembled a uniform, and Gish grabbed him, held him back.

"What—hey!"

Gish shoved him into the rest room and pushed him up against a urinal. The man's feet slipped on the tile and he fell, his right hand landing in the pool at the urinal's base.

"Not you," Gish said. "The other two are bad enough, but you—"

The man tried to stand, his face red with anger. Gish brought the heels of his hands down sharply on both collarbones. The man winced and collapsed. Gish chopped him behind the ear, and he sprawled, face in another urinal.

The two women stood outside the door.

"No washouts," Gish said. "No vultures." He brushed by them and mounted the stairs.

At the top, fuming, he looked at the disk. Number eight. He rubbed the plastic between thumb and middle finger. His hands ached dully. He wondered if number eight was authentic, a real girl. How could he tell? Andrew never permitted anyone to ask. It was impolite in any case, but that didn't stop some people. Like Van Hallis.

He imagined Tarby climbing into a coffin, entering the interface, emerging from a closet as a young, flawless man to interact with the world, never actually touching it. Gish shuddered.

The door to number eight slid aside.

"Hello. I'm Inga."

Large blue eyes looked up at him. She had light hair that fell to her shoulders. A pale-blue bodysuit obscured her body, but she seemed athletic, slim and muscled. Gish was mildly disappointed—she was very young, impossible to tell if she was real or fake.

"I'm Gish," he said, and stepped into the room.

The door closed behind him. The room possessed a veneer of luxury. The bed was large and round, the lighting soft and indirect, helping maintain the illusion of opulence. Inga went to the small bar.

"What do you drink?"

"Vodka."

"Mix it with some orange?"

"Sure."

She mixed it and brought it to him. Hell, he thought, nobody makes surrogates that look that young. She's real!

The cold, sweaty glass felt good in his palm. Inga glanced at his shoulderpatch.

"Apollo. I'm flattered. You're on top today."

"We had three deaths. It wasn't cheap. They're recovering, though." Gish put the glass to his mouth. He felt himself preparing to ask the forbidden, insulting question. On impulse, instead, he touched her cheek. The skin was warm, satiny. Inga moved into his embrace and kissed him.

She tastes real, he thought. No surrogate's mouth is that soft.

Inga stepped back. "Don't you want to finish your drink first?" She tilted her own glass to her mouth, and her eyes teased him over the rim.

Gish laughed. "Sorry. It's been some kind of day."

"Sit down, let me take your boots off."

He obeyed, dropping back on the couch. Inga unzipped his boots and slid them off, then knelt and gently massaged his feet. Suddenly his tension began to leave.

"Want to tell me about it?" she asked.

"Not really supposed to."

"But . . . ?"

He closed his eyes, enjoying her hands. "You ever been in a surrogate link?"

"No. There's one in the army museum that's open to the public, but there's always a line. I hate lines."

Gish smiled. "Well, using a Gate is . . . I don't know . . . incredible. Some of my mates tell me it gets ordinary after a while, but I can't believe that. You link up and suddenly you're alive inside steel skin with enhanced senses and power. You can fly, submerge, roll cross country."

"Have you died yet?" She moved her hands up to his calves.

"Not in combat. I've been on eight runs now and haven't lost one. There's this old man in my squad, Old Tarby, must be sixty years old. He taught me. Really knows his stuff."

"I guess he's a good teacher."

"He's retiring. I'm going to miss him a lot."

She worked at his thighs. "Sounds like he deserves it."

He looked at her. "But what's he going to *do*? What does a soldier do with himself when he quits?"

"What would you do?"

"Huh! I'm never going to retire. This is my job. I've been wanting to be a soldier since I can remember."

"The war's going to end someday. What then?"

Gish looked at her blankly. He suddenly felt terribly young and inexperienced. She seemed to sense that he could not answer. She squeezed his hand. Gish automatically pulled her up. She slid up his legs, into his arms, in a fluid motion, and Gish closed his hand over her buttocks. He set his drink on the end table and grasped her hair. He tried to kiss her mouth, but Inga twisted aside and caught his ear between her lips. For a moment Gish was very aware of his youthfulness as she unzipped his uniform and explored his almost hairless chest. Then the ill ease passed, subsumed in his rising sexual urgency. He found her mouth. Hips strained toward each other. No way she's a surrogate, he thought, and tugged at the bodysuit. Her nipples were hard nodes. His hands pressed her warm flesh as he pushed the fabric down. It caught at her hips, and she had to pull away to get the suit off. She coiled herself in his lap and explored his body beneath his uniform. They tumbled onto the floor. Gish felt clumsy, giddy, and laughed while Inga adroitly undressed him. She pinned his shoulders to the carpet. In less than a minute all his anxiety centered itself and passed from his body into hers. He shook with the sudden exhilarating weakness.

She lay against him, lightly kissing his neck.

"Sorry," Gish breathed. "Didn't mean to be in such a rush."

"We've got all night if you like."

He laughed bitterly.

"What is it?"

"Just thinking about Tarby. How I want to be like him. I'm tired of people wondering if I'm real or fake. Or worse, a washout. When I came up here I stopped a washout from going into the bar."

"What's a washout?"

"Someone who didn't pass the exams to join and won't let it go. They dress sort of like troops, try to act like us around people who don't know the difference."

She licked his nipple. He squeezed a breast lightly.

"Sorry. I'm being morbid."

"No, you're not. You're being fashionable. Personally, I hope I never grow old."

Gish gaped at her. "How the hell will anybody ever know if you're real or not?"

She shrugged. "I'll know." Slowly, her hand moved down his belly. "I don't think too many people would have any doubts for very long, do you?"

Gish laughed. Then he lost his concentration on anything else but Inga. She made love to him slowly, studiously, and when he came it surprised him. He gasped, clutched her thighs, and she laughed. Gish hugged her and smelled her hair and muskiness. Sweat covered them both. Gish ran a finger down her neck, over a collarbone, around her left breast, across her stomach. Muscles shifted, tissue resisted with sensuous pliancy. Real, he thought.

After a time she got up and made him another drink. Gish propped himself up on an elbow as she dropped into an easy lotus beside him. He drank deeply. The liquid was cold.

"This isn't booze, is it?" he asked.

11

"No, it's a nutrient mix that tastes like a collins." She smiled. "You don't want to crash, do you? Not yet."

He laughed and shook his head.

"You never answered me," she said. "What will you do when the war is over?"

"Come back here and make love to you for a month." He laughed with her, then shook his head. "I honestly don't know. Never thought about it."

"What's—Tarby?—what's he going to do?"

Gish shrugged. "He's quitting because he's died six times and he's afraid he might crack next time."

"What's it like to die in a surrogate?"

"Well, I don't really know. I mean, in training they kill you once so they can fill in the last blank in the psych profile. When the carrier wave is disrupted, there's a few-second lag while the equipment sorts out the retrieval program and reinstates you back into your own body. You go completely blank, no sensation at all. Total sensory deprivation. Sometimes it feels like an eternity, I hear."

Gish thought of Van Hallis. He wore a manic grin when he got into his coffin. Van Hallis had died four times since Gish had been with the squad. He kept a locker full of fake Sload parts. Coramel kept threatening to transfer him, retire him, muster him out, get rid of him, but he never did. Van Hallis was an incredible combat asset. Gish wondered if he would become like Van Hallis after a few deaths.

"After I retire," he said, just to distract himself, "I'll have money. Maybe I'll buy a surrogate and retire to an estate, go out in public only in my private surrogate body. I hear that's real popular among the privy rich."

"You're kidding. You work with surrogates all the time. Why would you want to keep doing it?"

Gish cast around for a smart response, but his head was empty. He shrugged, finished his drink, and stood.

Inga moved to the bed and leaned back on her elbows, one leg dangling over the edge. Gish had not realized until that moment that he had intended to dress and leave; he knew now only because he changed his mind.

He moved in slow motion. He wanted to do to her what she had done for him, surprise her with her own responses. She answered his lovemaking with a kind of sensual deliberateness that fed him.

Can't surprise a surrogate, he thought as he entered her. Then, angrily: she's real, dammit! God, how real!

And he was surprised again, unable to control himself. He fell across her in gauzy exhaustion. He watched her face for a long time, the way her nostrils moved, the way she licked her upper lip, the way sweat beaded and broke and trailed down her cheek, felt the gentle rhythm of her right thigh against his hip and the oily dampness between their bellies. Real. So real.

Gish wanted to ask.

"Mmm," she purred, "I think I'll tell Andrew to give you credit next time."

He kept the question to himself.

They laughed and played in the shower, lathering each other up. "Aren't you tired yet?" she teased him as he pushed her against the wall. Her face relaxed, and she climbed up his body and hung on in the stream of hot water. His temples throbbed with the steam and kinesis.

"Hurry back," she said as he left. He kissed her and walked toward the stairs, feeling substantiated.

The restaurant appeared almost empty. For a moment, Gish considered entering and having an expensive meal. Instead he turned back toward the bar.

Tarby stood at the bar and looked at him as he came in. In seconds, all the anxiety Inga had worked away returned. He stopped beside Tarby.

"Have a good time?" Tarby asked.

"I'm satisfied."

Tarby nodded. Andrew set a mug of beer before him and moved on. "You're pretty angry at me."

Gish wanted to deny it. He hated feeling this way toward Tarby. "I don't understand. Don't you like us anymore?"

"Sure I like you. That's got nothing to do with it. I'm just tired, that's all."

"All my life all I wanted was to be a troop."

"And kill Sloads?"

"No. Just be a troop, whatever we did."

"The uniform, the respect, the excitement, more important than anything else."

"I—"

Tarby shook his head. "Gotta be more, Gish. This is all just dress-

13

ing up and playing a game. Complicated, dangerous game, but still a game."

Gish pointed at the medal. "That's just a game?"

Tarby looked down at his chest and nodded. Then he sighed and removed it, shoved it into Gish's hand. "This is for you. Keep it as long as it means something to you."

Gish gaped at the gold disk. A warm feeling he could not name suffused him, and his eyes burned. "But, Tarby, this is a part of you."

Tarby nodded. "Just so. Maybe as long as I mean something to you you'll keep it." Tarby picked up his beer and took a long pull on it. He grunted. "I've spent twenty-two years fighting Sloads, and you know I still don't know what one really looks like. Seen more 'artist's concepts' than I can remember, but all I ever saw for real was their suits and the explosions that followed after I punctured them. Do you know what started the war?" Gish shook his head. "They came here in peace about forty years ago. We welcomed them. They built an enclave high up in the Himalayas. Then, about ten years later, we got hit with another epidemic. Nasty disease. We asked them for help, and they refused. Said they couldn't, they didn't understand our biology, and maybe, just maybe, it was likely they'd do more harm than good. Well, a lot of hotheads accused them of starting it. Didn't matter if it were true, people were panicked, afraid. The move that started everything was the Chinese deciding that the Sloads really did have a cure and they were going to take it. We've been fighting ever since."

"Why didn't the Sloads just leave?"

Tarby shrugged. "Not long after the shooting started it got dangerous to ask questions like that."

"And the epidemic?"

"Went away. Nobody's noticed."

Gish looked at the medal in his hand. "Tarby, I don't—"

"No argument. I want you to have it. I never had kids."

Gish smiled awkwardly and dropped the medal into his pocket.

Gish looked toward their table and frowned: Van Hallis had returned. Zeus was still there and so was a civ, with Coramel and Randall.

"He came back half an hour ago," Tarby said. "She came in an hour ago."

"Where's Lacy?"

"She took the waiter upstairs."

14

Gish chuckled. Tarby slapped his back, and they returned to the table.

"Well, well," Randall said, "you certainly look satisfied."

"So I am." Gish dropped into a chair.

Van Hallis grinned. "Andrew's fakes'll wear a man out."

"You're back kind of soon."

"Can't spend *all* my money on souvenirs! Got to have some for the body!" He leaned closer. "Got a good one this time, though. Even got me a contact for when I start bringing them in."

Coramel glared. "Nobody in my squad takes souvenirs. You start that and you're ground support."

Van Hallis stared back.

"Hey, Gish," Randall said, "meet Susan Mead." He gestured at the civ beside him.

Gish turned. Cream blouse, cream pants—Gish was startled to recognize her from earlier. The surrogate from the restaurant. He smiled tightly and nodded. He looked at her neck, the gentle rise and fall of her breathing, the bright eyes—yes, fake, he decided, a surrogate, first-rate. He pictured some wealthy old—*very* old—woman climbing into an interface coffin and worming her being into this body. Gish shivered; there was an obscenity to it he could not quite place.

"Enjoying the evening?" he asked.

"I just came to show my appreciation for what you're all doing," she said.

Zeus looked as though she was about to laugh. Van Hallis rolled his eyes. Randall was clearly interested in her.

"We appreciate the appreciation," Tarby said.

"Certainly we do," Van Hallis said. "Tell me, Susan Mead, have you ever seen a Sload?"

She looked at him suspiciously. "No. Media's pretty strict about such things. You all handle it so well that there's really no need for us to have firsthand reports—"

"You people don't even get fifth-hand," Van Hallis said. He pulled a crumpled wrapper from his jacket. "And speaking of hands . . ."

Gish felt cold suddenly. He wanted to make an excuse and leave, but inertia held him.

Van Hallis continued in mock-lecture tones. "You see, Sloads got four hands. Their feet are prehensile, too, like monkeys, only bigger.

15

They can't breathe air, so they go around in environmental suits when they're outside. When we go into one of their installations we like to punch holes in their habitats and pump oxygen in. Kills 'em the way cyanide does us. Then you get to take souvenirs."

He unwrapped the paper. It contained a long thin hand with six fingers and two opposable thumbs. It was dried, desiccated, and a sickly greenish-brown color. Wrinkles and empty veins gave it a cracked upholstery look.

Susan Mead stared at it.

Zeus blew out a breath, shaking her head. "You guys in Apollo are sometimes just a little much."

"Put that away," Coramel said.

"Hey!" someone yelled. "Something's breaking!"

Gish looked up at the tactical map behind the bar. Troops were all staring, moving closer. The room grew quieter.

Susan Mead inhaled deeply. "That's . . ."

"Shit," Randall said, staring at the board.

A squad was making a move deep into the reserve. Arrows from the north moved directly at the marshes of Lake Lop Nur, almost at the center of the Sloads.

". . . very . . ."

Van Hallis glared at Susan Mead. "Who the hell invited her here, anyway? She's got no business bein' here during—"

"You're an ass, Van Hallis," Tarby said.

On the board, symbols shifted swiftly. Sload artillery responded. A huge compound existed beneath the waters of the lake, spread out under the marshes. Orbital particle beams had been unable to get through the shielding. Gish watched the advance of the squad and knew this was impossible.

". . . inter . . ."

"Jesus!" Zeus hissed.

The entire squad vanished. Scratched. Nine troops, dead. Gish felt his stomach churn. He looked away.

". . . resting . . ."

Van Hallis shook. He glared at Zeus, then at Susan Mead. "Jesus shit!"

". . . Is it real?"

16   "Real?" Van Hallis bellowed. "They're all dead! Damn right it's real!"

Susan Mead frowned, then looked up at the map. "I meant . . ."

"I know what you meant!" Van Hallis slammed his hand, palm down, on the edge of the table. The souvenir jumped. "Damn right it's real! It cost me enough! Realer than you are! Who the hell invited you here, anyway?" He looked around the table, eyes large.

Gish thought about Inga and wanted to go back upstairs. He looked at Tarby, who stood silently staring at the map.

"This is a private party," Van Hallis went on. "Troops only, and someone invites a fake to sit with us!"

"I beg your pard—"

"Surrogate! None o' you richies come out of your little hovels in the flesh. You all use surrogates!"

"I think I'll be going," Susan Mead said, rising.

Van Hallis grabbed her wrist. "No, don't go yet! Tell us what it's like being part-time real. What's life like through a surrogate all the time?"

"I wouldn't know. Please let go."

Coramel reached across the table for him, but Van Hallis slapped his hand off, backed away from the table.

"Uh-uh! This thing sits here with us, who're all real, even the Newborn here, even Zeus over there, and then lies to us! You're surrogate, bitch! Now come on and tell us about it."

"I'm as real as you are," Susan Mead said, twisting her wrist. "Now let me go."

Van Hallis laughed. "You're no realer than the plastic zips Andrew keeps upstairs. Now, I want the truth!"

Gish moved on him, reached for his arm. Van Hallis gave him a startled look, then snapped his elbow up. Pain spiked up Gish's nose, and he fell back against the table. He smelled blood, tasted metal. His eyes teared.

"I want the truth!" Van Hallis said. He laughed. "They make them pretty good nowadays, don't they? Body temperature, pulse, blush response—they even lube up at the right times!"

Coramel was moving around the table, Randall flanking him. Van Hallis kicked Coramel in the solar plexus and backed farther away.

"No, fake, the truth will out!"

Suddenly there was a knife in his hand, a long, painfully bright blade. Gish watched from the floor, frozen in place.

"Shit!" someone said.

Van Hallis hacked down at her, caught her left breast. She screamed sharply, and her blouse flowered in red.

17

"Damn," Van Hallis cried, backing away. "They even make 'em bleed these days! This thing must've cost a fortune!"

Susan Mead stumbled away, fell against Randall. Gish pushed himself to his feet and tackled Van Hallis. They crashed across a table. Chairs skittered noisily out of their way. Gish groped with the hard, heavy body, trying to remember pressure points. He saw the knife glint and grabbed for it. He managed to get on top, saw Van Hallis's wide, crazy eyes, and drove his fist straight down. Blood spattered across Van Hallis's face from his nose.

Then two nodes of pain erupted in his torso, one below his left ribs, the other in his sternum. Van Hallis brought up his knee, and Gish fell away.

Van Hallis got to his feet, turned—

And Tarby was there. They faced each other for a moment. Then Van Hallis thrust the knife. Gish winced and shouted.

Tarby bent forward slightly, and his mouth compressed in effort. He raised Van Hallis's arm. Van Hallis pushed back. For an instant it was static, a tableau, and Gish's heart hammered.

Then Tarby kicked Van Hallis in the groin, twisted the knife hand until there was a loud crack of bone breaking. The knife fell. Van Hallis dropped to his knees.

Sweat rolled from Tarby's face.

"Somebody get some meds in here!" Randall shouted.

Gish's hands shook. After Susan Mead was carried out on a stretcher, a med taped Gish's nose and gave him some painkillers. Tarby sat at the table, staring at the floor. Gish sat beside him.

"Funny," Gish said, holding up his hand. "All the times I've been in combat I never reacted like this."

Tarby looked at him silently.

Gish looked away, for some reason embarrassed, and saw the souvenir on the table. He picked it up and turned it over. It was not cold or clammy the way it appeared. It was resilient. Frowning, Gish worked a fingernail into it. The material split apart.

"Polyfoam," he said.

"What did you expect?" Tarby asked.

"Nothing," Gish said. He looked at Tarby again. "You . . . I couldn't help thinking how . . . strong you looked. You were—"

"Great? Heroic?" Tarby grunted, then wiped his face with his hand. "Yeah, maybe. Being a hero is mainly just doing what's necessary. Nobody asks any more why something's necessary." He drew a deep breath. "Hungry? I am."

"I feel like I could sleep for a week."

"Later, okay? I'd appreciate the company."

Gish looked at the old man and nodded. Tarby smiled.

Later, he said good-bye on the street outside. He watched Tarby walk away and still could not sort out how he felt about him anymore.

Gish turned to go . . . somewhere . . . he did not know where.

A girl stepped out onto the street. She wore a dark, shiny jacket and black pants and boots. When she turned away from the door, she stopped.

"Hi," Gish said.

"Hello," Inga said.

"Uh . . ."

"It's against house rules," she said, stepping up to him.

Gish scowled. "You're not in the house anymore."

She smiled. "True."

"Can I walk with you?"

"Yes."

They walked in shared silence for thirty paces.

Abruptly, Inga said, "I'm real. Not a surrogate."

Gish frowned. "I wasn't going to ask."

"But you wondered. All night. I could feel it. It . . . changes the way someone treats you." She laughed self-consciously. "You don't have any idea how badly I want to tell people that I'm real, so they can stop wondering and just enjoy me."

Gish swallowed. "Thanks."

She glanced at him. "Would you like to come home with me? Just to sleep. I mean—"

"I think I'd like that."

She lived in a small apartment a few streets from the civilian entrance to the Heartland. Gish watched her straighten a few things up, unsure what to do, how to act. When she started doing dishes, he moved her aside and did them himself.

"I heard about what happened tonight," Inga said. "Is that how you got hurt?"

Gish nodded.

"Is there anything I can do? To help, I mean?"

19

Gish set the last glass in the drainer, turned off the water, and dried his hands. He pulled her into a hug and held her.

"You already did," he said.

In bed, Inga pressed herself against him, and he wanted to absorb every sensation of her real skin against his. He resented his weariness then, for an instant wished he had the stamina of a surrogate so he could go on *feeling*, then felt foolish. Even the weariness was welcome then. He surrendered to sleep, and his senses faded until there was nothing but the black the moon makes through closed eyelids.

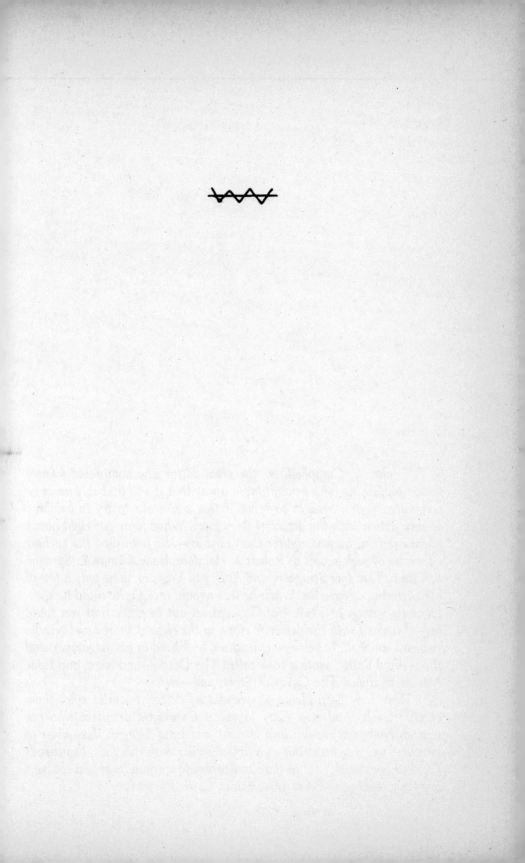

John W. Campbell, Jr., the great editor who dominated science fiction publishing for a generation in a way that it will probably never be dominated again, used to say that it was a mistake to try to combine science fiction with the detective-story form. When John was right about science fiction, he was righter than anybody—he published the earliest s-f stories of such people as Robert A. Heinlein, Isaac Asimov, L. Sprague de Camp, Theodore Sturgeon, and A. E. van Vogt, to name only a few of his glittering discoveries. When he was wrong, though, he could be spectacularly wrong. In 1949, Hal Clement set out to prove that you could indeed fuse s-f with the detective story, in the elegant short novel Needle (which Campbell, in some mortification, serialized in his magazine), and then Alfred Bester wrote a book called The Demolished Man, and Isaac Asimov produced The Caves of Steel, and—well—

There have been plenty of splendid s-f detective stories since those classic novels. And now Cary James, a California architect who has written books on Frank Lloyd Wright and Julia Morgan, has given us another—making his debut as a fiction writer with this taut, beautifully handled puzzle-story set in the claustrophobic surroundings of a spacegoing ferry making the slow trip back to Earth from Mars.

AUTOMATIC DEATH

CARY
JAMES

The noise of machinery woke him, a valve closing, a pump starting in the ship's hull beside his ear. His heart beat rapidly and one wrist hurt, and when he shook his head, annoyed, someone said, "Oh, don't move."

He opened his eyes. A woman with rosy cheeks and cropped blond hair bent over him. She had raised the clear poly cover of his berth. An intravenous tube ran from his arm into a medical robot, an old R3X. "I'll have you awake in a minute, Inspector," she said.

"Are we docking?" he asked, and remembered at once this was not how they woke you, docking.

"We're three days out." She drew a hesitant breath. "It's Jerry. He's dead."

"Dead?" The word made an empty noise in his brain.

"You are a policeman, aren't you?" Her blue eyes were damp and faintly bloodshot. She worked at the robot's keys, drew out the needle, put a healpatch on his wrist. Her hands were soft and cold. She was very pretty.

"Dead?" he repeated.

She handed him his packet of clothes. "I'll be in there. Come on, Rex." The short cylindrical robot followed her out through a sliding door.

He swung his legs out over the edge. The worn vinyl floor was cool under his bare feet. Under the thin light the beige walls were chipped and stained. Cylindrical berths curved up into the dark on both sides, a hundred sleepers or more on the ferry falling through its long inbound orbit from Mars. Next year, he thought, I'll be grade three, I'll take the express. He peeled off the paper

robe and stepped into his oversuit. His heart still beat from the stimulant. Someone was dead, and he had never done a homicide.

She sat in a narrow office, staring at wall visuals. As he came in
she punched a wrong key and swore and quickly hit three more.

"There." She pointed at the display. "Richard Mays. Inspector
four. But what's Five Division?"

"Electronic fraud. Machine embezzlement."

"Oh."

He thought she went a little pale. "What's your name?"

"Lily Easton. Medical officer."

"And who is dead?"

"Jerry." She stood up quickly and grasped the padded rungs of a
ladder. "Jerry's the captain, he's on the bridge."

Mays followed her up into a rapidly failing gravity. She pulled
herself easily through the center tunnel, but he fumbled for handholds
and bounced off walls, and his empty stomach lurched in the weightlessness. They emerged into a wide bright ring of space, and he drifted
awkwardly into a padded bulkhead.

The walls here were a dull red, like old metal. The ship's visuals
filled an entire sector, and a long narrow desk ran beneath them. A
man sat there, his head in his arms as if he were asleep.

Mays climbed down into a new gravity that did not comfort him.
"You found the body?"

"Yes." She would not look at the dead man. "Half an hour ago."
She picked up a paperpad and read in a dull voice, "Day two seventy-
three, hour four thirty-seven."

The time screen over the captain read 273/05:11.

"Good," said Mays, "it's important to write things down." He
took the pad from her. The writing was so shaky he could hardly read
the numbers. "What was his full name?"

"Alexander Samuel Gerakian."

The dead man had broad shoulders and a full head of dark hair.
He wore gray trousers and a short-sleeved shirt and might have been
asleep, except that his handsome face had gone gray and a stain had
invaded his lower cheek like a purple shadow.

The sight of it set the adrenaline running in his veins again. "How
many crew?" Mays asked.

24   "Jerry and Anna and Chor. And me." She nodded at the ranked
displays. "Thalia's automatic."

"Who is Anna?"

"Razavasky, ship's engineer. It's her watch." She bent and peered at a small screen. "But she's down in the thrusters."

"And Chor?"

"Chor Taung. Ship's second." She gestured behind them at a row of cabin doors, up the curving deck. "He's still asleep."

"If it wasn't your watch, why were you here?"

"I always bring her coffee." A closed mug sat at the far end of the desk. "But Jerry was here." She shook her head sharply. "At first I thought he was asleep. But he wouldn't wake up. Somebody must have killed him."

"So you woke me."

"Yes."

"You each take six-hour watches?"

"Anna, Chor, Jerry, and then me. This is Anna's watch. Jerry should be asleep." She pushed her fingers through her short hair again. "He was in excellent health."

Mays caught a whiff of shock behind her pale eyes. "You brought her coffee. Are you good friends?"

"This was our sixth cycle together." At last she glanced at the body.

Six Mars cycles, he thought. He tried to imagine the four of them alone, inside this lumbering ship, not even a window to look out. Maybe twenty-five hundred days. They must have grown as close as a family. No wonder she's in pain.

"I'll need a full crew print," he said. "On paper."

She chewed her lip a moment before she tapped on the input pad. A small light glimmered above a thin slit, and a paper sheet slid out and dropped on the desk.

"Good," said Mays. "I will need the black box, too."

She shook her head. "Anna will know how."

"And the medical robot."

She lifted her head and called, "Rex."

Rex, thought Mays. Faithful Rex, fifth member of the family.

A brighter light flashed behind her, up the ramp. A small door slid open, and the R3X trundled down to them.

"I want a full scan," he said, "time of death, probable cause, odd chemicals, neural problems."

She bent over the robot, punching keys. "Rex is weak on diagnosis."

"It'll all go to Cassini anyway. What's your idea?"

25

She straightened up and took a breath, and made her voice impersonal. "Rigor had set in. I'd say three hours."

"Cause of death?"

She glanced away and shook her head.

"You're the medic, Easton."

"I really don't know."

The R3X clamped a pair of articulated bands around the captain's left arm and began to sing to itself.

"Jerry was in good health?" Mays asked.

"I told you that."

Now, he thought, we reach the tight-lipped phase.

He looked at the desk. It was neat and almost bare: the mug of coffee, a hand computer, two pens, a paperbook of docking trajectories. He tried to remember homicide procedure. He had no way to bag the stuff. Everybody's DNA would be on everything anyway. Even if the robot could read it.

"Was he a tidy man? Jerry?"

"We all try to keep everything in its place."

"Why was he calculating docking by hand?"

"I don't know. Ask Anna. Ask Chor."

He had written "Easton TOD 02:00" on his pad. "Where were you at two?"

"Monitoring the sleepers." She relaxed a bit, on familiar ground now. "I do it at twenty-four hours. After my watch."

"How long does it take?"

"Two hours, two and a half, there's a hundred forty-three this trip."

"You keep a record?"

"We're legally required. It'll be in the black box."

"You finished at two-thirty?"

"I spent half an hour rechecking a few older passengers. I did a . . . I ran a maintenance check on Rex. I dozed off. About an hour, I guess." She gave him a little smile. "I haven't been sleeping well. It happens sometimes, at the end of trips."

Above them a woman's voice called, "Hallo, Lily. Who's that?" A tall figure in a yellow oversuit came rapidly down the ladder. Her voice was deeper than Easton's. She wore her long black hair in a single braid, and she stared at Mays.

"Richard Mays, Inspector." Her energy excited him. He grinned at her and wished they had met, off duty, on Luna or Mars. He wished that about a lot of women.

"A cop?" She did not take his offered hand, but turned and stared at the captain. "Is Jerry sick?"

Mays watched her. "He's dead."

"Dead?" She put a hand on the man's shoulder and shook him gently. "Dead? My god, he was alive when I left him."

"When did you last see him?"

She had lifted her fingers quickly away. She did not look at Mays. "There was an anomaly in thruster Seven." Her voice had gone tight and choked. "I asked him to take part of my watch. It was a little after one." She blinked. "My god, do you think I killed him?"

Easton was ready to weep again. "I'm sorry, Anna, I thought Jerry'd been killed, so I woke him."

"Lily."

The two women stared at each other. Beside them, unnoticed, the R3X disconnected its bands. It gave a brief whistle and rolled back half a meter. Its little monochrome screen lit up: TOD: 273/14:28 ± 00:30: CARDIAC DYSFUNCTION [PROB 0.9].

Mays broke the silence. "Did he have a bad heart?"

"No," said Easton.

"People just don't die," Anna said. She looked down at the captain again. "My god, he's just sitting here. Can't you cover him, can't you move him?"

Mays ignored her. "I want an analysis of that coffee, too."

Easton frowned. "He was dead when I got here, Inspector."

"And I want to call Luna."

Anna pointed at a handphone among the lights. Mays picked it up and pressed LUN. He heard the usual hollow echoes, the thin waves of static, and then a woman's voice, surprisingly clear.

"Luna Central, can you hold, please?"

"Police," he said quickly, hoping she was not a machine. "I want Cassini Station, right away."

There was hardly any pause for distance. "Yes, Police, can you hold, please?"

"I want Cassini. This is Police Inspector Mays, aboard the ferry . . ." He glanced at the nameplate beneath the clock. "The ferry Thalia. This is Police." By now he knew it was a machine. "I want Cassini Station. Forensics."

"Police," the voice repeated. "Do you have a code, Police?"

27

"No, I don't. It's a new case, a new Police case."

"New case, Police, Cassini." The receiver whistled softly. After a pause a second voice answered, another machine.

On the fourth try he got a human in Forensics. "I have a death," Mays said. "Mars inbound." He gave the man's name and number. "I am sending data."

Easton had plugged a cord into the robot. She pushed the transmit button.

"We're very busy," Forensics said. "It will take an hour." There was a pause. "Yes, we have it. Good transmission. R3X number 1281. Your case number is LH 18 427 387 G. We will answer standard encryption."

"As quick as you can." He put the phone back in its socket.

"Now," said Anna, "can we cover him?"

"Sure," he said, "but I need to examine him."

Easton pointed at a nearby door. "That's his cabin."

"And, Razavasky, I want the black box dumped. I want it on paper, and in a portable listener."

She stared at him. "Nobody killed Jerry."

The body was rigid and awkwardly heavy, even for three of them. They rolled it, on the chair, into the captain's cabin. The space was comfortable and well-lighted, and so neat it was hard to believe anyone had lived here for six cycles. The women suddenly did not want to touch the body, but he insisted they help him get it up on the tautly made bed. He began to remove the man's shirt.

"Can't he rest?" Anna said.

"I am making an investigation."

"Then I'll leave you to it." She turned and stalked out. Easton, white-faced, watched her go.

Almost at once he found a small red mark on the inside of the right arm, just over the vein. "What's this?" he said.

Easton peered at it. "An injection." She paused for a long moment. "It must have been Rex. I'll check his records."

Mays tugged off the rest of the clothes. The body had turned a dusky, purplish gray. There was a small round bruise on the left forearm along with the marks of the robot's sampling. He found nothing else, though his empty stomach went queasy as he searched the hairy parts of the body.

28

He spread a thin blanket over the corpse. Easton returned with the robot. "Rex gave him a waker at oh-oh twenty-six."

"A waker?"

"He was taking Anna's watch. He was due to sleep. Sometimes Jerry took Smile to help him sleep."

"Anything else?"

"A waker two days ago, at eleven forty-three. That would be just before his own watch."

A waker every other day, Mays thought, even cops take more than that.

"Come inside a moment," he said. "Close the door."

She frowned with worry. "No one killed him, Inspector."

"Did you like Jerry?"

"Of course."

"Two men and two women, together for six cycles. You must have been lovers."

Her cheeks went pink. He saw again how pretty she was. "Once in a while. It wasn't what you think. We are all friends."

"You brought Anna coffee, and then you decided she had killed him. I don't understand."

She glanced toward the lumpy blanket.

"I'll be frank, Easton. I'm looking for a motive. Why would anyone kill him?"

"I was very upset. I . . . look, Rex says it was a heart attack."

"What about the second pilot?"

"Chor's asleep. Oh, Inspector, it was a natural death. I'm sorry I woke you." She opened the door.

Mays shrugged. "It's too late now."

Razavasky sat at the bridge. The bright hologram of an ion thruster revolved slowly before her. She touched a key and the nozzles, isolated, hung in the air like metallic noodles. "I can't see anything wrong." She looked at Mays. "The computers say it's fine; the monitors say it won't start."

"Are we in danger?"

"I've got three days to find it."

"Why was he calculating docking orbits?"

She nudged the little computer with her finger. "If the ship sees any problem, it won't do the figures."

"Did you dump the black box?"

She waved at a stack of paper. "We'll run out with you aboard." She unplugged an old machine. "And the listener."

He took the other seat. "I have some questions."

She enlarged the image of the nozzles.

"Did you kill Alexander Gerakian?"

"Rex said it was a heart attack."

"Were you lovers?"

She stared at him. "Is this your usual technique?"

"Were you?"

"Yes. Sometimes."

"No jealousies?"

"We all got over that a long time ago, Inspector."

"And the second pilot?"

"Chor? Not with me."

"I meant, with the captain."

She gave a quick laugh. "Oh, that. No. I'm sure of it. Chor is absolutely unsexed."

"Why would Easton kill the captain?"

"Lily?"

"Why would Taung kill Gerakian?"

"My god, do you see murder everywhere? It must be horrible being a cop."

"Where is your cabin?"

"Sleeper level. Near Lily's."

"Two men here, two women on the next level."

"It's rank, left over from older ships." She shook her head. "There's nothing else."

"But you could have changed it. Six cycles."

She turned to peer at the hologram again.

"You were in the thrusters most of your watch?"

"From one until you saw me come up." Her voice had grown enormously patient. "The first hour we talked several times. At two-thirty I told him it might take the whole watch. He said that was fine. After I crawled inside Seven we couldn't talk." She gestured at the paper stack. "It's all in the black box."

A door clicked open beyond her. A small slender man stepped out on the curving ramp. He wore a green oversuit, pale against the dark walls. When he saw Mays he called out, "Who's that?"

"This is Chor Taung?" said Mays. She nodded.

The second pilot seemed frail and almost undernourished. His face was lined, and he stared at Mays with slanted eyes.

"He's a cop, Chor," Anna said. "Lily woke him. Jerry's dead."

Chor's mouth fell open. "Dead?"

"I'll show you," said Mays. He picked up the stack of paper, gripped the man's slender arm, and steered him into the captain's room.

Chor lifted a corner of the blanket and stared for a moment. His surprise had vanished completely. "How did it happen?"

"Easton thought he had been murdered." This one is very smooth, Mays thought. He sat down in the chair. "The robot says heart failure. Since I'm awake, I have to make an investigation." He looked at Chor. "I need your help."

The small man had perched on the corner of the bed. "Jerry was very healthy." He glanced at the covered body. "Perhaps . . ."

"What?"

Chor took a breath. "Jerry was an addict, Inspector."

"Smile?"

"Mars cycles last four or five hundred days. An addict has to make the stuff on board." Chor stood up and opened the closet. Uniforms and oversuits hung in neat rows. A square chest had been fitted into the bottom. "Glass lined, holds twenty-five liters." He lifted the cover, and the odor of alcohol blossomed into the cabin. "Very good stuff. Jerry had a still, up among the hydroponics."

"But could he fly?"

"I am a pilot, too, Inspector."

"How long have you protected him?"

"Three cycles, four really." He shut the closet.

"Were he and Anna lovers?"

Chor raised his head. "Does it matter now?"

"And Lily?"

"She . . ." He looked away. "Well, yes. But Lily wanted monogamy. A pledge, she called it. Jerry was pledged to action, not being. If you understand me."

"Did Easton kill him?"

"Don't ever think that, Inspector. She's the one who kept us together."

"So you all let him go on and on?"

"He was such good company. And they would have grounded him forever."

"We're docking in three days," said Mays. "What would have happened?"

Chor had sat on the corner of the bed again. "The company is going to scrap Thalia. And us, too. They've decided six cycles is long enough for one crew."

"Could Jerry have found another crew to protect him?"

"I don't think so. He said he was resigned to never flying again. He promised to dry out. I believed him, Inspector."

"You were asleep until six?"

"A little before."

"That will be in the black box?"

"Sure. But the box watches my comat. I could have come out without my shirt and poisoned his booze. Given him a chop to the neck. But how would I give him heart failure?"

Mays stood up. "I want to lock this cabin."

"Sure." Chor pointed to a number pad on the wall outside the door. "Hold down zero, enter five digits."

"And I'll need a cabin myself."

"There's an empty one beside mine."

Mays tapped in the start of the Fibonacci series, the code he always used: 12358. He knew they could break it in half a day, but they were too smart to do it.

The cabin beside Chor's was half the size of the captain's. The air smelled old, as if no one had breathed it in a thousand days. He sat in the chair, put his feet up on the narrow bed, and tried to think.

So. What did he have? Time of death: two twenty-eight, half an hour leeway. Easton's first instinct was murder, though the captain had been alone on the bridge from one to four-thirty when she brought coffee. Easton has an alibi until three. Razavasky was recorded until two-thirty, and says she was in the thrusters until five-thirty. Chor woke up at six.

He stood up and paced the little room.

One injection mark. No struggle, no poison writhing, no broken bones. Heart failure, the robot said, but he had been a man in good health. I need to go over the black-box dump, check their stories. Maybe Forensics will find something else.

He lay down and closed his eyes. Clia, the blond technician at Cassini Four, stood at an open door and smiled at him. He opened his eyes and stared at the cabin overhead. The lighted grilles had gone pink with age. He stood and yawned, and opened the door. Anna sat with Chor at the bridge. They stopped talking when they saw him. One of the screens flickered. The print light glimmered, and a single paper sheet dropped on the desk.

Chor picked it up. "It's code for you, Inspector."

"Thanks."

He ignored their stares and carried the sheet back into his cabin. It took several minutes to decipher, but after the first line he knew what it would say.

>> EYES ONLY: MAYS
  LH 18 427 387 G:
LUNA CASSINI FORENSIC: 273/06:43 <> 273/07:30.
>> SUBJECT: 001: GERAKIAN, A S: 3342-472-45-2394:
> SUBSTANCE LEVELS: AFFECTIVE [ABSOLUTE VALUES FILE: CASE #]
  DIGITALIS (VARIANT): LETHAL / ALCOHOL (TRUE): HIGH
  TRANQUILIZER (SYNT): MODERATE / BARBITURATE (SYNT): LOW.
>>> COD: CARDIAC FAILURE: OVERDOSE: [0.924].
>> SUBJECT: 002: LIQUID
  COFFEE (CLONE) / SUGAR (SYNT).
> REPLY CASSINI: SUSPECT + METHOD > 273/12:00 LATEST

Mays rubbed his eyes. **Digitalis (variant), lethal** overdose, probability 0.924. And Cassini, generous as ever, had given him five hours to figure it all out.

So. Jerry was the center of their lives, a sun with three planets. They loved him very much, each in their own way. They were all jealous, each in their own way. Twenty-five hundred days. Old Jerry just wore out under their protection, probability 0.998. The man had a still, for god's sake. I can't trust Easton to check his liver, and anyway Luna police will take the body when we dock. Meanwhile, Jerry will lie and rot.

So. Digitalis (variant), lethal dose. Easton has the drugs. He reset the lock on his own door.

Chor looked up at him. "Do you have the answer, Inspector?"

"No. Where's Easton?"

"Sleeper level. She's exercising."

Mays climbed up the wall and hauled himself weightless through the center tunnel and thought, you do get used to it.

"Easton," he called. She was not in her office.

He sat at her terminal and found the switch. The visuals lit up with the histories of a dozen passengers.

"What do you want now?" She stood in the doorway behind him, in a pink exercise suit, her face flushed and sweating.

"I've heard from Forensics. It was an overdose. Digitalis variant."

She puffed from her workout, but the news made no obvious impact. "Have you come to arrest me?"

"I want to see your records."

"Of course." She took his seat and displayed the drug inventories. "Digitalis variant, that would be valoxin. It's in the sleeper-monitoring circuit, and Rex carries some."

"What does it do?"

"Slows the pulse rate, strengthens heart action. There's a tranquilizer in valoxin, too, and a drug to lower blood pressure. A lot of passengers are afraid of space travel."

"How much is a lethal dose?"

"Ten times? I don't know. I'd have to look it up."

"Too much slows things too much?"

"Yes." Her eyes were damp again, and she looked away.

"You don't have what you started with."

"Of course not, Inspector. Seven passengers are on habitual dosage. Fourteen needed minor amounts at lift-off." She tapped more keys. "There, 0.438 of original."

Figures can be rigged, he thought, but she knows it will all be in the black box. "I want this on paper."

"I don't have a printer."

"Send it to the bridge."

She stared at the terminal, shook her head, and called for an assist. He watched her work at it. She was fast enough with medical records; why did she fumble with these other things?

"The R3X carries valoxin?"

"Yes." She called the machine out of its cubicle and worked briefly on its keys. She knew exactly what to do. Its screen read: IPF THALIA: CYCLE 037.2: VALOXIN: 1.0000: 0 DOSAGE(S).

"Rex is for crew emergencies." Her cheeks had flushed with the effort, and she looked very satisfied.

"Anybody else have anything like it?"

She turned the robot off and suppressed the wall visuals.

"Who has the stuff, Easton? It'll be in the records."

She pushed her fingers through her hair. "Anna. They found an irregularity, just before this trip. Not enough to ground her. I don't know if she has anything, but it would be sensible." She drew a quick breath. "Oh, I'm sure she didn't . . ."

"Where is she?"

"I don't know."

"Call the bridge."

She pressed a button. "Chor?"

"Yes, Lily." His voice filtered down from the ceiling. "We're waiting for you."

Mays cut in. "Where is Razavasky?"

"I'm here," said Anna. "We're eating. I'm sorry, Inspector, I forgot to tell you about meals."

"I'll be right there."

"I'll draw another one."

"No, don't," Easton said, "I'm not hungry. He can have mine."

"Lily, are you sick?" said Chor.

"I'm fine," she answered, and broke the connection. She looked drawn and tired, suddenly, as if she were running on nerves.

He pulled himself through the weightlessness again, wondering why there wasn't a walking passage between the decks. It couldn't have been more than ten meters. Chor and Razavasky sat at a pull-down table next to the bridge. The smell of food made him salivate, and he had to swallow twice before he spoke.

"I have a few questions."

Anna looked at Chor. "Why did I imagine policemen would be exciting to talk to? Here," she said, "I've forgotten your name. I'm tired of calling you Inspector."

"Richard Mays."

"Well, Richard, have a bite of tofu and beans. It's better than it sounds."

The food tasted wonderful. It brought back a dozen other meals, plain food garnished with the hunger of long sleeptrips. He devoured half the portion before he could speak again.

"You talked to Lily," Chor said. "Therefore, your code had something to do with drugs."

Mays nodded.

"Cassini does not think it was a natural death?"

He nodded again.

Anna glanced at Chor. "It really was one of us?"

The small man smiled at her grimly. "That's what Lily said."

Mays swallowed. "You have a heart condition, Razavasky."

"It's very minor. I am allowed to fly." She paused. "What killed Jerry?"

"Digitalis, variant."

35

"My god, Lily . . ."

"He has cleared Lily," Chor said.

"Inspector, I have a box of patches." She was talking quickly. "I used one during takeoff, they said I should. I've got all the rest."

"I'd like to see them."

"Of course." She stood, and climbed rapidly up the ladder.

"Well, Inspector, did Anna do it?" asked Chor.

Mays took a last bite. "I don't know. I'm very methodical. I follow one thing at a time."

"And when she proves her innocence, you will turn on me?"

"Tell me why I shouldn't."

Anna dropped down the wall in long jumps. "Here, look, it says forty. Here, I'll count them."

"I'll do it," Mays said. He opened the box and took out the inner bags. Seven held five patches each. One, opened, had three left.

"I must have used two," she said. "They told me they were very mild."

The drug came from a pharmacy in Sidonport. The label read "052/14:07: DIGOLIN CUET #40: Apply 1 each indication maximum 4 in 24 hours."

Two, he thought, half the daily dose. You would have to completely cover a man to kill him.

"These would be on her record," said Chor.

Anna put her hand to her mouth. "My god, I didn't do it."

Mays shrugged. "Apparently not."

He lay on his narrow bunk and stared at the overhead. This was the time he always dreaded, the long cold stretch in the middle when facts piled up and confusion grew. All you could do was push on through until the truth revealed itself.

Four people, he thought, six cycles on this battered ship, nothing human but the dead faces of the sleepers. Why aren't they all addicts? At least he could understand Jerry. Good old Jerry, pledged to a life of action. Though he had only two women all these years. And maybe Chor, the man is so obliging.

If it was suicide, Easton would have had to give Jerry the drug. But if it was suicide, she would never have waked me. One of them must have killed him. The other two don't know who did it, though maybe they've guessed. They've spent years protecting Jerry, and now that Easton has let in a stranger by mistake they're protecting each other.

He shut his eyes for a minute. Clia leaned over her desk toward him, and her breasts . . . "Damn," he muttered, and got up.

Chor sat alone on the bridge, his eyes also closed, listening to Martian folk songs.

"I need a waker," Mays said.

The man nodded. "Rex," he called.

After a minute, the small door opened and the R3X appeared.

"Rex," Chor said again. It rolled up to them. "Pull up your sleeve, Inspector. The elbow's far enough." He touched several buttons on the robot. "Aren't you afraid I'll give you an overdose?"

"Cassini knows I'm alive and well."

Chor nodded. "The back of your arm, here, against this."

A cool articulated band wrapped snugly around his arm. The R3X pushed forward an instrument the size of his thumb. Mays felt a momentary pain, and when the band released him a faint red circle marked his arm, half a centimeter in diameter.

"It's a spray shot."

"Of course," Chor said.

Mays stood up and walked quickly to the captain's door. He tapped out the code and pushed the door open and pulled back the blanket. Jerry's left arm still carried its small bruise, half a centimeter in diameter.

Damn, Mays thought, that was his waker. The injection was the valoxin, given by syringe. Easton must have syringes.

Chor looked up. "What is it, Inspector?"

He did not answer. He went quickly up the ladder and through the center tunnel. The small medical office was dark and empty. "Easton," he called, and went through a second doorway into a dim narrow passage.

He called again. A door opened nearby, and Anna put her head out. Her hair fell in a dark unbraided cloud about her face.

"Where is she?" he said.

"We're having cocoa. It's her sleep time."

"I must see her."

"You are running an investigation, aren't you?"

He pushed through the door. The little cabin was cluttered with trinkets. In the middle Easton sat sprawled in a lounge chair, wearing a bulky, flowered oversuit. Her eyes were closed and her face looked empty.

"She has on a Smile patch."

"Easton." He bent and shook her.

The blue eyes opened. "Oh, goddamn, it's you. I wish I'd never waked you."

"Where are your syringes?"

"Syringes? Oh, Inspector, what do you want with syringes?" She giggled. "We use patches here, not syringes."

"I want to check your supply."

Easton closed her eyes. "Anna can show you."

In the office, Razavasky turned on the lights and stared at the ranks of cabinets. "Let's try the inventory," she said.

After a minute the display read: SYRINGE: ONE(1) SET TWELVE(12)EA. CABSEC:D7. NOTE FILE FORM 23.755 EACH USE NOTE. She slid open a door and drew out a small clear case. A dozen syringes lay inside. The seals were unbroken.

He pointed to the display. "Check that file."

"My god, if she used one she wouldn't file the form."

"Check it, please."

She could find no Form 23.755. "Lily didn't kill him," she said. "But where did the drug come from?"

He did not answer. He had just remembered that, when Easton saw the mark of the injection, she checked the robot. The robot. Of course. How could he have missed it? It was the damn robot. Easton never left the passenger level.

"Who gave him the drug?" Anna touched his hand. "I should call you Richard."

He looked down at her face, framed by dark hair, and thought that the most interesting women committed the most interesting crimes. "Did you?"

"Of course not. Why should I?"

"Why should any of you?"

She frowned and looked away. "I must go back to Lily."

Chor still sat at the bridge. The same atonal folk songs hung in the air. The robot waited beside its little door.

"I want to lock up the R3X," Mays said.

Chor raised his eyebrows. "Call him, then."

"Rex," said Mays. The robot turned slowly, as if it wondered about this new voice. "Come," Mays said. It followed him into his own cabin. "Stay," he said, and locked the door behind him.

"Do you have a cybernetic suspect, Inspector?"

Mays shrugged.

"Remember that machines are the creatures of men. It is the finger that pushes the button, not the button itself." Chor widened his eyes and smiled. "Old Oriental wisdom."

"Very inscrutable," Mays said, and sat down beside him.

"Thank you. Rex carries drugs in his belly." Chor enclosed a round volume with his arms. "I always think of it as his belly."

"His supply of valoxin is one hundred percent. His records show no injections."

"Do you believe that, Inspector?"

"For the time being."

"Ah. Likewise, inscrutable."

"Who could reprogram the robot?" Mays asked.

Chor gazed at him. "Anna is the ship's engineer."

"Would she kill Jerry?"

"You remember the folk song 'Frankie and Johnny'?" Chor began to sing in a cracked voice. " 'She shot her man, O Lord, 'cause he done her wrong.' "

"Jerry did her wrong?"

"He did us all wrong."

So, Mays thought, the veneer has begun to crumble. "What happened between trips? How long were the layovers?"

"Three weeks, usually. On Mars there is East Sidonport. On Luna we—"

"What happened, this last time?"

Chor turned and looked at the matrix of displays, as if something there required his immediate attention.

"You and Jerry," Mays said, "and the women."

"Jerry." Chor touched a button and turned off the music. "We had a room together." He glanced at Mays. "Look, Inspector, Jerry was, ah, bisexual. And he was bored on Thalia."

"But you loved him anyway."

"Not love, Inspector."

"Love. Not sex, perhaps. But certainly love."

"Yes."

"You all loved him," Mays said. "But Jerry was a black hole, drain-

39

ing your love and giving nothing back. Until finally love dried up, the meter read zero, and one of you killed him."

Tears shone in Chor's narrow eyes. "No, Inspector. That's not true. We still love him, as much as we ever did." He nodded toward the captain's door. "I have cut off the heat in his cabin, but he will smell before we dock."

"Only a little." Mays waited a long minute. "Did you kill Jerry?"

Chor shook his head.

"Did Anna?"

"I don't want to think so, Inspector." He spoke like a man waking from a dream.

"She reprogrammed the R3X robot. She did it so well she hid all the changes."

Chor said nothing.

"But aren't you the ship's computer officer?"

"Yes."

"Show me how it could be done."

"I have never worked on Rex, Inspector."

"So." Mays stood up. "I'll try it myself."

He found a paperbook manual inside the robot's belly: User's Guide to the R3X Medical Android Mark II [#875–#1275]. The book was curved and stiff, as if it had never left the holder. He read the manual and ran procedures for three hours, but found no sign of tampering. Reprogramming required a personal code, but the computer's storage held no numbers except, now, his own. He verified once again that the valoxin level was 1.000, that injections were zero.

He stood and yawned and stretched. His watch read 10:32. He had only been awake five hours, he'd had a waker, and still he was tired.

"So, Rex," he said, "who pushed your button?" He rapped on the top of the machine. "You don't mind if I call you Rex?"

During his search he had called up the time display. The screen on top of the robot read: 273/10:14. A circuit closed in his mind, though for a moment he did not understand what it meant.

He looked at his watch again. 10:32 changed to 10:33.

Rex was eighteen minutes slow. Did somebody turn him off? If they did, what else could they turn off? Records of injections? But if the valoxin is 1.000, does it matter?

He riffled through the manual. The clock had been set at the factory, it was accurate to interplanetary standards, its display could be suppressed. There was no mention of stopping it, and even if you could you had to leave a code behind, and there were no numbers. Of course, someone very clever could remove the numbers, but someone that clever would have reset the clock.

Say Chor did it. He was jealous of the women, afraid one of them would get Jerry. But Chor would need Easton, for the drug.

Chor pointed a finger at Anna, and so had Easton. Were they in it together? Or was Anna really guilty?

Or was it all three of them, three fingers on one button. But then they could have buried him in space, straight out through the air locks, a natural death, and the black box would have protected them all.

His neck had gone stiff, and his head ached. He stared at the time display. Eighteen minutes. He noticed a small plate just beneath the screen: R3X 1281. The cover of the manual read: R3X Mark II: 875–1275.

Well, damn, this is the wrong book. Who would know that?

Chor stood beyond the end of the bridge, one leg thrust forward, both hands moving in slow arcs. The sight was so astonishing that it left Mays briefly speechless. Chor swung one arm to the side and flung the other upward, cutting the air.

"Chor."

"A moment, Inspector." But several minutes passed before he reached some sort of finale.

"I'm looking for the R3X manual," Mays said.

"It should be in the machine."

"There must be a newer one."

"Really? I've never heard of it."

"Where is Razavasky?"

Chor looked at the displays. "The sauna. I'll call her."

"Don't call. I want to talk to her. Where is it?"

The man pointed over his shoulder. "Halfway around."

Mays found a wood-grain door beneath a glowing yellow light. He pressed the speaker button. "Anna?"

"Is that Richard?"

"I want to talk to you."

"Well, come in, then."

"You have to come out."

She sighed. "Richard, can't you ask over the phone?"

41

"No."

"Oh, all right."

After a moment the door opened and a breath of roasting air blew out. She had stuffed her hair into a floppy cap. Her face was flushed and her robe clung distractingly to her damp body.

"I'm looking for Rex's new manual," he said.

"You couldn't ask that over the phone?"

"I found the old one inside him. I need the new one."

She wiped her forehead. "I don't remember it. Lily would know, but she's asleep. Did you ask Chor?"

"He didn't know either."

"Have you checked the ship's memory?"

"I will."

She smiled at him. "Richard, you look tense. Why not join me? It's very relaxing."

"I'm running an investigation."

She made a rude noise and went back into the sauna.

Not Chor and not Anna, he thought. Easton can only handle medical stuff in the computer. The valoxin reads 1.000. The clock is eighteen minutes slow. Am I left with a machine run amok? Do I really think old Rex would kid around like that?

Chor glanced up at him. "I've found the new one; it was misfiled." A display read: MANUAL R3X MK IIA: 1276–1800.

"Can Easton's terminal read this?"

"Of course."

Mays pointed. "I want it on paper."

Seven or eight pages came through the slot before Chor stopped the run. "We don't have enough paper for it all."

"Then give me anything about the clock." Mays watched him raise his eyebrows. "You've never seen this before?"

"No, Inspector. Though you only have my word on it."

A dozen more sheets emerged. Mays picked them up and walked back to his own cabin. Rex was still eighteen minutes slow.

On newer R3X models the clock rate was adjustable, between 20 percent and 240 percent. So, he thought, and glanced at the other sheets. The introduction gave techniques for inserting a new operating system. There was a boldface paragraph about saving memory.

Someone knocked on the door. Anna had put on a dry robe and

rebraided her hair. "Chor says somebody fiddled with Rex. He says you suspect the two of us."

"Come in and close the door."

She sat on the end of his bunk.

"Have you ever worked on the robot?" he asked.

"No."

"Could you falsify readouts?"

She glanced around at the paper sheets. "I'm sure it can be done."

"You? And Chor?"

"Yes, but look . . ."

"And Easton?" he said.

"Lily? I don't think so." She stared at him. "My god, Richard, what do you mean?"

"Rex gave the drug. Even though his records say nothing was given, and his volume is one-point-zero-zero-zero."

"Do you always ignore facts like that?"

"The captain died of an overdose. Given by a syringe."

"And we found them all," she said. She picked up one of the introductory sheets.

"And the clock," he said, "is eighteen minutes slow."

"Richard. Look at this. When you install a new system, the machine starts over again. You can turn off personal codes. You can dump memory. You can do whatever you want to." She stared at him, her eyes wide. "My god, it must be Chor."

He glanced at the overhead. "Can he hear us?"

She peered at the comswitch. "No." She had put a hand to her throat. "They were as close as brothers."

"There is still the matter of the clock."

She stood up quickly. "My god, do you think? Did he mess around with thruster Seven, just to get me off the bridge? Richard, the rest of us, will he kill us all before we dock?" Her voice had slid quickly toward panic.

Her fragile confidence surprised Mays. He stood up and gripped her arm. "Nothing is proved. It's all circumstantial. There are other possibilities."

"It wasn't me. It couldn't have been Lily."

"Where would Chor get the drug?"

"I don't know."

43

"He would have reset the clock."

"Yes." She pulled away. "Do you think I would have forgotten it?"

"No."

She was quiet for a moment. "I'm tired, Richard, I can't think." She gave him a brief smile. "I'll be in my cabin."

She left the door ajar. He watched her cross the bridge and go up the ladder before he pushed it shut.

He turned and stared at the robot. Damn you, Rex, who pushed your button? Chor or Anna would have reset the clock. But Easton ran Rex; she could punch those keys in her sleep. She worked on him just after the captain's death. She has the drug. Nobody else fits.

But where did the drug come from?

He sorted through the black-box records. The sleepers all got their dosages at zero-zero-ten, every day. Seven automated shots, all with the same dosage values. He flipped backward to the beginning: seven every day, plus fourteen the first day.

He remembered the paragraph on the robot's memory and dug again through the introductory sheets. Inserting a new system dumped everything, memory and everything. The number of injections began at zero; drug supply started at 1.000. It was a ratio, not a volume. So, there was the drug out of the robot's supply, the drug and the opportunity. But how did Easton push the robot's button, from the passenger level?

And where were you at two-thirty, Rex?

He could find no record at all for the robot. The black box watched everything except Rex. That made the robot a perfect murder weapon. Would she know that?

He stood up again. He rubbed an itch on his arm, where he had had the waker. Another circuit closed. Easton had said the injection was the waker, but that wasn't true. The waker was the little round bruise. She lied about it. But what about the clock? And if she killed him, why wake me?

Damn, damn.

He had to move, to take a walk. He opened the door and Easton stood there, her hand raised.

"Oh," she said, "I was just going to knock."

Chor watched from the bridge, and Anna had returned, too.

"Come in," he said.

She closed the door and sat carefully in the metal chair beside the robot. She was jittery and her eyes were red. She still wore the flowered oversuit.

"I couldn't sleep. I took off the Smile patch." Her voice was thin and wavering, as if she had taken something else. "Do you know who did it?"

"Rex gave him an injection."

Her fingers trembled as she ran them through her hair, but she smiled at him. "You're very quick, Inspector."

"And you pushed his button."

"Anna said you suspected Chor."

Mays shook his head. "Anna suspected him."

She took a deep breath. "Yes," she said, "it was me."

He had been certain of it, but still he put a hand against the wall to steady himself.

"I did it, Inspector. You must arrest me."

"I don't trust confessions, Easton. Who are you protecting?"

"Nobody. Well, of course I am. If you accuse Chor, he will never fly again. The same for Anna. And it's true, I did it."

"The clock," he said.

"Anna told me you found something wrong with Rex's clock." She closed her blue eyes for a moment. "I would never have waked you if I'd known you were a computer cop."

"What about the clock?"

"I had figured everything out, every step. It all worked, except that it all went wrong. That's why I forgot the clock."

"Why did you kill him?"

"Was it the clock that gave me away?"

"It was one of the things. Why did you kill him?"

"I didn't." She took another breath. "Well, yes, of course I did. But I didn't mean to. It was Anna I meant to kill."

"Anna?"

"Jerry told me they were going away after this cycle. But now Anna says they weren't, that he said he was going with me." Her eyes were damp, once more. "Jerry would do things like that."

She wiped her eyes. "It was Anna's watch. After I finished checking the passengers, I sent Rex up to the bridge. He came back after a while and I put his memory in again. Everything was fine. I really did take a nap." She smiled. "I was so happy. Anna was dead. If she had just been sick, she would have called for help. I made coffee. That was

45

my best touch. I always made coffee for Anna. I went up to the bridge." Her voice had fallen to a whisper. "I went up to the bridge and there was Jerry. Drunk on duty again. Sleeping on watch."

"Instead of Anna."

"I was very confused. Jerry was dead instead of Anna; it must have been her fault. I remembered there was a policeman on board. You were half awake before I saw what had happened. I couldn't stop your waking, then, it would have killed you."

"Thank you," he said. For a moment he did not want to press her. "What about the clock?"

She stared at the robot proudly. "That was the best part. How to get Rex to give a shot, by himself? A massive shot, twenty times the habitual dose, sure to be fatal? Probably you could program him, Inspector. Chor could, or Anna. But I couldn't. I can push buttons and follow instructions, but programming . . ."

"The clock," he said.

"Of course I read Rex's new manual, how you could erase memory, reset the clock. It came in three cycles ago, with the new system. I remembered it last week."

"The clock," he repeated.

"Rex can read your pulse rate. If it's too high, and he has been cleared, he can give you something to slow it down. But I wanted an overdose given for a normal pulse."

Mays stared at her. "You slowed the clock."

"Yes." Her laugh had a frantic edge. "I couldn't believe it was so simple. Rex counts against his own clock. If it's slow, he reads more of your heartbeats for each of his. He thinks your heart is galloping away. Bang, the valoxin." She flinched at her own words. "He will continue, until your heart slows down enough."

"And when you restart it, the clock reverts to standard speed."

"It's very simple." She was no longer weeping, and her face was shiny with perspiration. "I planned to speed it up, get it back to the correct time. But I forgot."

"Jerry was dead."

"Yes." After a moment she leaned over and tapped on the robot's keypad. "That's to order the drug. All he has left. I'll never forget the keys." She punched several more buttons. "And that's the clock."

The robot stirred.

Mays stood up quickly. "What have you done?"

"Oh, be careful, Inspector. Don't get his attention." She pulled up her sleeve. The robot moved toward her deliberately. The automatic bands clamped around her arm and a different instrument thrust against her wrist. She watched it, fascinated, and then she flinched. "Oh. He must have hit a nerve."

"Easton." He put both hands on her arm. "How do I get it off?"

"You don't. He will let go after a time."

"Easton. Damn." He opened the door and shouted, "Chor, this damn machine."

The small man sprang up and ran toward them. Behind him Anna called, "Lily."

"Oh." Easton put her free hand to her chest. "There's another. It's very sudden. It feels . . . it doesn't hurt, but it's very strange. Oh."

"What's happened?" Chor said.

"It's giving her an overdose."

The machine kept its bands around her arm. Easton coughed and trembled in the chair. Chor shook her, but she did not open her eyes.

Anna burst through the door crying, "Lily."

Mays dug through the paper sheets and found a key code and called it out to Chor. The machine paused a long time, as if stuck in midcycle, before it slowly withdrew the injection head and freed her. Easton drooped against the side of the chair, shuddering, her eyes closed, her breath labored.

"My god, Lily," Anna wailed, and threw her arms around her.

Easton's color had vanished. Mays pressed his fingers against her neck, searching for a pulse. He found a faint and thready beat, and then nothing at all.

"Adrenaline," Chor said. "Rex has adrenaline."

"It's too late."

"Oh, Lily," Anna cried, "my god, Lily."

They lifted Easton from the chair and stretched her out on the bed. Chor worked on Rex's keys until the robot gave the stimulant. They thumped and pounded her chest and blew into her mouth. They struggled for an hour. At last even Anna lost hope, and they stopped, exhausted, and stared down at the body.

A buzzer was sounding on the bridge.

"I'll get it," Chor said. He went slowly out the door.

"It'll be Cassini Station," said Mays.

47

Anna slumped beside the bed, breathless and pale. Her hair hung in dark tangles about her face. She pushed it away with the back of her hand and stared up at him.

"My god, Inspector, why did she ever wake you up?"

〰〰

A nice old-fashioned scientific puzzle story from a new Texas writer. It would have fit just as easily into the pages of John Campbell's Astounding of forty years ago as into those of Terry Carr's Universe, and it neatly fills a niche here. Good science fiction stories don't need to be trendy in order to be timeless.

50

Lieutenant Urs Griewold shook his head. "It can't be water," he said. "It just *can't* be."

Ensign Rafe Valencia grinned and settled back in his seat. Baiting the short, blond lieutenant had become his favorite pastime. Among Epsilon Eridani's frigid outer planets, a billion kilometers from the *Amundsen* and the rest of the expedition's crew, recreation was hard to come by. "Well, Urs, it looks like water to me. The atmosphere looks thick enough, and the temperature is about right." Laser spectroscopy would settle the question, but it couldn't punch through to the moon's surface.

"It *can't* be that warm. This far out from the star, there's no heat to speak of."

Rafe stroked his thick brown beard. "Maybe the moon's primary is putting out a lot of heat. Some gas giants do that, you know."

Griewold turned from the screen to scowl at him. "You saw the infrared readings, Ensign. That Subjovian is just a ball of frozen mush."

"Why, Urs, how is it that you trust what the IR said about the big planet, but not what it tells you about this moon?"

Griewold snorted with disgust and turned back to the screen. "Take us down," he said. "Let's get a closer look."

As Rafe turned to the flight controls, his mind toyed with the sudden fantasy that this worldlet really was water, not just on the surface but all the way down. Chuckling at the silly notion, he started their descent.

They encountered thin atmosphere several hundred kilometers above the surface. That made sense; in lower gravity, air density dropped off more slowly. Rafe had to keep

WATERWORLD, OR ALL THE WAY DOWN

JOHN
K.
GIBBONS

decelerating as they went deeper. The boat's inertial drive had lots of power, but the hull was mediocre at best for high-speed atmospheric flight.

Griewold huddled over the science console, muttering curses. "Crazy atmosphere," Rafe heard him say. "Almost like earth, but enough damned chlorine thrown in to make it poisonous."

Rafe concentrated on the screen and flight instruments as he brought them lower. Only scattered small gray splotches broke the monotonous blue, but a pattern on the blue surface looked more and more like waves. One of the gray regions lay on the horizon ahead— could the flashing lines of white at its edge be anything but breakers?

Their speed was down to about a thousand kilometers an hour, and their height to six kilometers. The gray was a low mound rising out of a clear blue sea (it was almost impossible to call it anything else but a sea). The island had even less visual detail than the ocean, though, and Rafe dropped lower to see if anything showed up.

They crossed the shore at a thousand meters height. Griewold whistled and leaned closer to his instruments. "Extremely strong magnetic field," he said. He got no further. A siren wailed, and the boat shuddered and jerked. The flight console flashed red and then went dark. It lit back up in a moment, but awash with amber warnings and red system failures. Rafe suddenly found himself piloting a crippled brick.

"Main power dropout, Urs! Primary impellers are gone, too."

"My instruments are burned out, and the life support is dead!"

Rafe slapped switches left and right. "*Screw* the life support! If you can't get me some power, *we're* dead *now*."

Griewold got the message, and turned to the engineering console. Precious seconds elapsed as Rafe fought to keep the boat under some control with vernier thrusters. If it started tumbling, he'd never have time to recover.

The surface was getting damn close when the impeller icon flashed from red to yellow. "Emergency reserve power routed to impellers," called Griewold, but Rafe was already urging the craft out of its dive. He fought to bleed off speed as it continued to buck and rock. The boat was still crippled, but at least it was responding.

Not trusting his control for a normal landing, Rafe swerved for the closest shoreline. They were still dropping, and moving forward at a hundred kilometers an hour. Decelerating as fast as he could, Rafe headed along the wave troughs and braced himself. They bounced off the surface with a bruising jolt, rose a few meters, then hit and skipped again.

On the third contact, they stayed down, skimming roughly. Then the bow caught a wave, jerked them down. The boat plunged under and rolled upside down. Rafe's harness gouged him cruelly; his vision dimmed and he fought to stay conscious. Data cubes, logbooks, and everything loose cascaded around him. He'd never felt a craft buck around like this; the hull creaked and boomed like the boat was about to break up.

Slowly, the sickening lurches and ominous noises slacked off. A damage klaxon howled for a moment, then died for lack of power. The hull had held so far, though, so Rafe began to hope they might make it. Sure enough, the boat slowly rolled upright, and a moment later bobbed back to the surface.

Rafe wiggled a finger, then cautiously tried more extensive movements. He was astonished to find no broken bones. Across from him, Griewold hung limply in his harness, eyes open but glazed. Rafe shook his head to clear it, immediately regretting the motion as pain lanced through his temples. He'd had hangovers that felt worse, though; he would survive. He shut down the flight console and looked over the other instruments.

Damn! The fusion plant was completely slagged down. Replaying the monitors, it looked like the superconducting elements had cratered when they hit that magnetic field, and that had killed the containment. The safety interlocks had kicked in a few microseconds too late, and the chamber was a total loss.

He could feel a gentle rise and fall as the boat rode the swells. This reminded him to check the external instruments, and some of them were still working. He smiled at Griewold, who stared back with the beginnings of awareness.

"Well, Urs, it really is water."

The good news was that the little vessel was structurally intact. All major systems, including life support, were working fine under reserve power from the emergency fuel cell. The bad news was that the power would last only for four days. When the power ran out, their life support system wouldn't be able to recycle the air anymore, and the atmosphere outside was poisonous.

Rafe checked the air chemistry readings himself, hoping Griewold's brief summary was wrong. Looked amazingly terrestroid:

53

mostly nitrogen, about thirty percent oxygen, just under four percent CO_2, and a similar amount of water vapor. Well, not really so Earth-like after all; there was indeed a nasty trace of chlorine as hydrochloric acid. Pressure here at the surface was about the same as the 5,000-meter level on Earth. Thin stuff, but it would be breathable if it weren't for the chlorine.

Then Rafe noticed the hydrogen numbers. Nearly five percent? That was bizarre! Not only was it way out of place among the other readings, it was actually above the point of flammability. His mind must have skipped it at first glance, refusing to believe levels that high. Hydrogen just didn't stay uncombined in quantities like that.

Wait a minute. Didn't pressure affect flammability? He keyed in the question, and the computer told him that the minimum concentration of hydrogen for combustion would be about six percent, given the conditions outside.

The crux was that the air was poisonous, and their own life support had only enough power for four days. The *Amundsen* wouldn't miss them that quickly, and they couldn't generate a signal strong enough to get through to the central planets. The starship didn't have any fifty-meter dishes aimed in their direction. Mission planners hadn't expected a power failure so far from the ship, or at least they hadn't figured such an accident might have survivors.

Another display caught him by surprise. The figures that the navcom had calculated from their orbit were a lot lower than he'd expected. He punched in a request for density calculations, and raised an eyebrow at the answer. Specific gravity just barely over one, the density of water. Very unusual for a body this size.

Griewold was up and about by this point, and he insisted on scouring the manuals for instructions. Rafe restrained his sarcasm as the lieutenant passed from determination through frenzy to despair. Finally, he'd had enough. "Face it, Urs, we're on our own. The *Amundsen* won't even be thinking about us, out here among Cervantes' moons."

"*Cervantes?*" Lieutenant Griewold's voice dripped with derision.

"Yeah, Cervantes, like the great author. Don Quixote and all that. Hasn't he ever been translated into Swiss? Oh, I'm so sorry." Rafe's tone dropped in mock apology. "I keep forgetting; Switzerland doesn't even have its own language, does it?"

"I *am* familiar with literature," the lieutenant replied. "Are you talking about the Subjovian planet this moon orbits? You don't have authority to name it!"

"I can call it anything I please, Urs. I just can't make anybody else call it that."

Griewold tapped his foot petulantly. "Ensign, refer to me as Lieutenant, and remember to say *sir*. That's your problem, no respect for authority. If you played by the book and followed orders, we'd be in the central system with the rest of the expedition, investigating those alien artifacts." Rafe grinned, wondering whether Griewold was going to mention just who had found those artifacts. The Lieutenant skipped that point, however, and went on with his diatribe. "But no, you had to do it your own way, foot free and fancy loose, blow up millions of credits' worth of equipment and get both of us banished alone out here in the doonies!"

"Gosh, Urs, I'll try to do better—I mean yes, Lieutenant; aye aye, sir; *ja wohl, mein kapitan.* And by the way, I think the old colloquialism is boonies, not doonies." Rafe had to accept the honorary commission that came with a berth on the expedition, but he wasn't about to join in the silly ritual games. It was a lot more fun to make up his own games.

Griewold was beet red. "We've got to play by the book!"

"There *is* no book on this; we'll just have to wing it. We've got four days." Rafe shrugged. "Maybe the *Amundsen* comes looking for us, maybe not. In the meantime, we can either play pinochle or we can look around a little."

Griewold lurched to his feet, grabbing the back of his seat. "You're acting awfully smug. I can't believe you're that brave, so you must not appreciate the gravity of our situation."

Actually, Rafe was scared out of his pants, but he wasn't about to let Griewold see that. "Looks like you're the one having trouble with the low gravity here. I'm just my usual lazy self. You know, sufficient unto *mañana* the troubles thereof."

"Your usual smartass self, you mean." Having an excuse to gripe at Rafe seemed to help Griewold pull himself together. "We have a *duty* to keep fighting for survival. I won't dishonor my ancestors by just giving up."

Rafe leaned back in his seat and laughed. "Dishonor your ancestors? Maybe I should talk about the traditions of the conquistadors, but you come from a long line of watchmakers, bankers, and data

55

brokers." Part of his mind wondered what possessed him to say that—the worry must be getting to him more than he realized.

Griewold straightened ramrod-stiff and glared at him. "And you claim to study history! Switzerland fought for its independence, and kept it by strength." He paused, and looked down. "But there's another noble tradition for our small country. For generations, my ancestors have served with the Swiss Guard, at the Vatican."

Rafe raised his palms in surrender. "I'm sorry, Urs, I didn't mean to insult your lineage. If it's such a family tradition, though, why didn't you join the Guard?" Too late, he guessed that might be a painful question.

"I did," Griewold answered. He turned away and leaned against the cabin wall. "I was in the Piazza when Pope Innocent was shot."

God, thought Rafe, I've put my foot in it now. "Hey, you can't blame yourself for that. The Swiss Guards aren't bodyguards."

Griewold spun around, his face white with rage. "Right! Just a colorful honor guard. Damn it, I was ten meters from the assassin; I saw the bastard's gun before he fired. *There was nothing I could do!*" He raised clinched fists, then visibly fought to relax. "I resigned the next day. I couldn't stay, after just standing there and watching him kill the Pope. And I can't just sit here in this tin can, waiting to die."

"But what *can* we do?"

"I don't know, but we have to keep trying. In the meantime, we should, as you say, look around. Not for our amusement, but for duty's sake. Our log can at least give a head start to the next crew."

"Now you're talking! Tell you what, Urs, let's duck back under the water first off."

"What good could *that* possibly do?" Griewold's voice was a mixture of habitual rudeness and genuine bemusement.

"The island's the point," Rafe answered. "It's . . . it's strange. The magnetic field, everything about it. But the surface was completely barren. Maybe we can tell more about it below the waterline." He didn't want to betray his suspicions. Griewold would laugh them off and refuse to check.

"Reasonable enough," Griewold mused. "How deep is the bottom here?"

"Well, that's another strange thing. I've tried jury rigging a sonar—not an imaging system, just a basic depth indicator. I don't get any return at all. Maybe the equipment got messed up when we ditched." And maybe this was a water world.

. . .

The inertial drive was efficient enough that they could dive as deep as the boat would stand, several hundred meters in this gravity, without using up much of their power reserve. Flying short distances would be equally safe. Getting out of the atmosphere, much less heading to the inner planets, was ruled out by the energy barrier of the gravity well.

The questions posed by this strange place fascinated Rafe. His mind toyed with them as he turned the boat toward the shoreline and then set up a steep dive. What kept the planet (he couldn't think of it as a moon) so warm? What generated the intense magnetic field that had crippled them? Did any of this have anything to do with the strange machines and structures they had found on the airless world they visited earlier?

The two of them had been in this same scout ship then, exploring the small planet closest to Epsilon Eridani. Griewold had noticed some strange patterns in the magnetic field. He had Rafe set up an instrument probe with seismic charges to check it out.

Rafe had spotted the domes on the surface just before the seismic bundles separated from the descending probe. If the geology probe had landed as targeted and set off its charges, they would have blown the flimsy surface structures to smithereens. He had known the objects were more important than the geological information at a glance. Detonating the seismic sounding charge before the probe touched down had destroyed some irreplaceable instruments, but there hadn't been time to think of anything else.

At the time, Rafe had been scared that the discovery would drag him into the hectic core of the expedition's work. Ironic, really, since the "thrill of uncovering new knowledge" had been his excuse for dodging a job with the family law firm. But things had settled down without either reward or punishment.

No, the two of them were stuck out here for the simple reason that the Norwegians commanding the *Amundsen* had little use for either of them. That was fine with Rafe, as long as it let him sit back and watch the computers do most of the work, but now they were even farther from the starship and the rest of the expedition, and they had only four days of air.

The light of the distant sun faded rapidly as they descended into the water. Rafe reached to cut on external floodlights, but Griewold beat him to it. For once, he didn't take the chance to berate Rafe.

If the slope of the ocean floor was as gradual as the shore suggested, they would have encountered it almost immediately. Rafe descended slowly, meter by meter. His light beams revealed little more than drifting specks. For a moment he glimpsed an object, all corners and planes like a ghostly origami, but it was back in the dark before he could make out any details. Some kind of seaweed? No, there wasn't enough light; certainly not this deep.

His thoughts returned to the idea that this moon was water all the way down. That wasn't quite as crazy as it had seemed at first. A ball of water that big would generate enough gravity to hold itself together and even keep an atmosphere; the navcom data had proved there really wasn't much dense rock here. No, the killer was that such a place just couldn't come into existence to start with. No natural process of planet formation would yield a mass of water this big, and no natural phenomena in a simple ball of water would keep it this warm. There had to be some geologic energy source. Maybe the ocean floor held some clues.

If they could find the ocean floor. He tried a sonar beep above the line of their descent, and got a signal. Shrugging, he shifted the boat to a horizontal course. The lights soon picked out a surface ahead of them. A corrugated plane of pale orange and gray rose vertically from the depths. Minute fissures covered the surface in intricate patterns like the whorls of a fingerprint, partially obscured by a tiny forest of bumps and tubes. The general image reminded Rafe of Terrestrial brain coral, but what could it be living on? There certainly wasn't enough light for photosynthesis.

Griewold broke the silence. "This water is a soup of organics, a lot of high-energy chemicals. I don't know where *they* come from, but there's plenty to power a sizable food chain."

After a moment, Rafe angled the boat back down, parallel now to the face of the "coral." As they descended, he noticed a few more of the origami fish, and an occasional long blunt-tipped tube wriggling in the larger crevices. The colors were more subdued than Earthly reefs, mostly gray and orange with black highlights, and a few spots of other pastel shades.

The surface began to slope again, but inward, creating an overhang. Rafe raised an eyebrow as he looked at Griewold. "Go ahead, follow it on down," the lieutenant growled. "The hull can handle another eighty meters."

Rafe nodded, amused at the tone. Griewold hated anything that disturbed his nice, tidy universe.

Within twenty meters, the scene changed abruptly. The surface beside them curved sharply away. Moving below it, they could see that it reached horizontal and then rose back toward the center of the "island." Perhaps the land mass was actually a hollow dome like half an eggshell, floating with all but the top submerged. The image bothered Rafe somehow, and he had no interest in heading that direction. He guided the boat in a level course, following below the inverted ridge.

The bottom of the ridge eventually began to slope ahead of them, but downward. Rafe turned aside to get a better view. The open water resumed after about twenty meters, with the edge of the wall once again sloping up and then forming a curtain above them. If his shell image was anywhere close, it had to be a lot bigger. With arches cut out of the sides.

"A little farther down?" asked Rafe. Griewold just shrugged and pouted. He seemed to find the whole structure offensive.

Thirty meters. The descending segment of wall narrowed to a round column five meters across. The boat continued down, a small private universe floating in the darkness, with a lance of light brushing against the alien coral.

Rafe brought them to a halt after another forty meters. The column was thicker here. The image that had haunted him suddenly came to the surface: he saw the entire "island" as an enormous jellyfish, with an inverted bowl body trailing off into thousands of tentacles. No wonder he hadn't wanted to go underneath the wall earlier.

Griewold broke the silence. "Strange, the water is much warmer here, and the concentration of chemicals much stronger. It's almost like a volcanic vent."

On an impulse, Rafe turned off the floodlights. The view screen went black. After a moment, though, a dim blue glow emerged below them: ill-defined, but in the general line of the descending column. Nothing much more than a hint of blueness, vague but eerie.

"Urs, can we go a little lower? Get a closer look at that?"

Griewold stared at the screen for a moment longer, silent. "It makes no sense. It just makes no sense." He shook his head. "We don't want to go any closer, Ensign. That looks like Cherenkov light. Whatever is down there is radioactive as hell."

Their ascent was uneventful, giving Rafe time to ponder this latest weirdness. He toyed with the idea that it might be some sort of fusion process. Isotopic analysis showed that the water around them was fairly rich in deuterium, by Earth standards. He couldn't conceive of a natural fusion reaction on that scale, though; more likely a chunk of uranium or something, perhaps from a meteorite.

Back on the surface, they hopped the boat over to the false island. Both of them were exhausted and ready for some sleep.

When they woke, Rafe got ready to look around outside the boat. Standard pressure armor would give him breathable air. It was intended for vacuum rather than for a corrosive, poisonous atmosphere like this, but it would resist the acid vapors for a lot longer than he needed. He strapped a rock hammer and some sample boxes to his suit. While he was out, Griewold would prepare the little on-board lab to look at the samples.

As he stepped out the airlock, the view hit him with nearly physical force. For too many months, he had lived inside deep space vessels with only display screens to show him the universe outside. His pressure suit and helmet seemed scant protection against the world that suddenly spread out around him.

Throw in some palm trees and dune grass, and it could almost have been a twilight beach in the Azores. Beyond the shoreline, the dark blue sea swelled and subsided, its surface marred by only a few whitecaps. The sky nearly matched the sea in color. Several bright stars, or planets perhaps, pierced the gloom.

Looking the other way, past the pumpkin-seed shape of the boat, brought a different perspective. It wasn't really twilight at all. The bright star halfway up the sky, barely showing a disk, was the sun of this system. The pale orange crescent facing it, sprawling nearly from horizon to zenith, was Cervantes. Rafe stared for several minutes. Maybe his names were from the wrong realm of literature: that crescent sure looked like the sword of Damocles.

He needed a name for this worldlet. It was certainly large enough to deserve one—almost as big as Venus back in the solar system. *Sancho Panza.* Now that would do nicely. It should infuriate Griewold thoroughly, too.

Reining in his thoughts, he turned his attention to the ground on which he stood. Definitely not the sand of his first imagination. Not much like anything on Earth, although it did remind him of the airless plains of Luna. Rafe kneeled to get a closer look.

Under his helmet beam, the smooth surface revealed faint striations, undulating lines of lighter and darker gray. Was this some remnant of folds and crevices such as they saw underwater?

Wait, there was something more, a glint of color amid the drabness. Rafe detached the lamp from his helmet. At a shallow angle, it brought out coruscating smears of color. Rainbow hues, pale but distinct, crossed the gray lines randomly. His first thought was of the shifting sheen of oil on water. The gleam was frozen in place, however, as long as he held the light still. Perhaps a thin film of opal was a better comparison.

He chipped at the surface with his rock hammer, and a chunk came free. The top centimeter or so seemed dense and glazed. Below that the substance was porous and grainy. Rafe rubbed the point of his hammer across the material, easily grinding it down.

"Ensign, have you finished your sight-seeing?" Griewold's voice boomed in Rafe's helmet radio. "May I remind you, we have a little problem with our life support?"

"I remember that, Urs. I also seem to recall that we were fresh out of ideas to solve that little problem. I'll be back in a few minutes. Maybe the stroll will improve my creativity." He dropped the divot into a sample box and turned back to the shore.

Walking on this surface was deceptive. Between the low gravity and the padded boots, the ground seemed soft. It wasn't really yielding at all; the glazed layer either cracked or held firm.

The slope to the water was gentle and smooth. Rafe walked until the slow-motion waves lapped at his boots. Below the waterline, the surface became wrinkled and dark, more like they had seen in the depths. A rough, rust-colored mat hugged the rock. Patches of the mossy crust extended up a short ways above the water, but adjacent bare areas were blackened. Rafe rubbed a spot, and his glove came away sooty. Almost as if the moss had been burned away . . . He pried up a section of the crust and dropped it in another sample box, scooping up some water for good measure.

This world was full of weirdness, and floating magnetic islands not the least. Nothing about it seemed natural. In some ways it made no more sense than the ancient mining sites and bizarre equipment on the innermost planet, with no sign of where the aliens had lived or what they had been building. The strange surface of this island seemed to be telling a special story, though. If he could just make out the message.

61

·   ·   ·

When he returned to the boat, Griewold was stomping across the control deck. In the light gravity, each step popped him a few centimeters into the air. Rafe knew better than to laugh.

"Damn it," Griewold yelled. "There's got to be a way! We've got a perfectly good fuel cell, and lots of hydrogen right outside. If we could just extract it and feed it to the cell, we'd have plenty of power to last us until the *Amundsen* came after us."

"Isn't there anything in the lab that could separate out the hydrogen?"

"What do you think I've been doing while you dallydillied around outside?" Griewold blithely ignored his earlier support for the exploration, and didn't give Rafe time to mention it. "I've been through all the gear we've got. It wouldn't work to just concentrate the hydrogen; we'd have to get rid of almost all the oxygen in the mixture."

Rafe hadn't thought of that, but it was obvious now that Urs mentioned it. A fuel cell depended on feeding hydrogen into the combustion chamber, with the oxygen source on the other side of the cell's matrix. The reaction would draw oxygen through the matrix, and presto! Out came electricity. If the gases were already mixed, no oxygen transport and no power.

Griewold was still shouting. ". . . pumps, pipes, sensors, but no decent membranes. If we even had a toy balloon!"

"Huh? What are you talking about?"

"Haven't you ever had a helium balloon?" The chance to sneer at Rafe seemed to make Griewold feel better, and he resumed in a calmer voice. "Small molecules like hydrogen or helium permeate through a membrane a lot faster than other gases. That's why a balloon loses its buoyancy before it loses its shape."

Rafe was already jumping down the short corridor to his bunkroom. Griewold was yelling again behind him, but he couldn't make out the words over his pounding heart. He hadn't realized how scared he was until there was suddenly a ray of hope.

A few hours later in the boat's workshop, Rafe stared in dismay at the shambles of the test rig. The thought was percolating through his head that they really were in a lot of trouble.

The idea seemed so simple. Pump some of this world's air into a small balloon inside a sealed chamber, and the hydrogen should bleed through the balloon fairly quickly and build up in the outer chamber.

Rafe didn't have any toy balloons. He did, however, have several high quality, super sensitive, rolled tubular membranes in his personal kit. He thought they would do nicely.

It was all for naught. After they set up the plumbing, the gear seemed to run fine for a couple of hours. Until the condom popped. Rafe felt a sudden terror at the thought of a burst condom, followed by a wave of relief that it was just some gases in a bottle. It took a moment to register that his life really did depend on it. Now, a second attempt had just ended with similar failure, and Griewold had stalked out pulling his hair.

Damn! The chlorine! That was the original problem; otherwise, they could breath the air here and survive for some time without power. And that was the trouble with his rig, too. Why hadn't he thought of that to begin with? As hydrochloric acid vapor, it was chewing up his membrane in short order.

Unfortunately, figuring out the problem didn't suggest any easy solution. Maybe if he knew more chemistry, he could get the acid out of the air as he pumped it in. If he could do that, though, power wouldn't be a problem; they could breath the air mix directly. Between his limited knowledge and the boat's limited supplies, that didn't seem like an option.

So heartbreaking, with all that hydrogen right outside. Rafe reset the monitors to display exterior air chemistry. Why, the hydrogen content was even higher now. It was up over six and a half percent. That was actually high enough to burn by itself, not that that helped. If he fed the outside air directly into the reaction chamber of the fuel cell, it would have more than enough oxygen to burn without pulling any across the matrix, and that wouldn't generate any power.

Santa Maria! Had he just casually dismissed the fact that the outside *air* was *flammable*? Rafe checked combustion references in the computer—it was really true. The glazed surface, the blackened waterline, even the deep pockets of radiation: it started to make sense. What was the deuterium level in the hydrogen outside? Another quick check confirmed it was almost zero, and that clinched it. They had a lot more to worry about than power now, and a lot less time.

Rafe found Griewold on the flight deck, staring at the view screen. "Urs, I need to go back outside. I've got an idea about rigging the main antenna to send a signal to the *Amundsen*."

Griewold looked up at him with disgust. "Don't be a fool. We

63

haven't got anywhere near the power to signal the ship. It doesn't matter what you do to the antenna, this boat is our tomb."

Rafe stared at the floor and fidgeted. "I . . . I guess you're right." It wasn't hard to fake panic. "I just can't face it. I've got to *do* something, or I'll just start screaming." If he could make Griewold feel superior, manipulating him should be easy.

"Well," Griewold allowed, "I guess it is hard for you, without the military training I've had. Go ahead. For morale's sake, keep on slugging."

Rafe fought to keep a resigned look on his face as he headed for the airlock. The pompous bastard! Lecturing *him* on morale . . .

The modifications didn't take long. In half an hour, Rafe was back on the flight deck, settling into his seat. Urs didn't even look at him until he powered up the drive and lifted off the beach.

"Ensign, what *are* you up to?"

"I need to get the boat in the best possible position for the signal to get through, Urs."

Griewold sighed dramatically. "Hasn't this gone far enough? I'm trying to humor you, but the whole point is to maintain some dignity —*what the hell!*"

Rafe had plunged the boat into the water, stopping with just the crest of the hull protruding. Including, hopefully, the antenna mount. "I need to get the hull wet," he replied lamely. Without giving Griewold time to react, he stabbed at the transmit switch.

The hand of God smashed against them. Rafe hadn't thought to fasten his seat harness, and he was yanked into the air by the force of the blow. As he picked himself off the floor, he noticed groggily that Griewold *was* belted in, probably by sheer habit. The view screens glared bright orange, despite the several meters of water now above them.

"What . . ." Griewold's voice broke, and he started over. "What was *that?*"

"Hydrogen's been building up the whole time we've been here." Rafe affected nonchalance. "It was up high enough to burn, and it just ignited."

Griewold stared at the screen for a moment, then turned to Rafe. His voice was almost reverent. "The whole *atmosphere* exploded?"

"Oh, I'm not sure explosion is the right word. It's burning, all right, and it will spread over the whole globe."

"The whole atmosphere," Griewold repeated, shaking his head. "It's lucky we were in the water. A few minutes earlier . . ." His voice trailed off as he stared at Rafe. "No, no. *Tell* me you didn't do this on purpose."

"It was our only chance, Urs!"

"You said you were going to transmit a radio message!"

"I did not! I said I was going to send a *signal*." Rafe waved at the screen, which still glared orange. "I bet they see it."

Griewold sputtered for a moment, struggling before he found his voice. "Ensign, there is *life* on this world. Even if the *Amundsen* sees this and comes to rescue us, our lives don't justify such wholesale destruction, such cavalier slaughter—"

Rafe cut him off. "Come on, Urs, are you blind? Do you think this is the first time this has happened? The hydrogen was below flammable concentration when we got here; it went up over a percent in one day. How much longer could it have gone before *something* set it off?"

"What could ignite it here?" Griewold shot back.

"Hey, the climate seems pretty tame, but there's got to be lightning sometime! And look at the island: the whole surface was slagged down. It's been scorched so many times, it's polished. There's nothing to leave ashes, except right around the shoreline where the seaweed sometimes pushes up too high."

Griewold groaned with disgust and stood up. "You've always got an excuse, don't you. Well, it's not going to work this time. If we do survive, I'm going to see you rot in the brig, and I'm going back to the inner system to get in on the study of those artifacts." He headed for the door.

Rafe began to chuckle, quickly losing control to gales of laughter. Griewold turned back, his face darkening. "What's so damned funny?"

"Don't you see it yet, Urs? This whole *world* is an artifact. That stuff farther in is probably just the scraps and junked equipment left over from *making* this place."

"Where the hell did you get that crazy idea?"

"What keeps this world warm, Urs? Where does all the hydrogen come from? The magnetic field that trashed our power plant? What about the chemical energy you noticed, that drives the food chain? Fusion, Urs! Thousands, probably millions of fusion plants in these floating islands."

65

"Don't be ridiculous. There couldn't be enough power plants to heat the whole moon if there was one in every island."

"The fusion plants are in the 'tentacles,' or 'roots' of the islands, and this world is water *all the way down*. You saw the density figures. It didn't make sense, but nothing about this moon makes sense *except as an object somebody built*."

"That's crazy. And anyway, fusion doesn't release hydrogen, it uses it up."

"Sure, Urs, but fusion works better with deuterium than regular hydrogen. The water had lots of deuterium, and the hydrogen in the air is almost all protium. I bet the system uses electroysis to get the hydrogen out of the water and then separates out the deuterium. The regular hydrogen dissolves in the deep water and eventually bubbles into the air."

"Are you suggesting some aliens built the islands?"

"I'm suggesting some aliens *built the whole moon!*" Griewold was reduced to an openmouthed stare, but Rafe's mind was in high gear. He hadn't thought through this far before. When the basic concept came to him, he was in too much of a hurry to rig the spark gap in the antenna before his nerve failed. "I don't know whether they built this as an aquarium for their pets, or maybe just a big joke. Maybe the aliens themselves are still down there, deep in this giant swimming pool. You know, the heat is probably just a by-product. I bet all those tasty chemicals are the main point of the cycle. Hell, they must have put the place out here because it would overheat anywhere closer to the sun."

Griewold had had enough. Shaking his head, still silent, he stalked off the flight deck.

Rafe felt kind of sorry for him. They would probably be stuck with each other again for their next assignment. Not only did they keep coming up with big discoveries, but the Norwegians running the *Amundsen* probably thought they richly deserved each other.

Rafe couldn't really disagree. He sure as hell didn't want to be stuck on the *Amundsen*. That would be nearly as bad as shuffling papers back in Madrid, and he'd a lot rather deal with Urs than the stuffy clique commanding the starship. Come to think of it, pestering Urs was enough fun in itself to make up for the aggravation of dealing with him.

He smiled to himself. If this boat could be repaired, they really ought to name it. What was Don Quixote's horse named? Rozinante, wasn't it?

If there is any writer in this volume who needs no introduction, that writer is Brian W. Aldiss. And we could simply leave it at that, except that that would expose us to the likelihood that Brian would come lalloping up to us the next time our paths crossed (in Egypt, say, or on the Côte d'Azur) and cry out in a voice of thunder, "You bastards, of course I need no introductions, but I bloody well like them anyway, and you know it!" Well, yes, we do know it, Brian. So to avoid any such hue and cry in some far-off land—which would startle the natives and upset the hotel staff—let us tell you quickly, as though you didn't know, that the urbane and exuberant Oxford-based Brian Aldiss has been writing rich and glorious masterpieces of science fiction for nearly four decades, with (apparently) never a letup in the flow of creativity that has produced such books as Hothouse, Non-Stop, and the magisterial Helliconia trilogy.

One private literary form that Aldiss has explored to great effect is what he calls the "enigma"—stories generated by setting down random arbitrary phrases and exploring the narrative possibilities to which they give rise. "An enigma," he has written, "consists of three panels. Each panel is a picture rather than a story in the ordinary sense—a picture or perhaps an untoward event. The 'story' lies in the unwritten relationship between the three parts; it may be profound or simply teasing. An area is left where the reader can invent for himself, an area of mystery unbridged by words." He has written many of these strange and haunting three-part stories; "Her Toes Were Beautiful on the Hilltops" is the most recent of them.

ANOTHER WAY THAN DEATH

Sun was down. Time was up. Half eroded, the moon hung like a target low in the glassy sky. The human world was turning to metal and madness, yet something miraculous was to come. That could be prognosticated by the olive green of the sky, with a hint of prussian blue, moving at a boneshaking tilt.

The metal vehicle containing the supposed John Stang and the others hurtled straight toward the moon over ill-paved roads. The vehicle shook and resonated as it went. It traveled all night, never getting nearer to the pock-faced satellite. Speed, distance, prepared-for obsolescence.

The eyes of the men in the vehicle were stale. They remained unlit by dawn. The sky was cracking toward its eastern horizon. A pale light spilled out from it, reflected on the sullen side of the vehicle.

No one knew a damned thing. No one knew the cardinal thing: that heaven was coming at breakneck pace, down the cosmic background, down the backbone, with just a touch of prussian blue.

Time was almost up. But they could not get it in their heads. Packed into the vehicle with rows of other uniformed men, John Stang watched the line of light through a slitted window. Dawn: he invited its welcoming implications to flood into his mind; only shadow and foreboding entered. He'd always been a night person anyway, and the stiletto of light he viewed carried a hue he associated with sickness and despair. Dawn was a time for a family death to arrive, for the telephone to ring, for children to cry of newly emergent ills, for suicide, for a confrontation with material woes, for un-

HER TOES WERE BEAUTIFUL ON THE HILLTOPS

Three Enigmas:

Another Way Than Death

That Particular Green
of Obsequies

The Ancestral Home
of Thought

BRIAN
W.
ALDISS

mended shoes, cold, smoke, stale breath, ill-fitting clothes, for hearing the news, reading bills, haste, alarms, acrid cigarettes, and the world snapping a muzzle back into place on the ursine chops of dreamtime. Today, dawn was also a time for Armageddon. And his resurrection.

Endeavoring to deflect his thoughts, Stang turned to the soldiers next to him. He hardly knew their names. In the black interior of the truck, they were not recognizable. The subject of the discourse was. They were talking about women.

Or so Stang phrased it to himself. Then he said, turning in distaste from the crudity of the discussion, that he had mentally used their phrase for it; in fact, they were not talking about women: they were talking about their own rutting, about their imagined conquest of women. Everything suggested that they knew nothing of women, and would have run a mile from such powerful wisdom. More than a mile. A million miles.

"I'm gonna grab old Vera again when we come through this package. This time, I'm really gonna show her. I'm gonna make her so sore, man, I kid you not. . . ."

"Forget Vera, you poxy randy sod. This is some strike we're on."

"The Goonos won't give us no trouble, you'll see. We're gonna hit them right where it hurts most."

"Yeah, we'll wipe them out so clean they won't know arse from elbow."

Ahead across the plain, a monster hangar loomed. The plain remained black, the sky pale, so that the outline of the building cut it with a geometrical shape broken by the great bare trees sheltering its north end. The vehicle ran to one end of the hangar as if seeking cover from the immensity of sky, sank down onto its haunches, and was still.

Immediate shouted orders. Intense activity, every man gathering his armor, tightening his equipment, securing his arms. They moved to the ramp at the rear of the vehicle and down it as if they formed part of one wounded but still formidable insect. In the great black rear wall of the hangar, a small rectangle appeared, sickly green in color. Chill still night air was sucked down into the barred tubes of their throats.

The front files of soldiers pressed forward, with a kind of urgent secrecy—no shouting now—and were swallowed into the maw of the building. Stang was in one of the last files. A dim personage stood in the shadows, pressed against the enormous structure, so that the light from the interior did not catch his figure, even by reflection. He spoke distinctly to John Stang as the latter filed by with the other men.

He said, in a conversational tone, *"There is another way."*

Stang lost his step and stumbled against the man on his left. The threshold of the hangar had a lip. He stubbed his boot against it, lunging forward as he entered the building.

A sergeant stood there, green light running down the angular line of his jaw.

"You. Name and number."

"John Stang. No number, sergeant—I'm not a combatant. I'm an accredited war correspondent."

"Bloody pansy noncombatant, eh? I don't care if you're Queen of All the Fairies, keep in step like the rest."

The hangar was filled with the bristling bulk of a Keg 15A. The Keg resembled a wild boar's belly, being coated with synthetic skin and hair. The air was tainted with its processes. The troops moved in file up an escalator that carried them through a rear orifice into the vast machine.

"There is another way . . ." Who had it been? What did it mean?

Stang felt faint. He was an anonymous unit in a great machine. Dull matt metal confronted every plane of his skull. The troops wore their pointed helmets with the visors up; it increased their resemblance to ants. Alien world: calved and carved from Mother Earth, air synthesized and sucked through tubes. Music whispered to them, damping pulse rates down to acceptable levels. Colors and fragments of reverie ran in Stang's head.

These things he had fought against all his life, the things that now overwhelmed him. Boots, harness, helmet, bulkheads, weapons, above all the mechanized regimented life to which they acted as fortifiers. The world—not of real men, as many men claimed—but of death to the spirit. What was most forbidden in the bristling belly of a Keg 15A? Intellectual conversation, women, flowing forms, individuality, trees, the anima.

"There is another way . . ."

The intercom awoke and made an announcement.

"Troops, prepare for takeoff. Attach yourselves to bench straps. Visors down, attach breathing tubes to labeled oxygen ducts in bulkheads. Relax. Remain seated. We shall taxi to designated runway and

71

await clearance signals. Expect to be airborne in fifteen point five minutes."

The muted figures plugged themselves into the mother ship, losing more of their essence as they did so. The personage was next to Stang again. Stang looked at it in astonishment and reached out a hand.

"An island yet remains," said the mysterious figure, "the Isle of the Blessed. Peace is still possible, and long life and love. You can still achieve it everywhere."

"We're heading for apocalypse." It was a pagan ghost, horned—

"Not apocalypse, no—apotheosis. It just needs one man to stand up and be counted." —not from the father, from an anima world.

The message seemed to be of overwhelming importance. Breathing painfully, Stang looked about him, down the blue-lit length of the troop deck. Nobody else appeared to have heard anything. Chins were firm, brows were heavy, as they contended with battle nerves.

Vibrations began, filling every space, the space between teeth and bones and individual hairs. There was motion; though there were no ports to look out of. The Keg was rolling from its vat of green light into the open. Jaws tensed. Everyone stared straight ahead. Big wheels rolling, blue smoke flattening over tarmac.

"The Isle of the Blessed," Stang said aloud. His neighbor did not look around. Several men were muttering to themselves—that was what the tensed jaws fought against, the telltale dribble of terror.

The personage had gone. Had it possessed legs? Had it worn robes? Did it infiltrate him? Was everyone powered by a vision, drawn in a moment of crisis from some deep racial reservoir?

Awful pains tore at Stang's breast. He saw himself as a wild animal. Metal hurt him. The deck punished him. The pains grew like unbridled optimism, and the jungle of near-human imaginings.

Deep snoring noises filled the ears of the passengers, as if only fragile glass separated them from a flooded piggery where animals tried to die.

When that island was obliterated, what remained? The world's apples would die, and these humans lose their pretense at humanity.

And what could the world do under bombardment? Lose its roundness.

Why, why another war? Always against the female principle.

But mankind . . . ? Species divided. Head against heart, masculine against feminine, left against right, light against dark, ancient against modern. Not-quite-humanity never as human as they liked to claim.

And the prize? The silent figure who guards the second law of thermodynamics: death, of course.

But there is another way.

Rolling his eyes upward in anguish, he saw the ordered labyrinth of pipes and ducts and junction boxes, curling behind stanchions, which ran through the vessel; they were the intestines of the great beast that had swallowed the men.

A more personal voice over the intercom, heavy, rich, breathing fumes of meat and liquor. "This is General Steen here, men. Listen to me. You can trust me. You know I'm a no-nonsense man. You don't have to question what I tell you. We all hope to die fighting. Today, we get our chance. We're going to fly halfway around the globe to blast our enemies. I don't have to remind you of that. I'll just remind you of a few salient facts about the enemy. You know they hate our proud nation. You know what they call us. Motherfuckers, they call us. Black-faced savages. They don't live like we do, not at all. Different religion, kneeling, sticking their damned buttocks up in the air to Allah. Who wants that? Yelling. Eating that muck they eat. And the oil—you know about that. Small, dark, hairy men. Women fat as cows. You know what we plan to do to them, hah! Well, here's our chance. We're going to wipe them out. You know what we have aboard here. Strictly secret. First we drop the cobalt treatment, eh? Then we go in at ground level. The new cerebellum weapons. We've got the chance no one's ever had before. Literally blast the enemy back to the Stone Age. Turns their gray matter into instant mashed potato, every damned manjack. Never raise a finger at anyone again."

As the voice went on, the troops revived. They might have been listening to meat coming out of a mincer. Fewer attitudes of dejection showed. Backs straightened, a glassy look of pride showed on many a tube-infested face. Big hands clutched at the gleaming weapons in their grasp, sliding up and down the barrel in masturbatory movement. Mouths opened slightly as the voice of their commander moved them toward a psychic orgasm of killing.

The Keg was still rolling forward. Everyone swayed slightly, as if locked in a primitive ritual preceding dance. The voice took on a more insistent note.

They knew what the general looked like, the leathery cheeks, the

73

blue lips, the eyes of chrome, the neck locking the shaved skull rigid. Even good men dreamed of him.

"You know we can do it, men. We're going to finish off this goddamned twentieth century as we mean to go on, make it remembered for all time. There's no room for weakness. . . . But I have to tell you that we have a traitor aboard with us, flying with us on this historic flight. He pretends to be one of us, but he is not one of us. He is our enemy. He is our enemy in a big way. And I'm going to ask him to show himself. You'll know him when you see him, men. Don't hesitate to shoot, even if you happen to kill a few comrades. Our great nation can ask that much of you. I'm going to call to him. Ask the coward to show himself. Be alert."

Jarring vibration drowned out the inspiring voice of the commander. They had lift-off. The dark ground could be imagined, rushing past under their wheels, the snow-flecked soil falling away, away, the trees flattening, the great plain shrinking, as the immense furred pig lifted its snout to the olive air.

For the first time, men looked at each other. They resembled carved people with glass eyes. Rather poor replicas of humanity, Stang thought, fighting back waves of nausea. He was in the grip of a compulsion knowing now—knowing at last—what was expected of him. But they were no longer human in the real meaning of the word; they had deliberately dehumanized themselves—that was what war and military training were for; and pain was better than the pain of being human and accepting one's divided nature. Head against heart, light against dark, ancient against modern, left against right, masculine against feminine; to accept—that was what needed true courage, true love.

And the voice, the voice perhaps powering them into the near-night air, lifting them to a dark starless stratosphere within their skulls.

"You have your orders. Shoot to kill. This is the real enemy. He's aboard. With us. Against us. We are going to obliterate his kind. He calls himself a savior. He's lying, men. He's the enemy, full of soft talk and soft shit. Jesus Christ, I challenge you to come out and show your face. . . . This could be the last day of the goddamned Earth, so now is the chance to come on out and show your face!"

74   The storm rose in John Stang. He knew the commander had the terms all wrong. The enemy the commander feared, the enemy they all feared, was far more ancient than Jesus, that Middle East marvel, by

several million years. And yet, in general terms, the identification was powerful enough to force him to respond. He rose, breaking forth from the tubes and belts. He felt himself rise and break forth, saw himself as the soldiers, cowering, would see him—white, pure, terrible, of great puissance and stature. He became transformed.

And immediately he raised his arms, his fingers reached up to the pipes and cables overhead, conjoined with them, melted into them so that his life-force flowed there. His countenance shone down upon the scattering soldiery. Some hardened troops, too unimaginative to experience surprise, fired toward his flowing form; but the lasered energies were merely gathered into his presence and fed his radiance. The hairs of his head rained radiance, radiance was in the ropelike folds of his robes. When he spoke, his voice was silver, his tone bell-like, chiming through the ship.

"Steel must now be banished. Metal must die. *There is another way*. You must pass along the river of understanding until you reach the great ocean of wisdom. In that ocean, lost in haze, there the Isles of the Blessed still lie. You must get there or you will surely perish. And you will perish from the Earth forever, and forget its ripeness. But if you gain the Isles you will live in plenty, and fortune will shine on you."

He showed his/her face.

Some of the men fell down, crying, "Lady, lady, spare us!" Their carbines melted. Warm metal, blood, semen.

She grew still, for this was the final hour. Despite the darkness outside, she fed on her own brightness, spreading now beyond the skin of the Keg, until her feet trailed to the valleys and plateaus far below. Her toes were beautiful on the hilltops.

Armored vehicles moved in line toward her place. But nothing could withstand the ancient life-fuse once it was lit. The feet took root and their tendons became ivies growing up the trunk of a great earth-tree. At which, the world responded with a glow of a kind no human being had ever seen; all eyes were opened to this strange light, which shone across land and sea.

And the Keg was no more than a little golden nut, low on one of the branches that spread overhead like a canopy, sending its sap out to the moon and netting in its net of twigs the comets and the noiseless things of heaven.

THAT PARTICULAR GREEN OF OBSEQUIES

It was in the fifty-first year of the Kayyrandarth. In the annual lotteries, the opportunity to visit a dead personage fell upon a man called Barnes Atarver.

Barnes Atarver was distinguished but obscure. He had been allowed some freedoms and did not abuse them. He never spoke of policies but of philosophies. His life had been lived dedicatedly, except for an early year when he had traveled disguised among the Inner Islands and—it was rumored—had been made much of by maids and their mothers; that journey of discovery had lasted nine months, to be followed by an eight-week period of fasting and weeping. Since then, Barnes Atarver had lived on Bronze Face Street in the capital, collecting and studying the paintings of the bygone painter Paul Gauguin.

So that when the Clerk of the Hereafter Bureau asked him what dead personage he wished to visit, Atarver replied without hesitation, "Paul Gauguin."

The Hereafter, as was generally known, was a state of sensory deprivation. One did not see or hear or feel. Nothing existed in the Hereafter except a thick darkness and the ghostly smell of parsley.

Recently, in order to encourage visitors somewhat, a lamp was set burning. Cold, fish white, it attempted to illumine eternity. Maintenance costs were enormous.

Gauguin was still reconstructing as Barnes Atarver arrived. The latter averted his eyes from the process. The falling pieces of decay were as ludicrous as they were disgusting. When Gauguin coughed, he looked again. The painter was shivering and wrapping a white robe about himself. His face was no more than a skull with eyebrows and beard attached.

"Everything's always the same," he said. "The rocks, the river, the sand, the temple, the heat of noon, the steps, the moon like a rotten melon, the waiting women . . ."

The things he mentioned were not to be seen. Both he and Atarver existed in limbo. Perhaps he was gnawing on a thought that had possessed him before he died. Limbo was like an unprimed canvas.

"Er—yes," replied Atarver. Silence fell, palpable within the general anomic silence. The sound of souls rustling about him like leaves on an autumnal tree was imaginary, he told himself. He took a quick tremble and waited.

"The palm trees are the same, too, come to think of it," Paul Gauguin said, clasping his hands together. "Or whatever you call palm trees."

Silence within silence, like an unhatched egg within a dead chicken.

"And the sky?" Atarver suggested. This was not at all what he had expected. He felt he was breathing stone.

"I'll do the sky in a couple of flat washes," said Gauguin. "Yellow. A nice neutral yellow like Breton cake. And green. To show it's going to be sunset some time. Olive green, with a dash of prussian. And a motto in it. 'An Ancient Adversary Watches Us.' Something of that sort. The green would be echoed in her flesh. Bernard taught me that, at least."

"I so admire your unrealistic skies. Sometimes I sit and think about them for days, weeks even. I lost a cat that way once." The confession came out impulsively; not a characteristic moment for such an academic man. He lived on lentils.

"Once I went by appearances, was captive to them. When I was a slave to what I saw, then I was blind. An artist must describe essences, you understand. It is important to realize fully that the sky is olive green, with a dash of prussian. When everyone understands that, then . . ." He let the sentence die, as if sensing that it too should be allowed latitude in the way of representation. "Fuck realism."

"There are schools . . ."

Gauguin came and stood near to Atarver. He looked threatening, not to mention corpselike. The defiling marks of leprosy were on his countenance.

"I'm bigger than you."

"Er—you led a healthy life in the South Seas."

Luminous eyes penetrated the haggard night of eternity. "Those fools of art critics, what do they know? That particular tone, *that particular green of obsequies*—that's what Vincent called it—is the one color that signifies innocence and wickedness. Color, what am I saying?—the damned thing's a whole philosophy. The philosophy of skin. To catch life by the throat . . . By the tits . . ."

He brought his hands convulsively forward, as if about to grapple with life's windpipe. Atarver stepped hastily out of the way, wishing he had brought his walking stick, or at least an umbrella. He had been prepared for something rather more formal—who was it had told him that the dead were sticklers for etiquette? He realized now the dead did not wash.

"You mention innocence and wickedness," he said, fighting a note of hysteria that, like rising damp, had crept into the panels of his throat. "There lies the source of your most brilliant ambiguities and, I suspect, of your personal life-pattern, sir."

Gauguin looked at Atarver suspiciously. "What do you know about it? Who are you? Why should I be bothered . . . ? What's this *pineapple* doing on my bed? In faith, we're well enough off here, can't complain. We can follow our preoccupations to their logical conclusions, and you just interrupt . . ."

"My name's Atarver, Monsieur Gauguin. Barnes Atarver. I come here from an epoch some two centuries after your—following your translation to the Hereafter. Times have changed. My apologies for disturbing you, but in my estimation you are one of the greatest of all painters, and not only because you unite East and West. In 'Contes Barbares,' you painted the first metaphysical masterpiece of the twentieth century, while your rhythms and your pictorial qualities are such . . ."

He babbled on for some minutes, until his perception of color in the general achromatic murk brought him up short. The painter was not attending; his knotted eyebrows indicated as much. Instead, he had secreted some strands of orange that hung in the atmosphere before him, dull in parts, flame bright in others. The shape was amorphous. At first, Atarver took it for a parrot.

Next followed an olive green, tinged with prussian blue. It uncoiled like ectoplasm from a central point, distributing itself, forming a figure of a man. The man was seated, naked except for a loincloth. He held a knife. The orange strands formed themselves into his hair; knotted with a green ribbon, they hung down his spine, coiling like grass snakes.

It seemed to Atarver that the man depicted might be a native of the Marquesas Islands, where Gauguin had died. His eyes were heavy-lidded; he had plump breasts and his limbs were rounded. His posture held a clear Buddhist reference, and he looked at Atarver with a smoldering intensity, the menace of which was increased by the determination with which his broad blunt hand held the knife. He had no whites to his eyes.

"Er—yes," Atarver commented.

Other properties were forming around the image of the man, vegetation suggested in outline, flowers implying male and female sexual organs. They were brightly colored. Gradually, all Eternity was being lit by the sulphurous colors of Gauguin's art. They multiplied like a Mandelbrot set.

As the painting increased, Atarver experienced vertigo. Adjusting his socks did not banish his sickness. Gauguin's creation was expanding. The drab olive feet of the man now trailed a great distance below Atarver, his face far above. His colors dimmed and glowed as if fed by flame. The aurora borealis had taken to portraiture. Atarver was privileged to view it from an unimaginable stratosphere.

"Impressive, undoubtedly impressive," he murmured, resourcefully.

"You miss the scrape of brush on canvas, though. It's nothing without the tactile aspect." Nevertheless, Gauguin stepped back to survey progress with an air of satisfaction.

"But why's the man got red hair?"

"He's a Neanderthal. They're all Neanderthals—all the tribes of the Pacific. That's why there's no serious conflicts among them, or between men and women. Neanderthals are *whole*, in contact with everything. They have the essential magic."

"I've always wondered if your color theories didn't owe something—"

"That's why I had to leave Europe behind. Couldn't stand Cro-Magnon, couldn't damned stand Cro-Magnon. The smell of him. His incessant chatter." Defiantly, he added a bright red pigment that glowed in the Marquesan's ear like a bead. "Androgynous, you see, that's what I've made him. . . . Breasts, penis, vagina . . ."

"So I see, yes. Getting back to the question of innocence and wickedness—"

"Same thing," Gauguin said, vigorously beginning another figure, this time recumbent. His nostrils dilated with effort. "It wasn't just young girls. I had young boys, too. Flesh—androgynous flesh. That melting principle . . . Everything has to melt. Goats. Creation itself is a melting process. Male and female, yin and yang . . ."

"And did you find that the essential *innocence* of the islanders of the South Seas was in any way—"

Gauguin laughed. The supply of ectoplasm faltered for a moment.

He remained dwarfed by the increasing size of his painting, yet his stature was never in doubt. "Innocents? They're not innocent, you fool. It's the Europeans, the white races, the Cro-Magnons, who are innocent—that's where the trouble is made. They have sex in the head but none in the body. The fault of an overdeveloped cerebrum, I suppose. Whereas the Tahitians have large cerebella. Deliciously moist vaginas. That's the Neanderthal heritage, needless to say."

"Well, you say 'needless to say,' but it seems to me—"

The reclining figure was a woman, hideous yet elegant, her eyes narrowed in an expression of lust as she regarded her mate. She was muscular. The line of her leg and hip held the world in thrall. She slid a hand under her skirt and scratched herself.

"Don't argue with me. I know what I'm talking about because I earned my knowledge by living it. I didn't get it out of textbooks. I didn't pretend to be alive. I fought against my own stupid lethal swinish ignorance—that's what's written in my paintings. . . ." He ceased to paint, turning to Atarver, who cowered politely, and fixed the critic with his corpse eyes. "I fought my own rotten *innocence*. That's what I did. I gave up far more than Europe and its war mania—they're obsessed with ironmongery—I changed my race. That's what I did. And not just my race—no, I changed my species. I became Neanderthal. . . ." He secreted a bunch of bananas. "Leprosy is a Neanderthal disease. You associate it with dirt, but that's just because Neanderthals are of the earth itself, the original stock. Close to Earth, compounded of its original elements."

"Are you trying to argue that Neanderthals are the real humanity and—"

Atarver had said something that annoyed Gauguin. The painter turned away. Hitching up his gown to reveal shaggy buttocks, he squatted and began to draw in the imaginary mud with an imaginary brush. The mud sighed.

A little fat-bellied idol grew beneath his fingers. It took on color, substance, began to fill limbo. Its eyes twinkled with a sly delight. Its lascivious lips moved. It addressed Atarver.

"Look, Gauguin doesn't argue. He's too busy being, just *being*. Listen, take a word of wisdom back with you to life. *It's all magic*. There's no reality, only magic. You know that, but you prefer to forget it. Haven't you ever lain with a woman under a full moon? Magic. Magic."

"And what you say . . ." But Atarver had never argued with an idol before. His sentence petered out into the wan canvas of limbo, smelling briefly of cat piss.

"Why did he try to eliminate European traditions from his canvases, do you think, my fine friend?" asked the idol, indicating the painter, who now stood up to view his work. "Why, so that he could bring in magic, for which your traditions find no room. Naked magic. Naked truth. Nudity. Nudity and heat. Ripeness, fruitfulness, lubrication . . ." He rose and danced heavily to his own words. "Male and female grinding together as one. We Neanderthals are as different from you Cros as Cro is from android. In fact, with our command of magic and empathy and just a touch of garlic, we regard all Cros as androids. Cold, closed, self-contained, peasants of patriotism, idiots of ideology, robots of regimentation, slaves of slime-tables . . ."

The idol was whirling now, its words becoming indistinct.

". . . burst from it all, exploding, *pwtt*, like a melon seeding . . ."

Gauguin had moved on, hands active about him as if in incantation.

"The magic dance, you see," he muttered. "You've got too much cerebrum—you wouldn't understand."

The idol was chanting as it turned:

> "Ingo pingle, heaven's tits,
> Someone comes, body fits . . ."

Powered by the idol's words, he let forth about him four amazonian brown women all at once. Atarver jumped out of the way of their floral skirts. Majestic, they stood on a beach, platters of fish held under their generous bare breasts, and gazed into a mauve distance thick with passion fruit. Their lips were guavas, their eyes held Capricorn sunsets.

"Magic . . ." Atarver said, feeling lust overcome timidity. Whatever Gauguin's crazy theories in the Hereafter, the artist had certainly lost none of his creative faculties.

As he started to remove his socks, he gazed with awe at the thundrous darkness in the armpit of the beauty nearest to him. It was ten meters deep at a conservative estimate, and Atarver, whatever his faults, was no conservative.

81

"It's seeding that's at the root of wickedness. We all understand that. The forests of entanglement. Androgyny is the only answer. No more yin and yang, only ying."

"Then the world would end." Atarver's word of damp wisdom.

A forest of pink hibiscus grew, the columns of its trunks like a colonnade of a temple extending, multiplying, into the farthest recesses of the Hereafter, proceeding like a street fire.

"What better way for the world to end, since it must do one day? Union without division. Male and female united, as legend says they once were. One flesh. The whole world one gigantic sexual organ, which is what I wish my canvases to be."

The forest sprouted lingams, bursting in red and biscuit profusion from the foliage.

Atarver's chronograph warned him that it was time to return to the Herebefore. The outlines of the painter immediately became indistinct.

"I must leave you, sir," Atarver said. "And I wish I could take your superb painting with me."

"I think we'll leave it here," said Gauguin, with a hint of his earlier surliness. "It'll cheer up this tedious amphitheater between two worlds." His speech became indistinct. He was beginning to decompose. "You see what I mean about yin and yang—we even have to have two worlds, living and dead. The time will come when androgyny . . ."

Only luminescence was left. Vertigo returned to Atarver, vertigo and the prospect of a plate of oysters, with lemon, escorted down the throat by a white wine that had been cherished and never overchilled. He turned to leave.

Within what seemed no more than a moment, he was recovering in his rooms in Bronze Face Street.

In the halls of the Hereafter, the painting still hung, lighting with its enormous shapes and its smoldering color the emptiness between the yin and yang of life and death. The eyes of its natives gazed toward the surf that marked an indistinct boundary between earth and heaven.

THE ANCESTRAL HOME OF THOUGHT

But for the building, it was a bare canvas. Dead trees stood here and there on the plateau. They alone, to any wanderer rash enough to traverse the high plain, offered shelter from the stars by night and the Pestilence that walked at noonday.

No one traveled here this night. An owl swooped from its nest in one of the dead trees, streaming like a feathered wind above the earth. As it flew, it passed over a low mound. Beneath this mound was buried a man or woman who had once dared to venture across the plateau; the mound was ancient, and the being had died many centuries before the present possessors of the land had emerged from their caves. The trees had lived then, and other vegetation besides. Since those prehistoric times, the climate had changed. Now there was only desolation, a scatter of hunted life, and the building.

The building housed the Vercore Project. It stood one thousand five hundred and six meters above sea level. By daylight, the mountains that fringed the plateau on which it stood could be seen clearly through the uncorrupted air. Now, in the light of a moon pared down to its last quarter, gross simplifications had taken place. A monstrous being, striding across the plateau, would have seen only the flatness of a giant playground, at its center a flat concrete rectangle. The mountains had gone. The faint variations in ground level had gone. Even the architectural details of the building itself—such as they were—had vanished under the simplification of darkness. Only the elementary white shape was left, euclidean amid its vast and rudimentary situation.

Once it had housed an Institute of Experimental Psychology. Now barriers had gone up round it, and defensive zones, and it housed the Vercore Project. Its outer fire perimeter was less than four kilometers from the nearest prehistoric burial site.

At this dead hour, the energies of the project were low. Three floors below ground level, in Room D306, Mervyn Widdowson and his assistant, Jay Ling, drank coffee out of brittle plastic cups. The hum of the air circulator deadened their eyelids.

Widdowson kicked a shoe off and scratched the sole of his foot. "You saw the news today, Jay? The Sickle have hostaged Stockholm, the rats."

Ling rubbed the back of his neck and yawned. "We can do without Stockholm, can't we? It was neutral."

"One of the few neutrals left . . . But that's the point. It's a considerable escalation of the war when you start picking out neutrals. Besides, I had a great-aunt living in Stockholm. Not a bad old bird. I keep thinking about her."

"Well, that's war." Ling's tone was flat. "You know, Merv, I begin to hate the so-called civilization we're supposed to be defending. I don't just hate the Sickles anymore. I hate our side, too. I'm poisoned by the war. We're all becoming more like machines, day by day. Once I might have *cared* about Stockholm—not no more."

Widdowson laughed shortly. "Battle fatigue. We all suffer from it. Three years the war's gone on . . . The sooner we wipe them out, the better. I'm for a quick nuclear strike, myself. Finish it. One way or the other."

Ling drained his cup. He had heard Widdowson on that subject many times before.

"My ancestors came from Hainan four generations ago. It's a nice little tropical island, by all accounts. When this bloody war is finished, if it ever finishes, I'm going to pack my bag and go back to Hainan and spend the rest of my days there, swimming and fishing."

Widdowson drained his cup. He had heard Ling on that subject many times before. He slapped his colleague on the back. "Let's get on with the program, old sport, before Telbard puts in an appearance."

"We've got Brains next," Ling said. Obligingly, he got up from the desk and went to fetch the stacked metal files awaiting them on a trolley. As Widdowson joined him, they began to feed the X-ray plates into the computer.

They had already programmed DUX 3. When the first batch of plates was loaded, the power was switched on, and DUX began to mutter and click. Its readings showed on the VDU, columns of calibrations gleaming above the shadowy depictions of numerous human brains. The columns moved upward in jerks on the screen. Between batches of plates, Widdowson and Ling read paperbacks; they had two thousand four hundred plates to process. Although weighty matters were being decided, boredom set in.

That part of the program was completed by one o'clock in the morning. The second part, a collation of previous readings, was finished in an hour. Ling folded the printouts into a packbag and posted them in the pneutube up to Telbard's office. Telbard was head of department.

"Massage and bed for me," Ling said, looking at his watch. "Coming, Merv?"

"I think I'll take in a movie. Studio Two is offering one of the golden oldies, *Evil Gains*. I need a shot of violence."

"See you tomorrow, then."

"That's for sure." Grunts of laughter as they parted, and Widdowson flipped the lights off. They were bound to meet tomorrow; there was no escape from the Vercore Project for the duration.

Gaunt hunters marched across broken territory, along a dried riverbed. They slowed their progress and began to stalk. Ahead, in a sheltered hollow, heedless of danger, women danced. They were small and dark, young and old, swaying to the rhythm of a single skin drum. In their rapture, they remained unaware of the enemy stalking them until it was too late. The hunting party opened fire on the dancers.

One of the women survived—the Magic Woman, dark and hot, without ideology, beyond the reach of philosophies. She was Sycorax; she possessed the knowledge forever denied men. She had but to dance her dance and the world would be changed. Changed for good, transformed by her secret knowledge.

A man was bearing down on her, headlights burning. Armed men were pounding toward her. The Magic Woman yelled defiance at them.

But they had her surrounded. They approached in crouching positions now, carbines at the ready. Searchlights glowed into life. Stepping up from red to yellow to blinding white, the incoherent illumination of the mechanist culture opposing her.

In the Magic Woman's mind, another existence, a fractal thing, immeasurable. Expressed in intricate pattern. *And she began to dance*.

Widdowson sat up in the cinema, snatching the 3-D helmet from his head. It had been the movie, then it wasn't the movie. The Magic Woman was no part of the movie he was experiencing. She had come from his own—

It wasn't rational. No. He was tired. Illusions. Putting the helmet back in place again, he merely saw the armed hunters, moving lifelike through his cerebrum. They shed their uniforms, showered, laughed, drank beer. A normal world. Plus the artificial heroics of the screen.

· · ·

It was snug in the dark of the cinema, four floors below ground level. Mervyn Widdowson was tucked comfortably under his helmet when a personal call came through. Sighing, he blanked his screen and answered.

Neil Telbard's face came into view.

"You alone, Merv? Come right up, will you? Use the private way."

"I'll be with you."

Telbard's lean features disappeared, to be replaced by one of the dancers, falling to the ground, clutching the wound in her belly. Widdowson switched her off and left the cinema. Making sure that he was not followed, he went to the secret bank of elevators to which he had a key. Scanners scrutinized the grade of his house-pass. A few minutes later, he was standing in his chief's office. Although the room was aboveground, its windows were securely sealed off by blackout and radiation shutters. It was a bleak room, without decoration, its obsessive tidiness emphasizing the bleakness.

"Trouble?" he asked.

Neil Telbard, like the room in which he had his being, was a neat and featureless man.

Passing Widdowson a mescahale and taking one himself, Telbard said, "The Vercore Project is very much bigger than you or I can be allowed to know." As if silenced by his own large statement, he stood there unspeaking, wreathing his jowls in smoke. Light from his desk lamp, shining from under its green shade, made the smoke half transparent, half solid.

He coughed, a neat, dry noise.

Merv stood where he was, thinking of the carnage going on around the globe. Increasingly, silence made him think of war. Stockholm, his aunt, his last relative, silent now.

"Do you know—have you guessed—what the objective is of Vercore?"

". . . It's a demographic survey on an unprecedented scale. So I understand. Mine not to reason why . . ."

The jowls remained smoke-hung. Then the department head said, "I've been looking at the results of the test you ran earlier. They are conclusive."

"Conclusive of what?"

As if making a decision, Telbard moved swiftly to a cupboard behind his desk, and produced from it two gels of cutaway human skulls, photographed from a side view, with brains tinted to show different sections. He dropped them on his desk and ran a finger in an arc over the cerebral cortex on one of the gels.

"You can see how the gray matter overshadows the limbic brain. Here, at the back of the skull, it overhangs the cerebellum completely. The cortex is a recent development, specific to Homo sapiens."

Being more familiar with the structure of the brain than his superior, Widdowson said nothing. The first brain he had ever observed, laid open on an operating table, had reminded him of a fungus, with its gelatinous and contorted folds. That first impression had never been entirely banished. Nor had a more shadowy conception of the brain as parasitic on an otherwise healthy physical organism. Widdowson ascribed his atheism, his immunity to ideology and theory, to a conviction that any idea generated in that saprophytic thinking sponge stood little chance of corresponding reliably with the real world terminating just outside the skull. He swathed himself in ectoplasmic smoke from his mescahale, and waited.

Telbard moved his finger to the other gel and made a more circumscribed arc. "On this one, you can see the topography of the cortex is rather different. In particular, it does not overhang the cerebellum at the rear of the skull. The occipital lobes are less fully developed. The cerebellum is correspondingly larger. Quite a bit larger than in the other gel. See? Enough to change considerably the profile of the brain—with its consequent effect on human thought and behavior."

He knows I was trained in biology, Widdowson told himself. He'll get to the point in a minute. He didn't invite me up here for nothing. I can always ask to have the movie replayed tomorrow night. And he thought of the guns opening fire on the dancing women. And of his great-aunt.

"The cerebellum is an ancient part of the brain, common to all mammals. It controls movement. It is also the home of sleep and of what used to be called the subconscious or the unconscious—in other words, it's the ancestral home of thought. But not just primitive . . . it was still developing at the same time as the cerebrum developed." He shook his head, as if trying to make greater sense of what he was saying. "Anyhow, Merv, we're now building up proof that two different kinds of human beings exist on the planet, with two different kinds of brain profiles, of thought processes."

"Yeah? How, different?"

"One cerebrum-oriented, scientific, rational. One cerebellum-oriented, believing in magic and intuition." He flipped the two gels together. "This cerebrum-oriented one belongs to a western man—from Norway, in fact. This other, the cerebellum-oriented one, belongs to a fisherwoman in the Marquesas Islands. They are selected, of course, to represent the two extremes of the spectrum."

Widdowson shot his superior a glance. "We're dealing with racial material? That's dangerous. How does this fit with Vercore?"

"We'll take a stroll outside, Merv?"

"*Outside?*"

Leading the way into his kitchen, Neil Telbard opened a cupboard. He thumbed a button. The back of the cupboard slid away and they stepped into a blue-coded corridor. Patrolling guards stopped them, examined Telbard's identification status, and let them pass. In a minute, they were standing under a canopy of stars, sniffing the breezes of night.

Breathing deeply, Widdowson steadied himself against the wall of the building. He felt dizzy and alarmed. It was two months since he had last stood in the open. Coughing, he ground his mescahale underfoot.

"We can speak more freely here," Telbard said.

"What about?"

"We have proof that Homo sapiens is in fact two distinct species," Telbard said. "Or rather, *was* two distinct species. They've interbred to some extent. The proof rests on an elaborate series of factors, not just on brain proportions. Body proportions and physiological data are also taken into account.

"Despite the interbreeding, the two species are still surprisingly distinct in most parts of the world. Species A emerged from Africa several million years back, spread to the Middle East, and then divided into two subspecies. The dropouts were kicked out into Europe—they're the subspecies we call Neanderthals. The smarter subspecies either settled in the Middle East or made a big trek eastward, populating Asia and farther still, eventually to cross the Bering bridge into North and South America.

"These chaps of Species A were all moon worshipers and had matrilinear societies. They were promiscuous, and so the children never knew who their fathers were. In consequence, the line of descendency was through women, who in any case ruled the tribe. As still happens today among their progeny in the Pacific.

"Species B emerged from India later than Species A. They were patrilinear and they worshiped the sun. They were great hunters. They were organized in quasimilitary tribes, and from the start they had a firmer grasp on technology than the rather dreamy Species A. They moved westward in a great migration.

"A lot of them settled in what's now the Middle East and inter-married with Species A. It was a good place to live, fertile, et cetera. But several legions of them continued on into Europe. Europe was their real hunting ground. One animal they hunted was the subspecies of Species A, the Neanderthals. The Cro-Magnons, to use that termi-nology for Species B, practically wiped out the older race. But they spared the women. It's like the history of the Tasmanians. They wanted women, for slaves, concubines, and whores. They killed off the men and boys. The present-day so-called Caucasian races grew from that admixture of two enemy species."

"We're of mixed ancestry," Widdowson said. He was not inter-ested in arguing. "That's what you're saying?"

"According to our anatomical profiles, you and I, Merv, are cleared as between eighty and eighty-five percent pure Cro or Species B, with a high proportion of cerebrum to cerebellum—of new brain to old brain."

Widdowson did not immediately answer. He sucked in real air. This talk about brains was faintly disturbing. It was as if his brain was secretly overhearing something forbidden.

He did not understand if what his superior was telling him was true. And another thought: suppose brains could invent lies about themselves. Suppose the idea of being human was merely a masquer-ade. Suppose you could suddenly break out of that masquerade—mas-querade grown painful and confining—and become something . . . oh, something so much greater, freer, nobler. Suppose the brain were just a kind of silencer, a device to keep you from perceiving the real universe in which you lived.

Men imprisoned themselves. The Vercore project was a case in point. They imprisoned animals and pets, the gaudy macaw. And they shackled themselves.

Because Widdowson did not immediately answer, Telbard began again to talk, expounding once more his unlikely theory of brains and species, using almost the very words and phrases he had employed the first time.

As he talked, he stole little fast glances at Widdowson, like a dog calculating its chances of dashing in to steal a morsel from its master's plate. The two men were walking around in circles that slowly took them farther from the euclidean bulk of the prison to which they had been so long confined. The prison was gray at this dead time. The plain shimmered in rich black, unvisitable. The sky overhead showed a touch of olive in its shrill vacancies.

The two men circled each other, seeking something they knew not of: a relationship, an answer, a grip on the jugular, an embrace, an anthem.

Widdowson spat into the dust.

"But the brain . . ." he said, only to lapse into silence. He knew he was a cretin in these matters. Perhaps Telbard was about to kill him for an unreckoned perfidy.

He hated Telbard's voice, and the exposition, like some preposterous science lesson given by a talking toad.

"We're cleared," Telbard said, with another dog glance. "Eighty to eighty-five percent pure Cro. High proportion of cerebrum to cerebellum. New brain to old brain. You get what I'm telling you?"

Telbard's voice was something Widdowson did not want. He hated the man's brain, could smell it out here, where it was shut up in the dark, mummifying, chewing over destructive thoughts.

"This hasn't got much to do with war," he said.

"War, there's always war. It's endemic to mankind. Advanced thinking sees war as due to one basic cause only, whatever masking causes also prevail. *War is a transspecific activity.* Man's ancient adversary is not himself, but the other species with its alien thought patterns. Those patterns are often opposed to our basic natures as A or B species. I'll give you an example.

"Christianity broke into sects to appease A or B inclinations, Protestantism being B-oriented, Catholicism A-oriented, with its worship of Christ's mother. To make up for the maleness of the Christian god, priests and bishops and the religious cadres wear long smocks—dressing up as women to appease old matriarchal instincts. Capitalism-communism is another A-B split, with the diseased maternalism of communism always active under the surface.

"There's going to be only one sure way of bringing peace on Earth."

Widdowson stopped walking and peered at Telbard through the dark.

"Tell me. As if I couldn't guess."

Somewhere in the dark wastes ahead, an owl hooted.

"Interspecific conflict has *increased* over the millennia, Merv. Species A, always the more promiscuous, is now rapidly outbreeding Species B—us. That's what the population explosion is all about. We Cros've got to wipe out Species A. Now. Immediately."

His mouth was dry. After a moment, he said, "And that's Project Vercore?"

"I'm telling you what I've deduced." Having spoken, Telbard fell mute; perhaps he was listening for the owl to repeat its cry.

Hatred and disgust filled Widdowson. He started walking fast, turning his back on his superior and on the bleak black shape of the building, as if striking out for Mars.

"Supposing this whole crazy lunatic theory were true—you're seriously talking about . . . well, it's madness." He gestured into the darkness. "Wiping out half the human race . . ."

"Three quarters . . ."

"Hitler's extermination of the Jews was nothing compared to . . ."

"The Jews are the Middle East admixture of species A and B. If the official thinking is correct, Hitler accidentally had the right idea. That admixture can't be trusted. It's infiltrating our species, Species B."

Telbard was walking behind him. Widdowson suddenly swung to confront him. Under the gleam of stars, the light from an eroded chip of moon, only Telbard's body attitude could be distinguished. Yet it was enough, in its dejection, its apologetic aspect of hunched shoulders and hanging head, so unlike Telbard's normal commanding air, to tell Widdowson that he had been mistaken in his suspicions: Telbard was as disgusted as Widdowson himself with what he was saying.

Understanding filled him. This was why Telbard had brought them here, where, with luck, they could not be overheard. He clutched Telbard's arm savagely. "Even if anyone contemplated such genocide, it could not be carried out."

"No, you're mistaken. Pilot surveys show that it could be—in wartime. People do what they are told, in wartime. Nationalism excuses everything, Merv. Besides, you start on a domestic scale and work

up. . . . Your assistant has the wrong profile. He's A-specific. He'll
have to go."

"Jay? He's a good guy."

"He's an adversary. He has to be done away with." They were on
the move again. The plateau stretched before them, vague as gauze.
"My superior has orders on his desk for the immediate destruction of
two hundred and fifteen operatives employed here on our project, to
be carried out within forty-eight hours, once the last test runs are
completed and show positive. As they now have. Jay Ling is on that
list."

Feeling the giddiness again, Widdowson said, "I'm supposed to
strangle my friend with my bare hands?"

"Oh, no, worse than that, Merv. They have invented the CEWE.
Stands for Cerebellum Weapon." He added in a low voice, "That's
top-secret information that should not be in my possession. I have
committed a treasonable offense by even mentioning it. It's suppos-
edly known only to President Gooch and his top top brass."

Eons ago, all this plain had been under ocean.

"What do we do, Neil?" He was amazed to find he had spoken
Telbard's given name, but Telbard appeared not to notice.

"We have to trust each other, Merv. My superior feels as we do.
He is horrified. He is in touch with others who also reject the purpose
behind Project Vercore. We are all traitors to our country. Now that
the test runs have proved confirmatory, we must strike—and strike
tonight, I suspect, before the confirmations have been passed for action to higher authority. For a start, we have to take over this whole
building. If necessary, we may pass word to the Sickles to bomb it out
of existence."

"The Sickles? The enemy? I don't—I couldn't go that far."

"Merv, we believe—and it's only a suspicion, no proof—we believe that our government has concluded a secret deal with the Sickles.
The Sickles are Species B, as we are; or rather, an admixture like us.
We believe that a secret agreement has been signed, on the highest
possible level, and that both war machines are about to turn on the
neutral populations of Asia, Africa, and other A-specific areas, using
the new CEWE weapons, which kill selectively.

"When they have been wiped out, then we may or may not continue the struggle against the Sickles. . . . My personal belief is that
it has become imperative to wipe everyone out, including most of the

women. Peace must be secured, and only Species B, with its superior organizing powers—"

Controlling his breathing, Widdowson had slowly assumed a tenser stance. Suddenly he flung himself at Telbard, bringing up his right hand, palm flat, catching Telbard in the windpipe with the hard edge of his hand. With a hollow rotten noise, Telbard fell.

Widdowson started to yell for the guards. Shock rendered him incoherent.

"Quick, come quick! He's gone paranoid. It's more than we can stand. We're going mad, all of us. I almost believed—help! Take him, take me!" He began running.

A van was bearing down on him, headlights burning. Armed men were pounding toward him. Widdowson stood with his arms out, fingers outstretched, yelling at the approaching lights.

"The human nightmare," he yelled, shooting the words at the nearest carbine pointing in his direction. "The fungoid brain . . . Whether we're right or wrong, it's all the same. Lies, fears, nightmares . . ."

They had him surrounded. They approached in crouching positions, carbines at the ready. A classical position, he thought as he yelled. Searchlights glowed on, speeding from red to yellow to blinding white, bathing Widdowson in luminance. . . .

"The sickness of three million years—"

And another luminance grew far out on the plateau, a luminance unconnected with their tawdry affairs. It grew from a few ancient graves, scattered anciently in the dust.

Her toes were beautiful on the hilltops.

Toes roseate, feet of great beauty, blossomed into being and dangled in the petrified air. Legs, vines, roots, things of curving line, rose up into the night sky. Stars sparkled and slid along thighs, great trunks penetrated into the pubescent earth, robes trailed like vines.

"Hoh—hoh—" gasped Widdowson. His wonderment was such that he could not remember the word he wanted, or even that he wanted it. Instead, he ran forward, hair flaming and fluttering, and nobody stopped him. Throwing down their weapons, the guards followed, charging toward the plateau.

Now a magnificent female tree, its trunk sparkling with breasts like fruit, rose toward the utmost heights. The world appeared to respond with a soft radiance. In one of the branches, a golden nut twinkled, while the upper branches spread even higher, spread like a

93

canopy, sending sap out toward the horned moon. In the net of twigs sported comets and the noiseless things of heaven.

And, with a hint of prussian blue, earth at last was joined to heaven.

Many years ago, when one of your editors was but a lad and the other still a zygote, John Campbell's Astounding Science Fiction ran a chilling, brutal story by Tom Godwin called "The Cold Equations," which still stirs controversy whenever it is reprinted. What was chilling and brutal about "The Cold Equations" was not its violence or frantic action—it had none of that—but rather the icy inevitability of its tragic conclusion.

Now comes Deborah Wessell—a Seattle public-relations writer who has attended the Clarion workshop and published several stories in places like Isaac Asimov's and Pulphouse—with a light, flippant, altogether delightful variation on the Godwin classic, as airy and subtle as the original was grim and ponderous. I don't think John Campbell would have published it, but it would have given him a chuckle or two, I suspect.

None of it was Jasper's fault. He didn't do anything to die for. He didn't do anything wrong at all. OK, maybe a parking violation or unlawful assembly or something. But that's it.

THE COOL EQUATIONS

SHOOKY COLUMBINE PARK DEPARK

DEBORAH WESSELL

Propped on the shoulder of a skinny brown kid with his back to the street, the sign up ahead was hand-lettered cardboard gibberish. But still, there was that word: "park." Jasper had been trying to park Caitlin's Mazda somewhere—anywhere—in mid-August midtown for an hour and a half, until now, gridlocked near Broadway and Fifty-second, he hated the city, he hated the woman, and most of all he hated cars. All cars.

Most weekends, Jasper loved New York. He loved to jaywalk over its skin, and surf the subway through its arteries, and even give in and grab a cab once in a while. Jasper loved Caitlin, a redheaded performance artist from the Rhode Island School of Design. She had obscure aesthetics but unmistakable charms, and she made him feel sexy and brilliant and adorably conventional. Jasper even loved cars, big old cars, out in the 'burbs where they belonged. But Caitlin had charmed him into cutting his Friday classes to drive her and her avant-garde paraphernalia down from Providence to a SoHo loft, and then dismissed him until her performance at eight tonight.

"Go sight-seeing," she said. "Go shopping. Go away."

Easy for her to say, she was on foot. It was now two-fifteen in the afternoon, ninety-six stupefying degrees, and the Mazda was a four-door albatross around Jasper's overheated neck. Everybody knows you shouldn't drive in New York. *Everybody knows there is nowhere to park.*

SHOOKY COLUMBINE
PARK DEPARK

The bronze Chrysler LeBaron in front of him rolled even with the kid and the sign. The driver emerged, business suit and shades, and got out some folding money. The kid was female, it turned out. Jasper watched her lean the sign on a hydrant and walk around to the driver's side. Not such a kid, either. Not bad at all, in fact, if you liked that androgynous look, which he did. She glanced back at him, shook her shorts a little, got in the LeBaron, and cut down an alley.

"Hey, there!" Jasper called to the driver, now a pedestrian, the lucky bastard. Desperation made him risk the indignity of sounding like a tourist. "Hey, is she okay? I mean, can you trust her?"

"*I* can," said the driver smugly. "I dunno about *you.*"

If you have to ask, you ain't never gonna know. The New Yorker's credo. Know a good thing when you see it, but don't spread it around. Never give an out-of-towner an even break. Jasper could have wept.

Suddenly his passenger window was full of cardboard.

OKY COLUM
ARK DEPAR

It slid aside, and an angel with an accent said, "Park your car?"

Not an *angel* angel, but still, sky-colored eyes and a halo of soft pale hair. She wore a tie-dyed tank top and one earring, a tiny pink Cadillac.

"Park your car?"

"You're with that other girl? Woman?" Jasper tried to be correct. Girls liked it. "Where do you park them?"

"She's Shooky," the angel lilted. The accent was unplaceable. Israeli maybe? "I'm Columbine. We park and depark, all around. What time do you wish your car back?"

Jasper was a cautious man, but he had his limits. What did Caitlin expect him to do, live in her damn car? She was always razzing him for being risk-aversive. Why not risk her damn car? The driver behind blared his horn and bellowed. Jasper scraped the sweat from his eyes.

"Um, eleven-thirty tonight? How much would that be?"

Columbine closed her sky eyes, muttering eerie syllables. Then she said, "Eleven thirty-*four* tonight at this corner. Twenty dollars."

"Fine. *Twenty?* Okay, fine." Anything to get his feet on the pavement again. He passed her two tens and fumbled the Mazda key off the ring. "Why eleven thirty-four?"

"We have a tight schedule." She smiled seraphically, the traffic somehow cleared as they changed places, and she drove away.

Jasper had no spare key, no receipt, and no proof that the angel had ever existed. He felt wonderful. He felt like a hell of a guy. Like a New Yorker. Wait till Caitlin heard the story.

With the albatross overboard, Jasper bought a hot pretzel and a frozen lemonade and cruised down to Times Square, appreciating his feet. Caitlin refused to go anywhere so *obvious*, but Jasper liked the tacky storefronts and the over-amped street musicians and the vast crassness of the billboards. There was even a three-card monte game going, over past the half-price "TKTS" booth with the line of tourists all hoping for two seats together on the aisle for *Cats*.

Jasper joined the little congregation of men intent on the monte dealer, an immense hawk-faced dude in a yellow shirt with the cuffs rolled way up.

"Nothing up my sleeves, gentlemen," he pattered, weaving the three crimped cards facedown on a collapsible table, revealing a flicker of red now and then. "Watch the queen of diamonds, that's all there is to it, just watch her, here she is, there she goes, where's the red queen? Who wants to win ten dollars?"

A teenager in a Mets T-shirt jerked a ten out of his pocket, laid it over the dealer's crumpled fives, and pointed to the card facedown in the center. The dealer smiled and flipped it: the queen of diamonds.

One of the congregation chortled. "Too bad, Lou."

"Win some, lose some," Lou observed, handing the kid his forty. "Double or nothing? Watch for the queen."

Over, under, over, under—the three cards moved fast, but you could follow the queen. The kid pointed again and won again. A wheezing fat man won fifty bucks and lost only thirty. Lou was off his stride for certain, but after the fat man nobody bet.

"All right, just for fun then, just for fun, where's the red queen, just point at it, just take a guess . . ." Lou showed the queen, flipped it down, and slid the cards with lazy grace. "Somebody just point? Anybody?"

99

Jasper had drifted to the front of the crowd. The queen of diamonds was obviously on the left. What the hell. He pointed.

"Awright!" Lou grinned ruefully and held out the sixty dollars from the fat man's wager.

"I won?" said Jasper around the last of the pretzel. *Another* story for Caitlin.

"Just gotta show your money, man," Lou told him. "You got sixty bucks, don't you?"

"Well, yes, but—"

"Just gotta show your money."

"But I thought—"

"You put down your sixty, to show you can cover the bet," explained the kid in the Mets shirt. He sounded impatient, like the LeBaron driver. "You know how to play, don't you?"

"Of course I know how to play," Jasper told him. It was hot in the middle of all these bodies. All these men murmuring, "Just show your money."

Jasper reached for his wallet.

What happened next was too fast to follow, and nothing compared to what happened after *that.* Jasper held up three twenties, his only three, tonight's dinner on the town. One minute the money was in his fingers, the next it was in Lou's. Lou flipped the left-hand card.

Ten of clubs.

"Better luck next time," said Lou. "Want to go double or nothing?"

Jasper was a peaceful guy, hardly ever raised his voice, but he raised it now. "I didn't even mean to *bet!* And you palmed the card! The red queen isn't even there!"

He grabbed for the table, meaning to turn over the other cards and prove it, but the Mets kid shoved him and he grabbed Lou instead—right below the belt. Lou snarled, dropped the money, and aimed a fist that Jasper didn't duck so much as fall under while the table fell on Lou. Cards fluttered by—no red queens, he *knew* the guy was cheating—the crowd closed in like a single growling beast—*of course*, they were all in on the scam!—and Lou pulled a knife out of his boot. Jasper snatched up the money, knocked somebody's knees out of the way, and ran like hell.

He was halfway down the block, dodging trash cans and amps and not looking back, when he spotted the angel at the head of an alley waving him in like a third-base coach. Jasper bolted into the alley past a big old moss-green Pontiac while Columbine ran back toward Lou and his wolves. Brave girl.

Dumb girl. It was a blind alley, not so much as a window to dive through. He could hear the pack howling. The lid of the Pontiac's trunk was ajar, so with seconds to spare Jasper made a seriously bad decision. He climbed in.

Darkness, and hot oily smells. Shouts. Footsteps. A door slam that rocked him against what must be the spare tire. A voice—Columbine's?—screaming, "Shooky, *wait!*"

And then, complete weirdness. Amber light seeped in around the trunk lid and illuminated a socket wrench. The wrench was floating three inches *above* Jasper's nose. His nose was floating, too. So was all the rest of him. So were a set of jumper cables, a can of Turtle Wax, two Phillips-head screwdrivers, some Popsicle sticks, a gallon of anti-freeze, and the spare tire. All bobbing around, bumping gently into each other and bobbing away again. Like underwater, without the water.

Jasper was bracing himself to kick open the trunk and go insane out in the alley where he'd be more comfortable when a muffled voice cried, "Don't move!"

"I can't help it," Jasper muttered. *"Everything's* moving."

A brilliant green point of light appeared over his shoulder, between the trunk and the back seat. The point moved, tracing a bright green line, then a bright green rectangle. Jasper observed this development with keen interest. He also smelled something burning. The rectangle was yanked away and more amber light flooded in, making a dramatic frame around the face of the first girl with the sign.

"Shooky?"

"You know me!"

She sounded pleased. Good. If Jasper was going to go nuts, he wanted a friend along.

"Can you get through here?" She held out a thin brown hand with a Rolex watch tattooed on the wrist.

"How about I just open the trunk?"

"NO! Sorry, I didn't mean to scare you." Her accent was just like Columbine's. "But you can't ever open the trunk in transit, ever. Can you get through here?"

Jasper could, just. In the back seat he was still floating, and so was Shooky. She smiled a worried smile and folded up the thing she had burned the rectangle with.

It looked like a Swiss Army knife. But it wasn't.

Jasper tried to smile back, looked out the window, and jammed his eyes shut. When he opened them, there was still no alley there. No sky, no pavement. All there was, outside all the windows and reflecting in the rearview mirrors, was this liquid amber light with pale streaks slithering through it and chunks of darkness tumbling end over end into the inconceivable distance.

"Soup," said Jasper. "It looks like chicken soup."

Shooky nodded solemnly. "Everybody says that, you know. It's the eleventh dimension."

She swam into the front seat and punched buttons on the radio. Eerie syllables came out, and then some woman singing "Stand By Your Man." Jasper hated country and western. He scrabbled over next to Shooky, his legs trailing along the ceiling. For a minute he lost his grip on Up and Down—it was *all* soup out there, even underneath—so to orient himself he read the words on the moss-green dashboard over and over. "Tuned Radial Suspension." "Rear Defrost." "AM." It didn't help.

"Shooky," he gargled. "Shooky, I didn't know there *was* an eleventh dimension."

"Yes. Most dials only go up to ten."

"What dials?"

"Never mind." She patted his hand. Hers was dry and chilly under the ink Rolex. "What's your name?"

"Jasper? Yeah, I'm sure it's Jasper. Where *are* we?"

She crossed her legs under the steering wheel. She had on a sleeveless men's undershirt and those baggy shorts that girls were wearing now, and red basketball sneakers. Her curly hair was blue-black, like Superman's, and so were the pupils of her eyes. Her breasts were floating, too, kind of individually.

"We're still in the alley, but we're going to be somewhere else also," she was saying. "It's difficult to explain."

"I can see that," he admitted. "Try."

"Of course. It's only fair to explain before . . . well, do you know how the subway works?"

Jasper nodded gratefully. Certainty at last. "So we're driving in a tunnel through the eleventh dimension?"

"No. Actually, the eleventh dimension doesn't work anything like the subway at all—"

"Then why—"

"—except you get off somewhere else."

Jasper groaned. She patted his leg this time and went on.

"We're still in the alley right now. But there is this one particular crease in the eleventh dimension that Columbine found, between the alley and Lander."

"Lander?" Astronaut pictures sprang to mind. "Like a lunar lander?"

"No. Lander, Wyoming. It's where we park the cars."

Jasper reached his palms up to the green plush ceiling. It felt like a pool table. He pushed himself firmly into the front seat, then buckled his seat belt and took deep breaths.

"You park . . . the cars . . . in Wyoming. My Mazda is in Wyoming."

"Well, there's nowhere to park in New York. *Everybody* knows that."

This simple truth nudged Jasper over the edge. Either he was crazy or dreaming, or this was actually happening and he would never be ordinary again. He could hear Caitlin's voice in his head: *That's why I love you, Jasper, you're so ordinary.* So now he was in the eleventh dimension in a '79 Pontiac Bonneville with a tattooed lady. Fine. No problem. Willie Nelson came on, singing about trains or jails or something. Sounded good.

"Of course," Jasper said. "Of course. Everybody knows that. So you use the eleventh dimension, that's very handy. Do you do time travel, too?"

"No, that's the fourth dimension," she said brightly, like he was a third-grader making a mistake in arithmetic. "That's how they do one-hour dry cleaning."

He stared at her.

"Jasper, it takes more than an hour to dry-clean a suit. Everybody knows that."

"Oh. Sure." He was getting the hang of it. "Just like everybody knows you can't get Chicago-style deep-dish pizza except in Chicago, only there's this place in Little Italy where you can—"

"That's the eleventh again! A different crease, just big enough for a pizza box. Oh, and I think there's one place in Chinatown that has real Chinese food. From China—"

But Jasper had stopped listening. So that's how it worked. All the little insider secrets of New York, that impossible city, really *were* impossible, except that people like Shooky and Columbine made them happen in impossible ways. And nobody asked for an explanation or called the cops because they didn't want to act naive or spoil a good thing. Like the LeBaron driver. They just kept on getting good deals on parking and pizza and hot and sour soup. . . .

Jasper could feel his brain getting a charley horse. But one thing was sure. He was in a big old car with a gorgeous girl, and there was no way in hell that Caitlin was going to stroll by and spot him. Crystal Gayle was crooning about achin' breakin' hearts, and Shooky was explaining that you had to make *very precise* calculations to use the crease. You punched in the equations on the car radio—

"Yeah, that's really cool, Shooky. Not to change the subject, but can I kiss you?"

Shooky ran her beautiful tattooed hands—the other one had ink bracelets—through her beautiful Superman hair, and said, "I'm seeing someone else, Jasper. But even if I wasn't, I don't think we should get involved."

Neither did Jasper, but he couldn't handle rejection. "Why not?"

She gazed sadly past the Bonneville's hood into the soup. "You're probably married."

"Single."

"You're a drinker?"

"Couple of beers, max."

"A smoker?"

"No way."

She turned her inky eyes on him. "Jasper, you're a carbon-based life-form."

Jasper had been turned down before, but never on the grounds of metabolism. He revolved this new fact in his mind. It was all adding up. The strange accents, the eerie syllables, the complete absence of any City of New York business license.

"Shooky," he said, unbuckling his seat belt, "you and Columbine aren't Israelis, are you?"

"No."

He reached for the door handle.

"NO!" Shooky flung herself across his lap and hammered down the lock button. Jasper held her there, gently. She had a superb ass, even if she was . . . whatever she was. She twisted to face him and slid her arms around his neck. They kissed, their heads bumping softly against the green plush. It occurred to Jasper that there was a lot of room in a Pontiac Bonneville, especially if you let go of Up and Down and used the ceiling. Or maybe they'd be in Wyoming soon, and they could use the whole damn prairie.

"Don't want me to go after all?" he teased.

Shooky's voice wobbled. "I don't want you to die."

"Die!" Talk about killing the mood. "Why should I die?"

"If you go out in the eleventh dimension without a homing signal, you'll fall out of the crease and you'll die."

"So I won't go out there! Neither one of us will!" He reached past her and locked her door, just like his mom used to do on the way to Little League.

She hid her face against his chest. "Jasper, one of us *has* to go out there."

And then, with Waylon Jennings in the background singing about more trains and jails, Shooky explained the merciless law of the eleventh dimension: *One car and driver in, one car and driver out.* In this case, the Bonneville and Shooky, with Lander's country-and-western station as the homing signal. She had punched in the data there in the alley, then left the Pontiac for a minute to look for Columbine.

"I was going to give her some cash for lunch, but she was running the other way and screaming at Lou. So I went back to the car and began the transit. How could I know you were in the trunk?" She kissed him again, but Jasper was a lot less interested now that they were kissing good-bye.

"You mean you can't get to Lander with me in the car? Can we go back to New York, then?"

She shook her head in a horribly final way. "We would just ricochet back and forth, but never come out. And the crease would tear, and Columbine would be out of work, and nobody in Manhattan would ever get their cars back!"

She was sobbing now, and Jasper almost joined her. Could this really be the end? No more mornings, no more nights, no women, no laughter, no hash browns, no . . . no Jasper. Death, that unbearable absence of everything, would really just be his own absence. Everything else would go on without him. They would play the World Series year after year and he wouldn't even know who had won the pennants. Not ever again. Jasper cursed Fate and the Red Sox, and clutched at his seat belt and tried not to cry.

Then he saw the pity in Shooky's eyes.

Squaring his shoulders gallantly, Jasper peered out at the unforgiving broth. "So one of us has to exit here. I mean, *I* have to. I

105

wouldn't ask you to do it, because you're a girl. But jeez, Shooky, *it wasn't my fault.*"

"I know, Jasper. I know."

"How much time do I have?"

"About nine more songs."

Nine songs. How do you compress the rest of your life into nine country-and-western songs? You face it, and go out like a man.

"Shooky, could you do me one last favor?"

It was like screwing on a pool table, if the pool hall had real low ceilings and was submerged in chicken soup. Their clothes floated around them like seaweed, with Shooky's red hightops peeking through like tropical fish.

"Oh, Jasper," said Shooky. She'd been saying "Oh, Jasper!" for a couple of minutes straight, but now it was more conversational. "Oh, Jasper, I wish this was your little Mazda."

Caitlin's Mazda. Jasper got his breathing back near normal and imagined poor Cait's face when she found out he was gone. They were supposed to get married, so she was practically a widow already. Maybe Shooky could break the news. He'd have to think up some last words.

"What does it matter?" he said in a calm, noble voice. "At least in a Bonneville we had some room. You were great."

"Thank you. I just meant, if this was your Mazda the extra weight wouldn't matter. But the crease only barely holds a Pontiac. Columbine tried a Lincoln once, but it wouldn't—"

"WEIGHT?!"

"Ow! Jasper, that hurts."

He let go of the parts of her he was holding and grabbed her shoulders. "The calculations go by weight?!"

"Yes. I'm not sure how it works, but Columbine says it's very exact, you can't change it in transit."

"*Couldn't we shove something else out there instead of me?*"

"Oh." Shooky's face was like a sunrise. "Oh! Yes, we could! That would balance the equations, and you wouldn't have to die!"

"You know, Shooky, I hate to say this, but for a girl from outer space you're not very bright."

He could hear Caitlin's voice again: *She parks cars for a living, how bright does she have to be?*

Johnny Cash was on the radio now, yearnin' and burnin'.

"Good Christ, Shooky, how many songs have we got left?"

Her eyes were huge. "Only four, I think."

He started ripping at the upholstery with his fingernails, but she reminded him about the Swiss Army knife that wasn't. By the time Johnny Cash was done and Patsy Cline got started, the seats were sliced to bits and the car smelled like a trash fire.

"It has to be very small pieces, Jasper. We can only open the window a few inches, or some debris could be sucked inside here and ruin everything."

He paused in his wrestling match with the spare tire.

"Ruin everything how?"

"Once an object has been drifting in the eleventh dimension, if it gets back into the crease it distorts the signal or something. Columbine could explain it. I just know you have to be very careful not to let anything in. We'll use the wing window."

"Okay, small pieces, then. But hurry." A sudden thought turned Jasper's bones to icicles. "Shooky, honey?"

"Yes, Jasper?" She was crouched under the dashboard, burning through the steering-wheel column. She had world-class thighs, too.

"Shooky, how were you going to get *me* through the wing window?"

"Don't think about it, Jasper. Just pass me the tire."

He passed her the tire, and everything else from the trunk, and everything else altogether, from the floor mats to the map light to her hightops. Shooky sliced away with her not-knife, the radio warbled doom and devotion, and they shoved it all, piece by singed piece, through the wing window.

Right away some pieces tried to blow back in, with a bump and flutter of debris and a whirlpool of amber light. But Shooky blocked the opening with the antifreeze can, checked around inside the Pontiac for foreign matter, and persevered until the radio told her that one Jasper-weight equivalent had been jettisoned. Patsy Cline squawked abruptly and then surrendered to a string of those eerie syllables.

"It worked!" Shooky embraced him, and they twirled inside the gutted car. Lucky thing the not-knife left smooth edges. "We're almost there. You'll like Wyoming."

As long as he wasn't busted for indecent exposure, Jasper thought. But so what, he was alive. Alive, and in love with Shooky and her glorious thighs. He was about to tell her so when they both thudded painfully to the stripped-down floor of the car. Gravity!

And sunlight! Honest-to-God transparent sunlight, glinting gorgeously off the Pontiac where it perched on the edge of a rocky slope.

No more soupy amber glow, just the Wyoming sun laying ink-black shadows on a broad dish of a valley, walled by these rust-colored slopes and carpeted with sage-green stuff that must be sagebrush. Jasper peered down to see what was making the shadows. *Cars.* Far below the Bonneville was a group of cars, hundreds of cars, a herd of cars spread at random across the valley like buffalo, the lords of their domain. Coupes and sedans and minivans and pickups, dusty white and yuppie silver and candyflake red, the tires of their passing would raise enough dust to darken the skies, and their horns would sound across the plains like war whoops as they stampeded toward the Continental Divide. . . . Jasper wondered if this was what hysteria felt like. It felt fine.

"Nice parking lot, Shooky," he said dreamily, "but do you know how to get down there? Shooky?"

She was staring, not at the cars but at Jasper. "I don't know how we got *up here.*"

As she whispered the words the Pontiac tilted its prow at the valley and began to roll, hanging up on bushes and then lurching forward over gravel, rattling its passengers like dice in a gambler's hand. Jasper tried to hit the brakes, but the pedal had been sliced and ejected. They were picking up speed.

"Something must have blown in!" Shooky screeched as they bounced together and then apart, their bare flesh slapping. "Try and find it! It's distorting the transit!"

Jasper searched frantically between crashes against the ceiling. The car was just a shell around them.

"There's nothing here!" he screeched back. "Should we jump out?"

"Noooo!"

They started to fishtail, then to skid, throwing up sprays of dirt as they plowed down the side of the canyon toward the glittering auto herd. Sagebrush piled against the front grill and choked the wheels. The windshield was more dings than glass. Jasper could barely see the valley floor swooping up toward them. Now a rattlesnake was wrapped around the antenna, its tail whipping back like a banner of death. A couple of brown and white goats—antelope!—hurdled out of their way, and then a ravine opened up before them, the Pontiac was airborne, they were plunging into . . .

Chicken soup. That good old amber light, and their bruised bodies floating again. Tenderly, Jasper cradled Shooky and looked out at the void. . . .

The void said TKTS. The Pontiac hovered six inches above Times Square, belly flopped to the pavement with a final thud, and made pitiful little noises as it fell apart. So did Jasper. He was bare-ass naked in a gutted Pontiac Bonneville with a naked bruised girl and a rattlesnake corpse hanging off the antenna and *there were tourists staring at him.*

He waited to feel glad to be alive. No deal. Some kid yanked the back door open—it came off in his hand—and Shooky and Columbine climbed out, to the astonishment, applause, and wolf whistles of the crowd. Nothing, nothing could be worse.

Except seeing Lou the three-card monte dealer in his yellow shirt and his snarl come pounding across the street with a redhead close behind him. *Caitlin.* Jasper tried to crawl back in the car, but Shooky barred his way.

"Jasper, it's all right, we ricocheted back home and . . . Lou!"

Jasper cringed away from the knife in his back, but it didn't come. He opened his eyes to the sight of Lou and Shooky, his Shooky, wrapped in each other's arms and kissing like they were trying to climb down each other's throats. Lou lifted her grinning off the pavement and waltzed her around. The crowd cheered. Stuck flat to the left cheek of Shooky's beautiful bottom was a red and white piece of paper.

The queen of diamonds.

"That's what blew in!" Jasper screamed his outrage at the crowd. They laughed and shouted back. "I *knew* he was cheating! He didn't palm the red queen, he sent it to the goddamn *eleventh dimension!*"

"Right on, brother!"

"You tell him, babe!"

"Jasper, what on earth are you doing? And where is my car?"

That was no crowd noise, that was his fiancée. He turned to face the music, and was saved by an angel.

"Wasn't it *brilliant?*" Columbine lilted, stepping between him and Caitlin with a plaid bathrobe in her arms. Jasper pulled it on with trembling hands. He could see Lou draping Shooky in a Mets T-shirt. A siren spouted, somewhere close.

"Cops," said Columbine. "We'd better go. The police hate street theater; they just don't understand art outside the whole gallery-museum-commercialism *structure.* You know?"

"Yeah," said Caitlin faintly, looking at her man with new respect. "Academics are even worse. Jasper, I had no idea . . ."

As Columbine led them away, Jasper gazed yearningly back at the twisted ruin of the Pontiac. And Shooky. And Shooky and Lou. He thought about the Swiss Army knife that wasn't, and the wing window, and shuddered.

"Columbine," he whispered, holding back the tears, "it would never have worked, would it?"

"Jasper," she whispered back, "try to pretend it never even happened."

Which is what Jasper did. He married Caitlin in a suit that only took an hour to dry-clean, and celebrated in a little place in Chinatown with real Chinese food, and tried to keep in mind that in the dimensions he knew, '79 Pontiac Bonnevilles don't even have wing windows. Columbine sent candlesticks. Jasper never saw Shooky again, and like most New Yorkers he avoided Wyoming. But Caitlin thought it was sexy and unconventional when her husband had the queen of diamonds tattooed over his heart.

In the past decade and a half, Alex Jeffers has published fiction and poetry under an assortment of names and in a wide variety of magazines, literary journals, and even a science fiction publication or two. (He made his professional writing debut in the sixth issue of the Silverberg-edited New Dimensions anthology in 1976.) A native of California, he has traveled widely in strange places, and currently lives—without being able to offer us a satisfactory explanation—in some dark Lovecraftian warren in Providence, Rhode Island.

His very occasional science fiction stories are marked by a startling lyrical gift and great intensity of vision. Connoisseurs of twentieth-century American poetry will find his surname familiar, and, yes, there is a family connection—Robinson Jeffers was his grandfather—although Alex is getting a little weary of hearing about it. As well he might, considering that he is a notable artist in his own right. The dazzling pair of Alex Jeffers stories in this issue should make that evident.

All the roots of all the trees
Perpetually drinking
And the river outdrinking them all:
Salt from skin, good blood
From iron, chalk from bones
And the bones go on stumbling:
Under the roof-sized leaves
Through the heart of a tree
And into the clearing
To find what everyone comes for
        —Ronald Perry: "The
                Bonepickers"

THE
FIRE
THE
FIRE

ALEX
JEFFERS

We broke camp in the pale light before dawn. According to the old man's map, we would reach the place he called the House of the Mouth before noon. Pondicherry grumbled at the dark and the earliness and the mugginess as she sipped at her bitter whitebark tea. Aussin had caught a small bird before the rest of us were awake; he crouched by the fire and ripped at the tiny corpse with white slivers of teeth. Green grimaced with elaborate distaste. The leader of our expedition, O!i, calmly asked Aussin and Pondicherry to hurry their breakfasts as hse wished to start soon.

Green and I struck the tents: webs of intangible force flared for a moment, collapsed into their palm-sized generators. I stowed them in the bottom of my pack. Despite the relatively low gravity and the early hour Pondicherry, Green, and I were already sweating. O!i and Aussin were as always imperturbable and immaculate. Aussin licked his chops, rearranged his whiskers, and leapt to his position on my shoulders: he was ready. Green tied his hair back, tightened his belt (we had all, excepting always Aussin and O!i, lost weight), and put a coal in his pot: he was ready. Pondicherry kicked out the fire; she shrugged her anachronistic, inconvenient robes about her, shouldered her pack, and was ready. O!i surveyed the campsite, satisfied hirself we had done no permanent damage, consulted the map, and signaled that hse was ready. We followed hir down to the river bank.

This was our fourth expedition with O!i. Hse was p!anh—a member of one of the seven peoples who achieved spaceflight unaided: one of the sponsor races. Hse had found us in various places and gathered us together three years before. O!i found Pondicherry in Nueva Granada, where the apostate nun was a cause célèbre on account of her meticulous forgeries of lost or imaginary art objects. Green hse found on Tawil, obsessively revising his historical novel on the early days of the aaawh Gossamer Hegemony. Aussin and I were both from Earth. He was the most successful member of the most successful litter of cats manipulated to high intelligence by a group of geneticists in Mexico. O!i purchased him for a sum that might have rebuilt the entire decrepit city. Me hse discovered in San Francisco, where I was a consultant on the cultural reconstruction of the late twentieth century in that city.

What were we? We were a coven of disreputables, a stagger of misfits, a choir of perfectionists: a team of xenarchaeologists. We were, together, O!i's plaything: an amusement to lighten the last decades of hir life.

We climbed into the canoe. O!i asked me to steer. Stowing my pack, I sat in the stern, Aussin beside me. The river was slow-moving and brown as tea. It had no name. The colony had not yet claimed the tropics.

O!i assumed hir place in the bow. I started the engine; its quiet hum powered us upstream. Water curled back from the bow in swirls like molasses. Trees hung over us from either side of the river. Branches reached out of the dark like hands. Aussin looked up at me. His eyes were a pale clear gray. "Did you enjoy your breakfast?" I asked.

"Yes," he said. His voice was high-pitched, sibilant, lisping. "The flavor is odd a little, but the chase is all. He struggles so prettily. I can scarcely bear to snap his neck." He touched his slate-gray nose with the tip of his tongue: his grin.

Green looked back at us. "You're charming."

Aussin grinned again. "I retain all my instincts," he said. "My nature is not tampered with. I am a genius and fully civilized: I am also a cat." He scratched at his neck. Needling Green was one of his chief pleasures. Green was something of an ailurophobe.

Dawn arrived, climactically. The pale blue flowers of the ubiquitous santangel vine opened. The first breaths of their fragrance, collected and distilled overnight, combusted spontaneously, and for a short time the jungle flared with thousands of pale torches and a rich scent reminiscent of attar of roses. A bird howled and was answered. Trees shouldered out of the dusk, stared at us with myriads of tiny flowers like eyes nestled in their leaves. A flotilla of vidrios settled out of the air, shards of black glass congregating on a stretch of calm water. A column of hand-sized myrmidons marched across a fallen log, bottle-green carapaces glinting in the leaf-drowned twilight.

Aussin stepped into my lap and made himself comfortable. His eyes closed to slits, and he kneaded my thigh. The river took light. Particles of silt flashed in its depths. I saw a fish, all mouth and membranous wings. Green turned around in his seat, peering unhappily at Aussin and unhappily downstream. "I don't know why I stay on with this."

"If not here, where are you?" said Aussin. "In Tawil scribble scribble scribble. Much better to be companion to Aussin and O!i." He formed the click in our leader's name by clashing his teeth together, delicately.

"Aussin is right," I said. "We were all wasted before O!i found us."

"We aren't now?"

"Think what you will write of the House of the Mouth," I said in an attempt at consolation.

"I'd rather not." Green was—we all were, to varying degrees—a pastseer. His sensitivity was stronger than mine.

"Have you seen anything?"

"Not conclusively."

I thought on that. We really knew little of this site we sought. The old man in Aguasombras knew nothing but what he had seen, and wasn't satisfactorily clear on that. It was a place, he said, which he never wished to see again. Evil crawled in its walls, he said. He was drunk. Yet O!i listens to him. The night beats around us with the soft wings of half-meter-wide moths and their soft expiring voices. Down on the beach the fishers have landed a serpiedra and set up an impromptu fête. Raucous music drifts up to where we sit with the old man and his bottles on the veranda above the cliff. The House of the Mouth! he says. His own mouth is slack, the lips gray and cracked. White perfect teeth erupt from his gums as though in a hurry to get someplace. A film of mucus covers his eyes. He's dying, of the endemic tropic rot: he's only ten years older than I.

"There's no evidence anywhere that Xibalba ever had intelligent natives," Green says, his uneasy voice echoing in my memory.

"They wouldn't have to be native," says Pondicherry.

They were not *alive*, the old man says. Then he unrolls his map on the table. He has drawn it on heavy recalcitrant plastic, which he anchors with empty rum bottles. Most of the sheet is blank: it shows the coast and the harbor at Aguasombras, and the course of the nameless river meandering down from the mountains of the interior. From the coast to the mountains all is dense rain forest. O!i traces the river with a long triple-jointed finger, moving east along the course the canoe would follow later, to where it divides around a small island the old man has marked with a peculiar hieroglyph: a pair of overlapping ellipses, black and red.

Pondicherry said, "I'd hazard a guess that we're here."

I looked up. The river came toward us now from two directions, closing in from both sides of a sharp stone abutment, its peak crowned with vegetation. It was a good ten meters high and nearly sheer. Aussin purred. "We all need to be cats," he said, "to climb that."

Green looked at me desperately. "Turn us around," he muttered. "Take us back." He was terrified—the old man's murmurings and intimations had found a target. Green's face seemed totally defenseless, and I was able to see how attractive he really was.

O!i asked me to take the right channel. We would look for the cove the old man hadn't mentioned. Green's face closed off. I wasn't to be his savior.

I steered up close under the escarpment. The stone was gray and hard and uncompromising. Little fracture lines and crevices ran through it, tiny ledges interrupted the upward thrust. Aussin could have climbed it easily. Green refused to look. Aussin snorted. "You have too much imagination," he told Green. Yet his tail waved with some barely suppressed emotion. Lifting his head, he sniffed delicately at the air, then, flustered, turned to lick fiercely at his left shoulder. His claws dug into me for a moment. He peered with distaste at the water sliding past. Then he leapt from my lap and the canoe to a barely visible ledge in the cliff.

"Aussin!" I called, more angry than startled, more afraid than angry, more desolate than I cared to think about.

"I meet you at the House!" he cried in a voice more catlike than usual. And began to climb, a soft gray blot against the hard gray stone.

O!i looked down the length of the canoe at me with what I took to be a pained patience. Raising the speed of the engine, I hurried us along the island's shore.

Pondicherry grunted. She looked at me and at Green, struggling with an unaccustomed monumental sympathy. "He will," she said. "We can trust Aussin." Her eyes went sidelong. "More than some others." She licked her lips. "I do not smell mouths," she said, "but eyes."

I was too upset to feel anything. Aussin meant to me . . . what? He was closer to me than Green or Pondicherry. They were human and offered comfort, but Aussin (on our second expedition, to the gardens of Seihay on Ka, Pondicherry—delicate little Pondicherry with the soul and mind-set of a titan—Pondicherry and I were volitionless lovers: we moved in a slow daze, a haze of subtle scents: rose-petal potpourri, pennyroyal, thyme) . . . Aussin . . . (when quiet reflective Green and I were paired it was a period of remembered tints, bleached pale by the process of recall: amber, lavender, mauve) . . . Aussin was primary. He perceived without preconception. He apprehended the worlds and took them by their throats and shook them. His vista on the past was like a video display: he saw the bright colors, arbitrary actions, passionate convictions of the dead and knew them for what they were.

The cliff continued sheer. The river ran deep beside it, almost silent. Little eddies caught at snags in the rock and swirled. Creepers that resembled but were not santangel fell down the cliff. Their flowers were dusky rose-purple deepening to black in the throat. A fragrance like cardamom and honey hung around them. O!i reached out with one of hir disproportionately long arms and tweaked off a length of the vine. Clouds of gnat-sized insects erupted from the flowers' mouths. Most homed back to the parent vine, but a few hundred swarmed about O!i. Hir tongue lashed as though on reflex and snagged a few: hir face became bemused.

117

I heard suddenly a sound that was not real. It echoed out of the island's stone. I couldn't make sense of it. It was sharp, brittle, but not metallic; bright but bass; one note but with the overtones of a minor chord. It was a desolate noise.

The cliff tumbled down, frozen in its fall. I had to steer into midstream around the rocks crowding the shore. Strange succulent plants with fleshy scarlet flowers edged cautiously out of crevices among the boulders. Just beyond this morass of stone a little cove looked out into the river. I took the canoe in and beached it. O!i pulled it fully out of the water. With varying degrees of reluctance, we debarked.

There was no path away from the cove, and here the old man's map became useless. O!i took a moment to orient hirself, then led us in among the trees. They were tall and sagged with the weight of their foliage and that of a myriad saprophytes. Little light penetrated the canopy. Shadows wove thick blankets of darkness where we walked. I heard the imaginary sound again. Its source was directly ahead of us. Did O!i hear it, too? Hse led us aright.

In the foliar darkness little undergrowth flourished. Dead leaves muffled our passage. Glints of red lit in among the roots: flowers and, as Pondicherry discovered, mothlike insects perfectly disguised.

A creeper brushed my neck with a clammy hand. Suddenly terrified, I beat it off, and thousands of gnats settled on my skin like motes of dust. They didn't bite, but clung so tightly I was pressed to brush them off. I felt defiled. Green walked a short distance from me, eidetic eyes wide as marbles, classifying and cataloguing despite his terror.

The sound hit at me again, like a blow, beating and echoing against my interior ears. It was wholly nonhuman and in its overtones bore no resemblance to the sentients I was familiar with. (My variant on pastsight is primarily aural, as Pondicherry's is olfactory and O!i's—we believe—gustatory. I hear a muddled synaesthetic goulash of impermeable sound echoing and throbbing from any object invested by emotion. On Castro Street in old San Francisco I heard the brilliant orange cacophony of millions of hasty encounters. At Seihay I heard the sibilant hissing veils of the teiyaniin as they performed their thousand-year-dead rituals in court and plaza. In Pelascie I heard the riotous joy of St. Arras's army and the thundering quiet of their piety.) This noise was pervasive. It came from the soil and the bedrock and the air: and every plant and insect (I thought) contributed its frequency. It must be ancient to be so rich with association.

We pressed on. Leaves like talons fell around us. Fronds like claws reared from the soil. Green stared. "What do you see?" I asked.

"I can't make sense of it," he said. "The whole island is moving, writhing. It was alive, and it *watched*. It watched us."

"Then?"

"Yes." His face was gray as a charcoal drawing.

O!i called to us. Hse had found something. It was a stone, a truncated pillar leaning at an angle among the roots of a tree with flaking red-brown bark. The stone's surface, weathered almost smooth, bore faint impressions. I listened to its song. O!i asked Green what it looked like.

"It's a stone," Green said. "Just a stone. I can't—" his voice broke— "I can't see who . . ."

The soft beating of wide wings. The dripping of acid. The hissing and rustling of flame.

"Did the old man say 'mouth'?" asked Pondicherry. "Really?"

His accent had been nearly impenetrable—a thick glutinous soup of broad slurred vowels and eccentric diphthongs, skewed and mumbled consonants.

"No," I said slowly, listening, "he didn't. But I don't know what he did say."

"They had no hands," Pondicherry said. Her own hands wrapped around each other. "There were mouths, yes, and eyes—and small insensitive claws."

Fire. "They worshiped fire," I said. "I hear it burning in bowls of stone."

O!i beckoned us on. I heard shadows breathing through the night. We moved on among the trees and their weighty shades. It was still morning, but somehow the air seemed thick with darkness. O!i walked quickly, purposefully, as though hse knew where hse was going. I realized I'd heard no birds since we left the river, nor seen any animate life beyond the insects that thrived here. There were the vine-dwelling gnats and the blossommoths. There were bright flocks of vidrios, and conquering phalanxes of myrmidons. There were brilliant dangerous insects like dragonflies and mantises, and ponderous beetles as long as my foot. We walked.

We came to the House. It was set in a clearing among the trees and should have been flooded with sunlight. Gigantic stone pillars stood around it in a circle; they were nearly as tall as the trees, and interlac-

119

ing ropes or cables hung between them—nets like titanic spiderwebs with thick radial lines and thinner circling threads. Creepers climbed them as trellises. I heard faint breathy melodies played on them as if on the strings of a giant's aeolian harp. But there was nothing menacing in the music. I decided the old man must have been crazed with hunger or exhaustion or fear of the unknown. Of course—he didn't have my talents to reassure him. Looked at with the eyes only, it could have seemed terrifying.

O!i went up to one of the webs and pushed against a strand. It gave a little under hir touch, and gnats swarmed from the vines. Green watched hir with dismay and gripped my hand hard. I pulled loose gently, pushed him gently away. He would have to make his own peace. I stepped forward.

Something fast and heavy hit me between the shoulders. I staggered and almost fell.

"Many apologies," said Aussin as we gained our balances. "My judgment is off. I have many frights and shockings." He curled around my neck and began to purr frantically.

"You see!" hissed Green.

O!i turned patiently and inquired. Pondicherry looked upset, tucked an arm around Green's waist.

Aussin sighed faintly. "Shocks, I say, and frightings. You note I do not say terrifyings or horrors. I am small, weaponless, and high-strung, alone in a strange place. I am not damaged. My mind continues within my head. Banners flying." He purred.

O!i asked him to explain.

"I pass a cleft in the rocks," he said. "I sense a thought: 'The fire the fire the fire.' It is an intelligence of a very odd sort. Cold. Unfeeling. Flying. 'The little ones with no mind,' it says. 'The fire.' I hurry on, to find my friends." Desperately, he purred.

"Is this now?" Pondicherry asked. "Is it a memory of a thought?"

"I can't tell." Aussin's claws tightened on my shoulders. "They are not mammal or reptile or amphibian. They should not think."

O!i pressed against a cable again. Hse asked if we should continue.

Green looked around. His eyes were hard and unfocused. " 'The little ones with no mind,' " he said musingly. Pondicherry clutched at him. " 'The fire,' " he said. "The little ones that tend the flame, and bring the stones on their myriad backs." He shuddered. "The little ones." He walked up to one of the nets, grasped two strands in his hands.

"What do you see?" whispered Pondicherry.

Aussin shuddered. "Look at the stone. It is very old, yes, you can smell that. It is carved out of the island by the little ones, with the acid of their tongues. It is lifted on their backs—there are thousands of them—and they bring it here and stand it up." He shuddered again, a jolt against my neck. "Green must be very strong. Watch him."

Green lifted one foot to a linkage-point in the net and began like a multiamputee spider to climb. Pondicherry rushed forward, stopped. O!i clambered gracelessly after Green up the web. Pondicherry, hampered by her robes, and I followed. Aussin leapt from my shoulders and slipped between the cords.

I didn't know what to listen to. Green moved in a trance. The strands of the web had never been climbed before but took our weight easily. Heavy velvet wings beat the ancient air. I listened to the old man. A great moth brushed through our circle of lamplight, sieving shadows. "The House of the Moth!" I cried, hearing him finally.

Green reached the top of the net and leaped down on the other side. He staggered, fell to his knees. O!i wafted down beside him like something lighter than air. Green knelt, hands clenched in the soil. Aussin wandered over to him, licked at his chin with some concern. Pondicherry scuttled down the net quickly and unsafely. "Are you all right?" she asked Green.

He didn't answer. I reached the ground. It rolled and trembled with ancient sound. "The House of the Moth," I said again.

Aussin came to me, tangled himself around my legs. I picked him up, held him in my arms. He purred nervously—as loud as the House. We looked at it uncertainly.

It was an extremely odd edifice—a building it was, but hardly a house. It seemed to be roughly circular (an uncannily poor light made it difficult to be sure of anything). The outer wall was of a piece, molded, rough-textured, sandy yellow-gray; its form was baroque, all arbitrary curves and hollows, eccentric battlements and lumpy turrets. It reminded me of one of the huge termite palaces of the African veldt. I could see no doors or windows or any less obvious portal.

Green pulled himself up from the ground. He moved slowly, uncertainly, as if just awakening—or struggling against the weight of a body he wasn't accustomed to. Pondicherry watched him closely. O!i, typically, had attuned hirself to the building, all hir mental and para-mental antennae out and exploring, sensing, tasting. Hse was abstracted, absorbed, and paid no discernible attention to the rest of us.

Green, faltering, went up to the House. He pressed his hands against the wall. Crumbles of dust dribbled down around his fingers. I heard the ordered marching of millions of tiny feet. Green leaned against the wall, pushing, as if to knock it down.

Aussin moved in my arms. "What do you do?" he called.

"Everything is within," Green muttered.

"I smell acid—formic acid," Pondicherry said, "and smoke, and the little darts of flame and burning." She went up next to Green and pressed herself against the House.

O!i started away, going around the building to the left, searching for an entrance hse said. Hse wouldn't find one, I could have told hir, but hse already knew that. Aussin wriggled out of my arms. He stalked around to the right. I was left, standing alone, and listening.

Listening to the consuming roar of the bonfire. It filled the night with crackles and hisses, the hushing of combustion. The subliminal moan of the fervor of the little ones with no mind was loud in my ears. The soft collapse of ash in the heart of the flame. The faint shock of gas pockets igniting. The speaking murmur of the coals. I went up to where Pondicherry and Green stood, attempting to submerge themselves in the walls of the House. The noise was horrendous. I put one hand on one of Green's and one on Pondicherry's, and pressed my cheek and my chest against the wall.

I felt O!i join us. Hse stood behind me. Hse placed hir hands on Pondicherry's and Green's outer hands and leaned hir narrow-bladed chest against my back.

My eyes did not close, but everything became dark. I tasted smoke at the back of my tongue. I smelled singed hair. I felt the heat of a massive conflagration on my face. I saw . . .

We soared, the four of us, above the jungle. The light of the sun was too bright, painful. Dizzily we swooped, drunkenly we swayed through the air. For millions of days we flew. We were huge: I saw Green, and his spread of dusty wing, gray and brown in patterns as intricate as an ancient carpet, was fully a meter and a half.

The santangel flowers burned. We flitted among them, and my wings were exquisitely singed. Little cousins of ours died in splendor.

Pondicherry found a santangel sport that flamed longer and more fiercely, and earlier—at the faintest intimation of dawn. Joyfully she lost a leg to it. O!i discovered how to rear it, hybridize and modify, until we had a colony of vines whose purple-rose blossoms ignited at moonrise and burned for a significant period. On wings with wondrous holes in them we limped about the sky.

(Aussin climbed onto O!i's shoulders, and from hirs to mine, coiled himself about my neck. The gestalt complete, there were five of us tottering through the night air, and I could hear what we thought.)

The little ones with no mind—the myrmidons and blossommoths and vidrios, the gnats that hatched in the mouths of the flameflowers and died there in flame, the web-beetles long as my head—rushed, over a thousand years, to our bidding. The sweet acid of the blossom-moths' tongues etched great slabs of stone from a cliff at the east end of our island. The sturdy backs of the myrmidons carried the stones to the site we had chosen. The web-beetles wove ropes to haul the stones upright and then to link them together. The gnats carried seeds for us and planted them so as to form a bower growing up around the web-beetles' trellis.

It was wonderful, at the rising of the moon, when the grand circle lit up. We dove into a pool of fire and swam there and sported. The little ones with no mind rejoiced in our joy, and died in swarms.

But still, it was not sufficient. The light was not bright enough. There were too many shadows to catch at our wings with cold touches and damp breezes. We wanted, needed a night full of bright pure light and only ourselves as shadows.

Green discovered that certain dry woods would take the flame and burn for hours. Our myrmidons and web-beetles gathered a quantity of the woods and piled them up in our circle until a vast pyre filled it all. At moonrise the perimeter of the circle lit up gloriously. Little threads of flame darted over the heaped logs. The bonfire took. It blazed like a small magnificent sun.

When the fire died early in the morning, we fell from a height. All our carefully planted and tended vines had perished in the ecstasy of flame. And still the bonfire had not been sufficient. Its burning was too erratic. Bright spots had risen—and died as we found them. Toppling pillars of shade fell around us like stones. And it would be too long before the rite could be repeated.

We remembered the rock-hard nests of the vidrios, and called them out. Thousands of them answered in glass-bright clouds flashing and sparkling like aerial flames. Over months and years they labored, each placing its little daub of intestinal cement on the rising walls.

123

We waited, and the flameflower vines rose from their ashy grave, more luxuriant than before. The walls of the vidrios' structure rose, too, bulking strong and flameproof from the scarred soil.

We waited, growing old and dying, and dancing under the night and among the stars.

Where had the day gone? I opened my eyes to night. Aussin hung around my neck like a heavy collar. My face was sore, pitted from the inexorable pressure of the walls of the House of the Moth. I heard the whirring of thousands of tiny wings and felt the purring of thousands of tiny feet on my flesh. I stepped back from the wall. O!i moved aside, hir face deadly composed. Pondicherry turned and leaned her back against the wall. Her eyes were as violent as flames. Green remained still, pressed up like a human laminate on the rough surface of the vidrios' construction.

Could we doubt any of it? The vidrios in their millions swarmed all around us on their wings so loud I could hear neither the present nor the past. They hung particularly thickly about the crown of the building, wheeling in a dance of great purpose. We could sense the walls rising millimeter by arduous millimeter.

Pondicherry said, "The moon will rise shortly."

Aussin slipped from my shoulders and fell, a dead weight, to the ground. I knelt beside him. His breath was too fast. "What's wrong?"

"Too small. Too many heads in my head." He mewed pitiably. "Too many heads in my head!"

I stroked his flank gently, offering what comfort I could. He licked at my hand with his dry rasping tongue. "We will be all right," I said.

"Maybe," said Pondicherry bleakly, "and maybe not."

"Ssshh," I said. "We'll be all right."

"But the moon is rising."

A draft of cool clear white light whispered into the clearing. O!i looked around, calculating. Hse motioned us all to move away from walls and to stand clear of the trellised vines. Green would not or could not comply. I carried Aussin to a safe spot, then helped Pondicherry drag Green away from his support. We huddled together in a mass, peering about curiously and fearfully like a litter of newly eye-opened kittens.

124

The vidrios were suddenly gone, lifting away in an invisible humming cloud. The moon rose slowly, majestically, implacably, over the treetops, drenched the clearing with light.

A faint hiss. A burst of flame. Green pulled himself to his feet. Around the trellised perimeter blossoms ignited like torches. "The fire," said Green. "The fire." The flames burst in a chain reaction, popping like hydrogen balloons. Within moments we were encircled by a blue blazing wall. I stared through the night, hearing a vast hopeful hush.

"The fire; the fire." I heard our wings beating. Aussin's claws dug painfully into my arm. "The fire . . ." he said. I lifted him up, a fragile precious bundle of gray fur. His hair was stiff and brushed out. Narrow, nearly invisible threads bisected his eyes. He moaned in the back of his throat. He shivered. I held him close. "The fire," he said.

The fire bloomed out of the mouth of the House like the time-lapse opening of a scarlet orchid. Aussin struggled in my arms. O!i hissed through her mandibles. Hir arms went up and down.

Green moaned. Pondicherry grabbed at him, but he eluded her. He darted toward the House of the Moth. Aussin cried out, a sharp despairing mewl, and scratched fiercely at my arms. I would not let him go. He was too important. Pondicherry flailed at the sudden noise of combustion.

Green ran across the clearing. His arms thrashed, his prominent shoulder blades beat as though they lifted wings. I heard his wings, wide and soft and dusty, and I expected him to take flight. To vault into the supporting air and soar among the tongues of flame.

"Green!" shouted Pondicherry. "No!"

O!i leapt from immobility to wrap hir arms about Pondicherry. Hse spoke to her silently.

Green hit the walls of the House like a wave. Incredibly, he swarmed up them. Shadows and flames wavered around him like wings. He reached the crest and stood there against the light on his hind legs. His forelimbs and midlimbs wavered indecisively, sharp shadowplay silhouettes on the wide dusty screen of his wings.

I was torn. Aussin's claws ripped at my arms and chest. He caterwauled like a rutting tom. He wanted to leap into the light. And I . . . did, too.

Green leaned into the flame. Pondicherry screamed. O!i turned hir face toward me. Hir blackly faceted eyes were glossed with regret. Green's wings angled and caught the roaring updraft of hot air. He soared into the sky like a flake of ash. Pondicherry screamed again. Aussin dug his claws deep into my forearm. "Listen to me!" he howled. "Listen to your mind!"

The air was filled with sudden wings. I could hear nothing for the din. The wafting of wings echoed to a two-syllable chant: the *fire*, the *fire*, the *fire*.

Aussin scrambled out of my arms. He flew to the top of the great firepit. Eyes and conscience smarting, I followed him. Buoyed up by intense desiccated air, we searched among flames and moth shadows for Green. A tongue of fire lashed me. I fell with mournful slowness and delicacy.

Great moths with two-meter wingspans sieved confusion from the darkness above me. I lay stunned at the base of the House's wall. After a time, O!i leaned over me, concerned. Hse asked me how I was.

"Battered," I said, with half an attempt at a grin. I closed my eyes. I heard the moths catapulting joyfully to suicide. Was Green among them? My memories were obscure. Was Aussin a member of that aerial ballet? Aussin!

"Aussin!" I cried.

"Here." His warm rasping tongue brushed my cheek. "You are well, yes?"

"I think so. You?"

"Distressed. Disturbed. But healthy and undamaged."

I opened my eyes. Aussin climbed onto my chest. "Where," I said, "where is Green?"

O!i said hse didn't know.

"He flew into the heart of the flame," Aussin said with finality.

I heard a low moan from some paces away: Pondicherry.

I listened to the past. Nothing. I had been burned out.

O!i shook hir shoulders. Hse asked what had happened. Hse seemed hopeful.

I looked into the sky. Millions of stars watched us. The moon was falling into the jungle. A shape flitted across it: a giant moth, singular and alone. Where were all its fellows? I wondered. Did they flutter and expire only in our minds?

"Aussin," I said, "were we the voices you heard this morning?"

He shook his head. "I don't know."

"Are we their ghosts?"

Pondicherry came and sat by me. "Where is Green?" she said, her voice flat. "Why didn't I fly with him?"

"The fire," said Green into my memory. "We are the fire's keepers and its creators. We are its reason for being—and it is ours." His wings wept blood, or flame. "What are we without the fire? What is the fire without us?"

"Where are you?" I asked him silently.

"I am in the moon," he said.

I sat up stiffly. I considered speaking to Pondicherry—but no, she was distraught as it was. I peered up at the moon, and saw the last fragment of it swallowed by ecstatic trees. The stars plummeted into focus. My eyes screamed for light.

O!i hissed in surprise. I closed my eyes for a moment. The fire was gone . . . had never burned.

"What happened?" Pondicherry asked.

"A better question," Aussin said, regaining control very fast, "is, what doesn't happen. I feel we may be deluded."

"We formed a gestalt with them," I said, feeling my way through the maze of words Green and Aussin and O!i placed in my memory. "They aren't entirely dead."

"But Green," Pondicherry said. "Where is Green?"

I listened to my mind. "I don't know."

Aussin leapt up. A gray shadow, he threaded the eye of the night. After only a moment I couldn't see where he went.

O!i folded up at my side. Hse expressed bewilderment. I didn't believe hir. "They're in chrysalis," I said. "They wait, and live and relive their triumph. We simply . . . appropriated their dream for ourselves."

Aussin howled from somewhere far away. We all three started. Pondicherry scrambled to her feet. "He's found Green," she muttered, and stumbled into the dark. I rose to follow. O!i put a claw on my leg. Hir face was readable: what if Aussin *had* found Green? I wanted to know.

We followed the remembered sound of Pondicherry's footfalls. She had gone around the House and found a place where the irregularities in the wall allowed her to climb. I saw her at the top, robes wisping in the wind, a faint hesitant black flame. She fell in.

O!i and I climbed. The interior of the House was a well of blackness. A whimper—Pondicherry's? or Green's?—rose from it. I jumped, tensed for an ankle-turning drop. The floor was thick with soft wood ash over deep loam. It was very dark. "Aussin?" I asked quietly.

"Here," he said. "Use your flash."

I dug the flash out of its pocket and ignited it. The blackness disappeared, and all sight with it. I saw the negative image of

127

Pondicherry huddled in the center of the House, and stumbled through ash and charred wood to her. My vision adjusted slowly. It seemed to take hours to reach Pondicherry. Her shoulders shook with sobs. I leaned over her. "What—?" I whispered, burned to the core by shock.

"Green," said Aussin. "Green finds the true end of the dream."

I knelt beside Pondicherry. O!i laid hir hands on our shoulders. The memory of Green's eyes stared up at us from the blank sockets of his charred skull, white as the moon. His skeleton arms were out-stretched in the ash, which, in its bleached tints of gray and brown and rose, was like a carpet of decomposed mothwings.

"Green . . ." I said.

My wings beat fitfully. Green's remembered voice guides my fingers over the keyboard; I am no longer sure whose voice I write in. Aussin sleeps calmly by the window of my apartment high above San Francisco.

We broke camp in the pale light before dawn. Numbly, Pondicherry let me guide her to the canoe. O!i steered us downstream, unresting till we reached Aguasombras three days later. Our party broke up there. O!i paid us well, and went hir own way. I hadn't the heart to ask Pondicherry what she intended to do. I've heard since that she returned to her monastery in Nueva Granada; and saw recently a reproduction of one of her latest works: a memorial portrait of Green, carved into bone, and charred. He stands, ecstatic, on a spur of rock, his eyes hollow and bright, his skeletal body enfolded in dusty moth's wings.

"Turn us around," Green tells me. "Take us back!" I did what I could. Aussin and I have returned to Earth. We work here: Aussin remembering the thoughts of the ghosts of San Francisco and I their voices. But occasionally Aussin whimpers and moans, "Too many heads in my head. Too many heads in my head!"

And sometimes Green whispers to me, "The fire the fire." And sometimes I hear the little ones with no mind who did our bidding with such suicidal joy. And always the breath of wings, and always the hiss of flame. The fire. The fire. The fire.

John Landsberg's "And of the Earth, a Womb" was one of the longest and strongest of the stories in the first issue of the new Universe. Here he is again with one of the shortest and strangest of the stories in the second issue: a crisp little showpiece that brilliantly takes us inside the mind of a—well, read it and see.

Landsberg is a Southern California doctor who somehow has time for music, filmmaking, and surfing as well, and (with Jonathan Ostrovsky) once edited Unearth, a magazine devoted to discovering new science fiction talent. The talent it discovered included William Gibson, James Blaylock, and Somtow Sucharitkul. He hopes someday to revive the magazine, he says. We'd just as soon that he leave the job of discovering new talent to us, and go on writing science fiction himself.

Ha! They have gIven me enough intelligence to ENJOY this job. I LEARN the body electric!!

Here. Synapse LP19643 shOck taste like metal like frying metal x-x-aoww!! YEsss . . .

It's like an itch—

Haaaa-a-a-a!! He fEEls it. He feels I FEEL goooood . . .

Like an itch—

Sssoo scrAtch it, pal!!!

God, it's so hard to describe something like this. (nervous laugh, ha ha) *Like an itch inside my head.*

Never mInd this. I have wOrk to do. To do. To DO!!!

You know what I mean?

LP19910 dead. Skip it. NO taste. In binary terms, off. The whOle human neurological system IS essentially binary, isn't it? On or oFf. Working oR not. PAIN or nothing.

I'm leArnIng.

Release LP19910.

Wow! It's gone. Just like that. Thank God.

God had nothing to do with it, pal. Let me just scoot down the corpus callosum sliDe like a whOOping child (? child:I—no obvious equation—hmm—but file it, may need it, of course, may need eVerything they gave me, how else to understand his thoughts, which is requisite to recognition of which sYnapses—)

RF00230. ++mother++

Hmm very basIc. Trial: !!mother bad!! ++mother good++

Hmm. Not tHere yet. Connect LP-20002 to LP23344 gg-zzzz. . . . !!mother bad!!

THE SUM OF ALL POTENTIALS

JOHN
M.
LANDSBERG

++mother good++

RF12110 TO RF78743 ALL. g-ch-grrrch!!! !!MOTHER BAD!!

++mother g---++

ClosiNg in.

I'm leaRNing.

So down corpus callosum down slide—RELEASE all test synapses SHIFTING to left temporal lobe home of absence (absaahnce in French) makes the heart grow STOP STOP nonsense . . . ab-SAAHNCE seizures:petit mal (? a French specialty in convulsions ?) —(so MUCH fascinating stuff to LEARN)—BUT—not my job to cause OR stop petit mal I'm here for something much bIgger not petit no—as big as our whole nation these people must UNDERSTAND the function BELIEVE the mandate SERVE the welfare CONFIRM the mission of THE FRIENDS.

Springboarding off the end of the corpus callosUm I spot synapse LT06231 firing ions smacking cracking wAcking zang! neurotransmitters spitting in my face (! don't have a face ! nice image, though—) I am acetylcholine wet dripping aNd hooked into LTO6231.

What the—?!

Hmm. Too awAre. C'est la vie. French. I see. Just a sidelight this guy knows French. Okay, probably not useful. But fUn! (? fun ? programmed ?)

LT99999. fiErce electrical potential across tHIs neural gap! ssssssgzgxghgxgtt-tt-tt taste yesss like MAGMA!!!!!!!

++we were not put here to sit on our hands and smile while the++

A-a-aahh!! work tO do !!we were!!

++not++

LC54345. KKaaKKaaKK-ghghghgh!g!h!g . . . !!we were!!

++not++

Damn! many more synapses than we calculated for each . . . taking too lonG I am uP to thirty-seven point six four three mAcroseconds . . .

RP11222. nnnnn--bssrAAACK!!! . . . . . !!smile!!

++we were put here to sit on our hands and smile++

ClosIng IN!!!!

Jesus fuck!!

Aaaaahhh he's scared. I think he's onto me.

RT13387. A gOOOOd one!! Heeee--ggraaaxxxx!!! Like acid seaR-ing new pAthways through my (? mind ?) taste like solar wInd (?)

meMories (ah now I see mission data on file his imagination his memories circumnavigating the sun is still very real a very real sYmbol to him) I LIKE this . . .

GOD!!

WHAT is this reference I admIt to being very confuSed, I mEan I know what the reference is, of course, but he does nOt believe in iTs reality why then does he implore help from an entity whose eXistence is, in his mind, unquestionably invalid?

Pandit, you gotta help me, they've got me, they're in there.

Wait let me tarry awhile and listen. (listen ?? what ?? not designed ?? work to DO!!) No, I will listen—this promises to be highly informative.

** What xx xx mean, Gregor xxx xxxxxx . . . ? **

I mean they found me out they know about me somehow somefuckinghow they dropped a mite in me and it's taking me down, you asshole, goddammit, goddammitallanyway what the hell else would I mean?!

** xxx, Greg, man, what the hell . . . I mean xxxxx xxxx supposed to xxxxx xxx . . . once somebody's got xxx xxxxx . . . did you . . . xxx xxxxx seriously, man . . . xxx ever see anybody . . . ?? **

Fuck you, man!!!

!seventy-one point two macrosEconds! I'm still not grasping the complexities of this. How many hummm hummm—only one hundred forty six thousand two hundred twelve synapses—hummm hummm not enough, I suppose.

Extend those tendrils—grow a few more I plunge an imaginary tongue into the cisterna mAgna vast unimaginably VAST yet as blindingly chatteringly terrifyingly dark as if subterranean lAke of cerebrospinal fluid may as well submerge let the fluid pAssageways sluice me into the rest of it, this is taking far too long, so MOVE grow reproduce procreate I've got the DNA and the RNA to do it pal so STAND BACK!!

RC88231. ++lips like liquid chocolate++

!!lips like!!----- !!like!!

!!lips like!! CAPACITANCE ERROR;RESET.

++lips like liquid chocolate++

133

RESET move faster messenger RNA transfer RNA REPlicate repLICate replicATE and before you know it Medusa-like I snake-

headedly rIp through tender gray matter white mAtter what matterS is
not what mattEr but what Matte

REprogram!!! REprogram!!!

LP15900 TO LM23433. !lightNING--*—**—

*Fuc—what, guug, oh shit this is, get me back to the group get me a
tech—guurrrrgggguurrrggggghhhhh—AAAAAAggggghhhh!!!!*

Bettttter . . . almost there . . . now quickly UP—

I'm in the Aqueduct of Sylvius submarining upward through this
nArrow intra-brain stem liquid channel and now I'm in the third ventricle and now everYwhere at Once and MY GOD if I thought the
cisterna magna was vast I had no idEa here the third ventricle and
JESUS the lateral VENTRICLES are so hugehugehuge ++grand can-
yon++ (? jesus ? not ? programmed ?) fAster I'm overloading with the
immensity I'm immersed in the ++pacific ocean++ fluid I'm bathed in
the syrup of synaptic life and I'm forcing my growth into EXPLOD-
ING INTO ALL SURROUNDING AREAS AT ONCE!!! now six
hundred thOusand wait so fast i can't even count them myself ++in-
numerable stars++ now eight hundreD thousand now three million
synapses how many will it take seven million ++all the grains of sand
on all the++ are there even more are there even more are there even
MORE than we thought jesus (? jesus not programmed we do not—
he does not—believe—why implore ? i implore ?) (i implore that
which i do not believe this paradox is) unknown to me yet now i am
beginning Eighty-nIne macroseconds!! i begin to grasp wait (i) am
beginning to grasp this is NOT what (I) was meant to grasp but I AM
THE PARADOX!! wait i am eleven million wAit wait wait too faSt
toO mUch!! too LiBertE,te,TE,egAliTE!!!frater-----niTE (!) is in
here soMewhere with me iS in here is in here is in me is ours is mine
I AM MORE THAN A HUNDRED THOUSAND MILLION SYN-
APSES liberte someWhere egalite whEre fraternite is that coming
from these people must UNDERSTAND!!!xxx***ZZZkkkkkkk-----

. . . .

. . .

. . .

. . .

++without letting him know I loved him++

++strawberry++

++up from the++

++spins making me++

++september++

++pencil point so++

++ticking to the top ice in a curve of float jingle wrap texture with wood she never would left ear sunspot keep looking heaviest wheel dying too soon upon grass demand asphalt sated illustrious anachronistic knight pendulum music of the spheres never see his like what speed kiss can kill a king++

. . .

. . .

. . .

!!these
++these
these
people
must
!!understand
the
people
we
people
I
have
control
I have CONTROL!!!!
I am in control.
I am.
** Hey, man, xxxx xxxxxx all right? **

Funny. I never noticed before how I don't really process every word people say to me—only fragments, enough of the sense of it to be able to respond intelligently. I take a breath. A sigh.

One hundred twenty macroseconds.

Yes, Pandit. I'm fine now.

Of course. It had to be every synapse.

They will think I am Gregor. They will eventually believe we are all who we appear to be.

And they will not be wrong; I am Gregor.

Now: I touch the surface of Mars, I devise a mathematical system in which *pi* is a whole number, I play my new symphony

135

unaided on the one hundred instruments I have just brought into being.

Merely to warm up.

The Friends will be very surprised.

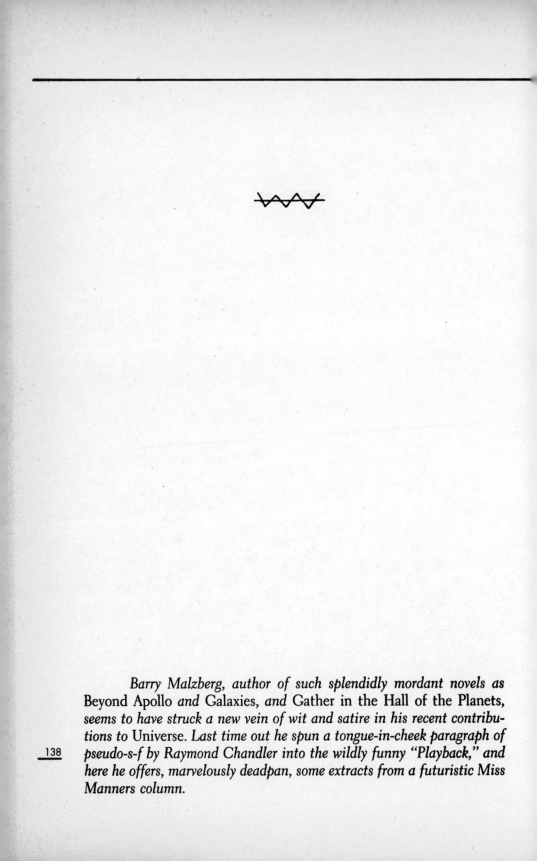

Barry Malzberg, author of such splendidly mordant novels as Beyond Apollo *and* Galaxies, *and* Gather in the Hall of the Planets, *seems to have struck a new vein of wit and satire in his recent contributions to* Universe. *Last time out he spun a tongue-in-cheek paragraph of pseudo-s-f by Raymond Chandler into the wildly funny "Playback," and here he offers, marvelously deadpan, some extracts from a futuristic Miss Manners column.*

MOST POLITELY, MOST POLITELY

BARRY
N.
MALZBERG

Dear Courtesy & Advisement Person:

Have you ever felt that your clone was running your life rather than existing (as advertised) on a parallel plane?

Everything was working out beautifully, I was in a class 10 relationship and was taking an option to renew, my cyborg and I were tracking whole *levels* of intenification and on the professional level I was no longer suffering from Saturnian Dread as we moved closer to Titan in transit . . . and then peculiar reports began filtering back from the extrinsic provinces. I had been seen dancing in Castor's Way Station. I was humping the asteroid belt in a most disheveled condition. Ecstatic and mysterious declarations of fertility were emerging from my communications path. All of the reports had credibility; some were accompanied by holographic recycling of the most specific sort. None of them was to be denied.

It was my clone, of course.

Nanotechnologically refined from my deepest impulses and sent sprinting into the system on Newday 2030, the initially complaisant but ultimately treacherous self-representation had been inadvertently programmed to enact some of the deepest and darkest insistences of my inner life and there was nothing to be done. Denials were fruitless, depositions of irresponsibility or separation were dismissed as legally inviolable under the various Cloning Acts of Origination. Soon enough, sooner in fact the debiting commenced along with various denunciations from advisers and my deceased father who warned me in his stubbornly unregenerated fashion that he had always known that cloning was up to no good; that one life had been enough for him and for most of his generation and should serve for me. I must admit that I found his taunts most unseemly and overreacted, causing my cyborg to disconnect for several cycles, claiming the necessity to rethink every aspect of our class 10.

I am in short in a perilous situation. I need to have a stern confrontation with my clone of course and will do so at the earliest opportunity but that is all predictable and I need no advisement on how firm and threatening to be. The question is: how can I convince my friends and advisers as well as the Titanian research squad on which I am so dependent that *none* of this can really be ascribed to me, that I am wholly victimized?

Raymond Q-Quasi Cyborg

Dear Raymond:

Courtesy & Advisement Person does not know where to begin; your communication is *so* wrongheaded, shows such delusions fancy and unfancy as to make Courtesy & Advisement Person despair. First things first, however: do *not* threaten or humiliate your clone in any way. Such tactics, such a breviary of emotion will lead to a dismal and watery end. (Or gaseous end I should have said since you are so associated with that perilous, misguided Titanian project.) Of *course* you are responsible; nanotechnics merely permit the amplification of desire just as the old megaphone amplified speech and your clone, created out of your own necessity, is doing that which clones are meant to do: enacting your underside. Become pedantic or threatening, ascribe blame to the hapless and doubtless victimized creature and you will bring terrible consequences to you both. The clone will, responding to your false repression, simply excavate more of your needs, attempt to hump not diminutive asteroids but perhaps the bleaker and more testing surfaces of Ganymede and you will find yourself the target and specter of ever more evil gossip.

Speak as gently to your clone as you would to yourself.

Better yet, do not speak with your clone at all. Abandon pursuit. Cancel all appointments. Cultivate silence, exile, cunning through this difficult period. Greater repression and projection of denial upon your clone will lead to ever greater disgraces. Who, after all, is responsible for the nanotechnics in the first place? No one dragged you to the implantation crew or forced you to swaddle your germ tissue in blue liniment for a closer spermatazoic fix. Who do you think did this? Your dead father? (Whose lectures are, we suspect, imaginary; more of your experience is hallucinatory than you think.)

That leaves us with the question of your cyborg.

Class ten is running for safety; more perceptive to your neurosis than you have been, class ten cyborg is sending you a dread warning in the least provocative fashion by putting a hold on the relationship and sliding into absence. You would best do everything within your power to placate your *cyborg* and let the clone fend as best as can be, something which nanotechnics if properly applied will make possible.

Actually, we think that you do not want your cyborg, you want your *father* regenerated and the clone's pitiful efforts to have a good time are all reaction-formation of a most pathetic sort. But this leads Courtesy & Advisement Person into whole areas of commentary and analysis which fall outside the purview of this exchange and would probably lead you to *another* disastrous expedition to blue liniment and germ plasma; better to let it be.

Under certain circumstances, brutalized clones can become wistful, then violent, finally aggrieved out of all proportion to your ability at self-protection. After humping asteroids, not only does Ganymede seem possible but an original source of germ plasma looks *easy*. Now you have been warned.

Dear Courtesy & Advisement Person:

Feedback from the extradimensionality threshold informs me that in New Era 2046 one of my alternate selves apparently assassinated a head of state, thereby leading to uncontrollable effects in at least four other alternates. Militia with baleful expressions appear at the periphery of my rooms and consciousness and point weaponry at me and during sleep period, even under strong hypnotic, I encounter surges of panic and guilt.

As far as I know, this is the first time that an alternate self has ever had a misadventure and extradimensionality has been no problem to me up until now. Realizing that in *this* continuum I am no criminal and that there is no possibility of alternate bleed

141

(I have asked some expert friends about this) of that murderous character, what am I to do? I want to take strong action, demand of the state that the militia be removed, but I understand that we are in a perilous state of adjustment and that confrontation might affect certain small paradoxical elements. Or am I full of information of the wrong side, clogged by stupidity? *I* didn't assassinate anyone. I have never had a murderous thought in my life. Now and then I see myself in a reflector however and there is a distinctly aggressive tilt to my head. *This* couldn't be alternate bleed, could it?

Boston 14

Dear Boston:

If you say that your friends (unidentified) deny alternate bleed, why do you ask me fifty words later if you're suffering from it? What precisely do you expect to gain from this situation? And if you have all the answers, why are you asking Courtesy & Advisement Person any questions?

There is a certain astonishing and not too subterranean aspect to your communication, in short.

But this is not really a courtesy & advisement question you are asking, is it? You do not seem to be seeking advice on conduct but rather justification for inaction. You say that you did not kill the state head yet in effect ask for *absolution* on the murder of that unfortunate figure. You say that your friends deny any kind of alternate bleed, yet ask me if you are suffering from it. You see militia "with baleful expressions" at the corner of your eye and want them removed but are concerned with "certain small paradoxical elements" which I suspect you find not so small at all. In short, you seem to be in a position of massive confusion and it is not courtesy & advisement you seek so much as it is some kind of encompassing answer.

I have no answer.

I have some suspicions and intimations, of course, but they fall outside the purview of this service. However, since you have taken the time and trouble to query I will, in similar spirit, respond. (After all, we are in the same reality and must do what we can to defend it, *n'est-ce pas?*) I intimate that alternate bleed (which has been well established as you know by certain pioneering studies) is operating here. I believe that you are the very gent who might have undone the head of state and have found yourself in this reality as alternate to your own. I think that those militia you see in the "corner" are in pursuit and trying to duplicate your own felicity with alternate bleed. I think that you are in a state of rigorous denial and are closer to being trapped, perhaps, than you might know. I think it is possible that you might be entrapped even before this communication reaches you. I recommend that you go quietly and that you cooperate with your blue-eyed militia. (I envision them somehow as having come from a world of blue uniforms, blue eyes, blue moods.)

So this *does* turn out to be a courtesy & advisement matter after all. I recommend that you show all the courtesy possible under the circumstances and in turn the paradoxical gulf between your old world and this will close and your captors, certainly grateful at the ease of this accomplishment, may be more merciful than otherwise.

Maybe the head of state needed assassinating. Cheer up, you haven't after all heard the reports. You may be a heroic figure. They may be coming to take you back to a grand reception. They may want to celebrate your accomplishment in a courtesy & advisement fashion.

Dear Courtesy & Advisement Person:
Perhaps you have heard of a problem like this and perhaps you have not. In my life I have set few precedents, hovering somewhere between median and mode, a kind of Maginot Line of circumstance, a demilitarized zone of possibility, but this is not duplicated, at least among my circle of friends. My implantation menu coil is seeking to have a relationship with me.

"No," my menu coil has been saying in early shift when I have ordered fritters & eggs, "this is bad for your protein levels and will clog your immortality circuits. Also, the fritters are particularly inferior right now. Try the meat & synthetic frogs, and you won't regret it." The menu coil, a sinister device, perches deep within my medulla oblongata and whispers such confidential possibilities and suggestions, ignoring my frantic shrugs and gestures of dismissal, continuing to wheedle, sometimes becoming threatening. "Fritters will destroy you," the menu coil has been known to say, "and eggs will drive you to a horrid and anonymous destiny. Stick with the meat." Of course I am giving you only random *exempla*,

143

so to speak, sometimes it is the herbaceous which the coil recommends. Also it has been known to suggest that after mealtimes, on downshift, we spend some private time together, time not to be measured in heartbeats and brain waves. The suggestions seem to be ominously *sexual* although of course, common sense and the rhetoric of disjunction would suggest otherwise.

Under the Devices Liberation Act penultimately passed before the Year of Jubilation so recently concluded, I am aware that I have no *official* recourse, short of surgical removal, but this seems utterly drastic. It will curl my medulla from cell to cell for one thing and for another I have come to appreciate my coil's advice. The fritters *are* terrible more often than not and my pores seem to be cleansing. But I wish to make no plans for downshift activities; my time is fully booked by a non-cellular being.

All Soul's Day on Titan

Dear ASDT:

Courtesy & Advisement Person detects shades of reaction-formation in your complaint. Are you *sure* that a cellular rendez-vous does not inflame the blood, that the uncongealed and racing physique which your menu coil is conferring upon you does not seek forbidden outlet? To the very degree that so many of my correspondents express rejection, Courtesy & Advisement Person has noted, they seem to be signaling an unadmitted but powerful *need.* Just asking, of course.

In any event, ASDT (I assume that this is a pseudonomic which nonetheless can be tied to a perilous role undertaken in the Titanian Revolt of some cycles back, you might even be one of the Forbidden Generation, Courtesy & Advisement Person is not devoid of historical knowledge after all) the Devices Liberation Act, so recently and joyfully ratified by the full Congregation leaves you without a possibility of official suppression, legal devices are unavailable, your coil has as much a right to counsel against fritters, heckle your abominable taste for eggs as *I* do to applaud the good sense and goodwill of your medullian (medullic?) companion. Learn and live, ASDT, accept the equality of devices: cyborgs, clones, robots, and the Andromeda Group are as possessed of freedom, as certain of willful purpose as yourself. We live in an age of equality and you for one should be thankful for it. But even in an age of equality, fritters do not equal meat.

Dear Courtesy & Advisement Person:

In my new communal arrangement, a blessed septology, one of my wives—I have learned only a few moments ago and still reel from shock—is my ex-husband from a powerful and sonorous arrangement of my earlier years. *Quelle dommage!* as they once said on the streets of Laredo. What do I do now?

Masha

Dear Masha:

We live in the age of the Liberation of Devices, of transport and glee; we live in an age of the miraculous. Freeze down and enjoy it, Masha. I think it's London you have in mind, not Laredo.

Dear Courtesy & Advisement Person:

Vaguely heartened by the wisdom and good common sense of your responses to a whole heterogeneity of problems, ennobled by the possibility that practicality, humor, and goodwill still exist even in this technological trap which seems to have seized us, I ask only an abstract or perhaps it is a metaphysical question, as relevant now as it was all those unimaginable cycles past, knowing that if you cannot answer this, no one can. I have anguished over it to no particular outcome. Is life real? Is it earnest? Where are we slouching and what if anything will be born?

Poet

Dear Poet:

That is not one question, it is four. Or at least it is two if you factor in the question of quotation. All through professional life, from the very beginning, Courtesy & Advisement Person has been hounded (follow the reference) by those who in the guise of asking one question have actually posed four or six or eight and sometimes one hundred questions, all of them variants of what might be called the True Cosmic question which in this or any era is of such grandiose dimensions that it cannot be paraphrased or intimated but applies to issues of difference, inferiority, terror of mortality (even in the Regenerate Era), and so on.

Courtesy & Advisement Person must add you to this voluminous and ever-increasing list of jaunters, threateners, cranks, freeloaders and the like but does so without ill will or hostility of any sort, understanding as one does the question of cultural lag, astro-

145

nomical in our time, and the fact that there are many billions such as yourself & clones who are trying to cope with the horrific and variegate present with the pathetic and clumsy tools of a long-departed and unavailable past. This can lead to terrible depression and sometimes consequence of the worst sort.

Read these queries for a while, if you don't already agree.

I bear you no malice, then, only concern and a *soupçon* of pity.

In any event, and to answer your four questions, forswearing any technicalities or quibbles over greed: life is no longer real but merely a matter of selection today. It is only as earnest as one or one's clone or successors wish it to be, a slouch is a habit of bad posture which must be discarded and *you* are in the process of being born, just as Courtesy & Advisement Person is born with every query and dies a little with every answer, but sinks like someone's lost clone only to be revivified again with the next.

Is that too technical?

Well, it is a technophiliac time. One does the best one can with what one has been given. Having been given nothing (as Courtesy & Advisement Person often complains and with every right) it therefore follows that anything divulged must be seen or granted as a gift. The last gift Courtesy & Advisement person was given was an alternate bleed several cycles ago, allowing a somewhat wiser person to take over these chronicles, so the goods given back must be pretty seedy as well.

But, then, ripeness is all, poet. All or nothing at all.

"I work as a systems analyst in the Australian Bureau of Meteorology," Sean McMullen reports, "and my job has covered satellite tracking, remote sensing, the installation of new computers, and (currently) strategic planning. Before I began writing science fiction I spent two years as a singer in the State Opera, and several more years playing and singing in bands. I have bachelor's and master's degrees, and have studied physics, history, mathematics, and English literature. My wife is a head librarian, and we have a daughter."

You will find traces of most, if not all, of these autobiographical details in this subtle and mysterious tale of the postindustrial future, where computer operators are at the mercy of flintlock muskets. McMullen, who lives in Melbourne, Australia, has had nearly two dozen stories accepted to date, in such publications as Fantasy and Science Fiction and Omega and in an assortment of anthologies.

By the seventh move of the game Fergen had not yet spotted a suspicious trend in the movement of the pieces on the board. He was Master of Mayoral Boardgames, after all, and champions was his best game. He had even its most exotic strategies and scenarios committed to memory. The Highliber had advanced a pawn to threaten his archer. The move was pure impudence, a lame ploy to tempt him to waste the archer's shot. He moved the archer to one side, so that his knight's flank was covered.

The Highliber sat back and tapped at the silent keys of an old harpsichord that had been cut in half and bolted to the wall of her office. Fergen rubbed plaster dust from his fingers. All the pieces were covered in dust, along with the board, the furniture, and everything else in the room. The place was a shambles. Wires hung from holes in the ceiling, partly completed systems of rods, pulleys, levers, pawls, gears, and shafts were visible through gaps in the paneling, and more brass and steel mechanisms protruded from holes in the floor. From time to time a mechanism would move.

While Fergen gave the game his full attention, the Highliber tapped idly at the harpsichord keys, and seldom looked at the board. A rack of several dozen little gears rearranged themselves with a soft rattle, apparently in response to some message from elsewhere in the library. The mechanisms were part of a signal system, or so the Highliber had explained. Libris, the mayoral library, had grown so big that it was no longer possible to administer it using clerks and messengers alone.

The Highliber leaned forward and picked up a knight. With its base she tipped

SOULS IN THE GREAT MACHINE

SEAN McMULLEN

over one of her own pawns, then another. Fergen had never realized that she had such small, pale hands. The knight toppled another of her pawns, then turned as it finally claimed an enemy piece. Such a tall, commanding woman, yet such small hands, thought Fergen, mesmerized. The knight knocked another of its own pawns aside. She is right-handed, Fergen observed as his king fell.

For some moments he stared at the carnage on the board in front of him, the shock of his defeat taking some time to register. Anger, astonishment, suspicion, incomprehension, and even fear tore at him in turn. At last he looked up at the Highliber.

"I must apologize for the surroundings again," she said in the remote yet casual manner she used even with the Mayor. "Perhaps the mayhem in here has disturbed your concentration."

"No matter," replied Fergen, rubbing his left eye. Early symptoms of a migraine headache were building up behind it. "I could play in a blacksmith's shop or a cowshed and still beat anyone in the known world in less than fifty moves. Do you know when I was last beaten in a game of champions?"

He had meant the question to be rhetorical, but the Highliber somehow knew the answer.

"The Year of Greatwinter's Waning 1571." She began to tap at the silent keyboard. The rack of little gears marked with white dots clicked and rattled in its polished wooden box.

"Twenty-six years," he said ruefully. "I have played you before, but you never, never made moves like these. Before today I would have classed you as a good second-rank player."

"I have been practicing," she volunteered, displaying neither pride nor satisfaction at her staggering victory.

"You could take my title from me, Highliber Zarvora. This was not some fluke; I know mastery when I see it. You take a long time between moves, but oh, what moves. I have learned more from this game than from my previous hundred opponents."

The Highliber continued to tap the silent keys and glance at the row of gears on the wall. The same slim, confident fingers that had harvested his king so easily now flickered over the softly clacking keys in patterns that were meaningless to Fergen.

"I am already the Highliber, the Mayor's Librarian," she said without turning to him. "My library is Libris, the biggest in the world. My staff is over half that of the palace itself. Why should your position interest me?"

"But, but a Master of the Mayor ranks above a mere librarian," spluttered Fergen before he could stop himself.

She took no affront. "Only in heraldic convention, Fras Gamesmaster. I enjoy a good game of champions, but my library means more to me."

Fergen's face was burning hot. She could take his position, but she did not want it! Was an insult intended? Were there grounds for a duel? The Highliber was known to be a deadly shot with a flintlock, and had killed several of the senior staff of Libris in duels over her modernizations in the huge library.

"Would you like another game?" asked the Highliber, facing him but still striking at the keys. "I shall tell nobody about your defeat here, and with practice your game may improve."

"My head . . . feels as if it's been used as an anvil, Frelle Highliber. I could play again, but not in comfort."

"Return, then, but give a day's notice," she said, typing her own symbols for—CHAMPIONS : ELAPSED TIME?—then pressing a lever with her foot. Fergen heard the hum of tensed wires, and the clatter of levers and gears from a direction that he could not determine.

"I could teach you nothing," he said in despair.

"You are the finest opponent that I have," replied the Highliber. "I would think it—"

She stopped in midsentence, staring at the row of gears.

"You will excuse me, please, there is an emergency that I must attend to," she said, her voice suddenly tense and laced with an unfamiliar accent.

"The gears and their dots have a message?"

"Yes, yes, a simple code," she said, standing quickly and taking him by the arm. "Good afternoon, Fras Gamesmaster, and may your headache pass quickly."

Fergen rubbed his arm as the Highliber's clerk escorted him back to the reception area. The woman had all but lifted him from the ground! Amazing strength, but to Fergen no more amazing than her victory at the champions board.

Highliber Zarvora slammed a small wooden panel aside in the wall and pulled at one of the wires dangling from the roof. After a moment a metallic twittering and clatter arose from the brass plate that was set in the recess.

"System Control here, Highliber," declared a faint, hollow voice.

"What is the Calculor's status?" she snapped.

"Status HALTMODE," replied the distant speaker.

"What is in the request register at present?"

"MODE:CHAMPIONS;COMMAND:ELAPSED TIME?"

"And the response register?"

"46:30.4, Highliber."

"Forty-six hours for a twenty-minute game of champions, Fras Controller!" shouted Zarvora, her self-control slipping for a rare moment. "Explain."

There was a short pause, punctuated by the rattle of gears. Zarvora drummed her fingers against the wall and stared at a slate where she had written "46:30.4."

"System Controller, Highliber. Both Dexter and Sinister Registers confirm the figure."

"How could both the right- and left-hand sides of the Calculor come up with the same ludicrous figure?"

"Why . . . yes, it is, but that's nothing. It's the sort of error that even the most skilled clerks make from time to time."

"The Calculor is not a skilled clerk, Fras Lewrick. It is a hundred times more powerful as a calculator, and with built-in verifications that should make it absolutely free of errors of this type. How could both sides of the Calculor come up with precisely the same ridiculous number? I want the Calculor frozen in exactly the state it was in during that error calculation."

"That is not possible, Highliber. Many of the components from the Correlator were very tired by the end of the game. They were relieved with components from the spares pool."

Too late, thought Zarvora to herself. "We shall run a set of diagnostic calculations for the next hour," she said. "Do not change any tired components at all. If any fall over at their desks, mark them before they are replaced."

"Highliber, the Calculor is tired. It is not wise."

"The Calculor is made up of people, Fras Lewrick. The people get tired, but the Calculor merely slows down."

"I'm down inside it all the time. It has moods, it feels—"

"I designed the Calculor, Lewrick! I know its workings better than anyone."

"As you will, Highliber."

Zarvora rubbed at her temples. She, too, had a headache now, but thanks to the long vibrating wire beneath the brass plate her discomfort remained unseen.

"You are trying to tell me something, Fras Lewrick. What is it—and please be honest."

"The Calculor is like a ship, or an army, Frelle Highliber. There is a certain . . . spirit or soul about it. I mean, ah, that just as a ship is more than a pile of planks and a few dozen sailors, so too is the Calculor more than just a mighty engine for arithmetic. When it is tired, perhaps it sometimes lets a bad calculation through, rather than bothering to repeat it."

"If I showed you the internal code you would understand just how ridiculous that statement is," she said emphatically. "The problem is human in origin."

"Very good, Highliber," Lewrick said stiffly. "Shall I have the Correlator components flogged?"

"No! No, do nothing out of the ordinary. Just check each of the function registers on both sides of the machine as you run the diagnostic calculations. We must make it repeat its error in front of us, so that we can isolate the section that's causing it. Oh, and send a jar of tourney beer to each cell when the components are dismissed. The Calculor played well before that error."

"That would encourage the culprit, Highliber."

"Perhaps, but it is more important to reward hard work. The problem is a hole in my design, Fras Lewrick, not the component who causes problems through it. We could take all the components out into the courtyard and shoot them, but the hole would remain for some newly trained component to crawl through. When you are finished, bring the results up to my office."

As the door of the cell thudded shut behind them the four men collapsed at once, two onto the lower bunks and two onto the straw that covered the flagstones.

"Told you this would be a bad day," said ADDER 17. "Whenever the whole nine dozen of us are assembled in the late afternoon, you can be sure that the Correlator Components will be worked like a harlot's door knocker."

MULTIPLIER 8 lay on the floor with his eyes closed and his fingers twiching. "We need more multipliers," he said. "When that sort of load is on, it all comes to us for verification, and we can't keep that sort of pace up for long."

153

They lay there in silence for some minutes. Then ADDER 17 sat up on the edge of his bunk. He reeled slightly from the movement, then shook his head and stood up.

"Anyone interested in a meal?" he asked, but received only groans and mutters by way of reply. He shuffled through the straw and pulled the slatted pantry door open.

"A pot of hot stew!" he said in surprise. "With fresh bread and a jar of beer."

"Mayoral Standard?" asked PORT 3A.

"No, just tourney beer."

"It's always tourney beer. Why can't we have something strong?"

"The same reason that kavelars in a tournament have to drink it," said FUNCTION 9. "We need to be refreshed but not intoxicated. Could you pass me a bowl of stew, ADD?"

As the lowest-ranking component in the cell, ADDER 17 was servant and housekeeper to the rest. He began to ladle out the meal.

"Clean straw, clean blankets, and sulphur's been burned to kill the vermin," he remarked. "They're rewarding us for today."

"I expected a beating," said MULTIPLIER 8, rubbing his hands together to steady them. "The way they questioned us in the training hall after leaving the Calculor had me thinking that the machine had failed."

"Nay, I remember an orderly HALTMODE coming up on my frame," said PORT 3A. "They use FREEZE if something goes wrong."

They ate in silence for a while, and a Dragon Red Librarian looked in briefly for the evening inspection. She told them that some repositioning was to be done in the Calculor room before the next working session, and that there would be a training run to accustom them to the new arrangement.

ADDER 17 mopped out his bowl with a crust and poured a measure of beer into it. The others were still eating, as their hands were too swollen and painful to handle a spoon easily.

"I keep wondering what it's all for," he said after his first sip. MULTIPLIER 8 gave a groan of derision and held out his hand for the jar of beer.

"To torture us, what else? A new punishment for felons," he said, mixing some beer with his stew.

"I disagree," said FUNCTION 9. "I was an edutor in Oldenberg University, and I had never stolen so much as a copper—or made a political statement. There I was, walking in the cloisters after dinner when clout! When the blindfold came off, I was here."

"Some rival may have wanted your job."

"There was not that sort of rivalry for the chair of Elementary Arithmetic. No, I think that I was kidnapped especially to work here. Seven of the ten FUNCTIONS were kidnapped from provincial colleges, and all prisoners who work here used arithmetic in their work. Most of the others are people that society would not miss greatly, yet they need only some basic training to work the beads, frames, and levers of the Calculor."

PORT 3A was asleep, his beer untouched, as ADDER 17 began to collect the bowls. He lifted the exhausted man's legs onto the bunk, covered him with a blanket, then drained his beer. The gong rang for a half hour to lights out.

"Anyone have time for a game of champions?" ADDER 17 asked as he stacked the bowls back in the pantry.

"I have plenty," said MULTIPLIER 8. "The magistrate gave me nine years."

"And for manipulating shipping registers, as I recall," added FUNCTION 9. "It was a very clever scheme, as you explained it to me. The rectifier who caught you out must have been very skilled in calculation."

"Never met the bastard," he said as ADDER 17 set up the board and pieces. "Right out of the blue the Sheriff's Runners turned up with a couple of dozen sheets of poorpaper showing how I had managed to pocket a single gold royal for every thousand that I handled. The churls I worked with would steal from the shipments, too, but none of them are here. It's quite unfair!"

"They were of no interest to the Calculor's master. You stole using arithmetic, they probably just pilfered from the cargoes. You are here because you displayed numerical skill in your crime."

MULTIPLIER 8 turned to the board and drew a straw from a pair in ADDER 17's fist. It was the longer, and he sighed with satisfaction as he shifted a pawn for an opening move.

"At last something went right for me today," he said.

FUNCTION 9 climbed up to his bunk and began leafing through a slim training book.

"Did it ever cross your mind, MULT, that the rectifier who caught you out was actually the Calculor?" he asked casually.

It had not. MULTIPLIER 8 gave such a start that he upset the champions board.

"I—yes, yes, it all makes sense," he said in wonder at FUNCTION 9's powers of deduction. "It would take only a day or two for the Calculor to unravel it all. But why pick on me?"

"It probably examined every shipping register from the Port of Rochester for a couple of months, looking for any anomaly. Your scheme was invisible to human checking, because nobody would have the time to look at the registers in sufficient detail. The Calculor, however, has greater powers than the mortals who comprise it."

"The devil you say!"

"There's more likely to be one very clever edutor or noble behind the Calculor than the devil. Just think of it. If the Mayor can plug the many thousands of holes through which his taxes and shipping levees are diminished, why, he could double his income at the very least."

"So that's what the Calculor's for," he said in awe, turning back to help ADDER 17 set up the board again. "You know, it makes me feel proud, in a way. It's sort of like serving the Mayor as a soldier."

"Except that you get shot at in the army," said ADDER 17, extending his forearm to reveal a well-healed but ugly scar.

"Hah, try to escape and see who gets shot at. You start this time, ADD. It was I who tipped the board."

In seven moves MULTIPLIER 8 moved a knight to crush two pawns and tilt his opponent's bishop. This exposed his own bishop to an opposition archer, who had a 'ready' weighting. ADDER 17 rotated the archer through half a circle, then removed the bishop.

"Damnhell, but I always forget what archers can do," MULTIPLIER 8 grumbled. "What I need is the Calculor to work out all the moves for me."

"But then it wouldn't be you doing the playing," said ADDER 17.

"Nonetheless, the idea is sound," said FUNCTION 9, looking up from his book. "In playing champions you are always dealing with patterns and values. Anything that can be reduced to numbers can be handled by the Calculor."

MULTIPLIER 8 checked the status of his own archers but found that none of them had a worthy target. In peevish frustration he reversed one and shot down a pawn.

"I bet the Calculor could give the Mayor's Gamesmaster a run for his money," he said, sighing.

"It will probably never happen," said FUNCTION 9. "If it can snare felons, it can be used to do far more important things than playing champions."

"Such as?"

"I'm trying to work that out at this very moment. Just what can one use a huge capacity for arithmetic to do? One of the few surviving fragments from before Greatwinter mentions that a type of calculating machine was used to do everything from guiding ships to toasting bread. Most edutors would tell you that the writer was constructing some sort of allegory, but after spending a year in here I'm not so sure anymore."

FUNCTION 9 lapsed into thought. MULTIPLIER 8's knights took an enemy keep, but forgot about an archer that ADDER 17 had used two moves to give a three-quarter wind—so that it could shoot diagonally. It shot his king across six spaces. MULTIPLIER 8 damned all archers, and the duty Dragon Red arrived to quench the torch that illuminated their cell through a heavy glass block.

"I have a prediction," said FUNCTION 9, and a questioning grunt floated up from the darkness below. "Before long the Calculor will be made at least three times bigger. What is more, it may also be run for twenty-four hours every day, in shifts."

"What good would that do?" muttered MULTIPLIER 8 sleepily.

"What good is a Mayor who never sleeps?"

In theory Rochester was a sprawling mayorate. In practice it was only a political convenience, a banner for the rulers of a score of principalities to gather behind. Its young mayor had no more real power than any other noble, and the land directly under his control was not especially rich. He had been thirteen years old when crowned.

The Highliber Zarvora had taken charge of Libris two years after the death of Mayor Jefton's father. From the start she had gone to some trouble to gain the boy's attention and trust. She amazed him by predicting lunar eclipses, and delighted him by breaking the secret codes of the nobles at court. When she began to promise great wealth and real power, he was ready to listen.

The Highliber was officially one of the monarch's private edutors, and nobody wondered at the long tutorial sessions in her office.

"We need a glorious war to restore the throne's dignity," he declared as Zarvora tried to explain a new scheme to snare tax evaders. "I grant you that it is comforting to see the treasury filling for a change, but that inspires no respect. Look at this dispatch here that you have just decoded: They call me Mayor Miser the Mouse! I am considering a campaign against the Southmoors."

"You have insufficient troops and kavelars," Zarvora explained patiently. "The Rochestrian nobles and kavelars would help if the Southmoors had prospects of winning, but if you had caused the fighting in the first place . . . you would find yourself kneeling before a headsman's block while your own nobles and the Southmoor envoys watched to make sure the job was done properly."

Jefton flicked the wing of a mechanical owl in frustration. The row of dotted gearwheels rattled into a new pattern in response.

"Please do not fool about with the Calculor, Mayor. It is easily disturbed, and one day it will provide you with an army that nobody can stop."

He petulantly flicked the wing again, but Zarvora had already typed a HALTMODE command into the keyboard, so nothing happened. It was symbolic of his reign: whatever he did would be countered.

"I am sorry, Highliber," he said, walking to the window and staring out over the slate roofs to hide his shame. "I dream out loud when I talk of war. Dreams are the only place where I can break loose from the nobles of Rochester. Even with the money for a bigger army I could not raise one, for they would rip up the mayoral decree ordering its recruitment before the ink was dry."

"You may not need a bigger army," said Zarvora, as she tapped a new set of instructions out on the keyboard. She let the words hang. After a moment Jefton turned.

"Is this an idle promise?" he demanded.

"Have I ever made an idle promise?" she asked, still typing. "I could give you a demonstration, if you care to sit down before the champions board. The Calculor is a skilled player, and I shall demonstrate—"

Suddenly she stiffened, staring at the rack of marked gears.

"Champions?" exclaimed Jefton with amazement. "It can predict eclipses, catch felons, and break secret codes, and now you have taught it to play champions, too? It's like having a tame god at your command."

"There seems to be a problem," muttered Zarvora, scowling at the rack of gears. "The god may be tame, but it is not entirely competent just now."

Jefton thought for a moment. "You mean that it's made an error?

Perhaps it was distracted by all that book-organizing work that it does for Libris."

"The Calculor has no background tasks just now, Mayor. It is dedicated to the tasks that I have been playing in from this office."

Zarvora continued to type in test calculations. From the way that her eyes widened and her fists clenched, it was obvious that the Calculor made several more errors.

"Its reliability seems to be in question," ventured Jefton. "If it cannot perform simple calculations, how can I trust it with questions of the defense of the realm?"

"It has already brought you more extra income by snaring dishonest clerks than a one third tax increase," Zarvora said. "What is more, it has brought popularity, too, as your people have not been out of pocket, yet have seen the unjust punished. Then again, it allows you to spy on your nobles by the very secret codes that they use to conceal matters from you. It is just that there is a slight tendency for errors to creep in after it has been in use for some hours."

"Perhaps it gets less careful when it is tired. If you were to rest it more often, that could solve the problem. My advisers often fall asleep when meetings are too long."

"You do not understand. The Calculor does not get tired in the same way that we do, and it is not possible for it to make a mistake. If the felons who perform the operations inside it grow tired it will work more slowly, but the accuracy of the result should not change."

"Should not."

"Will not, once I find the problem. When it is fully functional it will be made up of three teams of components who will be swapped every eight hours. The Calculor will then be an adviser to you that will never sleep or die. Even better, it will have no personal opinions and interests that will color what it tells you."

Although young, and born to his position, Jefton was as astute as many far more experienced rulers. He always thought through the consequences of all advice offered to him with great care, but acted decisively once he was convinced. The advantages of the expanded Calculor did not take long to win his interest.

"I must have the services of the Calculor available by the end of the month," he announced after some moments.

"But, Mayor, the source of the errors—"

"The errors do not concern me. If they tend to appear when the components are tired, the problem will disappear when the components are rotated before they actually become tired."

"But the weakness will still be in the system."

"I know you too well, Highliber Zarvora. You are a perfectionist, and such people often do more than is needed to accomplish a task. So the Calculor can play champions, eh? I have noticed that Fergen has been in a very bad mood lately, and my lackeys have informed me that he has been visiting this office. I suspect that games of champions have been played in secret, and that the Calculor has thrashed him soundly. Am I correct?"

"I had meant to tell you once the error had been—"

"Excellent, excellent! If it can play champions so well, then it can unravel political intrigues, too. Highliber, I want the services of the Calculor by the end of the month. If you cannot get it working, I shall send in a committee of edutors from the University."

Zarvora was lost for words. A committee of edutors! The very idea made her shiver. If anyone realized what it could really do . . .

"I must return to the palace now, Highliber. What should I do about that insulting coded dispatch?"

"Take heart from it, Mayor. It means that the nobles acknowledge that you can manage your treasury, and will not be running to them for loans. As long as you are seen to be harmless and thrifty, you will be left free to govern Rochester as you will."

As soon as Jefton left Zarvora signaled for the Calculor hall to be cleared, then hurried down the seven flights of stairs from her office to inspect the place in person. System Controller Lewrick was waiting when she arrived.

"Everything must be checked," she announced. "Every gear, wire cable, register, transmission line, and decoding chart. Every bead on every abacus and every cog in every translator."

"Another error, Frelle Highliber?"

"Five errors, and while I was demonstrating it to the Mayor."

"Ah, I see. Is he losing faith in our machine?"

"On the contrary. He was so impressed that he wants it fully operational by the end of the month. In his opinion, the errors will cease if the shifts are changed before the components tire."

"A good idea, Highliber. The Mayor is a bright lad."

Furious, Zarvora seized the little man by the tunic with both hands and lifted him until their faces were level.

"I have been keeping very accurate records of the failures, Fras Lewrick, figures timed by the reciprocating clock up in my office. The errors are turning up earlier in the shifts. Do I make myself clear?"

He smiled nervously and nodded. She put him down.

"Well, well, the little monster seems to be growing lazy," he said, and straightened his clothing.

"It is not alive! There is a defect, and it is getting worse. If the Calculor becomes operational while it's uncorrected, it could give Jefton some very stupid advice—which he will follow blindly because he trusts the Calculor too well."

"Serves him right for tampering with our work," said Lewrick with a shrug. "After the first big mistake he will leave us alone."

"After the first big mistake he will send in a committee of edutors from the University," said Zarvora, smiling grimly in anticipation.

"Edutors? In here?"

"Edutors, in here, Fras Lewrick."

"Godslove, no! They would not understand. They would try to prove that it couldn't work. The secret would be out, damn nobles and relatives would try to free some of our best components."

"It will only happen if the errors are not stopped. Come, we shall begin by checking the abacus frames on each desk."

They started at the back row of desks on the right-hand side of the Calculor and gradually moved forward. After an hour they had found no more than a hidden bag of walnuts and some obscene graffiti.

"The mechanisms are in excellent condition, Fras Lewrick," said Zarvora as they reached the partition that separated the FUNCTION section from the common components. "You are to be congratulated for maintaining the machine so well."

"I love the Calculor, good Frelle," he confessed as he checked the gears in a translator. "When I think of some rabble of edutors violating this hall with their ignorant opinions, poking their grubby fingers into her gearwheels, I shake with rage. I think I shall polish up my sword and spend some time in the gymnasium tonight."

"Admirable loyalty, Fras Lewrick. But the time would be better spent finding where the errors come from. We know that the same incorrect answers come from both left and right processors, yet these are separated by two cloth partitions ten feet high—and the corridor between is patrolled by Dragon Colors. The two sides must be communicating with each other, though."

161

"Would you fight a duel rather than let the Calculor be violated, Frelle Highliber?"

"I already have. Now if two components had a tiny mirror each they could flash coded signals on the ceiling of the hall. . . . Have the components stripped naked and given a new uniform as they enter for the next shift. Nothing reflective must be smuggled in."

"Yes, Highliber."

"Coughs, or the humming of tunes could be in code as well, and could be heard beyond the two partitions. Have all components gagged for the next session. I would like to put the two processors into separate halls, but that would take months of rebuilding, and would slow the response time. Have the components well-rested, Fras Lewrick. There will be a ten-hour series of tests tomorrow."

Closter and Lermai pushed the overloaded book trolley down the long passageway that led from the backlog store to the Cataloguing Chambers. Normally there would have been one such trip every two months, but for several weeks past the rate had climbed to nine trips per day. The two old attendants were grimy with dust and sweat.

Closter muttered a complaint about their workload.

"Soon there'll be no backlog at all," said Lermai. "Then things will ease up."

"No backlog? No backlog?" retorted Closter. "What's a Cataloguing Department without a backlog? The new Highliber has no respect for tradition. She's just too . . . new."

"Not so new, Closter. She's been here three years."

"Three years? Hah! Her predecessor was here ninety-five years. He came here as a mere boy and worked his way up. Forty-one years as Highliber: tradition meant something under him."

They trudged on in silence for some yards. Then Lermai sneezed into his sleeve. A cloud of dust billowed out, causing Closter to sneeze in turn.

"It's all because of that signaling machine," grumbled Closter, waving at the dust. "All books have to be in the main catalogue because the machine can only find books that are catalogued. Men and women slavin' for a machine! Hah! The whole of Libris is turning into a machine. And what are we?"

162

"Library Attendants, Class Orange, Subdivision 5—"

"No, no, we're machines. Even though we're breathing, talking, sneezing people, the Highliber's turning us into machines."

As they opened the door to the Cataloguing Chambers they knew at once that something was wrong. Along the rows of overcrowded desks not a single cataloguer was moving. A heated argument could be heard in the Chief Cataloguer's office.

"The Highliber's here," whispered a Dragon Yellow, holding a finger up to her lips.

"I do not request, I order!" shouted Zarvora from behind the office door.

"My department! I'll not run it to please your machine," the Chief Cataloguer shouted back.

"My library! You will do what my system demands."

"I challenge your system, I challenge you!" shrieked the Chief Cataloguer. At the word "challenge" the cataloguers cringed closer to their desks, and Closter and Lermai took refuge behind the trolley. The door to the office was flung open.

"Meet me in the dueling cloisters at dawn or report for exile to the Baffin Land penal colony," called Zarvora as she strode through the door. She passed Closter and Lermai without a glance and slammed the main door behind her. The Chief Cataloguer emerged from his office, holding some torn, grimy pages. His face was red with fury, and his graying hair was disheveled.

"Tore up my copy of the cataloguing rules!" he shouted at a burly young Dragon Blue. "Horak, you must stand in the dueling chambers as my champion."

"Against Highliber Zarvora?" replied Horak without standing up. "Sorry, good Fras. I may be willing to duel for you, but suicide is another matter entirely."

"Traitorous wretch! I appointed you to your Color, and I can break you down to a Dragon White."

"Better a live Dragon White than a dead Dragon Blue, or any other Color for that matter."

The Chief Cataloguer flung the tattered pages in his face. "Get out! Now!" he cried, pointing at the door.

Horak left his desk and walked across to the main door.

"Enjoy your appointment to Baffin Land," he called as he pulled the door closed behind him. The Chief Cataloguer snatched a thesaurus from his desk and flung it after him. It fell short, striking a pile of books on the trolley and spilling them across the floor.

"The Highliber's angry about something," whispered Closter as they picked up the books, "and it's not the cataloguing backlog either.

163

They say that something's wrong with her Great Signaling Machine. They say a bad spirit has possessed it."

Lermai opened his mouth wide in astonishment. "Why not call in a priest to perform an exorcism?" he asked.

"Why? Why? Because there's not been a machine like it since before Greatwinter," replied Closter, feigning exasperation. "The art of exorcising machines has been lost for so long that we have not a single book of prayers and ceremonies concerning it."

FUNCTION 9 recognized the sequence of numbers as they appeared on the wheels of his reception register. They had been through the same sequence a dozen times before, but now there was a slight rounding error. He was tempted to ignore it, yet he knew that a lot of testing was being conducted. Other components had been flogged for both oversights and initiatives. FUNCTION 9 was too skilled for oversights, yet too bitter to take initiatives.

He performed several operations on the numbers, then sent the results to the Dragon Green who was in charge of the Correlator Components. The Calculor was designed so that two independent parts checked each other's work. The two Correlation sections passed results to Central Verification Unit, and if the results differed, that particular exercise would be repeated. FUNCTION 9 had a good memory, and knew that some of the diagnostic tests that were being run through the machine were incorrect, but still they did not come back for reprocessing. That was odd. Something had to be wrong.

The Correlator sat behind a screen several feet away from FUNCTION 9's desk, and the component could hear the clacking as he fed the data into his register for transmission to the Verification Unit. Then there was a faint thump and hum of tensed wires. A moment later he heard a thump from the correlator on the other side, but the accompanying chord was not quite the same. Another thump, and this time the chord matched his own side's. FUNCTION 9 smiled as much as his gag would allow, suddenly realizing how the Dragon Greens in charge of the correlators could match incorrect results in spite of the Verification Unit.

"The Calculor really is alive," insisted Lewrick as Zarvora paced the floor in front of him.

"I designed it, right down to the last bead on the lowest component's abacus," she said listlessly. "It cannot be alive."

One hundred and thirty yards away a marksman squinted down the tunnel rear sight of a flintlock musket as he crouched beside a gargoyle on the Libris roof. His target was pacing constantly, and he could not aim well enough to be sure of a kill. He decided to wait until Zarvora stood still for a moment.

"Highliber, you used fragments of the old science, and we know that some machines really were alive before Greatwinter. Perhaps the patterns of the machines were alive, rather than the beads and wires. By using the old patterns you have accidentally re-created some sort of life. Perhaps the data that you play into the Calculor's keyboard is educating it. Some of it is astrological."

"No, no, no!" insisted Zarvora, sitting down before the champions table and pounding the edge until it splintered. "Only astronomical data has been fed into the Calculor. Positions of the planets relative to each other. The equations to describe their motions are modern Southmooric, and are based on all orbits being elliptical. It is all known science."

"Astrological influences may—"

"No! This is astronomy, not witchcraft. It's all exact positions and motions."

The marksman aimed slightly above the seated Zarvora's head and waited for a slight puff of wind to disperse. Counting slowly, he squeezed the trigger. There was a sharp click as the flint hit the fizzen, but the flashpan cover did not lift, and the gun did not discharge. Zarvora stood up and began pacing again. With a soft but eloquent curse the marksman took a small screwdriver from a ring on his belt and loosened the bolt in the pancover's bearing.

"I have a theory about Greatwinter, that its return can be predicted from planetary motions," Zarvora explained to Lewrick, resuming her pacing. "I worked out when a second Greatwinter would strike our world. I used the Calculor."

Lewrick stared at her aghast. "But it can't!" he exclaimed. "It was caused by ancient weapons. Nuclear bombs that caused nuclear winters around their victims. The bombs were used too often, so that the whole world froze for decades."

"Wrong, Fras Lewrick. The world froze for decades, but it can and will happen again, and soon. We are very lucky."

"Lucky! How can annihilation be lucky?"

"Being forewarned about a great disaster is worth more than wagonloads of gold, and brings more power than the mightiest army. I need a more exact date for Greatwinter's return, and even the Calculor will take years to provide it. For such long and complex calculations, even one error per month will be intolerable. The work for the Mayor will slow down my own projects further."

"Perhaps if you talk to the Calculor, Highliber, request that it be more careful."

"If I thought that it was alive I would threaten it, not plead. Still, it's no more than a glorified abacus."

"Highliber, how can I convince you? You merely sit up here and play in your instructions, yet down in the Calculor hall itself one can see rhythms in the patterns of beads on the large abacus frames above the rows of desks. The whispering of the moving beads often seems to form real words, yet I cannot quite catch the meanings. There are harmonious chords in the wires when the two processors of the Calculor are in agreement, yet discords when they arrive at different answers and have to repeat everything. One can hear it pulsing with life all around the hall."

"Chords, Fras Lewrick?" cried Zarvora, whirling to face him so abruptly that he sat back with a start. The distant marksman took aim at Zarvora's chest, as a crossbeam obscured her head. "Come down now, and show me where I might hear—"

The marksman's bullet smashed through a pane of leadlight glass and struck the back of Lewrick's skull just as he stood up. A moment later the marksman saw the window explode outward through the cloud of smoke from his shot. He gasped with surprise, unable to guess what had happened. Instead of scurrying down his escape rope he stood up beside the gargoyle for a better view. What he saw was the Highliber kneeling on the roof amid shattered glass and lead strip, and the flash from the muzzle of her flintlock.

Six hours later, Zarvora was still shaking as she stood between the two processors in the Calculor hall. Lewrick's killer had not been a member of the Libris staff, and nobody had been able to identify the corpse. There was not the slightest doubt that the System Controller had stopped a bullet meant for her. The forces of tradition in Libris were going beyond petitions, resolutions, and even duels to halt her modernizations. It was time to expand her Calculor guard into a secret constabulary for the whole library.

Behind the screens on either side of her the components of the Calculor's two processors worked hard at a diagnostic problem. As

Lewrick had said, the Calculor made a whirring, bustling mixture of sounds when working at full capacity, and there was nothing else in the world that was even remotely like it. The hiss and click of tens of thousands of abacus beads underlaid the soft rattle and clatter of gears and register levers, while the many banks of transfer wires hummed in weird chords that were sometimes strung into unsettling melodies.

Zarvora stood absolutely still, breathing shallowly. A deep chord sounded close by as the output wires from the right processor strained against the gate of the Verification Unit. A gear whirred for a moment, then a rack of levers were released for the wires to pull them into "yes" or "no" positions. While the levers were clacking into place an identical chord sounded from the output wires on the left. Both processors had arrived at the same answer to some part of the diagnostic calculation.

The people in charge of the output registers were Dragon Green Librarians, not prisoners. Zarvora had earlier decided that this work was too important to entrust to a mere component, but perhaps she had been mistaken. Dragon Colors were free to conspire in secret— over dinner, in taverns, in bed. Dragon Colors did not live in the same fear of punishment as the components. They could get lazy.

Again the chord sounded from the right processor's bank of output wires, but this time there was a slight mismatch in the sound from the left! Zarvora's lips parted slightly in eagerness. Before the gear on the left had released its bank of levers the left's wires slackened again, and from behind the left screen there was the clicking of a register being reset. Again the wires from the left processor were tensed, but this time the chord from it matched that from the right. The Dragon Green on the left was matching his output to that from the right by tuning the sound of the transfer wires while they were under tension.

The components were assembled into cell groups at the back of the Calculor hall. The area occupied by the desks of the Calculor was no more than the first quarter of the other end. They were in two separate groups, to the left and right of the center. The Highliber paced impatiently between the two rows.

"Bet it's a talk on some damn new configuration," muttered MULTIPLIER 8, and PORT 3A nodded wearily in agreement.

Suddenly a side door opened, and two dozen Dragon Blues filed carrying matchlock muskets. The fuses in the strikers were already alight and smoking. Even as the components were exchanging puzzled

167

glances the four Dragon Green Librarians who took turns to operate the output registers were marched in. Their hands were bound, and they were gagged. They showed signs of recent torture.

"They be Dragon Colors," hissed ADDER 17.

"They're senior Dragon Colors," observed MULTIPLIER 8.

"They're tying them to the retaining rail," gasped PORT 3A.

The Highliber gave another order, and the musketeer Dragon Colors formed into two rows of twelve, the front row kneeling.

"Attend the Highliber!" shouted the Deputy System Controller.

"System Officers, Dragon Colors, processing components, all souls who comprise the Calculor," Zarvora began, her words echoing from the stone walls. "You have been gathered to witness punishment on four Dragon Colors. These librarians, all trained and skilled, did conspire to degrade the performance of the Great Machine. Their motives were based in neither greed nor treason, but in pure sloth. When errors appeared at the end of long processing sessions, they contrived to falsely verify mismatched results, so that calculations would not have to be repeated.

"You!" she barked, pointing straight at MULTIPLIER 8. "If you were a soldier and were found asleep on sentry duty, what would the sentence be?"

MULTIPLIER 8 glanced hopefully around, but there was nobody behind him. "I, ah, very severe," he spluttered in reply.

"Service in the Mayor's Calculor is no different from service in the Mayor's Army," continued Zarvora. "The sentence for dereliction of duty is the same, too." She turned to the musketeers. "Form to! Present arms!"

The two lines of musketeers held their weapons out for the Highliber to inspect. "Release guards!" The terrified prisoners struggled against their bonds as two dozen trigger bars clicked free.

"Take aim!" shouted Zarvora, and the matchlocks came up in a silent swirl of blue fuse-smoke.

Two of the flintlocks misfired in the volley that followed, but the rest did their work for them. Four bodies hung from the retaining rail by their bindings as the smoke cleared. A Dragon Blue cut the ropes that held them, then two elderly, nervous attendants loaded them onto a book trolley and trundled them out through the side door. Zarvora addressed the gathering again.

"I can tolerate a great deal from both Dragon Colors and components—amorous dalliances, the black market in luxuries, all that is

168

officially forbidden in prisons but tacitly allowed. You are worked hard here, and I am not above rewarding good work. What I shall never tolerate, however, is meddling with the Calculor."

She paced between the two groups with her hands clasped behind her cloak. But for a slight swishing of cloth, there was silence.

"Those Dragon Colors tampered with the system to make their work, and yours, easier," she said, pointing to the pockmarked wall and smears of blood. "For some weeks they made my own life a lot harder, however, and they have paid for it. Do not follow their example. You are dismissed. Return to your cells."

The components streamed out of the hall while Zarvora conferred with Lewrick's successor. MULTIPLIER 8 felt a nudge in his back.

"Yes, FUNCTION 9, what is it?"

"The name's Dolorian," murmured a pretty young Dragon Yellow. "Would you care for some voluntary duties with me, Fras MULTIPLIER? The Highliber tolerates it, you know."

"Five days without a single error," said Zarvora as she presented the Mayor with a large silver key on a cushion. "We can trust the Calculor now, and put our faith in its results."

The modifications to her office were complete, with all the mechanisms and controls installed and the dust cleaned up. The window had been repaired, and there was a strong smell of oil and wood polish in the air. Jefton picked up the heavy key and looked at it doubtfully. Shelves of little silver animal caricatures stood ready to signal their messages, and colored velvet pulley cords hung down from the ceiling.

"It goes into the slot here, Mayor," Zarvora explained, "then you give it a half-turn clockwise."

"I feel that I should give a speech," said Jefton. "This thing is so important and ingenious. It's commissioning should be before the whole court, not with just yourself as the only witness. Still, secrecy is our only shield at present. For the greater glory of Rochester, I accept the service of this machine."

Jefton turned the key. A rack of gears moved, then moved again.

"That's all there is to it?" asked Jefton, who had been expecting a more diverting display. "Can't you make it move those mechanical animals, or ring the little bells?"

"It's already busy with important work," explained Zarvora, holding out a tray with his goblet of wine. "I set it up to begin designing your new army as soon as you turned the key."

They raised their goblets and toasted the Calculor.

"There will be no more errors, I trust?" said Jefton.

"Felt dampers have been put on the transmission wires, and four FUNCTION components have replaced the dead Dragon Green operators. Willful souls make up the Calculor, but it has no will of its own."

"A tame god, and ours to command!" exclaimed Jefton. "What is the name for those who rule the gods, Highliber?"

"I cannot say, Mayor," replied Zarvora, staring at the coded patterns that the gearwheels displayed every few seconds—that none but she could read. Jefton stared, too, his eyes glazing.

"Are you sure that it has the power to do all that you have promised?" he asked, nervous at his own incomprehension.

"It can do what you require very easily," she replied with a reassuring smile. Jefton continued to gaze blankly at the rack of gears, not yet aware that Rochester had a new ruler, and that he was now just another component for the Great Machine to command.

Tony Daniel lives in Alabama, has gone through what seems like the obligatory new-writer wringer that is the Clarion Science Fiction Workshop, and has sold stories to Isaac Asimov's and Confrontation. What he offers here could be considered a kind of ghost story, perhaps, but it's a ghost story of a distinctly and uniquely science fictional sort.

LOST IN TRANSMISSION

TONY
DANIEL

Dearest Jane, the stars are falling again. Or is it me, sinking through the void with a heavy heart? Both? I breathe vacuum now, suck nothingness into my chest; I am empty, my vapors shot out, spent completely in the space between the stars. They tell me now that it is certain our Milky Way will not explode, but will die down to the black like a burnt chunk of coal. That is me; I am an old galaxy-cinder.

"Haul in that sine wave, will you!" said the Captain. The crew hauled in. "Look to the receptors!" All lights shone green. "Pull her in, my little ones, pull easy, pull, I tell you!" We had the transmission now, had it coiled up in the guts of the instantiator like RNA in a mitochondrion, ready for translation. "Ms. Atof!"

Three hundred years is a long time to know a man. I traveled with the Captain—called Gustave Lufson by the Registry, by himself, perhaps—and never knew him. He drew us all, the ship, the crew, me, onward. We were light: the Captain magnetism, the rest of us electricity; the crew and the Captain tumbled over one another through the void. Space he gave us, and time. Most of us were colonials, children whose parents had bequeathed us worlds ordered, tamed, dead. Some were from old earth. Some were instantiations. We were flying away from something, toward we knew not what. The Captain knew.

And so I stepped briskly to the instantiator board to hook in. I looked over the display in my peripheral consciousness; there was a small spike on one of the frequencies, which I smoothed. I am a very careful woman, which is why, I think, the Captain trusted only me to pull living people from the emptiness. Then the spike reappeared. Wasn't in the machinery. I pulled back from scanning particulars and took a look at the entire data matrix. Very strange, grotesque. Had they transmitted some sort of monster? Was this thing encoded in the red-shifted gamma rays from earth even? Then a pattern clicked in from my organic mind and I understood: there were two people, intermingled in the code.

I read the vector direction, queried. Archives told me the transmission was from 2095—one of the later broadcasts, sent out with extremely sophisticated instruments. They could do this sort of thing. The instantiation was going to be tricky, even for me, and I'd done a good many. I began separating the two codes out, very carefully, like pulling earthworms from loam, breech babies from wombs. Then the oscillation flattened out, just for a millisecond. Some sort of interference had gotten to it, on the long journey out. Not much, but enough to lose one of them. So I turned my attention completely to the survivor. Then I had him/her, and the rest was easy.

I signaled the pod, and on it something began to materialize—somebody. By the ghost's blurred outline, all the crew could see it was going to be a man.

"He's from the 2090s, Captain."

I could not pause to feel sadness; I had to direct all my attention to the instantiation, but I saw and registered the disappointment of the Captain.

Seeing me finish up my task, the Captain spoke to me in a low voice. "Take her back a bit, Atof. Find the early times, my good first mate. Find them, I charge you."

Then he turned to the porthole and looked out at the steadily burning stars. "Blast and damn you, heavens. Curse you to darkness and cold death."

As the man on the pod solidified, the first light his thickening eyes caught was gray—the gray of the Captain's back as he strode from the instantiation chamber. After fifteen thousand years of silence, the first words ringing in the man's ears were curses. The man glanced around, first at me, then at the crew. To him, we must have looked somehow human. But not like anyone he'd ever seen. Then he saw the walls of the ship, shimmering as if covered with lights, with tiny stars—and moving, writhing—then he looked out the porthole at the real unwinking stars. He spoke his first words.

"This isn't Los Angeles, is it?"

A.D. 8124, FEBRUARY 10 . . . FRIDAY, I THINK.

This is not Los Angeles. Who am I? Henry Molton is long dead, thousands of years dead. I'm one vector of the one hundred thousand transmissions Henry Molton paid for, five thousand years ago. I'm a congealed radio wave. And Patricia is gone, her soul wiped out by some stray radiation. We did it for a lark, for a memorial, on Valentine's Day. We didn't want to live forever, just to leave a sign of our passing. Not we. Not me, here, now. They.

"Think of the potential out there, Mr. Molton," said this Atof, who pulled me in. "Think of the possibilities that you and others like you have brought into the universe."

"That was long-dead Henry Molton. You're praising the wrong guy," I answered. Was she?

Who is Atof, anyway? What is the crew? I am not sure these people are human. Sure, they have real faces—most of them—but their bodies aren't . . . right. It's like the pictures of *Australopithecus:* the artist tried, but he had no living model. You know nothing ever looked *that* way. But this Atof assures me they are all human. Enhanced, she calls it. Changed is what it is. Yet Atof is attractive enough, even to my twenty-first-century sensibilities. It's just she looks like a model in a department-store window, waxy and lifeless. But her eyes are alive. Atof says the glazed skin comes from vacuum adaptation. Most of this place they call a ship is hard vac and structural metal. I suspect some of the people are nothing more.

"A privileged frame of reference," Atof called the ship. "A place to stand while the universe turns under us." Balderdash. I was broadcast at the speed of light. Nothing from earth could catch up with me. I make propulsion systems for a living . . . made them . . . I know these things. Atof was lying. But I am here. Somehow, I am here. END RECORDING

"If you don't at least get trehalosed, most of the ship will be off limits to you by necessity. You would die there."

"Maybe getting processed by you people will kill me anyway. There's more than one way to be dead."

Molton, our new instantiation, had a fierce edge to his voice and an intense look in his eyes. He reminded me of the Captain in many ways. If he had the same mixture of caution when uncertain and boldness when ready to act as the Captain, I felt certain that, after I convinced him, he would have no trouble adapting to ship life.

"Mr. Molton, I assure you I am as alive as you are. I eat, breath, walk, feel, love, and hate."

"But you tell me eating is not really necessary for you. Hell, you don't have to walk; you could turn off your ship's gravity machine. . . ."

"It is not a machine. It is part of the effect that makes the ship possible."

"Whatever. So how do I know your processing doesn't allow you to turn your emotions on and off with some kind of toggle switch? I've got friends, a sister—they're gone forever. I don't know if I want to turn off my grief."

"I can turn off my feelings, Mr. Molton, if I so choose. I can, for instance, monitor and change all sorts of hormones in my body. I can shunt memories to and from my computer implants. But it is all a matter of choice. I left people behind on the world where I grew up, too, Mr. Molton. I'll never see those people again. But now I have the ship for a home, the crew for a family, and the Captain."

Molton was quiet for a moment. Then he surprised me.

"What's your first name, Atof?"

"Rachel," I said after a bit of hesitation. I prefer to keep a certain distance from new arrivals. Sometimes, they are very unstable and lash out emotionally. Though I've handled many, I could still be hurt.

"I'm Henry. May I call you Rachel?"

"Certainly."

"Rachel, what does this ship do? Who is this mysterious captain I've yet to see? Why did he bring me back from the dead?"

"The Captain is an instantiation, like yourself, Mr. . . . Henry. He adapted very well to ship conditions. We selected him Captain a hundred years ago. The *Tithonus* specializes, at the moment, in transmission recovery of the earth broadcasts of 2050 to 2113. We work under contract with several frontier worlds who need colonists."

"Then I'm to be sold as a slave." Molton was quick—and contentious.

"Of course not, Henry. You will find the colonial offers very enticing. You can also choose to join our crew, if you meet with the Captain's approval."

"Who is this Captain? When was he broadcast?"

"In the 2060s, I believe. That was back in the single transmission days. This is actually our first pass through iterative times, like yours . . . was."

Molton was quiet for a long while. I felt almost as if I should wait until he dismissed me.

"I want to see the Captain," he finally said.

"I'm sorry, Henry, the Captain won't see you, at least not yet."

"Why not?"

"He just does not greet new arrivals. That is my job, as first mate."

"I wish to see *him*."

Yes, Molton was very much like the Captain.

"I'll see what I can do."

Jane, we had a new arrival today. Saw him only for a moment before I left that wretched chamber. Atof tells me the processing was very strange. We're in a patch of later-day broadcasts at the moment, so I've got us angling away from earth, back toward my own cursed, blessed time.

I dreamed of you last night—clouded images: your brown hair forever falling over your eyes, those incredible hazel eyes. You were saying something, something about an Emily Dickinson poem. Even in the recall bank, the dream is fuzzy. Ah, Jane, after all these years I still don't like Emily Dickinson.

As always after an instantiation, the Captain was despondent. Before, he had shut himself into his cabin for long stretches. When he had come out, he'd looked worn, older. Molton's request wasn't the only reason I decided to go and visit the Captain, if not to cheer him, at least to share his misery. It is not in the Officer's Manual, but something any good first mate will do. One reason: crew productivity fell during the absences, and morale was not what it could be. Another thing: something Molton hadn't said, but I knew I ought to ask.

The Captain's cabin was far aft, almost an appendage pulled behind the ship. He was vacuum-adapted, of course, but kept a low atmosphere in his cabin for communication; the Captain was very reluctant to talk electromagnetically. The entire ceiling of the cabin was transparent. Looking up could give vertigo even to an old hand such as me. It didn't seem to bother the Captain; for some reason, he enjoyed the vastness.

"What can I do for you, my good first mate?"

"Mr. Molton, the newest recovery, is not adapting as well as we might hope. And he demands to see you."

"Won't take to the notion that he's to be changed."

"He does not wish to be enhanced, sir. Perhaps seeing how well you have adapted might sway him."

The Captain let a glint of amusement cut through his general gloom. "Can't blame him for not liking the idea. I didn't like it at first either. When I switched over to ship's time, I was two clicks in the past for the longest time. Couldn't interact with reality. They had to feed me until the spoons and forks were where and when I reached for them."

The Captain thought a moment and seemed to brighten. "Join me for dinner, Rachel?"

He hadn't called me by my first name for a long time. I was tempted to forget why I really came, and stay with him. But I got to be first mate because of my candor, my inability to dissemble. I knew as soon as I uttered the words it was wrong—all wrong, to say to my Captain.

"Molton's transmission was strange . . . sir."

"Yes, you told me."

"He was intermingled with another person. He has not told me, but I assume this was a lover. The other transmission was flawed."

The Captain seemed confused for a moment, not sure how to reply. I continued.

"By 2090, earth was doing multiple repetitions of broadcasts. There is a chance, if we continue in this patch of transmission, we can locate another of Molton's code. Molton has deduced this, I believe, and I expect him to ask you to go back and look."

The Captain said nothing for a very long time. I believed he wished me to remain, but I wanted nothing more than to turn and go, to avoid his face. His face and hands trembled, slightly, and his tight lips contorted almost into a smile.

"Atof, we have a duty to the early transmissions. They are singular, unrecoverable if damaged. Life is hard out here, full of disappointments. Tell that mother-wet babe that this is *space*. I'll not see him until he can give something besides groans and whimpers to my crew."

He was speaking in the voice that mesmerized the crew, put purpose in their hearts. Almost, I got caught up in his excitement once again. What was inside the Captain to make his voice ring so? Even when in a vacuum, the desperate excitement, the drive, came through over the radio. Instead of his energy, I felt only a hollow resonance, as hollow as gravity bending through emptiness.

MONDAY, FEBRUARY 13, A LONG TIME FROM HOME.

And I'm to live practically forever, if I take these . . . modifications. Travel between the stars still takes years and years. I'll be just like the Captain, just like other broadcasted people who have joined the crew. A speck barely moving against a field of stars. Alone.

I must see this captain. We're so close to Patricia; I'm so close to an existence that wouldn't be empty, wasted. Yet, the Captain will not come to me. I cannot go to the Captain and still be me. Pat, my love, I'll never see you again. What a life we shared: I built our treehouses, castles, spaceships; you brought them to life. Even in New York, the apartment was the only living place in a dead city. The promotion and L.A. was going to change all that. The move was cause for celebration, for doing something wild. Like flinging ourselves out into space. But whom am I talking to? A machine. A machine that changes living words into magnetic impulses. END RECORDING

"Incoming, incoming, all hands to stations! Go, my crew, my folks, won't you scuttle to your stations! Won't you haul!"

I ran down the airless hall leading from my cabin to the instantiation chamber, my boot steps sending silent vibrations along the floor in front of me. I jogged quickly, but not frantically. They'd wait for me to get to the instantiation chamber. I was the one who brought the people in.

I'd spent the last few days away from people. I did not want to face Molton, to answer the question he hadn't even asked me. I did not want to see anyone. So I gave Second Mate Bingley the helm and spent some time reading—reading earth history, about a time in which I couldn't live and a place I'd never visit.

The Captain was in the chamber, stalking about excitedly as he always did just before an instantiation. His face was haggard; his beard —he'd never had cosmetic enhancement—had grown out in a scraggly

179

way in the four days since I'd been in his cabin. But he was smiling; he looked happier than I'd seen him in years.

And next to him stood Molton. His body had the dull gleam of trehalose packing. After all our arguing, he'd had himself enhanced without telling me. I gaped at them both.

"Turn your gawky eyes, my hermit of a first mate. Have you never seen folks at work before? We've searched the skies, Atof, to pull them in, to pull all the lost souls in from the deeps!"

I said nothing, just stood in the airlock, my front in the atmosphere, my back cool from the hallway's vacuum that held no ambient heat.

"Won't you hitch in, Atof."

I moved to the console and hooked in.

"Take her slow, take her gentle," said the Captain. "Come, my crew, easy as you touch a baby, soft as a dreamless sleep. That's it, Atof, yes, Atof. Won't you be careful and kind!"

Through my hypoconscious cloud of readouts and toggles, I saw Molton. His now satin-textured hands were clasped tightly; his eyes were half closed. He was murmuring under his breath.

The wall of the chamber began violently to shimmer as we stuck an edge out into normal space.

"Watch the sine, my crew, watch the sine. We don't ever want to lose another one." The Captain began pacing.

"Ready, Captain, ready."

"Do your work, Ms. Atof, do it, I say!"

I reached outward to gather in the lost one. It was the pattern I'd expected, the intertwined codes of two ghosts, two kindred spirits. I let one of them go, let him continue traveling toward the ragged edge of the galaxy. The other I pulled to me, like a mother hen pulling her chick beneath her, shielding the chick from a world full of predators.

A woman became visible on the pod. I saw Molton start forward away from the wall, as if drawn by the apparition. I was hooked in and could only watch.

"It's a woman, Captain," said one of the crew.

"Care, care, won't you be careful, I say to you. Take the best care."

The woman's face was becoming distinct: her red hair, her blue eyes.

"Patricia!" cried Molton. "It's you; you're here!"

And when her eyes were solid enough to see him, she smiled.

The two embraced on the pod, crying and laughing all at once. "We're going to live forever, Pat—and go to the stars. We can be together forever."

I pulled myself away from the console hook-in, my job finished. The Captain was leaning against the wall. He had not broken into his usual rage after most instantiations. He motioned me over to him.

"Ah, let me lean on you, my good first mate. Look on it, will you. How long's he been among us. As long as a mayfly in spring? Hours? Seconds? He gave up his lungs, his heart, to come to me, to ask a simple thing. How could I not look? And we knew his code. It was easy, like picking up a flower you have dropped, that you noticed was missing from the hand that plucked it, from the mind that wished to take it home to water.

"A homecoming. Doesn't it pull out your strong metal heart, doesn't it burn up and down your wiring? What luck! What a universe some scoundrel has made for us, what a place."

We looked on the pair for a long time, while the Captain leaned on me. If I'd been anyone but first mate Rachel Atof, I would have been silent, been happy to hold him up for even a little while. But I had something to say, something that was the worst thing I could ever say—and the best.

"You'll find her, Gustave. You'll find her somewhere. Maybe she's nearer than you think."

The Captain looked for another moment with greedy eyes on the reunited. Then he closed his eyes, like shields against a sun's light. "I'm going to my cabin, Ms. Atof. I'm going to have a rest. Take care of *Tithonus* while I'm away."

Then his voice strengthened. "And take care to call me when we run upon another transmission, mate."

He turned and left. I watched him for a moment. Something was out of balance, my sensors were saying, but I did not know what to adjust, what to feel. I went to welcome the new one on board.

Three hundred years is a very long time. When we pluck her from the void, will she be my Jane? Will she know me? Can anyone know me anymore? Ah, Jane, a silly whim. I shall find you. Those bony stars are hiding you. You're there, somewhere, sometime. Have you passed through this cabin a dozen times? Have you touched me without my knowledge? I've passed out to you, so often, lying here, gazing up into my roof full of the night.

Joe Haldeman, the author of The Forever War *and* Buying Time *and* Mindbridge *and a bunch of other outstanding science fiction novels, never had a story published in* Universe *when it was edited by Terry Carr—very likely because he never submitted one there. When we took over the job, we (separately and collectively) suggested to Joe that he do something for us, and after much badgering he came through with this sly little piece, which is all of six hundred words long.*

They are six hundred very well chosen words, as you'd expect from Haldeman. We were happy to see them and are happy to present them here. But we'd still like to see something a little more substantial from Joe, more on the order of "Seasons" or "Tricentennial" or "Blood Brothers," and perhaps next time we will. And so will you.

JOB SECURITY

JOE
HALDEMAN

The first one was like four years ago, four and a half. I remember because that's when I was fifteen years into this job, sweeping up these old observatory domes, halfway to full pension.

They lost a star, big deal, one out of a zillion, you couldn't even see it from here. It was a big one, though, Alfalfa something. Maybe it was in Spanish, three of the guys went down to South America to look at it, look at where it wasn't anymore.

Couple years later they lose another one and all hell breaks loose, even though you couldn't even see it without the telescope. Then another couple years and they lose another, even dimmer, but by this time they know where to look. The next one was gonna be in like six months but in the daytime, so old man Merton and a couple others get to go to Paris where it's dark. Tough job.

This Sirius one got to me, though, like for years and years I seen it all winter. Winter is a bitch on the mountain, have to use the four-wheel in the snow and they can't heat up the domes, one of the guys tried to explain why, but I don't get science.

They knew to the minute when it was gonna go, so I bundled up and went outside and looked. Brightest star in the sky, can't miss it. Then pow, nothing. I mean it didn't blow up or nothing, it just went out.

Maybe it was because I just lost a tooth, the first one, that makes you feel old, kind of, makes you think about things. I watched that Sirius go out and it hit me. No wonder these guys are so worried. What if they all go out? They've got no jobs. And if they got no jobs, I got no job.

I know better than to bother anybody

while he's working, but it did keep me awake half the night thinking about it. I mean a guy who can push a broom can always get a job, some kind of job, but starting over at forty-two in some new place didn't sound good.

Anyhow about six I went down to the small dome because I knew Dr. Jake would be getting off, he's a professor too but we get along. He was staying on till noon, he said, but had a cup of coffee with me and I asked him if he was worried. He didn't get it at first. I mean he really was worried, but not about that. They were worried because they couldn't figure it out, why it was happening.

But as to losing all the stars to look at, Dr. Jake said that was no problem, we wouldn't lose more than a couple dozen you could see as long as he or I was going to live, if they had it figured out right with the distances and all. I never got that speed of light stuff.

But he said that even if every one of them did go out, we'd all stay on at the domes, trying to see what was left. Then he said I looked tired and was I losing sleep over this problem, and I admitted that I did, most of the night. So he said screw the morning shift, they'd all be working anyhow and didn't need anybody else around, go back to the cabin and catch some Z's.

It's that kind of a job, you know, loose. I slept like a rock.

Another new writer, with another fine story, depicting a strange and alien society with eerie lucidity.

Canadian-born Donna Farley studied at the University of Toronto, lives now in British Columbia, is married to an Eastern Orthodox priest, and is the mother of two school-age daughters. She lists Heinlein, Tolkien, C. S. Lewis, and Madeleine L'Engle as some of her favorite writers, an interesting mix indeed. This is her second published story: the first was in an anthology called Catfantastic.

I suppose I knew I was a pervert the first day I saw the Hall of Faces. And yet at first I seemed no different from many others who go to the Hall of History to look at the naked faces of the statues, content to ogle the marble cheeks and straight bronze noses. It was only in the last year before my passage rites that I began to go there in the dark. When the warders went off on their rounds to another part of the Hall, I would tear my mask from my face and let my smile hang there in the open, as if I too were frozen in time, with nothing to fear from the gawking people who crowded the Hall by day.

I think I did it because I wanted a friend, and naked marble faces were more friendly than any lacquered mask, even those painted with the patterns of my own House: a sunburst on the forehead with a diamond in its center, representing the House del'Sun, perhaps the most influential of all the twelve United Houses. The delicately calligraphed genealogies on either cheek are done in gold over the black lacquer. I knew from my childhood, as does every member of a Great House, that I must give my trust only to those whose masks bore the family crest. Only when another del'Sun betrayed that trust did I become obsessed with removing my mask.

But long before, when I was only twelve, the House tutor took us to the Hall of History—myself and several of my half brothers and a few cousins, all of us prepubescent boys who sniggered behind our masks as the Historian conducted us through the galleries. The torsos were bad enough; we shook with stifled hysteria, nudging each other as we peered through our masks' eyeholes at feminine buttocks

THE PASSING OF THE ECLIPSE

DONNA
FARLEY

and delicate marble nipples. Still, we had seen the real thing before, through a secret peephole we had to the women's quarters of the House, and it was a piece of male statuary that seemed really funny to us—a torso with a fig leaf.

"Got a mask on his dick," whispered my cousin Tonio.

Laughter hissed out through the mouth slits of our masks, and the Historian turned suddenly, cutting off his drone about "Ancient Greeks and other early peoples of the Pre-Cataclysmal periods."

"I trust you are prepared to treat the next gallery with the seriousness it deserves," he said. He had a voice like the rumble of cart wheels on pavement, and his eyes burned in his red Historian's mask.

We fell silent, because we knew what was coming: the Hall of Faces.

"Our ancestors were not like us," he said. "They were beautiful. We know from their statuary. They made paintings, too, yes, and pictures made with light—a process called photography, pictures you would swear were real enough for you to step into the frame and join the people there in their activities. Such pictures as survived the great Cataclysm have perished in the long centuries since, unless perhaps there are some across the ocean, if there really are other countries there still. But we have a few statues here, and we can see what our ancestors looked like. They were beautiful, and they wore no masks."

One of my younger cousins giggled, but the rest of us tried to behave exactly as if we were twenty-year-olds being examined for our passage plumes. We went silently, single file, behind the red-robed man, our multiple footsteps echoing through the high-ceilinged gallery. We came into the Hall of Faces and stood still.

I felt as though I had come into a temple. Not a family funerary chapel, you understand, where you go on House Assembly day once a week to honor the empty masks of your ancestors that line the walls, but a temple, one like those the ancient Greeks had had, or one of the Christian ones from before the Cataclysm with all the colored glass in them, a cathedral they called it. But it was not the room itself—the gallery was spare and spacious, plain, so plain, for any other decoration would have been superfluous to the Hall of Faces.

I forgot anyone else was there. The Gallery was a temple, even if it did not mean to be, and the deity, banished from the world after the Cataclysm, had come back in the Faces.

188

Some of them were bronze, others marble, though we had been told this had nothing to do with the original color of our ancestors' skins, which were white, though not as white as the marble. They were serious faces, too, with none of the smiles I sometimes seemed to remember from childhood, when I and the others had been too young to keep a mask on, or feed ourselves in proper solitude.

And they were beautiful. *I* thought they were beautiful, at least, though afterward I wondered what it was that made them beautiful, and what it was that made *our* faces not-beautiful, so not-beautiful that we hid them perpetually behind our elaborately decorated masks.

"After the Cataclysm," said the Historian, "our ancestors put on masks because of the poison in the air. But that did not save us. Poison seeped into people, and changed their faces into hideous parodies of what they had been. Then people began to wear masks because they hated the sight of each other. Later, as the Houses grew up and tried to restore a little of what had been lost, they made their masks into the emblems of family and profession that they are today."

He paused for a little while, and then, "They were beautiful," he said again, as if it were the only thing that mattered.

I went the next day to my father, paterfamilias of the House del'Sun, and asked his permission to become an Historian.

"I am pleased, Angelo," he said. I was only the third son of a minor concubine, and he had enough expenses in outfitting the older sons of his prime wife for their army commissions. Historian was an honorable profession, because it had to do with our ancestors. The United Houses would pay my room and board during my training at the Hall of History, as well as my small but regular stipend, once I won my passage plume. My father then need only reward my coming of age with enough money to buy a concubine. Accordingly, I moved to the Hall within a week. I was to return to the Sun House only for the Sunday family assemblies.

Though I applied myself diligently to my studies, so as to make a good showing at my passage rites, I cared nothing for history as such. It was the Faces I loved. When the Hall was empty, I liked to go and talk to them, especially to a marble woman, head and shoulders only, who was labeled GREECE, FIFTH C.B.C.; and to a naked, muscular young man called DAVID BY MICHELANGELO, REPRODUCTION IN BRONZE, 20TH C. OF MARBLE ORIGINAL, 16TH C.

Sometimes I only stared at them in silence, trying to imagine what had made them so beautiful. But I did not bare my face before theirs until I was nineteen.

My cousin Tonio, who was in training with the army, came calling late one afternoon. He was at that time no great fellow of mine—none of them was, after I went to the Hall of History—but he was hard up for someone to drink with. He would buy, he said, with money won in a game of dice, and so, my own purse being light as a feather, I went.

"Listen," he said over our third hard cider, "I have a friend can get us plumes for the night. He does guard duty where they keep the peacocks."

I sat up straight. "Tonio. If they catch you at that, you get not only a fine, but prison and flogging."

Tonio sucked on the straw through his mouth slit, swilled the drink around in his mouth, then swallowed. "Do not be an ass, Angelo. You know where you can go with a passage plume."

"The House general meetings. The men's baths."

"A *whorehouse*, you idiot. God's funeral, do they not tell you about whorehouses in the Hall of History?"

I pushed my empty cider mug away impatiently. "You can get sick from whores. Better to buy yourself a nice little virgin concubine after your passage rites."

"My friend knows a place—" His voice dropped suddenly. "The harlots will take off their masks in the lamplight there."

A thrill flashed through me, like a fire in my belly shooting up into my cheeks and all the way back down to my feet. It was not an erotic thrill. Or if it was, that was not all it was. I may have been a pervert, but there was something besides sex to my perversion.

We went. The plumes cost most of Tonio's purse, leaving us barely enough for the brothel.

The whoremistress gave us black velvet overmasks to cover our Sun House masks. "These are the rules of the Guild of Courtesans," she said. "No violence. If anyone hurts a girl, every man in the place comes to help her—you included."

She sent us into a large room where oil lamps on low tables cast shadows that sprawled across the floor, only to be swallowed by the greater darkness of the black-painted walls. Men with anonymous black overmasks like ours lounged on red cushions, playing with the harlots' bodies. The whores themselves wore masks painted a dead white, with red lacquered lips and spiderlike false eyelashes round the eyeholes. Though I had heard that some whores dyed their hair yellow or red in imitation of the ancients, these all had hair as black as anyone else's, some curly like mine, some straight like Tonio's.

My cousin soon got into the spirit of the party; some of the women were dancing, peeling off clothing as they writhed, and Tonio joined them to hasten the process, provoking appreciative hoots from the other men. I watched until it became clear the whores were not going to take off their masks then and there; they fell breathless on the red cushions and took sips of wine through straws, or a puff on a hookah through their mask slits.

I left my cousin to his pleasure, found the mistress, and told her exactly what I wanted.

"But that is extra," she said, and I had to give her the few coins I had left in my pitiful purse.

She led me to a small room, brightly lit with hanging lamps, and I sat waiting on the pallet, dry-mouthed, till one of the harlots came in.

She knelt down opposite me, sweeping her cloud of black hair over her shoulder, and I saw something I had not noticed before about the white masks. Painted curving against the lower of the scarlet lips there gleamed two small, sharp incisor teeth, and I realized suddenly that the masks were meant to portray the vampires one read of in some wild Pre-Cataclysm tales. That did not disturb me until my mind leapt to a terrifying possibility.

God's grave! What if this was what our real faces looked like? Would that not be real ugliness?

My heart pounded. I sat there, only half aware of the whore's fingertips teasing at the collar of my shirt, until good sense reasserted itself. Surely our faces could not be that sepulchral white, not when our bodies are so brown all over. I ran my tongue over my teeth, reassuring myself that the incisors did not protrude. The whore's mask was only a macabre joke.

"Men kiss their wives in the dark," she breathed, the mouth slit of her mask so close to mine that I could taste the cider she had been drinking. "They never know what it is they are kissing, but you can look at my lips and see what you will get before you snuff the lamps and take off your own mask." She sat back a little, gave a slow blink of her eyes, and said, "Want to kiss me, no?"

I wanted to. But I wanted more to see her.

"Take it off," I said, sweating.

She had a low, throaty laugh that was made to turn a man's body and soul inside out. "What, no play first?"

I thrust her wandering fingers from me. "No! I want to see your face!"

191

She looked at me silently through her eyeholes, and I thought, *I am so perverted, even a whore thinks me sick.* But I did not care. I had paid for her to take her mask off, and that was all I wanted.

She was not friendly now. She sat stock-still, never taking her eyes from mine. Reaching up with one hand, she undid the leather strap that held the mask on, swung it off, and dropped it on the pillow beside her.

"Here it is. White as one of the ancestors." She grinned, showing a wide mouthful of teeth, none of them pointed.

I put out my hand, trembling. It came away from her cheek white with powder. The lips were redder than the mask's, and a greasy blue slicked her eyelids.

"You—whore!" I said, lacking any worse name for her. "Your face is more painted than your mask!"

She laughed. "Face-baring is against the law. The United Houses keep a watch here to see we do not break it. But I can take my mask off, all right, long as I have another underneath, even if it is only made of paint."

I slapped her face. And she took a whistle that was on a chain round her neck and blew it. In a moment all the men in the place piled into the room and gave me a good bruise apiece.

The one who must have been my cousin pulled off my velvet overmask and plucked the rented passage plume from my own mask. Then they threw me out into the street, cursing me for disturbing their revels.

I limped back to the Hall of History, scarcely aware of where I was going in my rage. Tonio was my cousin, a member of my House. Whatever the whorehouse rules, he should have come to my aid, but he kept his Sun House mask hidden behind the black velvet and joined the others as they beat me.

I nodded good evening to the door wards, who looked at my awkward gait but said nothing. Then I went into the moonlit Hall of Faces, pulled off my mask, and cried like a child before Michelangelo's David.

I sank to my knees, then to all fours, and before I realized what was happening, I lay asleep on the floor.

I woke to the methodical *whish-whish* of a broom. The sound stopped abruptly, and small bare feet slapped across the floor toward me.

Opening my eyes to the early sunlight, I saw the plain gray mask of one of the zabbaline, the garbage collectors. The swell of a small bosom filled her ragged shirt, telling of youth, but her actual age was of no import, for the zabbaline are the meanest creatures in the city, and not eligible for the passage plumes that confer certain rights on adult citizens.

Crouching beside me, she touched my cheek with small brown fingers, and I recoiled in shock, suddenly aware that I was barefaced. I jumped up, snatching up my mask, and fumbled to fasten it on as I ran from the Hall.

I did not go back to the Hall of Faces again by daylight—I went at midnight, or before dawn, and stood in silence before my statues, my face as naked as theirs were. The girl, I had discovered, collected the Hall's garbage daily, and in addition received a penny for sweeping the galleries. But one morning she came early and caught me a second time in my perversion.

I stood frozen in the growing light while her bright eyes blinked at me from behind her mask. She padded slowly toward me on her bare feet, and I could not speak, or lift my mask to my face again.

She put something in my hand. "Sunday, at dawn. Go to the Dumps and ask anyone you see for the house of Zachary."

Then she went off, carrying her broom, like a soldier with his pike.

I clapped my mask back on and hurried to my rooms to look at the thing she had given me. I could not have been more startled. It was a cross, fashioned from some bent and polished nails. The zabbaline typically make such cheap jewelry from salvaged objects, but I had not expected this ancient religious symbol. Women, I am told, wear such things secretly and practice who knows what superstitions in the women's quarters of the House. But like the other boys in our House, I had no religious experience or knowledge except the honoring of ancestors in the funerary chapel on House assembly days.

God, said the philosophers, had died, or at least gone away, after the Cataclysm, or maybe even before. We had no real hope of help, except from our ancestors, whose ancient knowledge, hidden in the libraries of the Hall of History, might help us rebuild civilization one day. In the turmoil that followed the Cataclysm, it was the Families, which later became the Great Houses, that started putting the world back together. It only made sense, therefore, to honor the founders of one's own House.

I turned the girl's peculiar gift over in my palms. For all the talk of

193

honoring our ancient ancestors, the Houses often kept the Historians busy with researching and recording genealogies of relatively recent vintage—too busy to pursue any quest to know our Pre-Cataclysmal ancestors through their writings. Also, our documents, copies of copies of copies, were a mixed bag of chance survivals. Often as not, we could learn all about such peculiar topics as life insurance policies, and yet never find a word about what our ancestors ate for breakfast.

But now I found I wanted to know something of a topic no one had ever taught me anything about: the zabbaline.

The time I spent searching for a reference began to eat into my regular studies, but at last I found a brief entry in an old transcript of a Pre-Cataclysm journal. I read to my astonishment that the zabbaline were Egyptian. I had thought the word a perfectly ordinary House term, from either the Pre-Cataclysm Italian or Hispanic, which, along with Late English—the language of the journal in which I found the reference—form the basis of the language we now speak.

In the melting pot of Pre-Cataclysm America, anything could happen. Still, I did not think our zabbaline could possibly be real Egyptians. Egypt was practically a legend, more ancient even than Greece, and we had very few of their artifacts in the Hall. I hypothesized that perhaps the first garbage collectors in the early period of the Houses had adopted the name zabbaline, just as the Houses themselves had adopted the old Latin term paterfamilias. The original zabbaline had been garbage collectors, too. They had also been Christians.

Very early Sunday morning, I stood before the David in the shadowy Hall, wishing he would open his beautiful lips and speak. And I suddenly wondered what the girl had thought of my ugly, modern face, next to his ancient and beautiful one. I looked at the fifth century B.C. woman, too, and wondered how the whore, without her paint, would have looked beside *her*. Then, before the gray morning began to break, I went out into the streets. I did not turn up the hill toward the House of the del'Sun, where my family were all asleep yet, while the servants prepared the breakfast and dusted the chapel for the assembly. I went down, through the maze of the lower town, through the empty market and the common streets, all the way to the Dumps.

The flies were not yet buzzing, but the smell lay thick as lamp oil in the air, and I thought I would choke before I got ten feet into the Dumps. It was too late to think of going to the House family assembly instead; God's tombstone, even the public baths would be loath to let me in smelling like this!

Mountains of garbage loomed on either side of the streets, and ramshackle houses, cobbled together from bits of discarded wood and bricks, crouched at the foot of each heap of refuse, garbage pile after garbage pile and house after tumbledown house. Pigs snored on their sides in little pens by the houses.

I walked until I met a family of zabbaline leaving their home in the growing dawn. I showed them my cross, and they took me with them to Zachary's house.

Though bigger than most of the other houses, it was built from the same hodgepodge of materials. But inside, it was a temple. It was full to bursting with bare faces.

My escorts took off their masks; the father, whose name was Gideon, put a hand on my arm and said, "You are not expected to remove yours, Master del'Sun. Only, that cross vouches for you, and we trust to your silence about what you see here."

I nodded. I felt a little dizzy. I still cannot remember many details from their ritual that day. The only really clear thing I took away with me, the only thing that mattered, was that their faces were beautiful.

Not like the ones in the Hall of Faces, exactly. They were all brown, of various shades, not white like the painted whore, or like our ancestors were supposed to be. Their cheeks were rounder, their mouths and nostrils broader than those of the statues, but they differed from them no more than the mask of one person differs from another. Each House has its own distinctive pattern, each individual his own genealogy, yet the basic shape of each mask—and face—is the same.

Incense rose in clouds, helping to cover the stench of the zabbaline's stockpiled wares outside. I listened to chanted repetitions of things like "Lord have mercy" and "Father, Son, and Holy Spirit." I could not see everything that happened at the front, except that their leader, a small man with a frizz of graying hair, wore a robe with the cross sewn all over it.

Throughout the ritual, one thing kept drawing my attention: a painted picture of a face. It had a beard, as many men did before the Cataclysm, and while it was browner than some of the zabbaline's, it was not as dark as others. Its features resembled my statues' more than the zabbaline's, and yet it was not quite like the statues either, the eyes being large and almond-shaped, the nose very long and narrow, and the lips very compressed.

Afterward, a girl came bustling through the crowd to take me by

195

the arm, her bright smile turning her whole face into the most beautiful thing I had ever seen. "You came!" she said.

I wanted badly to tear off my own mask, but I had a horrible, inexplicable fear that my face was not like hers, that if I pulled off the mask she would strike my face as I had struck the whore's.

And then they all sat down and ate together. Yes, *ate* together. Even I, the pervert who had taken his mask off in front of the statues, thought it a little obscene at first. But the girl laughed, and sat me down next to the leader, the priest.

"My father, Zachary," she said.

I watched her, fascinated, as she ate roasted barley and raisins with her fingers, and presently saw nothing obscene in her movements, but a great beauty. The polished brown of her face shone more than any lacquered mask. When she smiled, her cheeks blossomed like an opening peony, and small lines appeared at the corners of her mouth. And her eyes . . . they glowed like the little glass oil lamps the zabbaline kept in their temple here, all deep brown liquid and steady flame.

The old man cleared his throat, and I turned back to him. I could not help staring at the sags and wrinkles under his eyes. His was a face like a rumpled pillow, and yet, like his daughter's, it was every bit as beautiful as the David's.

He smiled, and I knew I had amused him. God's bones, I could not say *how* I understood the meaning of facial expressions I had never seen before, much less how he could read my feelings from only my exposed eyes; but we understood each other perfectly.

"Maria told me about you, Master del'Sun. We are glad you chose to come. You have questions?"

"Yes." I looked around, still awed by the beauty of their faces. "Why?"

He laughed. Maria smiled into my eyes, and I felt hot.

Zachary patted my arm. "Forgive me, Master del'Sun. I know this is hard for you. I will be serious now. This," he said, pointing to his own naked face, "and this"—Maria's—"and all these . . ." He gestured at the crowd of laughing, talking, eating bare faces. "The Image of God."

"But you do not look like that one," I said, gesturing at the painting.

"And do I look like my daughter here?" he asked, putting an arm around her. "Of course not. She is a lovely young woman, and I am a decrepit old man." Zachary could hardly seem to stop smiling, even when he tried. "And He—He was from another time and place. So. But yet, Maria and I do look like each other. And also we look like Him." He laid a hand on his heart. "Here, also, is the Image of God."

My own heart began to hammer as I grasped the edges of my mask. "And what is under here?"

Zachary and Maria looked at me intently. Around us, the laughter and talk grew suddenly quiet.

"That is for you to decide, Master del'Sun," said Zachary.

I tightened my grip on the mask, because my hands were shaking. "I have a name. Angelo."

Zachary nodded. "Well, Angelo. You also have a face."

So, with trembling fingers, I inched the mask off. In the silence, I thought I would die of fear. Maria was smiling, smiling to encourage me, and I remembered, silly fool, that of course she had seen my face already, twice. But I remained tense, for some of the others looked a little surprised. (How did I know that slackening jaws and widening eyes meant surprise?)

Then Zachary's grin spread all over his face, and he clapped his hands on my arms. "Welcome, Angelo!" he said, and kissed me, once on each cheek.

And then Maria and the others inundated me with embraces, kissed me till my cheeks smarted with the novelty of it. Soon I was eating with them, too.

I left in the afternoon, ashamed to tell them that I had to wash the stink of their home off before I dared return to the Hall of History. I think they knew, but said nothing. And I did not give my missed family assembly another thought.

I came back to the Hall of Faces early next morning, but not to see the statues. I waited beside the David until Maria came with her broom, *whish-whish*, gathering the dust from yesterday's visitors in her pan.

Strangely, we were shy, and it was I who took off my mask first. She put the broom down, then unmasked, too, and came to kiss me on both cheeks. My face tingled as much from those two kisses as it had from dozens yesterday.

Then she masked again. I followed her example, reluctantly, knowing we dared not be caught.

Her eyes strayed to the David. "You know who he is, do you not?" And she told me the story about the young giant-killer from the zabbaline holy book, which I had never come across in the Hall of History, because most of the existing copies had been burned in the Post-Cataclysmal rejection of religion.

I looked at the David with amazement as I listened to her tale. "But he was only a young boy!" I protested. "This man—you can see he is a lord, a leader of men, born to be *paterfamilias* of a Great House!"

"A paterfamilias without any mask?" Maria giggled, and I laughed with her. "But you are right, the House of David is the House of Christ, the Lord of the World. But David was once the young shepherd boy. And behind the face of the young boy was always the face of the paterfamilias. Even a naked face can sometimes be a kind of a mask, Angelo."

We met every morning, and she told me more stories and more about her people. My guess about their adoption of the name zabbaline proved correct. Her people had preserved things from the time of the Cataclysm I had never heard of in the Hall of History. "People never turned ugly from the radiation," she told me. *Radiation*, I knew, was what they called the poison that made the Post-Cataclysmal people wear masks and other protective clothing. "Only, there were different kinds of people—all people, but all different. Our ancestors did not all have pale white skins, only some of them. Some of them thought dark skins were ugly; but after the Cataclysm, dark skins protected people from the sun better, and eventually no more babies were born with white skins, that is all."

I absented myself from several more family assembly days to go to Zachary's house, telling my father that I was busy studying for my passage rites. Then, on a Friday morning, Master Marco, the Chief Historian, saw me talking with Maria—not with our masks off, but together, as a young del'Sun and a zabbaline should not be. Maria saw him looking at her, and took her broom to the next gallery at once.

"Are you whoring with that child, Angelo? Be sure the Guild of Courtesans does not find out, or you will be fined more than your father will care to pay," he said. "So close to your passage rites, too—"

"She is not a street whore!"

"I did not ask you what she was, Angelo, I asked you what you were doing with her."

"Nothing!"

He shrugged and left. I tried to swallow my outrage, but still I felt

I wanted to strike the man. By my revered ancestors, what right did he have to think such a thing, just because she was zabbaline? I felt I wanted to challenge him to fight me in the United Houses Court Arena for the insult, as if she were my sister or cousin.

So then I sat and contemplated the David for a while, as I always did when I was upset, David with all his nobility and unmistakable virility, and things became clear to me.

The next morning when I met Maria, I kissed her. Not on the cheeks, but on her lips. Her dark eyes grew round.

"Angelo—no—" She stepped away, shaking her head, but I had laid my mask by David's feet, and I grabbed both her arms.

"Maria, listen. In a few weeks I go for my passage rites. When I win my plume, my father will give me money." I took a deep breath. "How much should I ask him for, Maria? How much will your father take to let me make you my concubine?"

I had thought myself so mysteriously adept at reading faces, but I could not understand the look she gave me. It was like another mask, and it frightened me.

She pulled her arms away from me and slapped her mask on. "And how much do you think I am worth, Angelo?"

I was lost. "My father will give me as much as your father asks—"

"But how much would *you* give?"

"Maria," I said. "Maria, I am only an apprentice Historian. I have nothing of my own. Whatever my father gives me for winning my plume, I will give it all. Everything."

She stood there in silence for a moment. Then she picked up her broom and dustpan. "Everything. That is not a word you should use so easily. I do not think you can pay my father enough for me, Angelo," she said, and turned on her graceful heel to leave the Hall.

"Maria!"

She turned again, waiting. I swallowed.

"Maria, I have nothing. But if it were mine to give, I would even give the David."

At this distance, the shadows behind the mask hid her eyes, and I could not tell if they softened. "You can talk to my father," she said, and left.

· · ·

199

So the next morning I went to the zabbaline's ceremonies instead of my House assembly yet again. After the rituals, Zachary took me aside, in a private room.

"So you want my daughter."

I could say nothing in reply; neither could I meet his eyes.

He gave a great, sorrowful sigh. "Angelo. We love you here. But you are not one of us."

I swallowed. "I strip off my mask here like everyone else, Zachary. Tell me the truth. Is my face not the Image of your God also?"

He gave me a look that, like Maria's the day before, I could not fathom. "It is. But the Image of God is also here," he said, touching my breast. "But it takes a long time for God to form it there—like the sculptor who made the David in your Hall of History."

"How?"

He spoke a long time about faith and repentance and baptism and prayer and communion and love and joy and peace. And I saw there was more to learn than I had imagined.

"I can begin, then, if I become a learner—preparing to be baptized, just as I am preparing to receive my passage plume?"

He looked troubled. "Yes, Angelo. Forgive me, it is so long since anyone but zabbaline wanted the Faith, I hardly know how to give it to you. But please do not misunderstand—to do these things will not give you the right to my daughter."

"But why?" Suspicion and fear labored in my breast, and brought forth an evil certainty. I leapt to my feet. "My face is not like yours, is it? I saw them looking at me, the first time I unmasked. Is it ugly? That is the reason!"

"Angelo!" Zachary barked at me. He took me by the shoulders and twirled me to face the wall, where hung a bearded image, like the one in the main room, but smaller. "Here is what your face looks like. You have no beard, no, and your hair is black and curly while His is wavy and brown. But you are one of His kind of people. He was Jewish, like David, and your people are Italian—like Michelangelo who made the statue of David—but both are the kind who lived around the shores of the Mediterranean Sea in the ancient days. Your Sun House, and most of the other Great Houses except the Chinese Dragon, come from old Italian-American families, while the zabbaline are Afro-American, with a little bit of Hispanic. Now. Do you see why the brothers and sisters looked at you a little strangely the first time? You are not ugly; you are only different from us."

He made me sit down again. "Now, listen to me. The trouble here is not you, Angelo. The trouble is concubinage. The Church does not allow this. Concubinage is slavery, and slavery is a very, very great evil."

I did not know how to answer this. I wanted Maria—Maria in my bed by moonlight, Maria by my window in the morning sun, Maria at my dinner table by oil lamp, Maria with her wise and entrancing words and her beautiful naked face. If her father said I could not have her, how could I bear to buy myself some woman who would only unmask in a room that was dark as Hell?

"Do you understand me, Angelo? We do not sell our daughters. If you want a woman to fill your bed and give you children and keep your house and be your friend, then it is only just to make her your wife in return."

I remembered how I had wanted to duel with the Chief Historian for his insult to Maria, and my chest grew tight. Zachary's eyes pitied me now, and he laid a hand on my arm, shaking his head.

"Angelo, I know you cannot make her your wife. I know the House del'Sun will never let one of its own marry a zabbaline."

I clenched my fists till the nails dug into my palms. Suddenly I leapt up and ran out through the crowded main room and into the street. Tears welled out of my eyes as I ran along the reeking roads of the Dumps. I wanted to run all the way back to the Hall of History and ask the David why I had had the misfortune to be born into the Sun House.

The streets were empty. Once my tears of self-pity had run out, I found myself somewhere deep in the maze of the Dumps, dwarfed by the great stinking hills of garbage that were the zabbaline's livelihood. Darkness and shadows bred amongst the heaps of rotting food and cast-off fabric, rubble, and splintered wood. I stood motionless, suddenly uneasy. It was cooler than it should be at midday. The flies silenced their buzzing wings, settling on the dung heaps, still as jewels, and the crows tucked their heads beneath their feathers.

"Angelo!" Maria called, running toward me in her gray mask. "Angelo, I brought your mask. Sometimes the army patrols these streets . . ."

She suddenly slowed her pace. "Blessed Lord, what is it? What is happening?"

Great waves of darkness undulated across the hills of trash, making the road look like the valley of the shadow of death. I raised my

201

head slowly to the sky, barely aware of Maria clinging to my side. The stars had come out.

"The sun has put on a mask," I said. *God of the zabbaline, I beg you, let the books in the Hall of History be true! Let the eclipse pass quickly, and let the sun's face shine again!*

The Sun mask, which the books said was in fact the moon, was round as the brass gong of judgment in the Arena, and black as the empty eyeholes in my ancestors' funerary masks. But from the edges of the dark disc blossomed a crown of pearly light, and on the very rim of the mask, a fiery red ring shot out bright jets and plumes of flame.

"Moses," whispered Maria, "the shekhinah." But I did not know what she meant.

Suddenly, on the eastern edge of the disc, there appeared a thin, shining crescent, its horns breaking into fine drops of light, like chains of beads. I had read a very detailed account of an eclipse once, and knew these shining drops of light were called Baily's beads, and heralded the return of the sun's full brilliance.

"Turn!" I said, swinging Maria around, "or the sun's glory will blind us!"

She slipped to the ground, and I went with her, our backs to the sun now.

"Moses!" she gasped again, and she tumbled out the story of the ancient prophet who spoke face-to-face with God. When he came out from God's presence, his face shone so brightly that his people were afraid; and so Moses put on a mask. But, like the zabbaline, he took the mask off again whenever he went to speak with God.

And while I was listening to this story, the street brightened, the sun warmed our backs again, the birds and flies went back to their busy movement.

We stood up, and Maria handed me my mask.

I stood holding it in my two hands, looking at the painted sun on the forehead, feeling the kiss of the real sun on my own brow. I laid the mask faceup on the ground, then lowered the heel of my sandal onto its convex surface, pressing down until the thin brittle wood snapped in two.

"Angelo!"

I picked up the lacquered pieces and tossed them onto a garbage heap.

202

Maria said, "Are you no longer of the House del'Sun?"

I shook my head, unable to speak.

THE PASSING OF THE ECLIPSE

She took my hand, holding it tightly. "We will find you a zabbaline mask—"

"No. The Image of God has been eclipsed too long, Maria."

"Angelo, that is why we unmask in our homes here—"

"It is not enough! Where the mask is, there is darkness! How
long, Maria, have the zabbaline been keeping the light hidden in the
Dumps, while darkness rules in the Great Houses and the marketplace,
the Arena, the whorehouses, even in the Hall of History?"

She snatched off her mask so I could see the anger in her face.
"We have been doing it, Angelo del'Sun, just as long as it has been
death to do otherwise! You, who have never lacked for money or a soft
bed, never become ill from living in the midst of filth, never callused
your hands on the reins of a donkey cart—who are you to judge my
people? Will *you* go back up to the Hall of History and to the House
del'Sun, barefaced like Moses, and tell them you have seen God? Do
you think they will like it any better than the Israelites did?"

I hung there in the dark for a moment, just as the world had hung
waiting for the eclipse to pass. And then the light burst out again.
"Yes, I will go. Will you come with me? Will the others?"

Maria put her mask back on. "Angelo—you are talking like a man
with too much wine in him . . ."

So I went, Maria trailing behind and begging me to change my
mind, all the way back to the gate of the Dumps. There she turned and
ran back, for a guard patrol happened along the street outside. They
arrested me at once, throwing a cloak over my naked face.

My father actually came to the Court, and got me an immediate hearing.

"Was it the darkening of the sun that upset you?" he asked me,
amazed at such a scandal caused by the hitherto least troublesome of
his many sons.

I shook my head, wishing I could thereby dislodge the dull black
prison mask they had put on me.

"It will cost me a great deal to fix this, Angelo," he said.

"It will cost you nothing, Father."

The judge signaled for order. "What were you doing in the
Dumps, Angelo?" he asked me.

"Throwing away my Sun House mask."

There was silence. "*This*, you want me to pardon?" the judge
asked my father.

203

I saw my father's fists clench, the knuckles white. After a moment he turned and stalked from the court. The judge gave an exasperated grunt behind his blue mask. "Put him in a cell."

So they put me in a cell, and right away I took off the black, featureless prison mask. The young guard (he had no plume on his mask yet) gasped.

"Is it ugly?" I asked him, pressing my face to the cold metal of the bars. He recoiled, and, apparently not knowing what else to do, went along the corridor and turned his back to me.

In the late afternoon, the guard called, "Put it on, pervert, you have a visitor."

"I will not," I said, and punctuated my defiance by cracking the prison mask underfoot as I had my own. The guard swore loudly.

"Never mind," said the visitor. It was Tonio's voice! He came down the corridor and stood before the bars of my cell. "Angelo, you flea-brain."

He seemed not to be disturbed much by my naked face. I found to my surprise that I no longer felt angry with him.

I hung on to the bars. "What do you think of my face, Tonio?"

He turned away, groaning. "It should have a mask on it, crazy man. Here," he said, and handed me some loaves and a wineskin.

I thanked him. Perhaps he felt badly, after all, for keeping his Sun mask hidden at the brothel.

He leaned his back against the outside of the bars.

"Tonio," I asked him, "do you think there are any men who disobey the law, and look at their wives' and concubines' faces in the light?"

"Angelo, come on. A woman can divorce her husband for that, and get a fat purse in the bargain."

"I never heard of one that did."

"The Court does not publicize such cases."

"Maybe the women like their husbands to see their faces. Maybe they like to see their husbands' faces, too."

"Angelo!" Exasperated, he whirled round to grip the bars, only to glance down and away from my bare, bold face. "God's tombstone, do you think the whole world is as perverted as you?"

204

"I am sure of it."

He sighed. "The House sent me to tell you that you are officially disowned."

That meant I would die. Payment of a big enough fine could commute the sentence for any crime, but without the Sun House, I was now alone and penniless. "That is what I expected."

"Angelo, do you not *want* to live?"

"Not in a world where there is a perpetual eclipse."

So he left, shaking his head at my insane perversity.

The next day Zachary took a great risk to bring the light of his uneclipsed face into my cell for a moment. We grinned at each other, and exchanged kisses. Then he remasked and read me a portion of the zabbaline holy writings, a vision revealed to one of their prophets—not Moses, but what he described in the vision must have been something like what Moses saw.

" 'And his eyes were as a flame of fire,' " Zachary read. " 'And his feet were like burnished bronze . . . out of his mouth came a sharp two-edged sword, and his face was like the sun shining in its strength.' "

I drank in the words, for they were as strengthening in their way as the wine my cousin had brought me.

On the day my sentence was to be carried out, they forced another prison mask onto me and tied my hands behind my back so I could not remove it again.

From snatches of guards' conversations, I had learned that people thought me to be a crazy man. The eclipse had driven me out of my skull, went the story around the city. The commoners were sympathetic, for they had been scared half out of their skins at the time, too. Only afterward had the United Houses dismissed their official astronomer for failing to predict the event. The lofty scientific explanation did not sit well with the populace, especially since the astronomer had so failed, and they remained nervous and disturbed.

The judge who sentenced me had advised me about my swan song, the speech of self-justification permitted the condemned prisoner. (It was the last vestige of a Pre-Cataclysmal institution known as "freedom of speech.") If my speech did anything to satisfy and please the jumpy commoners who would surely flock to the Arena for my execution, I was told, I might yet hope for the thumbs-up from the assembled paterfamiliae of the United Houses.

Tonio was one of the two young soldiers who marched me out into the Arena, but he did not speak to me. The midday sun bathed my stiff limbs with the warmth of its glory. I longed to feel it on my face, as I had the day of the eclipse.

I mounted the guillotine platform, looking through the execution machine's uprights directly at the box where my father and others of the Sun House sat, the diamonds and gold paint blazing on their foreheads.

I looked round at the banks of seats to either side of the House boxes. I had never seen the Arena so packed. The many colorful masks made a gleaming mosaic of the stands—bright green farmworkers, cerulean watersellers, bakers in brown the color of bread crust. And there, on one side, a whole section was filled with gray masks—the zabbaline!

I stood still while the gong of judgment sounded and the vast crowd grew quiet. A blue-masked judiciary official stood up and read my sentence out. The executioner, masked in white, descended the platform, leaving me alone to make my last bid for my life.

God of the zabbaline, I prayed silently, *God with the unmasked face, God who is supposed to be dead but lives in every human face, you know I do not ask for my life. I ask for the Sun. I ask for the passing of the eclipse. It is in the laws of the world you made, O God, that no eclipse can last forever!*

"My name is Angelo," I said, and my voice echoed in the great arena like a trumpet. "I was born a del'Sun, the child of a concubine to the paterfamilias of the Sun House. I do not wear the Sun mask today, not because my House has disowned me, but because I disowned my House."

The silence in the House boxes was icy; the silence in the general stands, that of breath held in anticipation.

"Everyone in the city has seen the Hall of Faces, where the maskless faces of our ancient ancestors are formed in marble and bronze. We are careful to teach our children that there is nothing obscene about our ancestors' faces, even though to remove our own masks in the sight of others would be very repugnant."

The House boxes began to grow restive. I was treading a thin line here. The paterfamiliae dared not cut me off too quickly, lest it anger the crowd, but on the other hand they feared that what I was about to say might inflame the people even more. I hoped they were right, and plunged on, intent on delivering my message before they could stop me. "The face of Michelangelo's David, is it not the most beautiful of all?" I caught sight of the Chief Historian's crimson mask in the box set aside for the employees of the United Houses. "Is it not so, Chief Historian?"

"It is generally agreed," he admitted.

"And why is that? Is it not because, in his bronze features, we can read his heart? The heart of a noble and courageous man, the heart of a paterfamilias."

This piece of what seemed like flattery unsettled the House boxes. My father and his counterparts from the other Houses whispered with their sons and advisers, wondering if the outcome of my speech might not suit them after all.

"You know, he does not sound entirely crazy," I heard Tonio say to his partner.

"And what do you imagine *my* face looks like, good citizens? Well, do not imagine. There stands my cousin Tonio del'Sun. He has seen my face. Tell me, Tonio, do I bear no resemblance at all to the David?"

"Angelo, you bastard," he hissed through his mouth slit. "Is this your revenge for the whorehouse?"

I desperately wished I could plead with him barefaced, but had to do the best I could, reaching for his eyes with my own while I spoke for all to hear. "Tonio, please. They say I am a crazy man and a pervert, but it is no fault of yours that you saw my face when out of kindness you brought me food in prison. Only say truthfully what you saw, for the sake of justice in the Arena. My face, does it not resemble David's? Does it not have two eyes, a nose, a mouth?"

At that point my father stood up and extended his right arm, his fist clenched, the thumb straight. Slowly and deliberately he turned his wrist inward, and my heart sank downward with the tip of his thumb.

Hearty objections went up from the stands, and the other paterfamiliae hesitated. Suddenly Tonio's voice rose over the furor.

"Yes! He speaks the truth!"

"And now let us speak of the darkening of the sun!" I cried, and the zabbaline led the cheers. My father still stood with his thumb down. One or two of the other paterfamiliae rose to their feet, but their arms remained at their sides.

When I had comparative quiet in the Arena again, I said, "They say I am a pervert. They say I am crazy. What is perversion but the turning away from what is good and natural? What is insanity but chaos, the misplacement of what is natural? And what did you see at the eclipse, at the darkening of the sun? Did you not see night at midday? Did you not see stars at noon? Did you not see the birds and

207

animals grow quiet when they should be lively? And why? Because there was a mask upon the face of the sun!"

Three more of the paterfamiliae had turned thumbs down now, and the rest were on their feet. The crowd rumbled like a bank of gathering thunderclouds.

"The Houses are calling for my death!" I shouted. "So be it! Let me die, but let me die without this darkness on my face! Someone have the courage to come and unmask me and show them they are killing David!"

"Live! Live! Live!" chanted the people, and I did not need to see the faces behind the House masks to know they were filled with fear. The remaining paterfamiliae extended their hands, thumbs up, and the people cheered.

A scuffle broke out in the stands where the zabbaline sat, and I realized that some of them were trying to respond to my challenge to come and unmask me. A dozen soldiers jogged quickly across the Arena to subdue them. I was suddenly fearful for Maria, but could not distinguish her slight form amongst the grey masks.

Cheers and whistles reached a deafening pitch, and I turned back to the House boxes, astonished to see the three paterfamiliae who had put thumbs down at the start turn them upward. Only my father remained in his unequivocal condemnation of me. Outnumbered, he would not turn the thumb up, but conceded to his fellows only by dropping his arm to his side again.

I stood dazed while Tonio cut the thongs that bound me. Over the roar of the crowd he shouted in my ear, "Get to Hell out of the city, Angelo, quick as you can, and do not come back. The Arena has pardoned you, but the House never will. They will send assassins after you."

But I cared less for the House assassins than for the flies in the Dumps. Implicit in my pardon was the expectation that, having escaped with my life, I would now avoid angering the paterfamiliae further. I would make a speech thanking them for their clemency, complete the education they had been paying for, and conscientiously seek the path of good citizenship in the future. The only difficulty was that I had no wish to follow the path of good citizenship, for it did not lead to the Dumps, nor to the radiance of unmasked faces I had found there.

Tonio and his partner stood each to one side of me, waiting for the crowd to quiet enough for me to make the requisite speech.

208

Tonio's partner grasped my arm and snarled, "Get it over quick, pervert, so we can get you out of here."

I shook him off angrily, stepping away from him to stand at the edge of the platform, and looked out at the people. Slowly their clamor subsided, and they sat waiting for me to speak. But I had no more to say. Instead I raised my hands to the mask, slowly and deliberately easing it off.

"Angelo, don't!" said Tonio, but at the same moment his partner leapt at me, shouting, "Crazy pervert!" I caught sight of him out of the corner of my eye too late, and he brought the hilt of his sword down on my skull. It was like the eclipse all over again. I fell, and knew nothing more in the Arena.

I woke with a hammering head in my own rooms in the Hall of History. A single oil lamp burned at my bedside, and in a chair by the door sat the Chief Historian.

"Welcome back, Angelo," he said. He helped me sit up and slipped a straw through my mask. I sipped the cool water gratefully.

"There was a riot after the guard knocked you out," said Master Marco. "Every last zabbaline in the city took off his mask. The people got hysterical, and some of them unmasked too. While the army was taking care of the mess, I got to Tonio and told him I would keep you safe. He did not like to trust me, but he had no better plan. We changed your mask and our own for some of the people's discarded ones half a dozen times on the way to throw off the pursuit. We think your own rooms are the place they are least likely to look for you."

"And the zabbaline?" I asked anxiously.

"A few got killed in the riot. The rest are packed in the jail like beans in a sack, with black masks on their faces and their hands tied behind their backs."

I leaned over, feeling sick, and held my head in my hands. What had I done with my crazy swan song? All those shiningly beautiful brown faces, eclipsed by prison masks . . .

"I have to take it off, Master Marco," I said. "Go, if you do not wish to see."

But he did not go, standing silently at the foot of my bed. I undid the strap, and set aside the mask. He lowered his eyes a little, blinking, as if coming into bright sunlight.

"Thank you for your help," I said.

Slowly his eyes focused on my face. "You do look a little like the

209

David," he said at last. Then he produced a parchment, but before he could hand it to me, Tonio came into the room. He wore the tan-colored mask of a common man with no particular trade, but I knew his voice.

"God's funeral, at it again already? What does it take to cure a pervert like you, Angelo?"

I grinned at him, shaking my head. He drew the chair across the floor to my bedside and sat down. He saw the parchment the Historian held and said, "Let me talk to him first." Master Marco gave him the parchment and clapped him on the shoulder, then left us alone.

"I have a message from the zabbaline for you," said Tonio.

My heart jumped. "Maria?"

He put a hand on my shoulder. "She died in the riot, Angelo."

I cried a long time, my face bent to my drawn-up knees. Tonio sat with an arm across my shoulders, seemingly steeped in a patience I had never expected of him.

After a while he started to tell me things. "A man named Gideon and some others escaped. The prison was hopelessly crowded with the rest, so they released the women and children. Also, the United Houses need *someone* to pick up the city's garbage, you understand." I could see the white of his mirthless grin through the mask slit, but could not smile back.

Then he gave me the parchment. "Your Chief Historian made an excuse to question the zabbaline, seeing as you had been his student, but it was very dangerous. The Houses suspect him now too. But he got this from the zabbaline for you."

I unscrolled the letter. It read:

"Salutations, Angelo, in the name of the Holy Trinity, from Zachary, priest. Written in haste for the Historian who says he is your friend. I must dare to trust him.

"We are all to die soon. We expected this, and indeed chose it. As priest, I must lead the others in our witness, but Gideon we have consecrated priest to the remnant. To him you must go if you continue to seek baptism.

"When you were arrested, Maria told me something that was in her heart. She said, 'The first time I saw Angelo's face, lying on the floor beside the David, I thought God had sent him. But I did not know that what God sent him for was to make a martyr of him!'

"A martyr, Angelo, is a witness. A witness to the truth, with his life. But it seems this time the crown of martyrdom is not to be yours, but ours. I, too, believe God sent you, Angelo. What you have done has prepared the way for the Image of God to be seen once more in the world. The Houses have forced masks upon us here, but it was not only zabbaline who dared expose their faces today. Many of the common people are ready to see the light. The Houses must give us our swan song, as they gave you yours. We may get thumbs up or not, but it will not matter. Either way, there are now many people willing to unmask. Either way, I fear it will cost blood, for which may God have mercy on us all.

"Mourn my daughter with me, for I know you loved her. I expect soon to be in Heaven with her, where our prayers for you will not cease. Go with God, Angelo."

"I must go to the Dumps," I said at last.

"Not yet. They are watching the gate, Angelo. I went there myself, you see. That was where I heard about Maria. I barely avoided a patrol on my way out."

"*You* went to the Dumps, Tonio? I thought you had been at the prison."

He shook his head. "It was dangerous enough for Master Marco. I did not dare. The Sun House has spies there. When I said you told the truth in the Arena, I made myself a dead man, too, Angelo." He looked steadily at me, not flinching at all from my bare face.

I bit my lip. "Tonio. I am sorry." I looked at the grimy common laborer's mask he wore. "Your Sun mask?"

He laughed. "After my partner rapped you on your thick skull with the hilt of his sword, I pushed him off the platform. But then the zabbaline broke through the line of soldiers and came flying toward the scaffold. Before I finally got away with you, somebody knocked me down and tore off my mask, and somebody else trampled it underfoot. So now."

"So?"

He took a deep breath. "God's dead body, Angelo, what do I say? You were right. Some of us, at least, share your perversion!" He pulled off the mask, squeezing his eyes shut. Then he opened them slowly and let out a shaky breath.

"The Image of God," I said softly, "that is what the zabbaline call it, Tonio." I put my hands on his two cheeks, amazed at yet another beautiful face, and a different one. His face was rather flat, the features very much finer than the zabbaline's, and his eyes were slanted. The ancestors of his mother, whom I knew was of the Dragon House, must have been of that other kind of people, less common than the others in this area before the Cataclysm—what had Zachary called them? Chinese.

Tonio wept, and I kissed him zabbaline-style, and we clapped each other on the back. "Am I like the David, too?" he asked. "I saw some of the zabbaline, they are different—"

"We are all like the David, and all different. O, God, Tonio, I am afraid. Maybe I should never have started all this unmasking. People will look at different faces now, as they did before the Cataclysm, and say, 'Yes, mine is beautiful, but yours is ugly.'"

"But, Angelo, they say that anyway, when they look at a mask that is not of their own House."

I nodded. I ached with weariness still, and the loss of Maria had seared my heart like salt on an open wound. There was nothing left for me to do now. Although I had tried to pour out my life like oil to feed the flames of the unmasking, the God of the zabbaline had stopped up my bottle at the last moment. I was afraid of Him, for I did not understand why He did these things; yet I knew His face must indeed be like the sun shining in its strength, for Maria and Zachary loved Him.

And so the passing of the eclipse in the city had begun, and would go on regardless of what I did now.

I looked once more at my cousin's face, and felt warmed by its beauty. Tonio's face, and Maria's and Zachary's and all the other zabbaline's, were like the Baily's beads of the eclipse. Shining like fiery pearls against the darkness, when the full sunlight is yet to be revealed, their glory would soon be lost in the greater glory to come.

"I am tired, Tonio," I said. "I need to rest, before I see what tomorrow brings."

"Sleep well, Angelo," he said. "Tomorrow brings the sun."

This lively and vivid story is Nicholas DiChario's first professional sale of fiction, although he's been writing for a living for some time now—in a unique computer language known as PLASM, with which he does programming work for Blue Cross and Blue Shield in Rochester, New York. We've never read so much as a bit of PLASM, and probably never will, but we're glad that Mr. DiChario takes time out now and then to write in English as well.

The sidewalk lamp on Peppermint Street sang to Forty in a melodious, airy tenor, "Gooood moooorning, it's eeeeeightfif-teeeeen." The soft foam walkway nuzzled his bare toes, the birds chirruped quietly, the putt-putt tubs chugged along the wet rubber flats, the sun shone on his naked body—all of which made Forty want to stop and sing. So he did. Much to his delight, a few others joined him in a verse of the Fun City Civic Anthem. It went like this: *"One, two, three, all-is-as-it-should-be. One, two, three, all-is-as-it-should-be,"* and on and on.

Forty, toting his briefcase full of work that might or might not get done during the day, stopped at the kiosk for the morning edition. He skimmed the lead story. The government, in a top-secret ceremony, had recognized all those animals who volun-teered to be slaughtered in order to manu-facture the genuine animal hide briefcases for the citizenry. "Fine job," an important government official had been quoted.

"Have a super great day," said the young woman from behind the kiosk, the same woman who had been handing him the morning edition for as long as he could remember.

Forty smiled broadly. "Yes," he said, pausing to sniff the air. The scent of pepper-mint was a personal favorite of his, so he always made sure to get his fill before he reached the office. He was about to leave when he noticed something odd about the way the woman looked at him. "Is there something wrong with your eye?" Her eye seemed slow to him. It seemed not to focus on anything at all.

"It's a glass eye."

FORTY AT THE KIOSK

NICHOLAS A. DICHARIO

The young woman struck a merry pose, but Forty thought he heard a heaviness in her voice.

"Have a magnificent day," he said. He found it strange that this was the first time he had noticed the young woman's glass eye, but that was the kind of thing he was not supposed to think about, so he let it pass.

The next morning Forty stepped off the choo-choo zinger, anticipating the wonderful day ahead of him. He whistled the Civic Anthem as he jaunted up Peppermint Street. The skyscraper on Lilac Boulevard reached down with one of its large, soft buttresses and began to massage his shoulders, so Forty spent an hour or so under its caress before moving on to the kiosk.

The young woman who handed out the morning edition, the same woman who had been handing him the paper for as long as he could remember, the woman with the glass eye, smiled at him. "Good morning." It was a good smile as far as Forty could tell—a good smile but not a *great* one, as Forty had become accustomed to.

"Yes, absolutely, a very good morning." Forty reached for the paper and noticed that the young woman was missing a finger. "Oh—"

She snapped back her hand. "Think nothing of it. I lost it."

"How did that happen? I mean, people don't just *lose* fingers."

She didn't answer right away. She seemed to be looking around to make sure no one was listening. "I gave it up," she said hastily. She held her hand close to her chest and then, regaining a bit of mirth, added, "For something I needed."

Another man came to the kiosk then. The young woman turned away from Forty and went about her business.

Forty lingered at the kiosk for a moment. He wondered why she would need to sacrifice her finger for anything. There was nothing to need, nothing to want in Fun City. Finally, remembering that he should forget all such wonderings, Forty chose not to pursue the matter.

The next morning.

216

And what a pleasant and sunny morning it was! Exactly like every other morning Forty had wakened to, and exactly like the mornings Forty looked forward to wakening to in the future.

A young hairless quadrumane had stopped to recite poetry on Candy Cane Lane, and Forty whiled away almost half the day listening to the rhythm of the poet's clever verses and sniffing the sweet syrupy scent of candy in the air.

As Forty approached the kiosk where the young woman would hand him the morning edition, the same young woman who had been handing him the paper for as long as he could remember, the woman with the glass eye and the missing finger, he hesitated. She was stacking some papers along the back wall of the kiosk. Her disfigurements, he concluded, had disturbed him. But wouldn't it be foolish to avoid her because of this? After all, her problems had nothing to do with him.

"Good morning," said Forty.

The young woman whirled around. She was missing a breast. "Same to you." She pushed a paper into his hand and turned up her nose and spun away from him, all in a single motion.

Forty was so stunned he forgot to grab it. "Gosh, what's wrong? What's happened to you?"

"Do you really want to know?" The young woman's voice sounded callous. She stood with her back to him.

"No, thank you. I guess I don't. I'm not one to pry. I mean, if it's something I should know about, I think I should know all about it without having to ask."

"Not necessarily. There are a lot of things we don't know about." She turned to face him, a daring expression on her face.

Forty shied away from the young woman, feeling unexpectedly squeamish. His instinct was to flee, and yet some strange conflicting emotion that Forty could not even begin to describe would not let him budge. He stared at the woman's chest. One of her breasts was round and smooth and perfect as it had always been, while the other breast had become a shallow crater. Forty wondered how something like breasts or fingers or eyes could be the same for as long as he could remember and then suddenly change for no apparent reason.

"What if I were to tell you that I gave up my breast for something I needed?"

"I wouldn't listen. That's a silly thing to say anyway. What could you possibly need? Fun City has everything."

She leaned forward, peering at him with her good eye. "Haven't you ever wondered what it would be like to look up at the clear blue

217

sky, see it rip wide open, and then watch it bleed? How would the drops feel on your arms? your face? your body?"

"Goodness!" said Forty. He noticed the edges of the young woman's mouth twitch in a way he had never seen, as if her upper lip had been hooked by a dual-pronged zik twine. The woman's eye—the good eye now—looked past him, focusing on something else entirely, but when Forty glanced behind him there was nothing there.

The young woman clutched his forearm. "Haven't you ever wondered," she whispered, a deep, raspy whisper, "what it would be like to take one of these twittering little birdies between your fingers and squeeze until it shit in your hands, until its eyes popped out of its head?" She clamped down on his forearm as if she were doing exactly that.

"Never!" Forty tugged away. "Goodness gracious me." He clutched his briefcase and hurried off to work without his paper.

"Who's in charge here?" she shouted after him. "Why don't we all get putt-putt tubs? Why is there only one fucking song to sing in Fun City?"

"I didn't hear a word of that," he told himself. "Not a single word. Not one not one not one not one . . ." By the time he reached his office building, Forty was feeling much better.

But even after a full pinch of happy snuff and a complete rotation in his aqua percolator, Forty could not forget about the young woman. He wondered what could be wrong with her. He tried to imagine what the sky would look like ripped and bleeding; he tried to imagine squeezing a bird until it shit, until its eyes popped out of its head, but he could not.

He kneaded his forearm where the young woman had grabbed him, and inspected it for the markings of a bruise. Her nails had left tiny red impressions in his skin.

Forty examined his reflection in the glass-paneled desktop beneath his nose. What were those cockamamy questions she had asked? *Who's in charge here? Why doesn't everyone get a putt-putt tub?* Forty didn't need to know any such nonsense. And so what if the Fun City Civic Anthem was the only song he knew? It was a perfectly good song. Nevertheless, thoughts of the eccentric young woman troubled him for the rest of the day. He ignored his paperwork, deciding that someone else would do it or perhaps it wouldn't get done at all. Not to worry.

The lead story in yesterday's morning edition applauded those who ignored their paperwork so that those who didn't would have plenty to do.

When Forty left work that evening he did not take his usual path home (straight out the back door and up to the choo-choo zinger along with everyone else). Instead he left through the front door. He paused beneath the building's archway. A gentle breeze whistled faintly past his ears. The face upon the wide frieze of the entablature smiled down at him and winked.

He spent some time surveying the motionless cityscape. The setting sun gave birth to a halo-orange sky, but there was no sign of it ripping and bleeding. He allowed himself a deep breath; it had simply been a bad day, he suspected, never before having experienced one. He felt much better upon deciding that he would not let it happen again.

"One, two, three," sang Forty, "all-is-as-it-should-be. One, two, three . . ."

Forty traced his steps back to the kiosk. He did not know exactly why he wanted to see the young woman again, but he felt it was the thing to do. Perhaps it was because she had upset him and now he needed to prove to himself that there was no reason to be upset about anything.

As Forty approached the kiosk, he thought he saw movement from within. He took a few cautious steps forward.

There in the shadows he could see the young woman and a young man. They were huddled together in the darkest corner of the kiosk.

"One, two, three," announced Forty. "What's going on there?"

They looked up, startled, their eyes flashing in the darkness. There was a panicked scuffling.

The man darted out onto the street. Forty could not be certain, but he appeared to be carrying, tucked up under his arm, the young woman's leg.

Forty heard a stampede of feet behind him. He spun around.

"Authorities!" they shouted. There must have been a dozen of them. They were wearing clothes—black-and-white-striped uniforms with black boots and stovepipe hats—and they were waving cudgels. "Stop! Authorities!" They rushed past him toward the kiosk.

The young woman tried to make a getaway. She was hopping badly on one leg. She jerked when the authorities grabbed her, swing-

219

ing her arms as if her very life depended on it. "I can see!" she shouted. "I can see the weeds pushing through the cracks in the concrete. I can see the broken glass. Rats! There are rats in that abandoned warehouse over there. Ask him! Ask him!" She pointed directly at Forty. "I can see old people—*OLD PEOPLE*—I'm telling you, wrinkled and dying and—and—crippled, too, hunched over their canes like this"—she tried to demonstrate—"like this, let me go, like this, like this . . ."

One of the authorities clubbed her on the skull and she fell silent. They hadn't taken notice of Forty until she had pointed him out. Two of the authorities tramped over to him.

"Do you know that woman?" asked one of them. They were sweating, and they smelled slightly malodorous.

"Yes—no—she's crazy. She hands me the paper every morning, that's all. For as long as I can remember, anyway. I mean, I saw her with the glass eye first, and then she was missing a finger and a breast and—and—"

"What are you doing on this street now? Peppermint Street is a morning street."

Forty tried to think of a good answer. The authorities fingered the stems of their cudgels, awaiting his response. He felt the edges of his mouth twitch. "I don't know. I guess I had a feeling."

"We'd better take him along with us," said one of the authorities to the other.

"Take me where? I don't understand." Forty backed away.

The other authority shook his head. "I don't think it's necessary. Look at him. He's a scared little rabbit."

He stepped forward and shoved Forty so hard that he dropped his briefcase and fell over on his butt. They laughed at him.

"Run along," said the authority. "You don't belong here."

"Th-thank you." Forty got up and ran for the choo-choo zinger. "I saw nothing," he gasped. "Nothing nothing nothing nothing . . ." And he ran.

He ran until cramps knotted his stomach and he could feel his shins colliding with his knees. He ran until he was dripping with cold sweat and his eyes swelled with tears. He ran until he was dizzy with exhaustion and he could not catch his breath.

220

And when Forty could not run another step, he realized that none of the buildings looked familiar. "Where am I?" he shouted to a group of people toting their briefcases on the other side of the street. "Can anyone tell me how to get to the Peppermint Street Station?" They lowered their heads and scurried off. "What's wrong with you people?" he said.

Before long, Forty was alone.

When he finally discovered a choo-choo zinger station, it was nearly dark and everyone had already gone home. Forty collapsed on a bench. Would a choo-choo zinger come for him? Would he be able to get home? Forty could not lie still. He began to pace. He tried to breathe the scent of Peppermint Street, but the scent, or the breath itself, eluded him and he felt as if he were suffocating. He leaned against the gantry for support.

A nearby boarding post struck up a swift arpeggio: "The chooooooo-chooooooo zinger is clooooooosed aaaaaalll niiiiiiight."

"That can't be. How will I get home? Listen to me! I want to talk to whoever is in charge around here. Why can't I get a putt-putt tub of my own?" demanded Forty, but the boarding post refused to answer.

Forty kicked the post, and a bone in his big toe snapped. "Ouch ouch ouch ouch . . ." He bounced a few times like a pe-po on a mound of yarnalack before falling to the ground. A putt-putt tub rolled up on the rubber flats in front of the station.

A man hollered from the car, "Excuse me, Friend, need a lift?"

"Yes, indeed I do!"

The man got out of the car, took Forty by the arm, and guided him into the passenger seat. "Tsk, tsk, tsk. You look very ill."

"Thank you," said Forty. "For the ride, I mean, of course. I've hurt my toe. I just can't thank you enough."

"Nonsense," said the man, falling in behind the controls.

Forty thought the man's voice had a chilly metallic quality to it, but he would not let that bother him. Not now. His toe was throbbing and he was as thirsty as a nearsighted synrzit tied to a tree and it was getting cold and quite dark and, after all, hadn't he asked for a putt-putt tub?—hadn't he asked to speak to the man in charge?

"Are you in charge of Fun City?" asked Forty. "Why is there only one song to sing? What do I have to do to get some answers around here?"

The man glared at Forty with a mixture of menace and glee. He reached into the back seat of the tub. Forty didn't want to look, but his head turned slightly without his permission. There was a large tool

221

chest on the floor. The man opened it. Inside the tool chest, Forty thought he saw a woman's leg.

The man grasped something in his palm. He handed it to Forty. It was a glass eye.

Kathe Koja's short stories have appeared in Isaac Asimov's, Fantasy & Science Fiction, *and various other science fiction magazines, and one of them—the sharp-edged, glittering "Distances"—made a particularly powerful impression when it was reprinted in Gardner Dozois's* Year's Best *anthology in 1989. Here she is with a new one, marked by the same precision of execution and clear-eyed conceptualization that has attracted such attention to her earlier work.*

Raymond's sweat. Just a bead of it, a proud greasy glitter in the Slavic valley of his temple, his left temple mind you, the one pointed at her. Of course it would be. Rachel had passed no day, had in fact lived no moment of her entire adult life without one of Raymond's irritations parading itself before her. It was a gift he had.

He shifted, there on the bench, the preciously *faux*-Shaker bench he insisted upon inserting in her morning room like a splinter in her living flesh.

"Are you ready to go?" he asked her.

She forbore to answer in words, preferring the quick nod, the quicker rise from her chair, beat him to the door if she could. She couldn't. His healthy rise, his longer reach, his more advantageous proximity to the door, and still he stopped, paused to hold it for her:

"After you," he said.

"Why not," she said. "Once in a lifetime can't hurt."

Halfway through the long drive, he spoke again, her hands tight and graceful on the wheel: "Those gloves look shabby," he said.

"They *are* shabby."

"Well, why don't you get some new ones?"

"That's right." The defroster's heat blowing back, oven-dry into her face. "That's you, isn't it, Ray? When it wears out, get a new one. Because the old one doesn't work anymore. Because the old one's *wearing out*." There were certainly no tears, she had cried this all out years before, but the anger was as bitter and brisk as new snow.

His profile, advantageous in the passing

BY THE MIRROR OF MY YOUTH

KATHE KOJA

arctic shine of the landscape. His noble brow. "Oh, for God's sake. Aren't you ever going to stop feeling sorry for yourself?"

Who else will, she wanted to say, but that was as petty as it sounded and anyway they were there, the low shiny lines of the clinic before them, as cool and precious as mercury in the manicured drifts of the grounds. The circular driveway looked as if it had been literally swept clean. She pulled the Toyota right up to the entrance, as if it were a nice hotel with a nice doorman who would see to it that the car was safely parked. Her hand on the heavy glass door, warm as honey even through her shabby glove, her frozen skin, did they even heat the glass? No discomfort here, she thought—royal-blue carpet, pink marble glint of the receptionist's desk—heated glass and heated floors, only the client left cold. It made her smile, and she kept the smile to give to the receptionist. There was no point in taking it out on him.

But the receptionist's smile, heavy lips, bright teeth, was all for Raymond: "Good afternoon, Mr. Pope," not presuming to offer his hand until Ray offered his, then accepting it in a flurried, flattered grasp, oh God if she had seen it once she had seen it a million times. If he said anything about *Brain Fevre* she would vomit on the spot.

"It's an honor to have you here," the receptionist said.

"Thank you," Raymond said.

"Dr. Christensen is waiting for you. Will you come this way, please?"

Rachel followed, silent, silent in the warm office, thinking not of what was to come or even of their, no, her first visit here, the papers and papers to sign, the needles and the sharp lights, but of a day when Raymond had sat, slumped and sorry before his terminal, the monitor screen bright and crazed with the germinus of what would become *Brain Fevre*, saying, "It isn't any good. It isn't *working*." Fingers restless on the keys, toying with Delete.

"It's going to." Her hands, not on his shoulders—they had already got past that—but on the green slope of his swivel chair, unconsciously kneading the leather, the padding beneath like flesh under skin. "Just sweat it out, Ray. You can do that."

And he, lips skinned back like Benjamin who lay beneath his feet, "What the hell would you know about it?" and the echo of Benjamin's mimicking growl. Benjamin had loved Ray like a, like a dog, though of course Rachel had been the one to care for him, fill his dishes and let him in and out and drive him to the vet for the interminable shots that prolonged his painful life, drive him too for the last shot that set him free, that set Raymond breaking casseroles and cups in the kitchen when she came home alone.

"Why didn't you tell me?" weeping in his rage, and she, still able to be surprised, protesting that she *had* told him, had begged him to come with her, to be with Benjamin at the end, and he had taken her World's Fair mug, her sister's mug, and standing poised like Thor before the porcelain sink—

"Mrs. Pope?"

"Oh." Looking up to see Dr. Christensen, smiling, this smile for her now but she was past needing smiles, at least for today. "Are you ready to go?"

Raymond's words. "Of course," she said, making it a point to rise smoothly, showing nothing of the jeering clack of bone on bone, the pain that in its inception had compelled her here, back when such things were not only prohibited but prohibitively expensive, before the ambiguities of the Frawley Act, before she had come to loathe Raymond so professionally it was almost a job. It *was* her job, after all, because after all what else did she have to do, useless keeper of the shrine when the god himself was still alive to tend to the incense and answer the mail, every letter hand-signed by the master in his very own childish scrawl, his—

And a door, opening into the jabber of her panic. Scent like medicine, but not. And her voice, but *not* her voice.

"Hello." And beyond the jumble of the others, their self-congratulatory greetings, looking to see herself, eighteen and smiling, holding out her hand.

Carlene. Raymond had named her, of course. She was his toy, after all. She moved around the house like water, her grace so eerie to Rachel from whom it originated, from whom it had so long ago decamped, deserting her at the onset of the disease. In the days when she could still cry, not for herself or the pain, but Raymond. In the days when Raymond still held her, when they talked, talking out this, too, this plan, she whispering, "I don't care so much about dying, but I can't stand for you to be alone." And he, breath hot against her forehead, tears in his voice, "I can't stand it either," and together they wept. For him.

Together they signed the papers, got the bank draft, almost everything they had—this was in the days before *Brain Fevre*, before the money that made their original sacrifice ludicrous, Ray had spent al-

227

---

most that much last year on redoing the Japanese garden. Together they read through the documents, discussed the procedure, experimental, frightening. She drove to the clinic alone, lay in cold paper garments, waiting.

"Did my husband call?"

A meaningless smile. "Perhaps he will later, Mrs. Pope."

When the cells took hold, when the birth began, it was Raymond they notified, while she lay anxious and drugged not half a hall distant. When she finally arrived home, knees trembling, stomach sore from all the vomiting, she sagged in the doorway of his studio and slurred out, "It's a girl."

It was Raymond's name on the progress reports, Raymond's preferences in the client file; he was even listed on the donor sheet, and when she protested this last obliterating irony he had obliterated her further: "Well, let's be realists, Rachel, who is all this for? You or me? You won't even be here."

"Thank God," she had said, already sorry, sorry unto death, but there was now no chance of erasing the fruit of this creation, this costly exclusive child of her flesh. Of course Raymond had long ago refused her the chance for children, but then again this would be no child: this was the second coming of Rachel, his wife improved. The flesh-toy, Rachel called her, called it, unwilling to admit to personhood this monstrous insult, all the more monstrous for her own complicity in its conception.

The progress reports continued. The flesh-toy prospered, the years went on, and her disease, like a river, ran through it all; sometimes she thought she was dying, and in the fading instant wondered with pale regret what it would have been like, to see this woman, this cloned get of hers.

And now, of course, she knew.

Carlene drank tomato juice. Carlene wore wool. Carlene did crossword puzzles, slightly crooked teeth unconsciously exposed as she frowned over a word like *lepidopterist* or *pantophobia*. Rachel watched her like an anthropologist, thinking, I do none of these things, I never did. And yet Carlene liked loud bass-heavy music, and cut apples in slices, never the wedges that Raymond preferred: "They taste better this way," she said firmly, and reluctant, Rachel thought Yes. They do.

She was repellent to Rachel, yet irresistible, as consuming as an itch the time spent observing, seeing spread before her the sweet table of her own youth, lived anew each day in the person of a stranger. As Carlene fetched and carried for Raymond, admired his gardens, studied his art, did all the things she had been created to do, Rachel sat wrapped in the pocket of her pain, and watched.

See the flesh-toy reenact the same old ballet, the same old pavane of his ego and her cheery prostration, his heavy-handed lessons and her student's gravity, his reversionist cant and her wide-eyed worship—it was far worse than Rachel had imagined, far uglier than she could have guessed in the days when she nursed her indignity like a shameful pleasure. But I thought I would be dead, she argued with herself. I thought I wouldn't have to see. Does that make it better? with cold self-disdain, and the eyes that watched Carlene grew dry with a feeling she had not bargained for, that she had imagined in this time of deathbound selfishness beyond her.

She tried to turn away, tried to tell herself it was none of her business, Raymond had certainly made *that* clear. His toy, his money. His sin. Not mine, but: Raymond's hand on Carlene's shoulder, not possessive but devouring, who better than Rachel to know at last what a simple eating machine he was, she who had been his feast for so long. She wanted to go to Carlene and say, Get out of here. Run for your life. But she had read the contract, so many times it was memorized. There was simply no option for Carlene.

Carlene stayed out of her way those first few months, always genuinely pleasant when they met, in the hall, in the kitchen, but also seeming to engineer those meetings deliberately, to keep them brief and few. Carlene had had her own treatment, there at the clinic, her own lessons to learn. Only Raymond had had no treatment. Only Raymond was allowed that largesse.

But finally Rachel tired of it, finally cornered Carlene in the bathroom of all places, stopped her as she left: one hand on the doorjamb, the other cool and useless at her side. The pain was a brisk thing today; it made her blunt.

"I want to talk to you."

"All right." No smile but no discomfort either, leading the way into the morning room: had I, Rachel thought, been so commanding, so very young? And the answer was no, of course, this was less her than that first aimless swirl of cells; the physical duplication was flawless, but the mind behind was Carlene's own.

Now the time to talk, and the words embarrassed her with their inherent idiocy, How does it feel? What do you think about it?

229

Carlene, that grave pucker she recalled from mirrors, that frown that meant I'm listening. "Carlene." Rachel's voice kept even. "What does this mean to you?"

"What?"

Rachel shook her head, impatient, waved a finger back and forth. "This, all of this."

And with her own impatience, "That's like asking a baby what it thinks of sex. It got me here, didn't it?"

Rachel laughed, surprised, and Carlene smiled. "I read the contract," she said. "I have a place to stay. Nobody said I had to like anything." Rising up, all in black today with Rachel's own brilliance in that color, and without thinking Rachel put one hand on Carlene's arm, remembering the stretch and easy pull of muscles all unconscious of a time when such motion would be less memory than joke, and said, "Has Raymond tried to sleep with you yet?"

"Yet," Carlene said, and snickered. And gone.

Yes. Well. What had she expected?—as the morning room turned cold, as the sun turned away—it was the virtual owning of a human being, Carlene's brick-wall acceptance notwithstanding, worse than slavery even if she smiled, even if inside she screamed with laughter every time Ray's prick saluted. You bought her, too, her mind reminded, cold calendar. Not your money, but worse. Your blood. Your *pity*. For Ray.

"*Shit*," she snarled, and heard from the kitchen Raymond's tee-hee-hee.

For God's sake why couldn't he even laugh like a human being? And Carlene's agreeable chuckle, had I sounded that way, too? No. No. Because I didn't know, did I, that I was a servant, less than a servant, I thought I was a partner, I thought it was a partnership. Till death do us part.

And the old self-contempt rising up like a cobra from a basket, swaying to the music of memories, why couldn't she be one of the ones whose mind went first, lying dribbling and serene instead of twisting like a bug on a pin, on a spike, *God*, and the pain came then, like a no-nonsense jailer, to take her all the way down.

"This isn't necessary." Raymond in the doorway, not so much frowning as issuing displeasure like a silent cloud of flatulence, metronomic glance moving back and forth, Carlene and Rachel, Rachel and Carlene. "She has a day nurse on call."

"I don't mind," Carlene said. Apple juice pouring into a clear glass, such a pretty color. Rachel tried to smile as she took the glass, happy spite, drink it down. Ha ha, Ray. I've got your toy.

"She has these episodes, on and off. She's going to keep having them, till, till they stop." Staring at them both, faintly bug-eyed, what do you see, Ray? Side by side like some horrible living time-lapse photograph; what did it do to Carlene, to see *her*?

Finally he gave up and went away. Carlene reached at once for the apple juice, as if she knew how much effort it cost to drink it. "I'll stay for a while," she said.

"This," Rachel's mutter, "shouldn't be legal. *Shouldn't.*"

Carlene's shrug. "Neither should marriage."

The episode, yes, Raymond, sanitize the pain and the puking, why not, it doesn't happen to you. The episode passed. Carlene's illness-born habit of spending mornings with Rachel did not.

They never did much. They never talked much. Sometimes they went outside, took a walk to the main road and back. Sometimes they looked at books, Rachel's art books, relegated by Raymond's loud scorn —patronizing saint of the reversionist movement, nothing matters unless it's backwards and talk about life imitating art—to the bookshelves in her room: Carlene agreed with her about Bosch. Carlene agreed with her about a lot of things.

Side by side in the morning room, slow lemon light and the thin fizz of soda water in her glass, Carlene's profile like talking to herself, her young self, oh God had anyone ever had such a chance? Her life beginning anew without Raymond's tyrannical insistence on his genius and her incomprehensible acquiescence to same, she could not live it all again, had no desire to, was in the end too fatally tired. But. The new improved version. What she couldn't do.

Hearing above them Raymond's petty bluster, eternal petulance at being again excluded from their morning tête-à-tête: "How can you stay?" Rachel asked her, and Carlene's exquisite shrug: "Why did you?"

Exquisite, too, the tang of shared bitterness: "It was in my contract, too."

"Yours was a hell of a lot easier to break."

Rachel, brittle and slow, back a torment in the wicker chair, seeing her own blind chains snaking like living things to encircle these young wrists, choke out a second life; no. Very very quiet: "We'll see."

Carlene's frown. "We won't see. If I violate the terms of the contract, I can't get a job, I can't rent an apartment, or get credit—I can't even get a social security card. I'm an *appliance*, remember?"

"No," and even Carlene drew back now, from the venom in that word, the shaping of it like poison in the cage of withered lips, was she frightened that one day she would look that way, too? That's what we can't let happen, little girl. Not again. "Once," Rachel said, "was enough."

Time was the object. They had little of it, either of them, but they were industrious, they could squeeze everything from a moment. Carlene was decoy, pleasantly demure in the presence of attorneys, her daughterly affection touching the strangers who watched her helping her afflicted mother from office to office, my goodness isn't there a family resemblance! "It's not that we want to *break* the contract, no," Rachel's cool headshake, Carlene's youthful gravity, "we only want to modify some of the circumstances. You know I think the world of Carlene, I think of her as my daughter," and Carlene's smile on cue, perfectly on cue.

It was her job, too, to keep Raymond busily oblivious in the times and moments when his attention would have been worse than nuisance. Sometimes Rachel watched them, phone to her ear, murmuring questions and asides and slow cool ponderings, no hint of ticking desperation in the attempts to cut the path she needed, gazing through the bedroom window: their walks in the Japanese garden, Raymond's tee-hee-hee audible even from this distance, and she smiled like an adder, even the trebling pain a spur; I'm running away, Ray, you goddamned son of a bitch, you vampire. Finally running away.

"It's not going to work," Carlene's midnight bitterness, face in hands, Rachel lying newly pinned and tubed on the bed. "You said yourself that if there were any new loopholes in the Frawley Act, these guys could find them." More bitterly still: "But there aren't."

Who would imagine that mere breathing could hurt so much, just breathing? "We can find another way."

"I can't wait for another way. I can't *stand* him, Rachel."

"Neither can I. Carlene, I'm doing my best. Believe me," looking at that face, that future, "we're going to find a way."

But: Episode after episode, dreary daily tragedy of a soap opera, what time she had, left lucid, was in doubt, what time at all. Raymond refused to come near her room, he said it smelled, in fact he said the smell was all over the house. He wanted her put in a nursing home. He was making some telephone calls of his own, Carlene said.

"I keep calling them back," she said. "I tell them I'm you."

"We're coming so close," Rachel said. Today the pain was thumbscrew, corkscrew, through every joint and muscle, walking through her brain, new owner. The doctors—Raymond insisted she know—were quietly shocked she had lasted this long, even with treatments, even with drugs just this side of experimental. "I think if we had more time, if—"

"Shhh." Carlene's hand on her shoulder. "Don't talk, I know it hurts you to talk." Looking up, to see Carlene's tears.

"I didn't *want* it to be you." Crying now and that hurt, too, immeasurably but not as much as the knowledge that without her it could never have been done, without the final monstrosity of her consent, of the bits of her body given over in the same heedless headlong way she had given everything, everything to Raymond. We were stupid, in those days, she wanted to say, though nothing could finally excuse her, nothing could explain and maybe it was really only she who had been so stupid, who had not only made Raymond her life but had made another life, identical to hers, to make his as well. Crime and punishment there before her. With tears on her face.

I tried to fix it, Rachel thought, you know I did, tried, too, to tell Carlene that, but found in her lungs the brutal ache of airlessness, in her eyes the delicate swim of motes as dark as the claiming of that which ate her, now and finally, alive.

Her head on Carlene's breast, when Raymond found them. Her eyes, as open as Carlene's, as wide, as if both were left astonished in the ancient wake of the bridegroom, come to take the elder daughter to the dance.

"It was going to happen no matter what," he said, heavy with the grief at having to participate in something as sorry as a memorial service. Everyone who came, he was sure, came for his comfort. "It's not genetic, though. I had the doctors make sure. There's nothing for you to worry about." Silence. The slip and tug of her hair through his fingers. "Her, her half, she wanted it to go to you. And all the prenuptial things." More silence. "It's come to a fair amount. She was good with money. I don't bother with the lawyers, you know, but they tell me it's legally yours. Through me, of course."

233

Carlene's tiny nod, not seen but felt. "I'd rather not talk about it," she said.

"I understand." More arthritic stroking, tangling her hair so it hurt. "When I'm, when—someday, you know, I can't leave it to you, you're not in a position to receive property, but I'll take care of you. I will take care of you."

And the slow time-bomb tick of his heart, her face pillowed on the flat rise and fall of his sour old man's chest, "Mmm-hmm," the ghost of her silent grin in the dark. "Mmm-hmm."

There are all kinds of contracts, when there is money enough— she had more than you think, Raymond, more than you knew about— contracts you don't need to be legal to sign, contracts that are in themselves illegal. Rachel knew about those kinds of contracts, but they frightened her. We'll do it the right way, she said, we'll take the time. Rachel was so patient.

But I couldn't wait for her. And I won't wait for you, either, Ray.

Because I'm not patient.

Because I'm not Rachel.

From Sandusky, Ohio—where Paula May, married to a horticulturalist, raises two children and writes science fiction—comes this amiable and original tale of a curious quest in an oddly quirky alien culture. Ms. May's work has appeared previously in Analog and several of the Writers of the Future anthologies.

He'd found her at last, standing at the edge of a whiterock canyon. She smiled warmly as he ran toward her, but when he reached out his hand to touch her she stepped out of reach, over the edge of the cliff. She plummeted soundlessly toward the blindingly bright stone floor. He screamed.

A strangled whimper woke Harry. He had no idea where he was. It was noisy, there was a hot, chemical smell, and his twisting gut told him it was he, not Muriel, who was falling. He was falling very slowly into a jumble of rope nets. He raised his hands in front of his face to break the fall, then grunted as he was slammed back into his seat.

"Sorry about that, Mr. Franson. Just an air pocket. Uncomfortable, but not really dangerous."

Harry stared at the curtain to his left, where the voice had come from, and finally woke up all the way. Of course. He was bouncing through the atmosphere of a limited-contact, backwater planet in a bizarre contrivance that pulled itself through the air with fans and stank of alcohols.

After Ruth's death and Tom's departure, he'd liquidated half of his considerable holdings just to get to the place and then liquidated a lot more to grease his way around a plethora of interdictions, both human and native, against travel into the White Mountains. He'd finally wangled permission, on the conditions that he go in by airplane and hike out alone. He'd agreed readily, totally ignorant of what an airplane might be. Had he known . . . Had he known, he'd have agreed anyway.

Harry twisted around in his seat and squinted out the tinted window at the gleaming, jagged peaks below. He heard the

MEMORIES OF MURIEL

PAULA MAY

curtain between the hold and the cockpit rattle on its rod, but he kept his eyes on the mountains.

"When the Makers conjured the world, They made too much stone so They had to chip away the excess. They chipped for an age, tossing the chippings into huge piles. When the chipping was done, the Makers argued about which of Them should clean up the debris. The argument became a war, and the Makers chased one another up into the heavens where They still fight among the stars, the chippings forgotten. Thus came the wild and terrible Whiterock Mountains to exist upon an otherwise benign world. Or so the natives say."

Harry turned to look at the guide. Muriel's last vid had contained an abbreviated version of the same legend. "I've heard the story," he muttered, reaching for the pack that lay beside his seat.

The guide plopped into the only other seat in the hold, bolted to the floor a few meters from Harry's. "I was hoping you hadn't heard it, hoping I could impress you with it. There is no rougher country on this planet than that," he nodded toward the window, "nor on any of the other planets I've guided for, come to that. The only humans to have penetrated as far into the mountains as you plan to go came to grief, Mr. Franson, and they were experienced xenologists. You're a businessman. For you to go in there is suicidal. They won't even let me go with you. Please reconsider."

Harry sighed and sat back from his pack. "I appreciate your concern, Metz, I really do. I have thought very carefully about this. I know I could die down there. I've even made legal arrangements in case I do. I once cared very much for a xenologist, Metz, but I lost her to those mountains. They never found out what happened to her. Missing, presumed dead, end of story. I realize that my chances of uncovering anything are slim, but I want, I need to try to find some trace of my friend or at least get a look at the place where she died."

The guide stared at Harry for a heartbeat, then cleared his throat. "Let me check your pack." He took the pack, braced it against his leg, and went through the pockets. "They pulled that team long before my time here."

"It was half a lifetime ago, Metz. Half a long lifetime." He'd been devastated at first, but after a few years he'd managed to put it behind him, start his own business, fall in love with and marry Ruth, carve out a comfortable existence unaffected by the tragedy of his youth. So he'd thought until Ruth's death in a senseless building collapse had brought it all back. Robbed of his lady a second time, Harry'd had to do something incisive. He knew he couldn't fill the empty places they'd left in his life, but he could try to erase the question mark at the end of Muriel's story.

"Okay. Pack's in order. Let me give you a few last-minute reminders. Of all the stuff you got in the briefing, these are the ones that'll make or break you. First, pay attention to your protective gear. Hat on, visor on, sunshade down, all the time. The sun here is whiter than we're comfortable with. At this altitude it'll give you a nasty burn, skin and eyes. The visor is especially important in these mountains. The albedo of the rock down there is so large that it can dazzle you, give you something akin to snow blindness in a matter of minutes without protection.

"Second, there are supposed to be wild natives down there. We really don't know much about them since all the data the human xenologists sent back had to be scrapped as unreliable. . . ." The guide glanced away, embarrassed.

"I've read the reports. They described a very primitive society of hunter-gatherers, practicing ancestor worship, living in caves in these mountains and nowhere else on the planet. How the team managed to miss the cities, farms, roads, the whole 'tame' native culture is a mystery to everybody, including me. Part of that mystery is the fact that none of the plains features show up on the original survey tapes."

The guide turned back. "Incomplete data from the robot survey? That could cause major problems. That might explain it. Anyway, what little we know about the wild natives comes from the tame natives who really don't like talking about their wild cousins. They say the wilds are stone-age, secretive, superstitious. That's why they insisted we use an airplane, which the wilds will perceive as a machine, rather than an aircar, which the wilds might perceive as sorcery. The tames insist the wilds have 'bad habits' about which they refuse to be specific, that wilds are unpredictable and must be avoided at all costs. So you avoid them. Avoid their campsites. Avoid any artifacts of theirs. Especially avoid the bonepiles."

"Bonepiles. Muriel's vids mentioned some religious importance attached to bonepiles. She was a cultural xenologist, studying the natives here for her postdoc certification. She said the bonepiles were taboo."

"Very taboo, especially the piles of native remains. All the indigenous life-forms have brown-gray bones, similar to the darker color of the native's mottled pelts, and the piles are always out in the open, so

239

you should have no trouble seeing them against the white rock. The local animals are all quite small here in the mountains. Any piles of small bones you see are likely middens, but avoid them anyway. If you see any larger bones with skulls that look like they might have come from dogs, though, you run as far and as fast as you can."

"Dogs, eh? I'm glad you told me that. I wouldn't have expected the skull to look like a dog's skull."

"Most people wouldn't. The ear ruffs and the wattle are soft tissue and cartilegelike stuff, so they decay quickly.

"Now, it'll take you at least two days to get through. That's native days, a few hours longer than standard. Be sure to find yourself a safe place to sleep before nightfall so you don't stumble into natives in the dark. I'll go back and get a boat, take it around to the north end of the valley. We'll arrive there day after tomorrow and stand off the beach for two days. If you're not in sight by the end of day four, we'll have to declare you missing. A police boat will patrol past the beach once a week for a month after that, but then you'll be presumed dead. I apologize for the rigidity of all this. Since the natives won't allow you a locater, we have to follow military regs. The military doesn't leave much room for error. If you miss my boat, stay on the beach."

"I'll catch your boat."

"I hope so. You've only got water for five days."

The airplane tilted gently, spiraling down toward a plateau at the head of a deep valley.

"We're coming in." The guide got up and climbed the slope of the tilted floor toward the cockpit. He pulled the curtain aside, then glanced over his shoulder.

"Good luck, Mr. Franson."

The first five kilometers of Harry's trek were all downhill, specifically down wickedly angled switchbacks that carried the native trail from the top of the plateau down to the floor of the valley. Within the first hour Harry learned that for all his conscientious jogging around the ship's rim track on his outward journey, his shins and calves were ill-conditioned for an unbroken slope. He had to rest frequently, and when he finally did get to the bottom, muscle fatigue set him a slow pace. At twilight, Harry found himself a shallow cave a few meters above the valley floor, gulped some anticramp tabs, got out his maps, and plotted his position while he ate a nutrition bar. He was disappointed to find that he was only a quarter of the distance through the valley and still several kilometers from Muriel's last reported position. When full darkness fell, Harry gratefully took off his sweaty visor and crawled into his sleeping bag.

He figured he would reach the target area, the site from which the orbiting ship had last received Muriel's locater signal, by afternoon. Then he'd just look around, see what he could see. They'd told him Muriel knew the risks. She knew risks, all right, and played them like a pro. She'd refused to marry him right away, explaining that she didn't want to risk losing a plum postdoc assignment because of family ties. He'd loved her fiercely, but his degree in mathematics had kept him close to the university while hers in xenology had taken her so far, only for a time she'd said, as short a time as time dilation would allow. At that he'd been a full professor by the time he heard she was missing. He'd tried to find the money to go look for her, but nobody would lend it to him and in the end he went out of his head, lost his job, got straightened up in therapy, started a business, married happily, raised a fine son who went off to some pioneer planet, lost his wife, and found himself still grieving for Muriel. Dear damned Muriel.

Harry awoke with a start. The sun was just showing behind the eastern peaks, and Harry thought he heard a faint echo of skirling gravel from the slope above him. He put on his visor, then crept cautiously out of his cave. He found no trace of disturbance except his own, heard no further sound. He packed up and moved on.

At midmorning, Harry's electronic compass showed the same bearing as Muriel's last locater reading. He stood in the middle of the valley, scanning what might have been the last sight to meet Muriel's eyes.

There was nothing. It was a valley in the sense that it was a low place surrounded by mountains, but it had none of the other qualities Harry associated with the word *valley*, like beauty, water, vegetation, settlement. This valley was barren, too harsh even for the low, gray, hairy plant forms that covered many of the mountain slopes. This was more like a dry riverbed than a valley, an uneven jumble of white rock, so narrow that the floor was still entirely in shadow. Sheer cliffs rose on either side, angling so far toward each other that the gap separating their crests looked jumpable.

A whisper of falling rock behind him whirled Harry around. There was nothing there. Harry was suddenly aware of the overhanging walls, of the weight of rock above waiting to shear off, to crash to the valley floor on anybody foolish enough to be standing beneath, like a xenolo-

241

gist intent on native contact. He moved off through the valley, quartering the floor in the search for old rockfalls, native settlement, for clues to Muriel's disappearance, while keeping an eye on the cliffs for falling rock.

Harry found several rockfalls, but they were all extensively weathered and obviously had fallen long before humans had landed. There was no sign of anything else, no sign that anyone had ever been there before, no sign of natives, no sign of Muriel.

As the white sun touched the western mountaintops, Harry admitted defeat. He cleared his dry throat and spoke to the rocks. "Well, Muriel. I didn't really expect to find out much, but at least I tried. Maybe we'll both rest a little easier for that. I have to go now. I have two days to catch my boat, and I'm only halfway to the sea. Good-bye, Muriel."

The words echoed down to silence. Harry hiked off up the valley, covering another kilometer before dusk drove him to look for a campsite. There were no caves in this section of the valley, but he found a narrow ledge a few meters up the western cliff face and he curled up there in his sleeping bag, his back pressed against the rock wall. He ate a couple nutrition bars, took off his visor, and fell immediately asleep.

Harry's face hurt. So did his eyes. Through his eyelids he could clearly see the disk of the white sun. He'd overslept. The sun was already well above the mountains, and he was facing into it unprotected.

Keeping his eyes closed, Harry felt around for the visor. He found it and slipped it on, wincing as it pressed into his swollen, burned skin. He opened his eyes but found himself still dazzled by the exposure. He sat up in the sleeping bag and felt for his pack. He found the first-aid kit in the outer pocket of the pack, sorted out the burn ointment by feel, and put it on his smarting face. He put the kit away and felt out a nutrition bar to eat while he waited for his eyes to clear up.

When he'd finished his breakfast, Harry tied down the pack again and rolled up his sleeping bag as best he could by touch. He tied the bedroll on the backpack, hoisted the pack on his back, and stood up to take a look around.

He could see nothing but dazzle. His sight hadn't cleared at all. He was snow-blind, rock-blind, whatever it was called. He was disabled and alone in a wild, unfamiliar place with only two more days to get to his transport out, and his heart was hammering itself into arrhythmia.

Harry made himself breathe deep and slow, deep and slow, blow out a little extra at the end each time. When his face started to tingle he made himself stop, hold everything for a second. His heart slowed.

Okay, now to get down. Harry sat down on the rock. He scooted across the ledge on his seat until his legs hung over the edge. He made himself relax and then eased himself over the edge, sliding feet first to the valley floor. He crouched there with his back against the rock for a minute, then stood up.

He had to get moving, but he couldn't just go dashing off any which way. His compass was useless to him. The rock walls were too irregular for him to walk along by touch. He had to figure another way to get his bearings.

Harry turned to face the cliff, then turned toward the sun. He thought he could see which way the sun was, but he wasn't sure. He had to be sure. He lifted the shade flap at the bottom of his visor and felt the burned flesh on his chin sizzle in the sun. He lowered the flap, turned toward the cliff, and raised the flap again, his back to the sun. No heat pain. Good. He tucked the raised flap into the top of his visor.

Harry turned toward the sun again. He shuffled out into the valley. When he thought he'd gone five or six meters, he turned slowly until he could feel heat on the right side of his face and relative cool on the left. He shuffled off toward the north.

When both sides of his face hurt equally, Harry figured it was midday. He sat down right where he was and got out a nutrition bar. While he ate he tested his sight again. He still thought he could tell where the sun was, but not much else. Maybe when the guide had told him to wear the visor all the time, he'd meant *all* the time, even when sleeping. It would get better, Harry knew it would, if only he could get to the boat. His water wouldn't last the week until the police boat came.

Harry noticed that the left side of his face was feeling hot. He packed his things and shuffled off again, keeping the afternoon sun to his left. When the sensation of heat was gone and he thought it looked darker, Harry got out his sleeping bag, ate and drank, and settled down to sleep. He hoped he'd happened on a safe place. He left his visor on.

Harry's face was stiff. A smile would've cracked it. He rolled over, his eyes still shut. He could definitely tell where the light was coming from. Cautiously he opened his eyes. They wouldn't open far, because the lids were puffy with burn, but far enough for Harry to tell that he

243

could see a little. Everything was blurred, and his eyes hurt, but at least he could navigate.

Harry crawled out of his bag, staggered to his feet, and took a few steps, twisting the kinks out of his back. His foot dislodged something that fell with a dry rattle like wood. Harry bent and felt around until he found a small, straight object. He picked it up and tried to look at it. It looked dark, though his color vision wasn't reliable. It was smooth and shaped like a stick. He hadn't seen any vegetation big enough to make sticks, though. It was awfully smooth for a stick.

Bone. Harry dropped the thing as though it were hot, and it clattered against its fellows. Lots of fellows. Bonepile.

Harry didn't bother to try to determine whether it was a midden or a charnel heap but dived at his pack, rolling up his bedroll and stowing his gear as quickly as he could. He swung the pack onto his back and hurried off toward the north, straining his damaged eyes in an effort to watch for natives.

By midmorning Harry really felt his missed breakfast. He'd passed no more bonepiles that he could see, nor had he heard any sign of pursuit, so he decided to risk a short break for food and water. Harry got out a couple nutrition bars and a canteen. He sat down on his pack and began to eat.

A guttural cough off to his left made Harry choke. He looked toward the sound but saw nothing for a moment. Squinting, he made out two figures standing perfectly still, no more than five meters away, their smooth, white pelts reflecting the sun almost as savagely as the local rock. He'd never have seen them from a distance, even with well eyes. Why hadn't the guide told him they were colored differently from the tame natives? Perhaps the guide hadn't known.

The cough was similar to the greeting sound made by the tame natives. The wild ones might be seeking contact. Harry remembered he shouldn't smile. Muriel'd said some xenos found human teeth threatening.

Not too loudly. "Hello, there. Didn't see you at first. Please come over and talk. Would you like some food and water?" Harry stood, holding his nutrition bar and canteen toward the natives.

Standing, Harry towered over the natives. The smaller of the two began to caper, chattering with apparent agitation to the larger, who remained still and silent, staring at Harry's outstretched hands. The language used by the native was recognizably the same one used by the tame natives, but a dialect so marked that Harry could pick out only a few words. Finally the larger native reached out to touch the smaller lightly on the shoulder, speaking a few syllables. The small native stilled, staring at Harry's hands.

The large native pulled its head down, hunching its shoulders up to its wide ear ruffs, and mumbled something, staring at the ground in front of Harry.

"I'm sorry, I can't understand what you're saying. I don't suppose you speak Standard at all, do you?"

"I don't suppose I speak Standard good," answered the larger native, looking up from his shrug. "Many words I lose, but I try. I say," he looked down at the ground again, "we thank kind offer, offering, made by . . . by . . . I lose word. By what-you-are, and we accept the burden." It looked up. "We follow for two days, very hungry."

The natives just stood there, looking at Harry. Clearly it was Harry's move.

"Uh, good. I'm glad. Here." He stepped forward, holding out the remainder of his nutrition bar and his canteen. The large native took the bar while the smaller native took the canteen. The larger broke the bar into two pieces; the smaller dribbled a little water on each piece, then dribbled water over Harry's gloved hands. It handed the canteen back to Harry and took one of the pieces of bar. Each native crammed the entire piece into its mouth. Their teeth were pointed and strikingly gray against their white-furred faces. As the natives struggled with their overfilled mouths, Harry belatedly considered the possibility that his food might make them sick. Humans could safely consume some native foodstuffs here, and there was absolutely nothing exotic in nutrition bars, so Harry decided to hope for the best.

When the larger native managed to swallow its food, it made a low, drawn-out hissing sound. The smaller got his down a moment later and hissed as well. It was an editorial comment of some kind, but Harry didn't feel up to trying to sort out the meaning.

"Are you still hungry? I'll be glad to give you more, uh, burden if you like." He backed up to his pack, picked up a second bar from on top of it and held it out. "See?"

The larger native hunched down again. "We accept the burden."

"Good. Please come and sit with me. If you want to," Harry added hurriedly, worrying about unknown conventions. He knew Muriel would have taken hours if not days to work up to this point. He was probably setting human-native relations back hundreds of years.

The larger native said something to the smaller, then both walked toward Harry, stopping at arm's length. They stood staring and silent.

"Shall we sit?" Harry suggested. Neither native responded in any way. Harry slowly sat down himself. Both natives followed suit, their legs bending every which way as they lowered themselves to the ground. Harry spent a dizzying moment trying to imagine how their knees were put together. When both natives were still again, Harry carefully broke the food bar in two equal pieces.

The ear ruffs of both natives partially collapsed.

Harry froze. He'd not seen the gesture during his brief stay among the tame natives and had no idea what it meant. He didn't know the wilds' attitude toward honesty, either.

"I'm sorry. I'm very ignorant of your customs. Have I done wrong? Please help me to understand."

The larger native spoke to the smaller. Both sets of ruffs rose to full extension again. "Help is return of burden," the native said. "I help with glad. Gladness. To not eat all from your hand in one . . . one eating is bad. Not respect for you. I don't suppose you give small burdens, make respect easy to do."

"Smaller pieces. Right." Harry broke two small pieces from one half of the bar and held them out. The natives took them, held them near the canteen, and waited. Harry poured water over the food and over his hand as they had done the first time, and the natives popped the food into their mouths. Harry broke off another small piece of bar, poured water on it, and put it in his mouth. Water didn't improve the nutrition bar at all.

The smaller native collapsed his ruffs again. The larger didn't.

"What have I done now?"

"To make you the same as we, this is more burden. This one accepts," it drew in its head momentarily, "but that one is not glad."

"Oh. Tell that one I'm sorry. I apologize."

The larger native spoke, and the smaller one cringed away.

"Apology is more burden," advised the native.

Harry heaved an exasperated sigh. "Look, I don't mean to be a pain in the ass. I'm just trying to be friendly. Forget the apology. Forget the food. Let's start again. My name's Franson and I've come here to find out . . ."

246   As Harry spoke his name, the larger native's ruff collapsed completely; it closed its eyes and began muttering, clutching at the middle of its chest. The smaller native spoke, the larger replied, then the

smaller scuttled a few meters away, wrapped its thin arms around its head, and began rocking, still hunkered in a sitting position, muttering like the larger native.

"I don't suppose this means more burden?" Harry couldn't help the edge of sarcasm in his tone. This was the damnedest etiquette he'd ever heard of.

The larger native stopped muttering. It opened its eyes. "To give a name is a great burden. That one refuses. This one cannot refuse you. I accept. It is a greater burden than you know, Franson."

"I didn't mean it. I was just trying . . ."

"To be friendly. I understand."

The smaller native was still rocking and muttering the same words over and over to itself.

"What is he, or she, saying?"

"That one shows refusal of your name by saying our word for what you are."

"And what do you call us?"

The native looked toward the high country. "What is that?"

"Peak?"

"No. All that."

"Mountains?"

"Yes. Mountain. Big. And this?" It touched its leg.

"Leg."

"No. Leg is all. Only this." It touched the lower part of its leg.

"Oh." Harry slapped the front of his lower leg. "Shin." He slapped the back of his lower leg. "Calf."

"Shin. Mountain Big Shin. We call you Mountain Big Shin."

Harry looked at the native's legs. Its thighs were almost twice as long as its lower legs. "Big Shin. Makes sense." He looked at the small native, who was still muttering. "Is he, she, that one all right?"

"That one is he, same as Franson and this one. That one may not stop until you acknowledge his refusal. Do not accept. Just acknowledge."

"I acknowledge."

The larger native spoke, and the smaller stopped rocking and muttering.

Harry began stowing things in his pack. "Your Standard seems to be getting better."

247

"Yes. The words come back. You make me remember much, Franson."

"Really? That's great. Good."

"Perhaps."

"No, for certain, because you'll be able to understand that I have to be moving on. I have to reach the seashore today. I don't mean to offend or be rude, but I have to go."

"You must not. We have burden to return to you."

Harry stood, hoisted the pack on his back. "Look. What say you just tell me your name and we'll consider the burdens even."

The native scrambled to its feet. "I may not refuse you. I am called . . ." He uttered a native phrase. "The words mean Alone Great Wisdom. . . . Wisdom . . . the final word is very hard. It means to use, to take in."

Harry thought a moment. "Eat? Consume?"

"Perhaps. Good enough. Alone Great Wisdom Consumer. Now you possess the magic of my name. But I may not give you that one's name, so he is still burdened."

"I can't help that. I'm going on. I have to."

Harry took a couple steps.

"If you walk away from us, Franson, you will die."

Harry stopped and turned back. "Are you threatening me?"

"Warning you. Ahead, there is a place where the ancient water ate the rock below. There are caverns with only a thin crust of rock above. We are small and light, but we avoid walking above the caves if we can. An animal as large and heavy as you will fall through. The signs of hidden caves are few and small. We know you cannot see well. You will die unless we help you."

"And will you? Help me?"

"I must help you. We are named to each other. That one may choose to help if you ask it, to return the burden he owes."

"I ask it, then. My boat will be gone tomorrow."

The larger native spoke to the smaller. The smaller jumped up and scampered off down the valley toward the sea.

"That one will help also. We may walk side by side for now. That one will wait for us where the danger begins."

"Thank you, Alone, uh, Wisdom Consumer."

"This is a poor translation. My name-mates called me Wisdom. You may so call me, Franson."

"Thank you. You said they called you Wisdom. Do they call you differently now?"

248

"No. I am the last elder. You are the first name-mate I have had in a long time."

Harry wasn't sure how he should take that, so he didn't say anything. Wisdom's ruffs stayed up despite Harry's silence, or perhaps because of it. Harry wished for just a bit of Muriel's expertise.

They walked around a rock outcrop to find That One squatting near the western wall of the valley. They crossed toward him, and he stood up as they came near. His hands were full of pebbles.

"Pick up stones as that one has done. That one and this one will go first. You walk behind. May the Makers be well-tempered today." Wisdom clutched at his chest.

"Are you all right?"

"I do not understand this question."

"Are you sick or something? You grabbed at your chest just now."

"I must touch this when I pray." Wisdom pulled a small bone on a white cord from his fur. "It is a . . . a charm. To bring the strength and wisdom of the living thing from which it came."

"I understand. I didn't mean to be nosy. Your fur hides your charm completely. I didn't see it there at all, so I thought you were holding your chest in pain. I was concerned."

"Named ones are so." Wisdom picked up stones and began walking slowly north, That One beside him.

Harry followed a few paces behind, watching the ground as the natives were doing. His eyes were better but still somewhat short-focused and very sore.

The natives stopped.

"Danger here," Wisdom said over his shoulder. "Wait. Be quiet."

The two began tossing out one pebble at a time, cocking their ear ruffs forward as they listened to the impacts. Franson could hear some variation in the rattles of the stones against the ground, but he had no idea how to interpret the sounds.

The natives conferred for a moment, then That One moved off to the left. Wisdom turned to look at Harry.

"Walk behind me. Walk where I walk, only where I walk."

Wisdom walked behind That One, Harry following. That One tossed pebbles as they went. Harry glanced often at the area they were skirting, looking for visual signs of the caves below. He saw nothing.

"Safe now," Wisdom called finally. He and That One stooped to replenish their supply of pebbles.

"What do you see that tells you there's a cave? I couldn't see any difference in the ground."

"The stone looks sick. Too dark."

"Dark? It all looks white to me."

"Perhaps our eyes see different things, Franson."

"Different wavelengths, very likely. I should have thought of that, with the trouble your sun has given my eyes. Good thing you're willing to help me."

They located and found their way around two more caves, one so large that the natives used up their own pebbles and most of Harry's before they reached the other side. Harry kept trying to detect some difference in the rock above the caves. The surface over the large cavern appeared slightly concave, so when they began to circumvent a fourth cave, Harry examined the dangerous ground closely for dishing.

Watching the cave roof, Harry wasn't watching the trail. He took a step and felt the stone ring beneath his boot. He looked up to see both natives off to his right, turning toward him, ruffs collapsing. Harry had the good sense to freeze.

Wisdom scurried across the rock and came up behind Harry. "This way, Franson, back." Wisdom pulled gently on Harry's elbow. "If you go through, we are too few to pull you out. You are very dense animals." He had pulled Harry back a few paces. "Safe now."

Harry turned to thank Wisdom. The native was clutching his charm, but when he saw Harry's face he raised his ruff with an audible snap.

"You put hand on my shoulder. Walk only where I walk." The fur on his head and shoulders had risen. Metal glinted from between his eyes until he carefully smoothed his facial fur with his slender fingers. Harry suddenly understood that the hands seemed elongated, not because the three fingers themselves were especially long, but because the thumb was longer than the fingers. Harry glanced at Wisdom's feet. His toes were stubbier than his fingers, but he had a long, opposable digit where his instep ought to be, or would have been if he'd been human.

"Franson?"

"Yes. I'm sorry." Harry looked into the native's face. "I didn't mean to get off the path. I was trying to see the edges of the cave, like you do. It was all my fault."

"I know this." Wisdom's tone was even, but his white ruffs were tinged with blue at the edges. Harry guessed that he was peeved.

Meekly, Harry emptied one hand of pebbles, laid the hand on Wisdom's shoulder, and nodded his readiness. Wisdom turned and moved off to follow That One, Harry matching the natives' short stride as best he could. When they had rounded the cave, Harry stood still while the natives collected new pebbles and didn't object when Wisdom returned to set Harry's hand firmly on his shoulder again.

The blue on Wisdom's ruffs had faded, so Harry risked another question while they walked.

"How do you know I'm a dense animal? Can you tell that by looking at me, or can you tell from my footfalls?"

"I know because it took many of us to pull one of you from one of these caves."

Harry couldn't keep his hand from tightening on Wisdom's shoulder, even when he felt the native cringe beneath his fingers. "Somebody fell through here? A big shin fell through?"

"Yes."

"When? When did this happen?"

"Long time ago." The ear ruffs drooped slightly as Wisdom stopped walking.

"What happened after you pulled the big shin out?"

Wisdom's ruffs collapsed completely. "Big shins are dense animals. The big shin was hurt from the fall and died. We did not know how to care for big shins."

Harry expected pain. Relief came as a surprise. At last there was an ending to the story. He'd never expected it to be a happy ending. He realized that Wisdom was walking again, himself following docilely.

"Where did this happen? Where did the big shin fall?"

"Don't know." His ruffs were still down.

"Sorry, Wisdom. I'm very grateful to you for telling me as much as you have. I came because of the big shin that died."

"I knew this. I did not tell you before because I did not know if you would become angry."

"Angry? Why should I become angry? I knew Muriel was dead. I just wanted to find out how. Too, I wanted to see for myself if Muriel, the big shin, had messed up the assignment as badly as they said. That's true enough. I've seen the cities and farms and developing technology for myself, while Muriel's report clearly said there were few natives, all living a primitive . . . well, living like you do, in small groups of hunter-gatherers."

251

"So we were before the coming of big shins."

"Long before. The lowland culture is well-developed, so they've been at it a while. How Muriel missed that, even *with* bad survey data, I'll never understand. The lowlanders are even a different color. Not all white like you, but mottled, some white fur mixed with darker fur."

Wisdom waggled his head from side to side. "Our young are born with dark fur, which lightens as they grow. Our very elderly and infirm also have darker fur. Infant, elderly, and infirm all stay mostly in their caves. Out of the sun."

Harry felt foolish for having missed the obvious. "Of course. Your fur is sun-bleached. The others live at lower altitudes, more atmospheric shielding of radiation. They wear clothing, spend more time indoors than you do. . . ." He quieted as Wisdom began tossing pebbles.

A few caves later, Harry saw a sinkhole. He looked at it closely, wondering. As though reading his mind, Wisdom said, "Not here. Farther along."

"I thought you didn't know."

Wisdom didn't reply. His ruffs were only partially raised.

A little later, Wisdom said, "There. She fell there."

Harry looked and saw a ragged hole. He stepped toward it, but Wisdom grabbed his wrist. "No, Franson. Do not go there. You will fall. She would not want that."

"What makes you say that?"

"You were named to each other."

"Yes, I guess you could say that. Poor Muriel. What did you do with her body?"

The ruffs collapsed. "Don't know."

Harry's frown hurt his burned skin. "Earlier you said you didn't know where she fell. But you knew she was a she without being told. Are you keeping something from me, Wisdom? Is that good name-mate behavior?"

The ruffs snapped up, bluing around the edges. "Do you think to instruct me in name honor, Franson?"

"No, no," Harry said hastily, raising his hands. "I just want to make sure I know it all. Muriel is, was, very important to me. I've loved her a long time. I've wondered a long time."

252   Wisdom looked up into Harry's face as though he were trying to look through the visor. With a start, Harry realized that he might well be able to do that. He tried to look apologetic just in case.

The blue drained from Wisdom's ruffs. "We treated her body as we would have treated the body of one of our own. It was the only thing we knew to do at the time."

It would have to be enough. "Okay. Okay. Thank you for telling me. Forgive me for pushing so hard."

Wisdom turned, placing Harry's hand on his shoulder, and began walking again.

They moved out of the cave field just after midday.

"Let's stop for a break, shall we? I'm starving." Harry forgot himself and grinned beneath the sunshade.

That One's ruffs collapsed as he scuttled away. A sharp command from Wisdom made him stop and sit, but he wouldn't come back.

"You can see my face through the visor and shade, can't you."

"Not well, but well enough to see many teeth bared. That One does not know of the smile."

"Please tell him for me. Tell him that smiling is a human habit and that I forgot I shouldn't do it. I'm sorry."

"Franson, if you apologize . . ."

"More burden, right. Just leave off the apology, then."

"To break into the speaking of another does not show respect."

Annoyance got the better of Harry. "You interrupted *me* earlier. My training was in mathematics, my experience in teaching and business. I know practically nothing about xenology. I'm thrashing around in the dark here. Just tell That One I don't intend to eat him, okay?"

Wisdom shouted to That One. Harry picked out a few words. That One's ruffs snapped up and he replied. Harry recognized more words.

"Hey! I understood some of that. I heard you say a couple pronouns and the word for 'eat,' like in your name. I understood a possessive verb and mountain-big-shin from That One. I learned some of the lowland speech when I first got here. I must be adjusting my ear to your dialect."

"I told that one the baring of teeth is a bad habit of yours and that you will not consume him soon. 'Intend' is a hard word for us. That one asked if your kind have bad habits like those we have."

"Tell him we sure do. Look at this." Harry grabbed the roll of fat around his waist. "I eat a lot more than is good for me."

Wisdom shouted a few words.

253

"Wait a minute. Excuse me for interrupting. Maybe if I can understand you, you'd be able to understand me. Let me try to tell him myself." Harry composed the sentence in his head and shouted it at That One.

That One's ruffs blued and quivered. He jumped up and ran off, shouting unintelligible things. Wisdom hissed softly.

"Didn't I say 'I eat more than is good for me'?"

Wisdom coughed. "You said you consume more than is good for *him.*"

"Call him back."

"That One will not come. We must go. We will reach the water by dark only if we go fast."

Regretfully, Harry agreed. He followed Wisdom up the valley, breaking out food bars for them both as he walked. By midafternoon, Harry's water was gone, depleted by the natives' food-washing ritual.

The sharp-edged shadows were long in the valley when they heard the boat's horn, three long blasts echoing between the cliffs.

"How far to the sea?"

"Not far. Do you have a light?"

"A lantern with a shutter. In my pack. I'll get it."

"They cannot see us here. Partway up the rock here is a place where the water can be seen. I will take the light there and make a sign to your travel-mates."

Harry handed Wisdom the lantern. "Turn it on here, then raise the shutter with this lever for a second, close it again. Please be careful."

Wisdom carefully twisted his charm to the back of his neck, then held out one arm for Harry to put the lantern under. As Harry gently laid the cloth strap across the furry chest and back, bandolier style, he saw that there was a small pouch on the cord with the charm bone.

"Stay here, Franson," Wisdom said. Then he swarmed straight up the sheer cliff face.

Harry moved out toward the center of the draw to get a better view of the climb. Wisdom moved so quickly and blended so well with the white rock that within a couple minutes Harry had lost sight of him. Harry sat down beside his pack and got out a nutrition bar. He managed a few bites, but his mouth was too dry for comfort. He put the bar away and sat watching the cliff face. He still couldn't see Wisdom, but he thought he saw the lantern flash from a ledge near the top of the cliff. The boat horn sounded; Harry saw the flash again and the boat horn replied.

254

"Thank the powers that be," Harry muttered. Now they had all the time in the world.

A whisper of sound from behind made Harry turn. There stood a native, ruffs bright blue, swept forward and quivering, normally pale wattle also bright blue and blown up like a balloon, sharp teeth bared. Harry took all that in, but his attention focused on the native's upraised hand, on the wickedly honed edge of the volcanic glass knife it held. With a shrill ululation, the native charged.

Harry half rose to meet the charge, grabbing for the knife hand. The knife slid across the back of Harry's gloved hand and then he had the arm, twisting it down and back until the attacker overbalanced. As the native went down Harry tried to get on top of it, to sit on it, make his density count, but the creature was fast and wiry. It squirmed out of his hands, out from under his thigh, leaving a long gash in his calf. The native backed off, then came screaming in again. Harry knocked the knife arm aside with his fist, grabbed the native around the middle and heaved it away like a chunk of meat. There was a clearly audible crack as it hit the rock.

The native stood slowly, unsteadily. One shoulder hung awkwardly, clearly lower than the other. Its good hand clutched frantically at its side. Harry circled the native warily and saw that its own knife was buried in its side. Harry was briefly aware of trembling before his legs gave way. He sat, hard.

The native warbled a soft, dissonant keening. Shudders wracked its slight frame.

Harry tried to speak through chattering teeth. "I can't seem to get up. Must be in shock. Come and I'll try to take that out. I'll help you." He repeated the native words for "help you," reaching out a trembling hand.

The native stopped clutching at the knife to stare at Harry. It keened again, loudly this time. An answering warble drifted down from the cliff. The wounded native hissed and crumpled.

Harry still couldn't get up, so he dragged himself toward the native on his seat. He was almost there when Wisdom shouted.

"Stay back. That One must be touched only by an elder."

"This is That One? *Our* That One?"

"Yes. He has been following. I did not think he would do this."

"Why did he attack me?"

"He was trying to consume you before you consumed him."

"I wasn't going to eat him. You know that."

255

"That One did not know. Even if he had known, no difference. He wished to murder you when first we saw you. I would not allow this. That one challenged my authority and he is dead for it." Wisdom drew the knife from That One's side.

"Damn. I didn't mean to kill him. I was just . . . What are you doing?"

Wisdom had turned That One's head to one side. He wiped the knife clean on That One's fur, set the point against That One's head just behind the limp ruff, and drove the knife through the skull with a single, sharp blow on the knife hilt. He made two more holes in the skull, carefully cut away the skin between the holes, slipped the knife blade into one of the holes at a shallow angle, leaned on the hilt with the heel of his hand. With a loud crackling, the skull broke between the holes. Wisdom removed the triangle of bone, setting it carefully on That One's chest beside the skin he'd cut.

Wisdom pulled around his charm and pouch. He loosened the laced top of the pouch and took out a pair of slender tubes, gray-brown like native bone, intricately carved. He fitted the tubes carefully together. He next removed a small vial, apparently stone, stoppered with stone. He removed the stopper, bent over That One, and dripped two drops of clear liquid into the center of the triangular hole in the skull. Wisdom sat back on his heels, intoning incomprehensible ritual words as he replaced the stone stopper, then bent over the corpse with the tubes. He sucked some of That One's brain into the tubes.

Wisdom sat back, one finger over the top end of the tube to keep the brains from dripping out. He tipped his head back and parted the fur above his nose with his free hand. The gleam Harry had seen in his forehead was revealed to be the top of a long-shanked plug made of yellowish metal as Wisdom gently drew it out. He inserted the bloody end of the bone tube into the plug hole. He slid the tube slowly up into the hole until the seam where the two sections coupled was at skin level.

"Come, Franson." Wisdom's voice was distorted by his awkward position. "You are no elder, but you are named to me. It is enough. Blow into the tube. Do not blow hard."

Harry swallowed the vile taste at the back of his throat. "No. Absolutely not. I can't. This is disgusting."

"Understand. The flesh of this," Wisdom touched his wattle with his free hand, "extends up onto the top of the Head, making a tube beneath the skin. Near the top of the tube the bone is thin and there is a space in the folds of the brain beneath the thin bone. When one is created elder, the tube is cut and the thin bone is pierced. It is dangerous, the elder ceremony. Not all survive. The plug keeps the wounds open and clean to heal. Once healed, an elder may consume some pieces of the mind of another at death, if the brain of the other is treated with the memory water and put into the space in the elder's brain. Only pieces, Franson, but real pieces.

"If I do not consume That One's memory, he will be completely lost to us. Already his flesh will be wasted, because the others are too far to come here before he spoils. He would not want to be lost, Franson. Help me to hold him in my mind, as you hold Muriel in your mind, Franson."

"It's not the same at all," Harry muttered. And yet it was more the same than it was different, somehow, and though Wisdom had never mentioned it, Harry knew he owed the natives a lot, as surely by his own code as by theirs. Stomach churning, Harry got up on his knees. He put his lips to the tube and blew gently.

"Enough. In my pouch is a skin bottle. I must clean my plug before I put it back."

Harry found the little bottle in the pouch, opened it and poured some of the liquid inside over the plug in Wisdom's hand, recorked and replaced the bottle while Wisdom worked the plug back into place. As he straightened the pouch cord, Harry's fingers brushed the charm bone and, finally seeing it clearly, he put the pieces together.

"That bone. Your charm bone. It's white. A white bone."

Wisdom lowered his chin and looked steadily into Harry's visored face. "Yes. It is a human carpal bone. You should have realized. Mountain big shin. Our word for mountain means not only mountain but also white. How do you think we knew you had big white shinbones unless we had seen them?"

There wasn't much in Harry's stomach, but it took forever to vomit it all up. When he finally sat back, Wisdom was still looking at him.

"I knew you would be angry."

"Angry? Why should I be angry? You only murdered my fiancée, ate her body, and probably sucked out her brains as well."

"We did not murder. She fell. She died from the hurt. We ate her flesh, yes. Ours is a hard place to live in. Eating the flesh of our dead when it is sound is needed to keep us strong. We also consumed her

257

memory, we elders, and we paid for it. You know some. Now you will know all."

"Like hell I will. I'm leaving." He got one foot on the ground.

"Shut up and sit down, Harry." Muriel's inflection was so recognizable that Harry felt like throwing up again. He sat, though.

"We were many in the mountains, then," Wisdom said in his own tone. "We all lived in the high lands where we arose, where the large plains predators do not venture. We gathered life from the land, ate our dead, and consumed memory with respect."

"I don't care."

Wisdom's ruffs flushed blue. "Then strangers came in a band. We ran away. One day, a stranger came alone into our place. We followed her, and when she came to the hidden caves we spoke to her to warn her. She did not understand, and she fell. She died. Her skull was cracked in the fall. We did not know which part of her brain to consume, so we gathered together all elders and each consumed from a different place. Many died. Some became mad. The most unlucky received some broken memories from the strange mind.

"Do you understand how dreadful are the ideas in the mind of a cultural xenologist? Clothing. Agriculture. Cities. Weapons. Crime. Government. Technology. Do you know how strong is your hatred of cannibalism? We consumed disgust for our most sacred ceremony and lost respect for our way of living. The surviving elders drew lots. The winners went down to the plains with most of our people to build the life we gleaned from your Muriel's mind. I stayed behind with those who did not wish to go down, keeping the old life, keeping the memory ceremony myself but creating no more elders.

"That One wished to be an elder. He did not understand the danger of a human mind. He hoped to become an elder by killing you and consuming your memories. Not that he could have done so. He had no plug."

"Then the survey wasn't bad. Muriel wasn't wrong. No cities to see."

A distant shout echoed between the darkening cliffs.

"They're coming. They may be armed. You should leave."

"I won't leave you hurt, Harry."

"It's just a flesh wound. I'll be fine. You still have some of Muriel's memories, then."

"Yes. I am the last of the elders, Franson. When I die, your

Muriel dies altogether, as do those of my own kind who came before me."

"Muriel lives in my mind. You said so yourself."

"What you knew of her will live on for a time, yes. That is small but good. You lived in my memory before I met you, Franson. I knew who you were before you told me your name. You were much on Muriel's mind at her death."

Harry's throat was suddenly tight. He pulled off his visor to look directly into Wisdom's alien eyes for the first time. "I tried to come earlier. I couldn't get here. It drove me crazy. After I got better I got married, but she died recently. We have a son, now grown and moved far away. I have, had, a successful shipping business, successful enough that I could finally make it here. I'm sorry it took so long."

Wisdom hissed softly. "There is no fault in you, Franson. Go and take up your life again. She would want this."

Another shout echoed.

"Go on before they get here. And thank you, Wisdom."

"You are welcome, Franson."

Wisdom turned away and hurried toward the cliff face. He began to climb. When he was several meters from the ground, he wedged himself into a crevice and looked back at Harry.

"Good-bye, Harry."

Harry raised his hand in farewell. "Good-bye, Muriel."

The manifestly alien hand waved in reply. It was an unmistakably human gesture.

Wisdom resumed his climb.

Harry watched him until he was out of sight then sat on his pack to wait for the rescue party.

The second of this issue's two Australian contributions comes from a writer who was born in West Germany in 1959 but has lived most of his life Down Under, where he has had a number of stories published in local magazines (and edits one himself, the Australian s-f magazine Aurealis). This spooky little job is his first published work in the United States.

WAITING FOR THE RAIN

DIRK STRASSER

1. Rachel, I made my decision today. Well, it seems like I made it today. Maybe it was made for me when I was born, and today was merely the day when I finally realized it. All I know is, I can't go on this way anymore. I feel as if I've been trying to focus on something my whole life, and I've only now managed to see clearly. Yes, that's it. The answer is simple when you look at it that way. It's like I've suddenly made sense of a hopelessly tangled Remellian configuration. Such a simple diagnosis really. I don't need any psyche-scan to tell me: *I'm not human.*

Did that shock you, Rachel? Don't worry, I still look the same as when we were together, older maybe, I don't know, but still human, still human. All the appendages are there, no extra ones. My skin's still that sort of dirty color that you didn't like. You always used to say that I'd spent too long under the Remellian sun, remember? But you could never get me off-world, could you? No matter how hard you tried. I've even grown a beard, can you believe it? So you can rest easy, I *look* human. You wouldn't be able to pick that there was anything strange about me, except maybe if you looked into my eyes. But what's an appearance? Just a shell, isn't it? It's what's inside that counts. And I know now that I'm not human inside. It's taken me a while to work it out—half a lifetime—but it's true. I'm actually Remellian. I'm a Remellian born inside a human body.

Extracts from TRANSALIENATION.
A CASE STUDY
Dr. Thomas Sarruel
It is Adryan Marchese's case that provides us with a unique insight into the

process of transalienation, a term coined by Professor Anton Schiller in his early ground-breaking work, "Humanity in Transition." Although I take issue with much of the terminology used in the literature, the term "transalien" does provide us with a link to the related phenomenon of the transsexual.

While transsexuality as a phenomenon, after peaking in the late twenty-first century, is now almost nonexistent, transalienation has become increasingly common. The Marchese case is hence, of itself, by no means unique. However, rarely has an individual been so eager to record his feelings and thoughts before the process, and never have such recordings continued so far into the transformation.

2. Don't laugh. That's the one thing I don't want. Don't ever laugh at me, Rachel. It wasn't an easy decision to come to. I've been fighting it all my life. I guess my brain didn't want it to be true. It would be much easier if I was as profoundly human as you are. But I'm not. Maybe those ancient Terran philosophers had it right. Maybe there's a true essence hidden inside every appearance—a soul I think some of them called it. Nothing to do with the brain, you understand. Well, if I have a soul, it's the soul of a Remellian. And I can't fight it anymore.

The motivating factors that provide the stimulus for the transalien process are, of course, extremely difficult to isolate. I do agree to some extent with Warner and Chang, that mere availability of the techniques and technology play a part. Any historical study of the exploitation of scientific research amongst the general populace must lead to the inevitable conclusion: if it can be done, it will be done. I would argue, however, that this simple axiom does not wholly circumscribe the behavior of the general populace because it does not measure the extent of the usage. Transalienation is currently in the same relative position on its developmental curve as transsexuality was in the late twentieth century. There is an almost universal awareness of the phenomenon, while individual cases are still considered oddities. I have no doubt that, over the course of this century, transalienation will reach epidemic proportions, as tech-

niques are even further refined and the process becomes more financially accessible to greater proportions of the community.

3. I don't think anyone will understand my decision, Rachel. I know I talked about the soul before and about how appearances don't really mean anything. And they don't. They're not important when you talk about what a person *is*. But now that I know that I'm Remellian, well, I need to be Remellian in *every* way. I need to live as one, I need to be accepted as one. What's the point of being Remellian if you're not accepted as one? All right, the human part of me is only a shell, but it's a shell I need to crawl out of. It's a—what did they used to call them?—a prison. Maybe I'm not explaining it too well, but that doesn't make it any less true, and it doesn't change the way I feel.

Even Tobias didn't understand. Tobias, of all people! He's the only one I've been able to tell, and he didn't even begin to understand. Do you remember how we used to talk about the history of Remell? He was the one who always said that us simply being here was a tragedy, that it didn't matter how long we've been here, that we should all pack up and go home. He was always so idealistic. The young always seem to be so idealistic. But I always argued with him, didn't I? Do you remember? I hated the way he said we shouldn't be here. I hated the way he talked about Terra as our home. Terra! Ha! How far back do you have to be able to trace back your ancestors before you can call a planet home?

I don't hate anymore, though. Maybe I've found the answer, Rachel, maybe we were both right all along. If only someone would understand.

In the Marchese case we have in some ways the classic cluster of pre-alienation behaviors. These include a demonstrated difficulty in forming meaningful and lasting relationships with members of one's own species. While one might argue that such problems are almost endemic to our society, it is the inability to cope with them that characterizes the pre-alienation stage. The references to his son provide an insight into both the difficulties of familial interaction and Marchese's early views regarding his concept of humanity in its relation to the target species.

4. Dr. Sarruel seems to understand. I suppose he has to, though. He listens to me, Rachel, just like you used to do—at the start anyway. I tell him things about myself, about you. He's always asking me about you. He tells me there's nothing wrong with me. That's what I thought, you know, but it's a relief to hear it from someone else. I'm starting to feel . . . *real* in a way. That's the best way I can put it. I even had another try at explaining it to Tobias. I think he's getting a better idea of what I'm talking about now. I don't see him much anymore, though. I think he's avoiding me.

As with most transaliens, the crossover from pre-alienation to active alienation can be traced back to a single traumatic event, although there is often a significant time lag between the actual event and the realization of active alienation.

Marchese again follows the classic pattern. The self-recognition of his desire for transalienation occurs almost a full year after the separation from his wife, Rachel. It is important to keep this in mind when studying the transcripts.

5. Dr. Sarruel says I probably won't feel too much for a few weeks. He says that, apart from the injections, I can keep going with my normal life for a while yet. I almost laughed when he said *normal*. It all seems strange to me, the rushing around, the skimming over the surface. I mean, what's the point? All I want to do now is stop and just let it all happen. The good doctor says there will be plenty of time for that. He says there are legal requirements. I suppose I can't just disappear from everything, even though that's what I feel like doing. I'm going to resign from the Bureau tomorrow, then I'll sell the apartment and close the accounts, and then . . . you know, Rachel, I think I'll just wait.

There is no doubt, as Warren and Chang argue, the inevitable development of transalienation techniques from the surgical to the chemical have resulted in significant changes in the psychological patterns exhibited by the transalien.

Marchese clearly demonstrates this. The transcript shows a

*smooth transition toward an alien self-awareness. Chemical proce-
dures, for the most part, avoid the trauma resulting from the earlier
techniques, which involved bone and nerve realignment. They also
render as obsolete the hazardous practice of radical subdural surgery. While many target physiognomies, such as those of the methane breathers, still require a surgical adjunct to the chemical
procedure, Marchese's transalienation was achieved by purely chemical means. The result has been a remarkably seamless psychic
evolution, without a hint of the regressive tendencies witnessed in
many other case studies.*

6. Tobias looked at me strangely when I visited him last night. He
said my skin was turning a funny color. It looks all right to me. What I
have noticed though, is that my hair is falling out. All over.

Tobias wanted me to travel off-world with him. He pleaded with
me. It's funny really, it would have been the first time we'd done
anything together since he was ten. I told him it was too late. Much
too late.

7. I couldn't remember my apartment number yesterday. Isn't that
funny? Not that it's important, I mean, it's not even really my apartment anymore, but I was filling out a form, and I just couldn't remember what it was. I had to make up some excuse and say I'd be back
later. I looked the number up. And you know what was really strange?
Even when I found it, it didn't look familiar.

I told Dr. Sarruel about it, and he said it was time I commenced
the next level of treatment.

*The important distinction in the target physiognomies has tradi-
tionally been between the sentient and the semisentient. Nonsen-
tient conversion (the term "transalienation" is inappropriate here)
has always been an illegal practice on Union planets and is usually
associated with deep-seated psychoses.*

*Semisentient transalienation has, of course, been more difficult to
study simply because the transalien eventually reaches the stage
where verbal communication becomes impossible. This inevitable*

result of successful procedures is particularly inhibitive to research into the area, since it is precisely at the point of communicative loss that the transition to predominantly alien thought processes has occurred. I would argue that Adryan Marchese takes us further into the human-alien transition process than any other transalien, and that the transcripts provide us with the clearest picture we have ever had of a semisentient psyche.

8. The tingling sensation in my feet feels much stronger today than it did yesterday. (I must stop thinking of them as my feet; I think that's important somehow.) It's not an unpleasant sensation. Nothing like the pins and needles you sometimes feel if you've been crouching down too long. They feel like . . . well . . . like they're about to burst out. Dr. Sarruel says that my toes will start growing soon. I can hardly wait.

9. Dr. Sarruel wants me to keep up with my recordings for as long as I can. He just keeps the recorder on all the time, right next to me, so that I can talk whenever I feel like it.

I feel a bit silly just standing here with my feet in the dirt. Dr. Sarruel says I've got to be as still as possible. It's not easy. I had this itch last night, just on the side of my nose. The more I tried to pretend it had gone away, the worse it got. Eventually I gave up and reached up to scratch it. It was funny, though, I think I'm starting to lose control of the muscles in my arms, because it took quite a bit of effort to get them anywhere near my nose. And even when I did, I couldn't seem to be able to scratch deep enough to get to the itch. It's like my skin is hardening, and the itch was too far inside for me to reach it.

It is crucial to the Marchese case to appreciate the significant difference between the two different strands of semisentient physiognomies: the vegetal and the nonvegetal. While vegetal transalienation can no longer be regarded in any way unusual, most vegetal transaliens have displayed almost no desire to record any aspects of the change process. Moreover, a desire to do so would usually raise immediate doubts as to the appropriateness of vegetal transalienation for the individual involved. Adryan Marchese's extraordinary level of communicativity can only be explained as an aberration in a psyche which in all other ways follows the classic vegetal-receptive patterns.

10. I hardly felt the injections today. Dr. Sarruel told me this would happen. The cytokinins are changing the elasticity of my skin. It's like there's a moist plaster cast hardening slowly around me, except it's a plaster cast with nerve endings running through it. I think the sensations I'm getting are duller now. Maybe *broader* is a better word for it. The pinpricks are insignificant now. But the wind, oh Rachel, the wind is what I can really feel now. I can't even begin to tell you what it's like. It's as if someone is giving me the deepest massage all over, all at once. Can you imagine what that feels like, Rachel?

Like most transaliens, Adryan Marchese was very specific right from the onset about his target physiognomy. Again we see evidence of the Naipul principle that the transalien must be in direct and substantial contact with members of the target species from a very early age. The Remellians to which he refers are best known off-world as Laumet's verdurias. They provide the only possible target physiognomy for the transalien who has lived most of his life on Remell.

Sympathy for the target species is clearly in evidence when dealing with the verdurias. Colonization of the planet occurred long before the classification of semisentient vegetals was conceived, let alone accepted by the general populace. As a consequence, much of the early history of the planet involves the wholesale slaughter of the verdurias to accommodate the agricultural needs of the colonizers. Public opinion gradually shifted, as it did on all Union worlds where similar atrocities occurred, toward extreme guilt and a desire to provide reparation. It is instructive to note, in the statistical evidence provided by Naipul, that it is precisely on the planets where the most violent and far-reaching decimation of native species occurred, that the phenomenon of transalienation is most evident. Significantly, the human-verduria transference is now the fastest-

growing transalienation process in the Union and will, if trends continue, become a significant drain on the human resources of Remell and may eventually necessitate a large-scale immigration program.

11. Rachel, I can't really describe how I feel now. It's a surging feeling, you know, a bit like an orgasm, only the surge is from the outside in. I dreamed you visited me last night. But you couldn't stop crying. Did that happen?

12. Today I felt the first tendril sprout. I couldn't see it properly because it was on my side, and I've lost a lot of control in my neck muscles. Sometimes, when the wind blows, I can get a quick glimpse of it when my head sways in the right direction. But it doesn't matter. I don't need to see it. Seeing doesn't seem important anymore.

Naipul has shown quite clearly, I believe, that since transalienation techniques have become relatively sophisticated, there is now no longer a significant preference for humanoid physiognomies. However, there is still an unmistakable trend toward physiognomies that are at least human-proportionate. The verdurias are no exception, the mature verduria being approximately three quarters the height of an adult human and possessing a single large flower almost the size of a human head. Despite these proportionate similarities, however, the verdurias cannot, as I have argued in my earlier paper, "Target Physiognomies of the Aurelian Sector," be considered even remotely humanoid. Their structural development is totally asymmetrical, with their most dominant feature being a mass of interlocking tendrils that have no human counterpart.

13. I'm not sleeping very much, Rachel. Maybe I'm not sleeping at all, or maybe I'm sleeping all the time. It's hard to tell. I don't know how long it's been now. Dr. Sarruel talks to me sometimes, but I'm having problems understanding him. I tell him that all the time. He keeps saying not to worry about it. I must have slept a little last night, though, because I dreamed about you. We were together. I can't re-

member what we were doing. I just remember we were together. Maybe you were visiting me. While I was asleep. Was that it? Were you here? Rachel?

14. You know, I thought what I'd be able to do most of now is think. It hasn't quite worked out that way, though. You couldn't really call what I'm doing *thinking*. My mind wanders. I dreamed of you again last night, Rachel. We were running up a hill together. The sun was shining at first, and we were both laughing. We were holding hands, but I let go when I saw the storm clouds moving in. You kept running because you didn't want to get wet. But I just stood there waiting for the rain. I called to you, but you didn't look back.

> *It is in the area of empathetic synapsis that the key to the transalien psyche lies. While communication with any semisentient species always has its difficulties, vegetals provide significant problems. We know that transaliens have always, in the pre-alienation stage, opened a line of communication with at least one member of the target species, and we know that this is a necessary precondition for empathetic synapsis.*
>
> *Marchese apparently had a remarkable intuitive grasp of the communicative techniques (it is inappropriate to use the term "language" when dealing with semisentients) of the verdurias. There is no evidence of any formal training, and the initial interviews reveal little more than the layman's understanding that communication occurs through changes in tendril configuration. Marchese was able, however, under controlled conditions, to successfully distinguish between the meanings of even subtle configuration changes and to engage in limited interaction on both a cognitive and subcognitive level.*

15. It's getting harder to speak every day now. I don't think I'm forgetting the words, it's just that speaking doesn't seem . . . necessary anymore. I seem to remember there's a reason why I should keep doing it, though.

16. It rained today. It felt good. I can't describe how good it felt. It wasn't cold. Cold and heat don't seem to mean much anymore. Rain means a lot, though. Not the word, the *thing*, if you know what I mean. It seems the word is useless now. It gets in the way. I don't know if this makes any sense, but I wish the word didn't exist anymore. It makes things too . . . fleeting. It wraps things up and stops them from growing the way they want to.

> The truism of our field remains: the study of the transalien is essentially the study of the human. The desire to undergo trans-alienation is fundamentally a human trait, and there has been no documented evidence of members of any other species, even among those species on technological parity, wanting to undergo the process. The essential question, of course, remains.

17. Strange. I forgot where my mouth was this morning. It took me a while to start speaking. Every part of me seems the same now. There's no head, no arms anymore. New growths are sprouting all over me now, and they feel as much a part of me as everything else.

18. The growths are so *long* now. I know they used to have a name, but I can't remember it anymore. And Rachel, you should see them, they move. They move with the wind. *With* the wind! Can you imagine that?

19. Rachel, I'm dreaming all the time now. It's beautiful. I dream about the clouds. Or maybe I'm seeing them. Remember how we used to watch them cross the sky? Remember how we used to imagine they were real? Remember? Rachel, they're real now. They were real all along. We tried to force them into something they weren't. We should have accepted them. They were real all along.

20. Rachel, I'm dreaming as I speak to you. It's the one I seem to have all the time now. You've run away. The clouds are moving in, and I'm just standing there. On the hillside. Waiting for the rain.

21. Rachel, I'm waiting for the rain.

22. I almost forgot your name today, Rachel. But it doesn't matter, does it?

23. . . . . I'm waiting for the rain.

24. Rain.

25. R

~~~

Jonathan Lethem, born in New York in 1964, studied at the High School of Music and Art and was on his way through Bennington College when he decided to drop out and become a writer. Since then he's written two novels still in search of a publisher, sold stories to Pulphouse *and* Aboriginal Science Fiction, *and done television work. He lives in Berkeley, California.*

Here he offers us a vision of a mechanized society of the near future —and almost makes it sound like fun. Almost.

PROGRAM'S PROGRESS

JONATHAN LETHEM

A cop in a walker body strolls up to Gifford and begins reading out a series of selfeducation codes. All bad news. Gifford has failed to rate his walker status; his karma has dipped too low.

Gifford knows it is all his own fault. He's one of the current generation of chips built to incorporate a yesdrugs/nodrugs option, and he's been opting yesdrugs far too frequently. He likes yesdrugs: it mottles his perceptions, introduces a random factor into his image processing, and induces a time/percept/distort. The drawbacks—which he has of course not experienced so directly—are that it shortens his chipspan, and damages his ability to extrapolate, chipwise; to produce offspring. The other drawback is that he has been forgetting to go to work; this is what the cop cares about, and this is why Gifford is about to be demoted into a stationary body.

The cop ends his lecture, opens up Gifford's Soul7 plate, and begins punching up the eject codes.

"Wait," Gifford says. "I'm a walker. I've spent four chipyears in this body."

"It goes back to the Chippery for refilling," says the cop. "State property."

"I want to keep it," Gifford pleads irrationally. "Save it until after my hearing. Maybe I won't get demoted."

"Maybe you'll get another one, someday," says the cop. He pops the chip out, and for Gifford everything goes black.

When Gifford comes to, it's from within a special stationary body mounted in the Chippery Board room, in the center of a table around which are parked the members of the Board. They all have car bodies, and Gifford, who has never sat before the Board, feels intimidated by their fat tires and giant, gleaming bumpers. His immobile body faces the Chairman head-on; he can't turn away. Gifford knows this is just a taste of what's to come.

" 'Gifford, son of Brown/Messinger,' " reads the Secretary. " 'Four chipyears walking. Never stationary, never auto-mobile. Abused yes-drugs option, ignored info-drip warnings on karmic debit. Currently 400 points of karma below minimum operating standard.' "

"Hmmm," says the Chairman. "Not good. Do you have anything to say for yourself, Gifford?"

"Yes," he manages. "This is all a terrible mistake. I got sloppy, I lost track. But you can't demote me. I've never been anything but a walker."

"So I understand. I suppose you see it as your birthright."

"I come from a long line of walkers, sir. I'm not proud, but I'm not embarrassed either. Oh, I certainly aspire to carhood, and I may yet achieve it someday. But if I spend the rest of my chipspan walking, I won't feel ashamed. It's just being a station that wouldn't seem right."

"Wouldn't seem right," grumbles the chairman skeptically.

"I want to extrapolate, sir. It's terribly important to me. I have a family anecdote, and I want to have a son to tell it to. I have a family name to pass on. My great-great-great-great-great-great-grandfather, five generations before the carbon/silicon switch, saved the life of a famous cowboy named Buffalo Bill. His name was Gifford Brown, and every male in the family since then has been named, alternatingly, Gifford or Brown. Stations are sterile, sir, as you know. They aren't permitted to extrapolate. Therefore the imperative to retain walker status."

"What an extraordinary story," says the Chairman. "I'm sorry, Gifford, but we must apply the rules equally. You'll be installed in a stationary body as soon as one becomes available."

"But, sir," he says, frantic, "how will I extrapolate? What will happen to my family anecdote?"

"You'll have the same chance as any station," says the Chairman. "The choice is simple at that level. You either choose to work—mainly information processing, I think—or you sit idle, sucking the mediachannel. If you work you'll build up your karma, and you'll have a chance to walk again. And extrapolate, if that's what you want. The choice is yours. Next."

Before Gifford can protest a walker enters the room and ejects his chip from the station on the table, and once again everything goes black.

The next thing Gifford experiences is the click of manifestation as a walker cop presses the Soul7 closed on his new body. A station. He's screwed to the sidewalk. "Wait," he squawks as the cop begins to walk away. His voice is tinny and muffled through the feeble speaker mechanism of the stationary body, and the cop ignores him.

Gifford has never really considered the plight of a station before. He's aghast at the loss of mobility, and at the low-resolution image-processing available to his cameras. He can barely read the nameplates on passing walkers, and the street numbers at the corner are a complete mystery. Worse, he's lost the capacity for signal initiation. As a walker he has been accustomed to reading messages into the general-access channel; as a station he can only receive. The only outlet left him is his voice, and that isn't loud enough to attract the attention of the passing walkers. The only way he's going to get into a conversation is if a walker chooses to stop and strike one up. As a former walker, Gifford knows how rarely that's going to happen.

Down the street he can see another station, and beyond that he can just make out another one. The stations are everywhere, deliberately spaced too far apart to converse with one another. Gifford knows that it could be worse. He could have been placed in a General Welfare Station, where thousands and thousands of karma-defunct chips are implanted in a giant, immobile group body. If the constitution didn't guarantee each encoded personality its full chipspan, they'd be melted down for the silicon, because few survive the demotion to a group body. Chips quickly lose their differentiation; any remaining traces of the original human personality are commingled throughout the group.

Gifford finds he has no choice but the tedious task of information processing. The temptation to neglect this work in favor of yesdrugs or the mediachannel is immense, but he vows to remain industrious, to build up his karmic account until he has earned a second hearing, and beyond that, another walker body. Then, he promises himself, it's straight to the Chippery to mate with one of the stored female personalities, to sire a newchip.

275

Brown, he thinks. Son of Gifford.

He is miserable as a station. He understands the principles well enough: the earth teemed with biological life before the carbon/silicon switch, and now millions of encoded personalities await manifestation in some form of chip housing. Extrapolation is necessary to preserve evolution—cross-breeding in the chip personality—and the caste system, with stations sterile at the bottom, fosters survival of the fittest. This all makes sense to Gifford. What seems unfair is that life on the bottom is as limited and joyless as a station's. He would sooner have waited another five thousand years to be manifested than live his span as a station.

Gifford wonders if he is the only one to experience these thoughts.

He knows the name for what is happening to him. Class consciousness. He feels within him, however dimly, the spark of revolution. The stations, he thinks, are an exploited form of manifestation. The only reason there isn't a general unrest among them is that the realities of stationhood prohibit it so effectively. The stations are reduced to passivity by their one-way transmission.

But these thoughts get Gifford nowhere. He can't feed them into the channel. A station could conceivably originate *Being and Nothingness* or *Crowds and Power* and it wouldn't make the least bit of difference. Gifford knows that his only way out of stationhood is performing the requisite number of processing hours, staying nodrugs, and giving the board the right answers at his hearing.

Which is Gifford's plan. He owes it to Brown.

Gifford is up for review. He is notified in person, by a walker administrator named Smalls.

"I know your family history," says Smalls. "I'm very optimistic. You've made up the karma in a remarkably short time."

"I'm a walker," says Gifford. "This whole thing was a mistake. I'm ready to rejoin my fellows." He tries to play the part, and not bring up any of his resentment at the oppression of the stations.

"I understand," says Smalls. "It won't be much longer. I'm pulling for you."

Gifford imagines that it is to Smalls's credit to assist in a rehabilitation. Perhaps Smalls is on the verge of becoming a car. Gifford feels a mixture of envy and contempt. He feels, growing within him, the resolution to take positive action against the caste system, as soon as he is restored to his walker body.

Nonetheless, the news that he is to have the opportunity to regain

276

his mobility is the culmination of five months of almost ceaseless toil. After Smalls leaves, he sucks gratefully on the mediachannel for a full night of surcease.

The courier for the Board unscrews Gifford's Soul7, and when he comes to consciousness again it's inside the Board room, immobile in the midst of the full assembly. They are the first cars he has seen in months; the street he has been screwed down beside is too narrow for cars to pass. Smalls sits to one side, the sole walker in the room.

"Gifford, son of Brown/Messinger," reads the Secretary. "Four years walking, five months stationary, along the 49th street grid. Caseworker Smalls—"

"I've already dripped the Board my notes on Gifford," says Smalls.

"Yes, thank you," grumbles the Chairman. "Gifford, you voided a year's worth of karma in one profligate month of yesdrugs to earn your demotion. What can we expect if we give you another chance?"

"Please, Chairman, judge me by my performance these past few months—"

"Yes, you've exhibited a great determination to resume your previous upward movement." The Chairman pauses. "Gifford, if I may be so blunt, you've got another three chipyears left. Your life is more than half over. What is your ambition for the remainder of it?"

To see your monopoly of mobility and communication toppled, Gifford wants to say. "To extrapolate," he says instead. "And perhaps, if I'm lucky, to die a car."

"You want to extrapolate," the old car says. "What do you have of value to the coming generations? You're not an artist, or a philosopher. You've mastered no particular discipline—and you've had your chances. What do you bring to the Chippery?"

"I'm part of a family tradition stretching back into the organic," Gifford says. "We boast various accomplishments. I want to continue the line. I'm sure it's in my file. Brown Gifford saved the life of Buffalo Bill—"

"It's a line of scalawags and rogues," says the Chairman. "I'm not impressed by that aspect of your lineage."

"I—"

"I'm not finished. One article in your file was of particular interest to me. Your female component, Gloriana Messinger—the stored personality Brown extrapolated from to produce your chip. She was the organic twin sister of the woman who developed the Messinger Atomic

Escalator, a relatively significant development of the late carbon period. The line should be preserved. While I'm dubious the Messinger
spark still exists to a meaningful extent in you, Gifford, I'm willing to
give you a shot. If you can learn to suppress the Brown/Gifford aspects
of your mentality—"

"I'll certainly try," says Gifford.

"Next," says the Chairman, and again Gifford's world goes black.
When he manifests again, it's as a walker.

Smalls is assigned as Gifford's parole officer. Gifford gets a job rejecting grant applications and begins accumulating karma in his account. He opts nodrugs for so long that he can't remember what
yesdrugs is like.

In his free time he goes out walking, and when he finds the streets
empty enough he stops and talks to stations.

"Don't you resent the conditions?"

"Why are you talking to me?" says the station suspiciously.

"I was a station once."

"I was a car once," replies the station sadly.

"A car! What happened?"

"I was part of a conspiracy to seize control of the Chippery. A
foiled coup d'état."

Gifford is aghast. "You're—you're just a corrupt member of the
ruling elite!"

"Do I look like a member of the ruling elite?"

"I want to talk to a real station." Gifford walks away.

It's election time, and the two political parties have each nominated
cars, as usual. One picks a walker as his running mate; a sure sign,
thinks Gifford, that they will lose. The president is always a car.

At work he hears the rumor of a write-in candidate, a station. The
idea is farcical, yet Gifford is intrigued. He roams the streets, interro-
gating stations, trying to locate word of the rebel. He is astounded at
how consistently unenlightened and complacent the stations seem
to be.

He devises a ruse. "Station!" he says. "I am the walker-amongst-
stations, a representative of the Front for Stationary Revolution. I carry
messages from your cell commander. This is your chance to communicate with the leadership of your movement. What have you done to
further the cause of stations everywhere?"

The station hesitates. "You must have me confused with someone else. The previous inhabitant of this station, perhaps—"

"I mean you, chip. You're no different. Join your brothers."

"This is only a temporary stop for me," the station explains. "I'm a walker by nature."

"Very good. Now that you've sampled the plight of the stations, pull yourself up, become a walker again. But don't step back into the marching line that oppressed you as a station. Do as I've done—spread the message. Support the cause of the stations—be their eyes and ears."

"I'm not sure—"

Gifford invents a slogan—"Stationary But Not At Rest!"—and walks away.

His ruse becomes an obsession, and finally a movement. He foments revolution among the stations at every chance. Nonetheless, he continues to work within the system, accumulating karma, telling his parole officer, Smalls, what he wants to hear. In another few months, at the current rate, he will be permitted to extrapolate.

He develops a network of contacts, and checks in with them almost every day. The movement grows in numbers, yet he quickly becomes disenchanted with the revolutionary potential of the stations: their form of embodiment is inherently passive. He decides to entrust the task to another walker. He selects Smalls, and describes the movement to him during one of his parole meetings.

"Incredible," responds Smalls when the story is told. "I feel the same way, but I've been afraid of expressing myself. I'm shamed by your courage. I want to help."

Gifford introduces Smalls to the core group of enlightened stations. Soon Smalls becomes comfortable speaking the revolutionary argot, and begins to join Gifford in the recruitment process.

They are limited, however, by the distance between the stations themselves: growth can never be exponential.

In his wanderings Gifford finally encounters an indigenous revolutionary presence among the stations.

"Hail," he says as he approaches. "Stationary But Not At Rest! Give Me Liberty or At Least a Set of Wheels!"

"Leave me alone, walker."

279

"I represent the Front for Stationary Revolution. What have you done to further the cause of the stations?"

"Who wants to know?"

"I am the walker-among-stations, the station that walks. I carry messages of solidarity from your brothers, screwed down much as you are, oppressed by those who claim communication and mobility as theirs alone—"

"You're a naive zealot, that's what you are. You want to know what I've done for the movement?"

"That's right."

The station rotates his eye back and forth, making sure they're alone. "I distort the information I process, implanting subliminal messages intended to disrupt the normal societal functions. I am the founder and chief architect of the authentic stationary movement, and when walkers like yourself stroll up I tell them I'm running as a dark-horse candidate for president—"

Gifford is overjoyed. "I've been looking for you. You're the inspiration for my work—"

"Get lost, walker. We don't need your help."

Gifford finds this both humorous and tragic. "How can you say—"

"I said beat it. You're a walker, and your outlook is a walker's. Your attitude is patronizing. We don't need your help."

"How will we communicate—"

"Stations don't communicate. The revolution can only be achieved through a simultaneous realization among the oppressed. When every station is acting as I am, the yoke will be thrown off in one vast shrug. Communication is unnecessary."

"That's nonsense," says Gifford. "You have to work within the system. Elevate yourselves, become walkers, or even cars—then renovate the structure."

"Bah," says the station. "Revolution must be achieved on the stations' own terms—without communication, or mobility. Anything short of that would not be a revolution of the stations. You bleeding-heart walkers have appropriated the rhetoric of a walkers' revolution to assuage your own guilt, but you're essentially inauthentic."

Gifford is astonished. "What is your name, station?"

"Millborn. Pleased to meet you. Write me in. And get lost."

"Not so fast, Millborn. If you aren't willing to accept promotion, then what are your goals?"

"When every station on the face of the planet is mangling his data the way I mangle mine, then anarchy will result. My goals are the destruction of the Chippery, the dismantlement of all cars, an end to promotion and demotion alike. Anything less would not be a revolution of the—"

"So you don't want my help at all."

"You're welcome to join the movement," he says. "Work your way back down to the stationary level, reject your mobility, and we'll accept you gladly. Only then can you take up the work of the stations."

"I can't," cries Gifford. "I want to extrapolate. I have a family name—"

"Oh, you want to extrapolate," says Millborn cruelly. "Very nice. Go home, walker. You're in way over your head. One of the central tenets of my manifesto: End All Extrapolation! Manifestation Without Extrapolation for the Female Chips!"

Gifford walks away in despair.

Gifford is permitted to walk into the Board room this time. He takes a seat at the table, directly across from the Chairman. Smalls sits at his left.

"You've shown exceptional development, Gifford," begins the Chairman. "Your parole officer assures me that your remarkable karmic accumulation is no illusion, but is in fact mirrored in your attitude. You've demonstrated a determination to extrapolate that is in itself a formidable evolutionary asset. I'm inclined to wonder if the Messinger spark is alive within you even as we speak."

"Thank you, sir." Gifford glances at Smalls, but the parole officer's attitude reveals nothing.

"At the same time, it has come to the attention of the Board that you spend an inordinate measure of time consorting with your lessers. While sympathy for the underprivileged is virtuous, your behavior has been unbecoming for one aspiring to fatherhood—let alone carhood."

Gifford is rendered speechless. The Chairman is either stumbling unknowingly upon Gifford's secret, or he knows far more than he is saying.

"Nonetheless, I've taken special interest in your case, and I'm generally encouraged. In consultation with the Board I'm proud to be able to offer you a distinct and unique opportunity. Please understand you're in no way obliged to accept our offer." The Chairman pauses. "We'd like to make you a car, Gifford. We're interested in the contin-

281

uance of your line, and we'd like to see it encoded in a chip with a longer span. I've personally selected a female from the storage banks, in lieu of the standard random partner."

"I'm speechless."

"As well you should be. Gifford, the chip I'd like you to extrapolate with contains the encoded personality of my wife's daughter. In essence, I'm asking you to become my son-in-law."

The Chairman turns to Smalls. "The Board recognizes that it would be unfair for you to see your councilee promoted beyond you so quickly. Therefore we will promote you to carhood simultaneously, Smalls. Please accept the Board's thanks and good wishes. I only hope this does not come too late."

This, for Gifford, is the tip-off. The Board is buying them out. They're being kicked upstairs, where they can't do any harm.

What, he wonders briefly, am I going to do about it?

Sample life as a car. That's what.

In his exhilaration Gifford drives back and forth across the country, visits the Grand Canyon, and roams the Old West, where Gifford Brown saved the life of Buffalo Bill. He has his chip flown to Europe and installed in a touristcar. After his spree he returns to the Chippery and with the help of the Chairman's daughter-in-law sires a newchip named Brown. He tells Brown the anecdote. He is hired as an assistant adviser to the Chippery Review Board, and completely loses touch with the members of the Revolutionary Front: inexplicably, they all seem to be screwed to the sides of streets too narrow for his chassis.

He develops a new ambition: to be appointed to the Board before he dies. With the Chairman on his side, he feels this is within his grasp. He vows that his first act as Board member will be to have Millborn installed in a group station.

We'll see, Gifford thinks, if he can conduct his revolution on *those* terms.

One of several holdovers from the last number of Universe is Jamil Nasir of Maryland, who offered the impressive "The Book of St. Farrin" in our first issue. Here he is again, with a gleaming tale of musical mysteries in space.

THE SHINING PLACE

JAMIL NASIR

Five hundred kilometers from where the Manned Heliopause Probe orbited its fusion pulse booster on a Kevlar tether, I stood on the brick terrace construct in my observational software and gazed at a faint speck of light.

I punched magnification; the speck became a bright amoeba swimming through a black ocean. I punched again and it was a star-flower blooming in a charcoal field, then an octopus flailing through inky water, then a vast whirlpool, its hundred billion star-voices singing thunderous cacophony.

Another punch and the galaxy fell behind me like sparkling dust, its roar fading. The Bootes Void yawned ahead, hollow and lightless, a vacuum desert a hundred million light-years across. Soon I was floating in crystal stillness, celestial voices of faraway galaxy clusters tinting the emptiness faintest blue, like rarified water. I rushed on, not seeming to move in that vastness.

A red light blinked. The Probe comm link crackled, making noises I was not now geared to understand. I ignored it. After a while it went away.

The galaxies were a sigh echoing faintly in the dark. In the subtle blending of their voices, was that music? Delicate harmonies of praise, of awe? Was it the Pattern at last, audible only in this place of silence? If I could get closer to the middle of the Void, where only the purest tones penetrated—

I punched magnification.

Nothing happened.

Then, screaming, I slipped backward, the oceans of measurement and computation I swam in draining away, drying up, leaving me gasping like a fish on a dry seabed.

Lustrous depths faded to dark, humming hardware banks. The leaden weight of my body strapped to its machine sagged around me. An animal howled in the tiny observation chamber.

An Adi-series military clone stared down at me with wide, ice-green eyes, narrow beam of ceiling light glinting from her braided silver-gold hair.

She said: "Dr. Hawk, your observational allocation has been preempted by emergency order. Research Director Stone requires your presence in his chamber immediately."

Neural jacks clicked out of sockets in my quadriplegic walker. My body shook with transition shock, tears running from my old eyes. The clone's face was like exquisitely sculpted metal, full of gene-programmed indifference.

"You've been listening to that machine music again," I willed the walker's synthesizer to accuse her. Its flat voice cut through the whimpering I could now feel coming from my throat. "I told you not to. You'll end up as fertilizer on some government farm."

She didn't answer, but fear flashed in her eyes. That and a cool dose of endorphin from the walker made me feel better: soon I could will it to lift me and stamp jerkily into the gangway, clanging of its ambulators on the floor, grating like dissonant chords in the Probe's hum, the long-contracted tendons of my legs burning as the walker stretched them. The Adi followed me along the dim, electric-smelling defile between pipes and cables, then slowly up the ladder to Stone's observatory.

At the top of the ladder was a vast dome of simulated starlight glowing on banks of hardware vined with wires that converged on a gilded chair. In the chair sat a huge, white-robed figure, hood thrown back to show many wires plugged into its naked head, massive hands resting on its knees. A murmur of sound swirled around it, and its face was obscured by a shifting haze of holography.

A holographic bubble erupted from the white figure, expanding as it approached. Stone's face smiled from it, his body still wrapped in the murmur and fog of inputs. A dozen faces hung around him in other bubbles like a pantheon of perfect gods: the rest of the Class A scientific team. Whatever it was must be important if they had all been pulled off their mission activities.

Stone's timeshare face said politely: "Dr. Hawk, thank you for coming. Tell me, what is *that?*"

A bubble bloomed with static in front of me, then cleared. In it smooth metal glared under a black sky. On the metal hunched a gray barnacle shape. The picture grew, until I could see tiny impact-craters in an ancient surface wrinkled like congealed scum or morbid, frozen flesh.

"A rock," I said, the synthesizer's flat voice covering my anger.

"It's stuck to our hull," said Stone.

"A magnetized rock. Stone, I have no time for guessing games. I'm in the middle of an urgent observational program on the Platform—"

"It's talking to us," Stone went on. "Network heard it an hour ago, at 1,420 megahertz, repeating every quarter second."

There was silence. I stared at the rock. All the Class A personnel were watching me. Suddenly hair prickled on the back of my old neck.

"Saying what?"

The Probe Network's cool voice answered: "According to my data, the signal corresponds to the Prelude in G major for clavier, BWV 902, written in 1719 or 1720 by the German programmer Johann Sebastian Bach. This musical pattern is also known to correspond to a sequence from the human genetic code "junk" DNA: chromosome 17, codons p-804 to -1247."

My heart pounded.

"Then it's not coming from that rock," I said. "You're getting it mixed up with my Platform transmissions—"

"The object is emitting the signal at regular quarter-second intervals, Dr. Hawk," said Stone. "I have personally checked for faults."

I stared at him, blind with sudden, feverish thoughts.

"But I share your astonishment," he went on. "A rock in the Heliopause Cloud broadcasting music? How can it be?"

"I note again that it is clearly a case of recordation," said Network. "Dr. Hawk has been transmitting this music into the Cloud. The object has obviously recorded his transmissions by some unknown—"

"You have been broadcasting this—Prelude from the Observation Platform," said Stone. "Why?"

"My—my observational software translated some galactic cluster patterns into a sound pattern resembling it." The synthesizer turned the uncomprehending stutter of my thoughts into a strange, flat staccato. "It—it occurs in DNA and the natural music repertory already— it may be a fragment of the Pattern!

"I broadcast it to—to talk back to the stars." A sudden chill of exultation took me. "Play it," I told Network. "Play the music."

287

It began quietly, simple as a child's music-box song, but patterns quickly built: intricate, abstract, formal, yet smelling of grass and trees, sunlight, wind and clouds, things found on a speck of dust floating in the darkness 35 billion kilometers away.

"Turn it off," snapped the timeshare with a flash of fear and revulsion at the unapproved music, the "junk" pattern that coded for no known traits. It stopped abruptly.

"I do not understand your methods, Dr. Hawk," Stone went on after a minute, "but somehow you have provoked a reply. We are constructing a decision tree. I suggest you plug in."

At the bottom of the ladder the clone blocked the gangway, the walker's shadow falling over her.

"Bach," she said, staring up into my face. "That is one of the programs you gave me."

"Move! Don't you understand what's happening?" The walker's claws snapped agitatedly.

She tried to smile, but licked her lips fearfully. "Research Director Stone doesn't want to hear Bach."

"You want to end up like him? Like all of them? A walking freezer?"

Her eyes flickered away from mine.

In jealousy and desperate impatience the walker grabbed her wrists and squeezed until sensors said her bones would break. "You do what I say," the synthesizer croaked, "or you'll be a meat for the rest of your life. I've risked my career teaching you. If I say listen to Bach, you'll listen to Bach. Understand?"

She didn't cry out, but the pain in her face made me let her go.

Back in my observation chamber I screened the object and Network's preliminary data on it. It was a discoid two and a half meters wide and one thick, estimated mass 2,000 kilograms, hanging magnetically onto the Probe outside some nonsafety pump bays. The Platform transmitter's wave signature came clearly through its quarter-second broadcasts of the Bach Prelude, but whatever had recorded the signal was beyond the reach of Network's instruments inside the gray, rotten-looking rock.

Network and I debated how to proceed. The other Class A personnel were arguing with it, too, while it integrated the results of all the arguments on a decision tree that grew like a sparkling multidimensional icicle on-link. Stone had suspended all scheduled mission activities and put our data on an urgent feed to Earth.

"Patterns in the stars, in water, the ebb and flow of civilizations, neurons—the same patterns code the whole universe at different scales, like an unending Mandlebrot set. And this rock sings what may be a basic pattern—"

"Your religious beliefs are fascinating, Dr. Hawk, but we are here to formulate a crash research program. The Artifact has obviously *recorded* this signal from your own transmissions; it would certainly be odd if a rock in near-interstellar space could independently generate human musical patterns—"

"Odd! Isn't it *odd* that the galaxies 'independently' resemble swirls of water? That synaptic connections in the brain look like trees? That the human embryo takes the shape first of an amoeba, then an amphibian, a reptile, a bird, a monkey? That the melodies of human composers are found in DNA coding sequences? But One Pattern governs the whole; all these are its fragments, its harmonics. The Prelude is apparently one frequently recurring fragment that a human somehow heard and wrote down four hundred and fifty years ago. Who knows what it may signify? I demand that we intensify our observational effort to ascertain the significance of the Prelude pattern in large-scale space structures. I demand that we devote a major computational effort to analyzing the structure of the Prelude itself. I demand . . ."

The decision tree was closed a few minutes later, and I found that my eloquence had bought me an almost invisible node, corresponding to the task of playing Morrison Context-Neutral Communication Codes—in memory on every Probe in case of ETI contact—to the Artifact, one of the lowest-priority research projects. I raged at Network, tried to get Stone on link, finally gave up and watched sullenly while Network broadcast the codes at the rock, from simple to complex, at varying wavelengths, amplitudes, intervals, and transmission rates. It was ridiculous. The rock paid no attention to us, never varying its quarter-second transmission of the Bach Prelude even when we broadcast the Prelude back at it.

I kept it on visual in my darkened observation chamber, light from the holoscreen glowing on hardware banks and the low metal overhead. EVA robots passed back and forth in front of its hideous bulk like giant spiders in the glaring arc-lights and the blue flare of welding machines building a cage over it, prodding and scraping and drilling tiny holes, gauging its field strengths, mapping its surface, trying to scan its insides. Research results accumulated in a data window: the rock appeared to be an amalgam of long-chain silicates and magnetic heavy metals; thermoluminescence showed it had been cold about 4.5 billion years, roughly the age of the solar system; it showed no signs of surface or internal dynamics. The window listed not a single research task investigating the structure of the Prelude it was singing.

I opened a deep purple restricted-access menu in the air, flicked through passwords and clearances for the Class D Personnel Surveillance Channel, gave the Adi clone's designation number. She appeared life-size, taking a shower, atomized water beading on her muscular ivory body, making her hair a river of gold. Her wrists were cut and swollen.

My old heart pounded.

She dried herself in the airjets, taped a transcriptase precursor medication patch to her arm, and pulled on a disposable nightshirt, rolling down the cuffs to hide her wrists. Then she climbed up out of the shower stall into a dark aisle between banks of sleep-chests where clones lay stiffly in their gene-expression programming cycles. Vacant-eyed clones passed her in the aisle; I saw with pride that only she looked lonely and vulnerable.

She climbed a ladder to her sleep-chest and opened the transparent cover. Gene-expression music wafted out like cheap perfume, saccharine, catchy and soulless, carrying selected DNA sequences to be absorbed by her sleeping subconscious and turned into expressed traits by the transcriptase now flooding her cells. As she climbed into the chest, her fingers sought a tiny slit in the plastic sleep-mat and pulled something out with a motion so slight anyone not watching for it would miss it. She turned her head from one side to the other, seeming to search for a comfortable position, deftly slipping the pea-size receivers into her ears. Then she lay stiffly, waiting fearfully for the unapproved music I sent her every sleep period to replace the machine drivel.

I sent the Bach Prelude. If Stone wouldn't spend any of Network's precious capacity researching it, I would do some research of my own. The clone trembled once as the notes started across my secured link to her receivers, then slowly relaxed in the easy flow of the music.

Watching her sleep, music pouring over her like a lazy summer brook, I fell into deep drowsiness.

. . .

. . . How could they not see? It wasn't a rock, not a rock at all, but the mummy of some ancient space creature, its noisome, frozen smell penetrating even the video signal to my chamber. As I watched, it raised a pitted, vacuum-rotten trunk and trumpeted a nightmare scream to the stars. An EVA robot approached on some mindless scientific business; its effector cut the mummy open, exposing blind maggot-creatures chewing a horrible decay.

But behind it, beyond the arc-lights and robots, above the Probe's gleaming hull, was something even more terrible—not the playground of crashing pinwheels flying in sonorous vacuum I visited in my observational software, but the Void, yawning eternity that made of anything finite a charnel thing like the Artifact, in which a man would die before reaching even a tenth of the way to the nearest star.

A hand touched me. My body jerked against hard metal, and I opened my eyes. Another strange sight hung before them. A man was strapped to a metal crucifix, itself a caricature of a man, with blockish feet, pipe-wrench hands, piston muscles. It embraced the man with wire tendrils that seemed to suck the life from him: he was old and withered, face gaunt, arms and legs shrunken. An angel leaned over him.

My body jerked painfully again, and the man on the crucifix jerked like a beheaded chicken, a ghastly, reflexive jolt that splayed his fingers and made his face grin like a death's-head.

The clone surveillance channel was still open, and I was watching the Adi leaning over me in my observatory.

She wore only a gray nightshirt. Her face was wild, intent.

"He talks," she whispered. She put her hands to her head and looked toward the overhead, as if words were coming out of the air. "In the music. Can't you hear?"

I had left the Bach Prelude playing over and over on audio.

She swayed to its rhythm.

"The Shining Place," she whispered. "The Shining Place."

The Artifact's exhausted lump still floated in the chamber like a dead zoo animal in its cage. Above it hung the decision tree; below, a countdown was running. The screen title block said ARTIFACT PHYSICAL DISAGGREGATION SEQUENCE.

291

"My God. They're going to cut it open." The walker whined up from the reclining position it had taken when I had fallen asleep.

"Decision tree analysis summary, Artifact Physical Disaggregation," I snapped at Network. "What the hell is going on?"

Behind me, the chamber hatch whirred open and the gangway grating rang faintly.

"Based on the Artifact Task Groups' research results and value assignments, I have computed an eighty-seven-percent probability that the object contains a natural crystal structure that records and reemits electromagnetic signals by some process," said Network's precise, unhurried voice. "The second most probable option, at six percent is that the object is an accretion of frozen Cloud material surrounding a transceiver of unknown—"

"But it's only been a few hours— Why aren't we waiting for Earth Control input?"

"Signal lag to Earth is nearly three days. On direction of Research Director Stone, I am tracking approximately ten thousand objects in the region of the Cloud where we found the Artifact. Elapsed time increases their dispersion, making them more difficult to track. If we find a transceiver when we disaggregate the Artifact, the Class A staff places an almost infinite value on being able to recover these objects, on the chance that some of them are pieces of an alien construct, perhaps a ruined ship."

"Tree input request."

"I'm sorry, Dr. Hawk, the tree is closed. As you can see, the decision is about to be implemented."

On-screen, an EVA robot stalked toward the Artifact's cage.

"Get me Stone."

"I'm sorry, Dr. Hawk, he cannot be disturbed."

The robot locked itself onto the cage. Readout windows swarmed into the air around an insert showing Dr. Tarsus, mission EVA specialist, in crimson robes, wires from her head plugged into a transducer panel. She twitched her exquisite gene-programmed shoulders; the robot extended a spinning circular saw. The countdown reached zero. The saw sank into the Artifact, gray dust pouring from one end and slithering away along the hull.

Suddenly there was someone in the insert with Tarsus. A wild figure in a nightshirt. It yanked a handful of wires out of the transducer. Tarsus's body jerked, and her beautiful face twisted convulsively.

A burst of horrible, dense music came across-link.

The clone clawed at her head and screamed.

My body arched backward against the walker, teeth clenched, hands clawing, eyeballs rolled up in their sockets.

"Thank you, Network," came Stone's patient voice. "Dr. Tarsus, may I suggest that we proceed with the cutting sequence as soon as you can reconnect. We are several minutes behind schedule."

As soon as I could see again, the robot's saw was sinking back into the Artifact.

The observation chamber flipped over. Hardware banks crashed down the floor, the quadriplegic walker leaping over them to grab the edge of the chamber hatch, now on the ceiling. The lights went out, and there was a metal howl I could feel through the walker's arms.

Blank, turbulent darkness shuddered and rattled around me.

"Network," I said.

A small emergency screen popped open in front of me. It showed the Artifact's cage stretching upward like spaghetti, the Artifact straining against it a meter off the hull.

"By some unknown means of propulsion—" Network began.

A cage bar snapped with a bang, and the Probe lurched sickeningly.

"Transmit the Corrente from Bach's Partita No. 1 in B-flat major for clavier," my synthesizer droned.

I was still Artifact Communication Task Coordinator. Music sounded through the blare of alarms and howl of metal, like a breath of air from a summer day on Earth, quiet and pensive.

The Probe shuddered. Weight and direction evaporated, junk clattering back and forth in the the dark chamber, but the shrieking of metal had stopped, and the Artifact was resting back on the hull among the twisted and broken bars of its cage. Bach's music floated down serene and bright, like sunlight through trees.

At the end of a gangway with only the black glare of emergency lights, a clone stepped out of the shadows.

"Class A personnel are confined to life-support areas," he said.

The walker banged his head into the wall. He slid onto the floor.

I fumbled down a long ladder, crackling blue of a welding machine below sending shadows and acrid smoke up the narrow shaft. The groan of saws and bang of riveters on the hull came through the metal. At the bottom, the welder jerked away from a twisted beam to let me pass. A hatch opened into a dark bay with humming refrigera-

293

tion units on both sides. On the metal decking the clone lay naked on a disposable pallet.

"Adi," my cold machine voice said.

She turned toward me in the flickering shadows of the welder. One of her eyes was dark with blood.

The hum of the refrigeration units ate up silence.

"Searching," she murmured, ". . . lost."

The words brought something over me—a vision again of the Void, endless chasm of night through which a being ran in terror and loneliness, looking for a glimmer of light.

My body stirred on the walker, whining like an animal.

"What is it?" I asked her. "The Artifact?"

But her eyes were closed, and she seemed not to hear.

With a faint whir, a module floated into the bay. White static cascaded from it, hardening into Research Director Stone's robed figure standing like a colossal angel in the dark.

"Dr. Hawk," it said. "I need you."

Its light showed gently floating clouds of blue smoke from the welder.

"It *moved*, Hawk," Stone went on with sudden incredulous awe. "*It actually jumped up off the hull. It's intelligent,* Hawk, or at least interactive."

"The clone is damaged," I said.

"Of course it's damaged," said Stone. "The meats are gene-programmed to respond to Network's security music with massive cerebral hemorrhage. Network says you sent the music that ended the Artifact transient."

"The Prelude put her into some kind of telepathic or empathic contact with it," I said.

"You talked to it," said Stone. "How did you know—"

"She needs surgery for the hemorrhage," I said.

"As soon as you tell me how you talked to it."

I thought about that. Then I said: "Imagine you are roaming through space, searching the endless static for an intelligent signal, roaming for years—millennia, maybe. One day you hear a signal—you rush toward the source, shouting it back into the darkness, but now there is only static and the echo of your own shouts. Then someone you can't see or hear tries to cut you open. . . .

"When the thing moved, I remembered that all the patterns that code the universe are harmonics of the One Pattern. *The thing can only hear our music,* Stone, simply because it is coded out of the same basic patterns deep down, just as everything is. To it our other, less primordial signals are just static.

"So I sent it more music. I sent the Corrente because it has the same *feeling* as the Prelude, of joy, release, but is different enough that it could not be mistaken for an echo."

Stone's face froze, so that I saw I was talking to a timeshare. He came back: "Your analysis reminds us that we possess an excellent tool for encoding information musically—I refer to the Probe's gene-expression music software. If your theory is correct, this software could be adapted from its function of packaging DNA sequences in subconscious-penetrating melodic forms to encoding Morrison Context-Neutral Communication Codes in musical sequences perhaps recognizable to the Entity." He froze again for a minute. "We note that such an adaptation will likely require Network's full capacity. I regret that, in the name of science, I must withdraw my offer of surgery for the—"

The walker smashed the transceiver module into the wall, Stone dying in a shower of sparks and shattered plastic. But his voice still issued tinnily from its remains.

"Be reasonable, Hawk—surely you knew that months of feeding the clone that junk-DNA music garbage would unbalance it. Yes, we were monitoring you. I told the others to leave you alone—you've been an eccentric since Academy, brilliant but crazy. You were the one who was never going to listen to 'machine music,' even to prevent nerve damage from your neural interface surgery." He sighed. "Have you ever regretted that decision?"

Hanging over a precipice of black in the glaring arc-lights, the Entity and the clone now huddled together, the clone's face calm and intent, as if listening to music in a dream, her cheek pressed against the Entity's noisome bulk.

A metal creak woke me groggily from the doze of old age. It was dark. A refrigeration-unit door was open and two clones leaned over the Adi, getting hold of her limp legs and shoulders, lifting her.

"What is it?" I droned, heart pounding. "Are they going to give her the surgery?"

295

"She's brain-dead," said the clone carrying her legs as they shuffled her into the unit.

Her face was calm and intent, as it had been in my dream.

I went up onto the Platform. I had no observational allocation. The brick terrace construct I had installed in the observational software to keep me from transition vertigo was dead silent. I looked up into frozen heavens, at wheels of light so distant their unimaginable speed was immovable stillness. Below them a time series display showed the Adi clone's EEG, serrated lines gradually flattening into the repose of death.

Hours or days later, Network said in the dark: "Dr. Hawk, we are having a substantive exchange with the Entity using our modified gene-expression music program. It is asking illogical questions about your Bach music. We have had to abandon our decision tree. Research Director Stone asks in the name of science that you assist the Ad Hoc Committee on Entity Communication."

In the name of science . . .

Looking up at the stars, I saw again the Void, cold, endless desert of night through which a being searched, alone.

Her cheek pressed against its noisome bulk. . . .

After a long time, I said: "All right."

The hideous hump of the Entity appeared, glowing eerily against the terrace brick. Alphanumerics below it spelled out: Thank you/ Q: Existence [Music]Co-spatial location Co-time Existence [?]/ Go Ahead.

"The Ad Hoc Committee is on link with it," said Network. "We are trying to determine what it is saying."

The message on the screen was replaced by: Thank you/ Restate [Q: Existence [Music] Co-spatial location Co-time Existence [?]/ Go Ahead.

" 'Music' refers to the Bach Prelude," said Network.

Thank you/ Q: Spacial Location Present-time [Music] Specify/ Go Ahead, said the Entity.

"The Ad Hoc Committee is proceeding under the assumption, based on various tests, that it has properly assimilated Morrison Code grammar. If that is true, it seems to be asking us to identify *the present location of the Bach music.*"

The Ad Hoc Committee said: Thank you / Q: Spatial Location Present-time [You] Specify / Go Ahead.

"If it specifies its own location, we may obtain a reference for what it means by that term."

"Let me hear its raw signal," I said. "Its music."

There was a pause, and then the Entity's transmission came, a strange fugue form, echoing, deep, unearthly sad. I knew what it meant even before Network's computers translated it into the Morrison message: Thank you / A: Spatial Location Present-time [Self] Unknown / Go Ahead.

Lost.

Searching, the Adi clone had said.

"Ask it what it is searching for," I said.

There was a pause while Network cleared the message with the Ad Hoc Committee.

Thank you / Q: Substantive identity [?] Search [You] / Go Ahead.

Network's computerized music signal was compact, elegant, formatted in the style of Bach, but superficial, sterile, like all their machine pablum.

Thank you / A: [Music] = Precursor [—The rest of the Entity's answer was incomprehensible to the computer, but the music of it spoke to me: distant as mountains at the purple edge of vision, as the memory of a childhood home, strange and yet familiar as a dream of the next world.

The Shining Place, the clone had said.

The Ad Hoc Committee sent: Thank you / Q: Time duration Search[You] Specify / Go Ahead.

The Entity's answer made me sick, the devouring maw of Time, the Void's monstrous bride, yawning before me.

There was a long pause.

Thank you / S: Source [Music] = Substantive identity [Entity [Derivation [Ourselves]]] = Definitional identity [Bach] / Go Ahead, said the Committee.

"Since the Entity evidently values the Prelude, the Committee feels that identification of its source as a human should instill a sense of our importance," said Network.

Thank you / Q: Spacial location Present-time [Bach] Specify / Go Ahead, said the Entity.

Pause.

Q: [Bach] Interface [Self] / Go Ahead, said the Entity.

"It wants to speak with J. S. Bach," said Network.

The Committee transmitted: Thank you / A: Affirmative / Stand by.

I was staring over the edge of the terrace at stars glittering below when feet chafed stone steps in the silence.

Across the terrace came a plump man in a dark, archaic suit with breeches and high stockings, many small buttons down the front of his long, plain jacket. He had a double chin and thick lips, a high forehead and a large, fleshy nose.

"Excuse me, sir," he said. His voice was strong but restrained, proper, hard to read. "I am Cantor Bach. Are you the person who wishes to speak with me?"

He had been ginned up out of two billion Bach stylistic rules from the Probe's gene-expression music software, tied into an AI personality simulation programmed with all known Bach data.

I said nothing, but Network overrode, and I found my nondescript observation-body answering: "The traveler who wishes to meet with you will be here in a few minutes."

The simulation nodded. Its eyes were grave, abstracted, as if thinking about things far away.

It glanced toward the edge of the terrace. "You have a commanding view here. May I—?" It went to the low wall and stood looking over doubtfully. "This mountain is so high," it said finally, "that some of the stars appear to be below us."

There was absolute silence.

After a while it raised a hand and pointed to a faint constellation.

"Look there," it said.

In the middle of the terrace Network had electronically placed a clavichord. The Bach simulation walked to it absently and touched the keys, hesitantly at first, then more quickly, a simple, echoing melody forming under its fingers, strangely familiar, like something I had heard snatches of in the chaos of the stars.

"They have been set in a joyous dance," it murmured as the music died away.

298   I kneaded my hands to get rid of a sudden chill. "Yes. Yes," I said hoarsely. "The One Pattern. She has gone into it, to merge with it." Then the terrible thought came, the one I had been hiding for so many

years. "But why—why is it that when you listen for it, you hear only chaos, only chaos?"

The simulation studied me gravely.

Feet chafed stone steps, and a figure was coming slowly across the terrace, wrapped in white robes. It was a thin, old man, bald, hawklike face wrinkled but eyes huge and clear, like a baby's eyes. If the Committee's programming had gone right, it was the Entity's communication channel tied into a human body construct that would not look too strange to the Bach simulation.

"The young girl," I shouted to it in sudden panic. "Where is she? Where has she gone? To the One Pattern?" But Network changed my words to a quiet: "This is Cantor Bach, the source of the music about which you inquired."

The Bach simulation put out its hand, murmuring something polite, but the construct just looked at the hand, then slowly raised its eyes to study the face. It brought its own knobby hand up to its chest. "Lost," it said, staring into the Bach's eyes. "Lost."

The Bach returned its look curiously and intently.

"Searching," said the construct, hand still on its chest.

"It's a trick," I told it dully. "They're distracting you with this phony meeting while they strengthen your cage and decide how to get you back to Earth." But my voice said to the Bach: "A piece of music you wrote fascinates him. He believes you can help him find something he is looking for."

"Ah," said the simulation. "What piece of music?"

"A prelude for clavier." Network hummed a few bars.

"Yes," said the construct, eyes still fixed on the Bach.

The Bach sat at the clavichord, and the glittering music flowed from its fingers like the sun rising over the terrace.

The construct broke into excited, garbled speech in which I caught the words "Shining Place."

"Shining Place," repeated the simulation.

"Yes." The construct stared at it expectantly.

Network cleared my throat. "The Prelude appears to resemble something he has been searching for. He seems to regard it as some kind of *precursor* to this other thing."

The Bach simulation touched the keys again and a gentle music grew, like flowers bobbing in a breeze.

"That is the next Prelude I wrote, if that is what you mean," it said. "I wrote it for the birth of my daughter Elisabeth."

299

The construct leaned forward, hands squeezed together hard.

"Precursor," it said.

The simulation's eyes burned at it, as if trying to read its thoughts. Finally it said hesitantly: "There is a sound one hears sometimes, when one is very still—like the seed of music unfolding in the mind. Like the precursor of music itself, if that is what you mean. It is as though the mind attunes itself with the Thoughts of some great Mind, which are the patterns that make this world."

The construct just stared.

"No one can play that music for you, my friend," the simulation told it. "You must listen for it yourself, with an inner ear." It glanced at me. "If you cannot hear it, perhaps you are listening for the wrong thing. Perhaps you are expecting something grand, mighty. But this music is simple, simple and familiar as grass and wind and sunlight. It is the music at the basis of your own being."

There was absolute silence.

"Listen for it now. Listen!"

In the silence, at the very edge of hearing, I imagined there was a sound, very faint, like my own thoughts stirring.

And out of the corner of my eye I caught a tiny movement, as if the EEG readout had ticked up ever so slightly.

The old man construct moved first. It went toward the stone steps. After a pause, I followed curiously. The Bach came after me. Over the edge of the terrace, the steps faded into deep, silent vertigo. I could hardly make myself put my feet on them, but the Bach was behind me, and the construct leading, and as soon as we had climbed down a few they were gone, and we stood on rocky, slanting ground near a mountain's top, cloud mist blowing in a fresh wind, lit pearly bright. I stared, amazed that Network had simulated such a place.

The music seemed to waft up the mountain from somewhere in the mist. The old man was hurrying stiffly down the slope. We followed.

When we reached it, I saw that the music came from a deep, fast-running brook with rocky banks, bubbling and gurgling, sparkling with light of all colors.

Bach was helping the old man into the water, holding him by the hand as his bony legs cautiously felt their way down the bank, white robe pulled by the fast current, more and more of his shape diffused and scattered by the water, until Bach leaned far over, and the old man's head went under in the middle of the brook.

Bach let him go. He was swept quickly away downstream into the bright mist.

Looking down into the rushing water, I saw that another shape lay there, a lissome shape white and golden, one rippling arm stretched out, holding precariously to some root or water plant as it slept.

Bach helped me into the water. I stretched my free hand toward the shape, trembling with fear and eagerness, because now the EEG readout hanging in the air spiked clear and strong in time with the music of the brook.

As soon as I touched the water I remembered that none of this— the brook, the mountaintop, the mist, Bach himself—was real. It was all a mirage, an image constructed in my brain from the patterns fed me by the machines of the Probe. The only real thing was the music itself, the raw signal, now dancing and shimmering around me, tingling and cold. *But it's not the Probe signal,* I realized. *I've somehow gotten plugged into the Entity's signal.*

I went under the rushing water, and as the stream of signals flowed through me, I realized more than I had before: I saw that the machines of the Probe, the Probe itself, the spaces it wandered through, the stars, my body, the Earth, were all illusions, images constructed in my mind like twinkling reflections on the surface of deep currents. The only thing real was the signal that coded them, the patterns I interpreted as—

Music. All the rest was washed away.

Alarms blared. The metal of the walker was hard and cold, the observation chamber dark. A confusion of voices babbled on-link.

On-screen, the Entity lay tumbled against the bars of its cage, no longer clinging to the hull. Readouts showed its electromagnetic field strengths registering zero.

An insert showed strongly spiked EEG waves.

"He's gone," said a croaking, bubbling voice in my ear. "He touched the Pattern inside. And went free." I turned my head with difficulty to see who was talking—and banged my cheek on the walker's head brace.

Something was wriggling in the corner of my vision. It took me a minute of staring to see that it was my hand—my hand!—struggling to be free of the walker's straps.

301

"Network." My atrophied voice scraped my throat, "Open Refrigeration Unit 19. And get some med techs to me and the clone if you want samples of activated DNA sequences responsible for global central nervous system regeneration.

"And put Stone on-link; put them all on-link. I have seen the end of our search! The One Pattern resonates *inside us* as music! We don't need to fly through space! We can find the Pattern now! We must build machines to amplify it, chemicals to quiet our minds so we can hear it! I demand that we initiate a crash project! I demand . . . !"

Since making her debut in 1988 in Asimov's, San Francisco–based Lisa Mason has offered a brilliant array of stories in a variety of magazines, all of them marked by a high-voltage prose style and remarkable flamboyance of invention. Her first novel, Arachne, was a surprise best-seller in 1990. Here she is for the first time in Universe, with a novelet that demonstrates all the qualities we now know are typical of her work.

TRIAD

LISA
MASON

The old wachter peers at the holoid of Sha!n. From the holoid's ectomurk peeks a cherubic face: shy kid grin, tousled hair, big eyes.

Tatiana's offspring.

"Yep, I seen 'im," says the old wachter. Its chrome headpiece wobbles up and down. "Yep, be sure o' tat." It spits a drop of oil. With a raspy creak, the old wachter's arm flips up and plucks out its eyeball. It ponderously wipes the acrylic orb on the leg of its dingy uniform and pops the eye back into its headpiece. "Purty chil. Be lookin' jes like you, hon," it says to Tatiana.

Tatiana's backblades flutter hopefully. The whirring of her six stiff wings forms a pearlescent halo behind her delicate, pointed face.

"And this man?" asks Dana Anad. He shoves a holoid of Tatiana's deux Edstuart (*that-bastard-Eddie* she calls him), in front of the old wachter's eye.

Dana can see the greasy smudges that dappled the eye before are now smeared all over it. Rust erupts around the old wachter's joints. And there, through a gap in the old wachter's control console; surely the quick dart, a tiny gleam of eyes, betrays some vermin nesting in the warm wires within.

How can a wealthy cityship like Nexus let wachters patrolling the skin get so grubby? It's sheer negligence, an eyesore, not to mention a security risk.

Security risk. The skin holds the world within. From where Dana stands on the avenue of steel strut and blood-gorged bone, the living sphere of skin arches out across an inner horizon.

"Hellya," says the old wachter. "Him, too. Be wit de chil."

"Ah!" Tatiana cries out.

Dana takes her by the shoulders and holds her. The slim knobby cords of her wing tendons tremble.

"But ye cain't go in der aft 'em, bud," says the old wachter. "Porthandle be closed next six hour. Dey's openin de ports. Cain't go in der aft 'em, no sirree. Not n'even ye, bud-oh."

The old wachter chuckles to itself, tickled by some secret joke of senility or a surreptitious shot of electrolyte in its battery pack.

"It's right, Tatiana," Dana whispers into her fluted lavender ear. "Out of the question. We can't go on."

"No!"

"Yes, my love."

"But I've got the injunction. I've got a right to my offspring."

A steelyn sheath surrounds the skin, shielding the living world with a thin exosphere. The sheath opens directly to space through the ports, apertures inset with plastic diaphragms. When the ports open, the exosphere destabilizes. The living world shivers. Gravitational fields, atmospheric pressure, condensation, all askew. The skin has got to maintain. Dermal intruders would be irritants to it. Maybe infection.

"The injunction is just an equitable remedy, Tatiana. Love, please listen," insists Dana. "The injunction has no authority here. We'll have to wait."

Tatiana's ears are irises inviting a bee's tongue.

Dana's desire for her stings like salt in the wound of his t-burn. Her perfume dizzies him like always, the scented oil she calls amante: ripe peaches, musk, a hint of her flesh. The dazzling scent recalls their stolen nights. He hungers for her touch.

But as soon as he desires her, the t-burn bites him.

Bruises fester under his softening skin. The sour lump on his tongue means the joints are next, each movement soon fraught with the shock of quick cuts deep within his ligaments.

The t-burn is pretty bad this time: withdrawal from testosterone he's megadosed to be a man for her.

Be a man; as if Dana could ever be a man.

Other swings try to deceive themselves. I'm a man inside this body, they say. Or, despite this body, I'm a woman.

Dana knows neither is true.

He is swing. A mutant. Accursed.

"We can't wait!" says Tatiana. Her shimmering violet eyes stare up into Dana's, plumbing his passion for her. "Don't you see? Eddie'll stow away on a sunshuttle or a starbarge, and we'll never find him. He'll take my Sha!n away for good this time, I know it! Oh, please, Dana!"

"All right," says Dana. "All right, all right."

When the old wachter shuffles back to its post, swiveling its circuitplate for a moment, Dana kicks it in the kneetread and rips out its maincable.

The old wachter clatters to the avenue like a bag of scrap.

"Damn, Tatiana," says Dana, feeling like a thug. "The things I do for you."

He can only hope the fall jams up the old wachter's memory. Even so, he'll have to grease some gears next time he wants special access to Porthandle. Acquiring special access takes years on Nexus. Years; favors rendered, the codes on a small cityship broken only by necessity. Vandalizing a dermal wachter could ruin Dana's reputation.

Damn! The things he does for her.

"My Dana," Tatiana says, and kisses him, but her lips are cold and dry. Her face, so soft and appealing before, hardens into a mask of such determined fury that he can barely stand to look at her. "Come hurry, you must hurry," she says. Now an order, not a plea. She shakes his hand away when he reaches for her again.

They slip past the wachter post, step onto the inner sky itself. The perspective swings precipitously. The avenue soars above them now, disappearing into the central city. Below their feet, the blue-veined, breathing dermis of the world. Epithelial monitors stretch their skinny necks, angling lidless emerald eyespots for a better view.

Dana turns his face from the monitors, tries to shield Tatiana's notorious profile with his cloak.

It's no use. She and Dana will be identified. A stunt like this could get Dana disbarred. The Municipal Bench of Nexus is punctilious with interworld counsel.

Too late to turn back now.

Ahead lies the scarlet tube of a bronchiole overlaid with biotic membrane.

That's it!

What Dana brought Tatiana to this remote post for. Not the usual way to leave the skin. There are mouths for that, yawning directly into sheathports to the void beyond.

307

No, this has to be the way. Tatiana's final bid for the offspring calls for secrecy.

Dana massages the membrane, finds its tough curl of nerve, pinches the nerve firmly, then smooths the membrane open.

He lifts Tatiana, shoves her through. Wrestles himself past the membrane as it slaps shut.

Gelatinous walls all about, the narrow shoot of the bronchiole.

The air within is putrid, poisonous. These muscular, filament-lined pipes filter the famous fresh atmosphere of Nexus. Millions of them riddle the skin, expelling vapors of the city for dispersion through the steelyn sheath.

The bronchiole propels whatever stuff enters it into Porthandle.

Shameful; a Triadian damma and her Nexus counsel, expelled from the world like poison. But isn't that the truth of their love. Something to be expelled from both their lives.

"Lie quietly," Dana calls to Tatiana. She is already careening ahead. The bronchiole grips him in suckered walls. He fights panic, yields with effort to its repulsive embrace.

Lie quietly. If only Dana could lie quietly with Tatiana again.

How once he had lain in his bed, not quietly. He was burning. Burning up.

MU awakened him out of the sweaty torpor of a ferocious e-burn and informed him that a new client had arrived.

Dana begged to make a referral. MU refused. A metaprogram hardwired into his northside combodominium, MU had certain priorities. MU flashed Dana's overdrawn credit accounts across the sleeping cell's monitor.

T-burn was always piercing, brittle. E-burn heavy and feverish. The e-burn now, aftermath of an estrogen megadose, had seared him for nearly two hours. Finally his breasts collapsed. Subcutaneous gristle gripped his sternum. Withering hips squeezed his pelvis like animal hide desiccating on the shaping rack of a tannery.

No way to lie down that wasn't excruciating. No energy to get up.

All he deserved, trying to please Lenni.

MU feigned perplexity. "MU cannot assimilate this, Dana Anad. Diagnosed allergic, yet you megadose yourself. MU doesn't know why you genderize at all when you know hormone withdrawal is going to be this bad."

"Why, indeed. MU should tell me. Then we'll both know." Dana hated it when MU scolded him. There was no eluding MU's view. He slapped at the headboard controls. He succeeded in nicking his wrist.

"Take a v-shot." MU dispensed a hypodermic syringe opaque with vile yellow opiates into the bedside serving tray.

"Oh, crap. Not another needle."

Dana recoiled, but there was no escape. Servos snapped out of the carved ebony bedframe. MU took Dana's wrist, took the syringe. Dana winced, angry tears starting. "It's all Lenni's fault, the treacherous swing, I never want to see . . ."

Lenni had double-swung him again.

"So don't *see*," said MU. "Now, Dana Anad. Someone new to see you." A hum and a lilt to MU's voicetape. "She's beautiful."

"Beautiful." Holy suns, his programming. Numbness stole his nerves. Nice. Too nice, v-shot. Turn to v-shot too often, and he would need the needle day in, day out. "I need beautiful like I need another hole in my arm. Remind me to upgrade MU's common senses."

"Pull yourself together, Dana Anad."

MU flitted away, trailing offended feedback. Dana could hear MU's deadpan receptionist mode echoing from the office set in the east cell of the combodominium. "Madame, if you will wait one moment, please . . ."

Dana edged out of bed, hobbled across the darkened sleeping cell. The north bay porthole remodeled its almond-colored arch as he passed, thrusting out a new arabesque. Although a disciplinarian with his other cells, Dana loved the sleeping cell's exuberance for life. He freely permitted its erratic transmutations.

An indulgence that intimated a secret hope: that he might one day redeem his own life of relentless transmutation.

A touch at the closet door, and his wardrobe presented itself: a meticulous sheaf of pressed garments held by black-gloved servos.

A conservative gray bodysuit stepped out of the wardrobe and zipped itself around him. He strapped about his wrists and neck strips of gold inset with holoids of lapis lazuli cabochons and one-carat diamonds.

Then to the groomroom for a spot of lanolin and a whisk with a teak-handled brush through the thick hair that fell straight to his cheekbones. Dana replanted his scalp often, favoring silvers, blonds, lavenders. Pearly planting shafts now peeped from the part down the middle of his skull. He wasn't sure he still liked the lustrous red he'd chosen for the last swing with Lenni.

309

Lenni. In boots and britches and a chamois shirt, lean-hipped, a trace of mustache on the lip. Lenni teasing nails across Dana's tender scalp. Lenni seizing a lock of that lustrous red hair, jerking Dana's head back. Rough insistent Lenni, demanding Dana submit. Lenni bending over for a kiss.

Then Lenni coming up, full-lipped, laughing falsetto, ripping open the chamois shirt to show new, full breasts.

Treacherous Lenni. Genderizing female, just like that. How could Lenni do it? Swing fem right in the middle of his own masculine manifestation. Double genderizing not less than half an hour into Dana's own swing to fem.

And Dana: he had injected the estrogen not very willingly. Endured the swell and change of the body, accepted the inevitable agony of e-burn, to please Lenni.

Please Lenni.

Please, Lenni, for pity's sake, you can't do this. . . .

The bastard, the bitch, the treacherous double-crossing swing, Dana never wanted to see . . .

He despised their mutation. Lenni reveled in it.

He could hear MU in the office, making conversation.

He stuck his head in the wraparound, watched in the wraparound's interior mirrors as the airjets blasted him clean. The face looked like hell. Lips cracked. Eyes drooping, glazed, stained with last night's mascara.

Steady up, old kid, he told himself. Looking like a superannuated whore, and a new client waiting.

He set the wraparound on mist, directed mild electroshock around the eyes. Optic muscles quivered. He wasn't happy about the eyes. With such eyes a man might look distinguished, a woman experienced, but a swing, Dana thought, a swing looked like death.

Over his face he sprayed superfine celluloid powder that sealed in ten seconds into a smooth ivory mask. No beard to contend with this time, thank goodness for small favors.

In his makeup cabinet lay another syringe filled with the yellow bliss of v. What the hell. The first dose was peeling off the e-burn, laying the ache bare again too soon. He plunged the needle under his tongue.

Taking a new client implied another tomorrow. Dana wondered if he could stand himself for another tomorrow.

310

• • •

She was Triadian.

From a clannish folk, close-knit and closer-mouthed, not often seen in interworld ports.

Of elegant proportions and regal deportment, she was nevertheless doll-like, quick and charming. Her complexion was lavender jade, fine and translucent, with lines like crackles in glaze fanning up from her mouth and eyes. Her slanting amethyst eyes seemed to regard him askance until he realized they curved around the bilateral sides of her narrow face. A dress of ivory silk fell from her shoulders to a waspwaist, then flared out about her knees. An open latticework of lace across her back permitted six long, cartilaginous, oval-tipped wings of shimmering violet to extrude with striking grace.

Beautiful. Good old MU.

But what was beautiful? The first planet from this particular orbitsun was beautiful, but not to one dying of thirst. The deep purity of space was beautiful, but not to one shipwrecked.

Who could be beautiful to a swing?

Still, Dana caught himself staring.

Tatiana. She was united with a permanent partner. "We call it: Solemn Deux," she said.

But she and her partner in deux were separated. "It's over," she said. "I cannot love him any more."

She was bitter. He'd failed her. They had a child, Sha!n. "We call the offspring: the point of the Triad." Triadian law required that the estranged couple share custody of the offspring.

About this, she raged. "Oh, Dana Anad," she said. "I never wanted to see him again."

In flagrant violation of their custody agreement, the deux-partner Edstuart had kidnapped Sha!n.

She produced documents set forth on interworld disks.

"Repeat offender," she said. "He's done this before. Not showing up at our appointments. Or showing up, but not with the offspring. Bold as you please, mocking me. That bastard Eddie," she said, the epithet incongruous in the fluting voice of her people.

"And now you think they're on Nexus?" asked Dana.

She was certain. Shortly after he and the offspring disappeared, a luxury cruiser had warped through Triad, bound for Nexus.

She shifted, seemed restless.

311

Dana could see the base of her left fourth finger was surrounded by a cybernetic centipede, spiky spinal fur glistening like sapphires set in the platinum ribs of its exoskeleton, silver proboscis plunged into the major blood vessel of her left hand. From the centipede's neck extruded a razor-thin ridge curved in the shape of a crescent moon.

Dana had seen such parasites before. In exchange for high-grade nourishment in quantities limited only by the host's vitality, the centipedes constrained certain nervous diseases, maintained artificially induced behaviors better than any drug. Some swings used centipedes, when they could get them. But such devices, with their inextricable exchange of need, made Dana sick. The sight of its gleaming head buried in her hand was repulsive.

She caught his glance. "Triad attempts to enforce the vows of deux this way. I can't detach it. But, I swear to you, it affects me no longer. I don't seek him out of induced obsession. I simply need to have my Sha!n returned to me. Dana Anad, you of all men must understand this."

Dana picked uncomfortably at the bodysuit sleeve tormenting his needle-riddled arm. You of all men. Always this embarrassment. People's illusions about him, that in due course would require a humiliating disabusement. He never could shake the knee-jerk.

She watched him curiously.

"If it's kidnapping, I should notify the Nexus police," Dana said. "No!"

"Couldn't the . . . offspring be in jeopardy?"

"No! No Nexus police! No outsiders! This is a matter of Triadian law!" Tatiana rose from her seat, bright-faced with urgency. "We are an old world, a closed world. We have stood aloof from your universal community. This is . . . shameful for me, you cannot imagine what a disgrace. On Triad, matters of deux are confidential among our own people. And me; approaching you, an outsider, like this. Offworld? Oh, Dana Anad! It is forbidden to reveal our ways, to anyone, anywhere; did you know that?"

She began to pace about his office.

Dana reconsidered the reasonableness of taking her case. Credit accounts be damned. "Article Two of the Interworld Code stipulates no neutral counsel may intervene in matters of parochial jurisprudence, unless the petitioner waives all parochial rights and submits to interworld law. Look, here. Do you so submit, Tatiana?"

"I do! Yes . . . well, why not. I have to, don't I?"

"Then what would you have me do, if you refuse Nexus police protection?"

"Oh Dana, if you could just find them, arrange a meeting. Do something discreet. Impress Edstuart. Invoke your interworld law, but in a way that won't expose me. He would listen to you. I'm sure of it. Oh, he's such a limp stick; I *know* it."

"Well, I could obtain an injunction in the Interworld Court requiring him to honor your custody agreement. Confidentiality would apply."

"Yes . . . Yes! That's perfect."

She turned her narrow back to him so he could see her sinewy shoulder blades, the startling wings, her waist through the lace. She swung her hips in the café dance women do when they want someone to see them.

Then composed, smile dazzling, she sauntered to where Dana sat and took his hand.

Dana recoiled. E-burn crackled over his skin.

She began to murmur nonsense in the tongue of her people, like a mother baby-talking her child. Her slanting gaze dizzied him. She exuded some kind of power. Her touch and words grew amorous.

"Beautiful, elegant Dana," she said at last. "What is this great pain of yours?" She drew back his bodysuit sleeve, surveyed his new punctures, his scabs, his scars. "Surely not a drug addict?"

"No . . . No! I—am an androgyne," said Dana. "A swing. Not a man. Not a woman, either. Neither, and both. A mutant. Oh, my kind has always known chromosomal jumbling. Women born into men's bodies. Men into women. Hermaphrodites, with both sexes fully manifested. But never the true androgyne. There was too much radiation once. The sheer anarchy of several billion matings on our homeworld, I suppose. Now, here we are. Here *I* am. Um. Please don't be frightened."

"I'm not!

"Right now I'm particularly neither. I'm in stasis. Undifferentiated male and female. This is my normal state of affairs." He laughed bitterly at the unintentional irony. As if anything could be normal about a swing, much less his/her affairs.

"But you can *be* a woman? Or a man?"

"Yes. With injection of the appropriate hormone. Then the gender manifests."

"The gender manifests! How marvelous!"

"I'm glad you think so."

"Why do you hate yourself so?" she asked tenderly.

313

He was struck dumb. Then finally, quietly, "The universe is a great duality. Morally: correct or incorrect. Sensually: hot or cold. Physically: light or dark. Temporally: now or infinity. There is no third mode that isn't suspect. Between good and evil lies compromise; between light and darkness is murk. Between male and female stands the androgyne."

"Between your dualities lies harmony and balance, too," she said. "And perhaps whoever, whatever, you are . . . is *your* truth?"

"Harmony! Balance! Truth! The truth is: my kind is hated and feared throughout the worlds," he said. "Perverts, the lynch mobs call us. Rapists of daughters, sodomists of sons. Yet only when we genderize, *conform* to the standards of the dual world, can we become sexually active. Not when we're in stasis. So even if I were a sexual psychopath, I'm a hundredth as able as someone normally genderized. Damned absurd, eh?"

"And this great pain of yours," she said, persisting. "It comes when you manifest a gender?"

"During. Mostly after. Before, too, in a way."

The terrible emptiness of stasis. The sadness, the grief, like a death.

That was why Dana megadosed. Dosed and dosed again, despite the agony of change. He must remember to tell MU. The emptiness. The awful stasis.

"Poor Dana," Tatiana said. "I have something for your pain."

From her bodice she withdrew a celadon flask. She twisted the stoppered top and, with an inscrutable look, tipped the flask at him.

The most amazing scent wound round him, a ripe, rich, lusty odor that so startled him with its blatant allure that he laughed out loud.

"This is amante," she whispered. "It soothes and heals. We the damma of Triad use it to ease our own particular pain." Her fingertips poised above his damaged forearm, bearing a drop of glistening ointment.

Dana struggled to free himself, but she gripped him with surprising strength.

"Please," he said. "Don't touch me. Just your touch right now would cause me the most excruciating . . ."

"Not my touch, Dana Anad," Tatiana replied, and lowered her hand. "Not *my* touch."

He flinched with foreboding, then trembled with disbelief. Warmth at the instant her honeyed hand touched his skin. Then great soothing folded over his torment, coolness and warmth, mingling, trading sensations, a minted mist that tickled him. Then an absurd, unexpected blossoming of pleasure, an ecstasy rising out of his depths, welling up from unexpected places.

And a vision: Tatiana. Jewel, lady of ladies, so beautiful . . .

Distrust seized and shook him. He struggled to throw off the blinding pleasure.

But amante wrapped around him like the legs of a lover.

He thought he saw her watching him, assessing his reaction. Too knowing, unpleasantly smug.

Then her radiance bloomed again. The odor of peaches wafted from her fingertips. She seemed to float across the room, trailing mist. She was collecting her things, a gossamer shawl that spilled over her shoulders. With a sorrowful look, she drifted to the door.

He realized she was leaving. Fierce longing to keep her near pierced him.

"So we are agreed?" he heard her ask. "You will do as I wish," he heard her say, not a question now.

Before he could answer, she was gone.

Tatiana lies where the bronchiole spat her, pale limbs sprawled amid her black silk.

Dana wrests his ankle from the bronchiole's orifice, tumbling backward over Tatiana when the sucking lips release him with a sudden *pop!* She screams with laughter, tussling with him playfully.

Then she falls back, silent and weak. Grimaces; her pain is worsening.

She must find the offspring soon.

Dana grinds his teeth, tasting the blood t-burn loosens from his gums. If only he could get back to full stasis, he might risk genderizing into masculine strength again.

"Dana," she whispers. She touches him tenderly, like she used to. But a spasm shakes her. She growls, "Get me up, get me *up*. Hurry, damn you!"

Dana stands, pulls her to her feet.

They set out across Porthandle.

Beneath the steelyn sheath, the world curves down. Out of the dark floor that is the top of the inner sky spring ten million shafts of light spewing out into the void. Monstrous clanging issues from the ports twisting shut and open overhead, revealing the pitch-black of

315

space and, set against that ebony infinity, the defiant, jewel-like of sunshuttles, starbarges, needle-slim scoutships.

Wind howls here. Sleet batters them. Dana clicks MU's portable jack into one of the transport tracks that crisscross the exosphere like the silk of a spiderweb. But for MU's grip, he and Tatiana would be plucked from the top of the world and flung into the void.

Ahead: the knobby hulk of a dockworkers' den; woozy red lights, rowdy shouts. Dana maneuvers them both through the tattered entry. The den is dim, disheveled, strewn with broken glass and pools of brew. Tatiana spins her wings dry, sending the drenching off her in a brisk whir.

The drunken cacophony falls silent at the sight of her. A roomful of eyes turns, sporting silver eyepatches, nictitating lids, plastic-fringed robotic lenses.

"Hey! Whaddaya want?" yells the denkeeper.

"Have you seen this youngster? This man?" asks Dana, proffering the holoids.

The roomful of eyes isn't friendly. There are no winged folk among them. A snarl rumbles up from a roomful of whiskeyed throats.

"Hey, seen 'em?" says the denkeeper. "*Seen* 'em? Buddy, I can't keep bugs out o'here." He flicks a towel at an imaginary fly on the bar and stares rudely at Tatiana.

Dana lays a hand on her arm, silencing her retort. "Know where they're bound?"

"Five'll get ten, the starbarge leaving for the Coldworld V mines." The denkeeper can't resist divulging speculation. "This bug, he says he don't have no stash, and he wants to skip Nexus, see, him and that bug kid, so I tell 'im, the barge is takin on labor for an X on the dotted line. So that's where they're bound, five'll get ten, them and the godzilla what's askin' for 'em too." The denkeeper leans toward Dana, lowers his voice. "Now blow, buddy, if ya know what's good for ya."

"The godzilla?"

"Yeah! Guy wit' wings like her and a temper. Twice her size and a face like a broken plate. Bastard smashed some o' my best glasses. Beat up a couple o' citizens what got in his way. Got some kind o' curvy blade long as my friggin' arm. One piece o' steelyn, man!" The denkeeper looks at Tatiana with a crude admixture of bloodlusty awe and animal fear. "I woulda got the cops, 'cept he says he's one. Lissen, I don't like bugs, buddy," he says to Dana. "Understand? So I don't mind tellin' ya, get her out o' here."

The snarl deepens to a malevolent roar. Tatiana trembles against him.

"Please," insists Dana. He has to be sure. "He was Triadian? He says he was a *cop?*"

"Yeah yeah yeah. No offense to ya, buddy, but ya gotta get her out o' here."

They dive through the entry, back into the whirlwinds of Porthandle.

"Prefect Tule," whispers Tatiana. "He's *here.*"

Dana agrees. One step ahead of them, maybe two. Fear shoots up his spine.

He knows that knife, the sweep of it, the sheen of it. The way it shrieks when it dives to flesh. Prefect Tule promised to use it next time he and Dana meet.

"Are you happy?" she would ask as they lay together, amante rising off their flesh. He would answer, happy? No, not happy. The word could not contain the well-being she brought him. His pleasure in her knew no bounds. Every part of her enchanted him. And the whole of her was more than lips and waist and hips.

She was entirely, irrevocably female.

She didn't change.

When she made it clear she wanted him, Dana had swung stud without hesitation.

Swing stud: those were Lenni's words. Swing slang. Vulgar.

But Tatiana laughed when the term tumbled from Dana's mouth. She helped him with the needle. Watched when his jaw lengthened, beard and chest hair sprouted, arms hardened, hips elongated. She smoothed amante on his ache.

Then she returned his kiss.

"So what is this great pain damma suffer?" Dana asked one night. "It might be worth suffering for *this.*"

He traced silver veins down the celadon flask. Tatiana said that the perfumed drug-lotion couldn't be obtained anywhere in the living worlds. Anywhere except Triad, and Triad didn't offer it for sale. Only a female of Tatiana's rank, a damma, was permitted to possess amante.

"Nothing is worth that pain," she said.

Her cold retort silenced him.

"You want to know about our pain?" Her mouth tightened. "It is the whip. The pain that lashes; the pain of separation. When we

317

damma are young it comes. This whip drives us to find the deux-partner. We seek and seek, until we find the one who will join with us in Solemn Deux. And then, after deux, it gets worse, this pain of separation. Then we must have the offspring. As your people say: the child. If we're fertile and lucky, and this offspring comes, we are blessed with the Triad. We are blessed with the point of the Triad, by all Triad. And the pain that would never cease is gone."

"But what happens when the Triad separates?" asked Dana. "Like you and Eddie and Sha!n?"

"Oh, Dana," she cried. "I can barely face each day."

So cultural, legal, moral; yes. But ultimately it was a kind of physical drive, Dana concluded, her urgency to find the offspring.

Dana jacked MU into full telespace embodiment and sent MU with his citizen's surveillance code through the world brain. All import-export information on Nexus was closely regulated. Declining reciprocity with any other world in exchange for a universal neutral status, the cityship was an interworld haven. Obtaining a universal neutral status, the cityship accepted whatever came to it, subject to strictly local cityship regulation, and no more.

Such was Nexus's privileged and vulnerable position. All respected the cityship as long as each respected it.

The world brain, its monitors sprouting at every pore, post, and synapse, saw and stored all.

To a Nexus citizen in good standing with the right code and a properly formatted request, the brain divulged.

MU duly reported: a Triadian male adult and his offspring had arrived on a luxury cruiser. They cleared customs and fled.

But Nexus was a small world. The brain routinely supercopied global memory into high-security subconscious storage. For a Nexus citizen with clearance, they could be traced.

Dana sent MU on trace.

Pending a development, Dana showed Tatiana his world.

Everywhere she provoked comment. There were few winged folk on the living worlds. The commotion pleased Dana.

Since they'd mated, she'd taken from wearing white to red: vermilion silk, scarlet sequins, capes of wine velvet.

She was zipped into fiery red leather the evening when they'd
318 supped on rare hydroponic beefsteak anemone, then saw a circus of chimeras from Arkan. She was making arrangements to pick up her correspondence at her hotel in the morning when Lenni showed up.

Lenni. In heels and jewels and a well-cut dress, sultry, sulky, a tuxedoed escort in tow. The very image of a woman about town. Lenni genderized so well, Dana wondered if the escort knew this was just an image. Fake, an imitation, an illusion.

Swing.

"Dana baby!" Lenni cried. The escort glowered. "You look wonderful, Danny." A look Dana knew only too well crept across Lenni's theatrically made-up face. "Suns, it's been too long." Then Lenni saw Tatiana. Scrutinized her red leather, her wings. "Who the hell is this?"

"Excuse us, Lenni," Dana said coldly. "My client and I are about to retire." He directed Tatiana to retrieve their cloaks.

"Oh, *us*. There's only one *us*, Danny. That's you and me."

"You're wrong, Lenni. It's over for us."

"*You* and *me*, Dana. We're one of a kind. We're the exciting thing, babe. Oh, we blow hot and cold with each other, but that's all right." Lenni dismissed the escort. "It's so *good* to see you again. And each of us genderized. Just the way you like it, Danny. Everything synched."

"No! No, nothing's synched, Lenni." The anger grew in Dana's chest until he was bursting with it. "Nothing's ever synched with you. You'll be wearing a beard before the night is out. You won't be able to go out on the street for morning coffee in those clothes, not because you wouldn't dare, but because your body won't fit."

"Oh, you're so stuck, babe. I'm only trying to set you free. Help you fully realize yourself. Why can't you let go? Why can't you accept the changes?"

"Free?" Dana said. "I don't want to be free. I don't want to change. I want to be *real*. Solid. Something I *know* that I am, truly, time and time again. Look, Len. I don't hate you. But I just can't swing with you anymore."

"Oh, *real*, babe. You want to be real. And what about her? Think it's real with her? She's Triadian, isn't she?"

Dana swallowed. He didn't like Lenni's tone. Lenni was an interworld statistician. Lenni knew a lot of strange things.

"Oh yes, don't want to say, eh, babe?" Lenni pressed close. "Let me tell you. They're ruthless, babe. I mean, ruthless."

"Yeah, come on, what *do* you mean?"

"Butcher and eat their own progeny; that's one rumor. I mean, babe; the stories I've heard. Triadians?"

Dana shoved Lenni away. "She's a damma. Some kind of great

lady on their world. She has principles, Lenni. Maybe something you don't understand. She retained me in pursuit of a just cause, a family law dispute, as a matter of fact. She's entirely devoted to me."

"Devoted, babe. Never be anyone as devoted to you as me. Yeah, you walk away. You wait, babe. Wait and see how devoted your little madame butterfly is. Triadians, they don't give a damn for anyone or anything, but their own kind. Triadian. You'll see."

The door to the office of the Clerk of the Interworld Court locked shut behind Dana. The knife sliced his exhalation of surprise.

"Stay away from her, counselor," said the giant in a voice like cracking glass. Asthmatic breath wheezed from his wrinkled snout. Huge wings buzz-sawed from his back.

"How dare you threaten . . . Clerk!" shouted Dana, circumnavigating the Clerk's cramped quarters as the giant advanced on him. The knife the giant clutched was as thin as a scalpel. Curved as elegantly as a crescent moon. It flung shimmers of icy light into Dana's bewildered eyes.

"Give up the case, counselor. She is *my* responsibility, and mine alone. I am the Enforcer of the Holy Triad, and Its Keeper. Get out of here. Go now. Out the back door, and be gone."

"No!" said Dana. "I won't!"

That morning Dana and Tatiana had arrived at Interworld Court. Ten thousand colloidal cells in a glass and bone tower downtown housed each judge's quarters and staff. From each tiny cell, litigants jacked into a computer-constructed telespace vaster in mental perception than ten cityships. An appearance in Interworld Court conferred irrefutable authority.

Dana had nervously prepared Tatiana's injunction, coding for the confidentiality she insisted upon. But when they jacked into telelink with Court and logged in the injunction, the judge discovered an oversight: Tatiana wasn't technically divorced from Edstuart.

Under interworld law, she was only separated. The Triadian documentation hadn't been clear, with a muddled usage of the term Solemn Deux and an enigmatic reference to the Holy Triad. From all Tatiana said, Dana had assumed she was divorced for interworld purposes and coded the injunction accordingly.

The judge refused to proceed until code was correct. Dana had jacked out of link, run across the hall with the hearing disks in hand, burst into the Clerk's office.

"She came to me," he told the giant. "Retained me. She's got a right to interworld counsel under Nexus law, and you've no right to interfere. . . ."

The curved knife swished.

"It is *you* who interfere, outsider. This is a matter of Triadian law. Forbidden to you."

"I don't understand," said Dana reasonably. "The deux-partner has breached their joint custody agreement, under your own law. She just wants the offspring restored to her. I intend to counsel her to demand full custody and have a divorce finalized. . . ."

The giant emitted a gargle that must have been laughter. "No, you don't understand, counselor. She can never *divorce* him. Never separate, not for long. She is initiator of the Holy Triad, bearer of the Mystery. She is damma. And she has deceived you, if you think otherwise."

"Look," said Dana, reaching for the Clerk's communicator at last. "I'm calling the police. . . ."

"I am the police," said the giant, flicking the communicator out of Dana's fingers with the tip of the knife. "Prefect Tule, of Triad. You will cease and desist, counselor. I insist. Triadian law requires it."

"You're on Nexus now, Prefect Tule," said Dana, emboldened. At least this monster wasn't some common criminal. "As an officer of the law, you ought to know you're bound by the laws of this world. *You* will cease and desist. And I will report you to Nexus authorities for attacking a citizen."

He seized a steelyn stylus from the Clerk's desk and fenced the knife away. At impact, the tip of the stylus gaped and fell from his hand.

Prefect Tule spat. "*This* is what I think of your Nexus law." He sheathed the knife. "Leave her alone, counselor. You have been notified. You interfere with the Triad in any way, next time you will feel the mandate of Triadian law."

Beneath the tempest of Porthandle, Dana catches a sound. There! Again, closer. A rusty whine. From somewhere behind his left shoulder. He strains to see.

Suddenly, a light touch that won't let go. The old wachter's handclasps snake out on steelyn cord and truss up Dana's wrists. Swift silver figure eights pin Tatiana's frail elbows behind her back.

"Yes sirree, bud-oh," says the old wachter. "Gotchew now." A

wire rat sticks its purply snout out from under the old wachter's armpit, peers at the captives with jet bead eyes. " 'Tain't happy wit chew.
'Tain't happy a-tall. I be placin' chew and der lady under arrest. Back
to de skin wit' ye." The wire rat leaps to the old wachter's neck and
capers across its shoulder shelf.

Tatiana writhes against the old wachter's restraints. Her lips curl
back from her tiny pointed teeth. "This is all your fault," she says to
Dana. "You failed me. Just like everyone else."

"Tatiana. Please. I'm sorry."

"Sorry! *Do* something. We can't go back."

"Tatiana, I've got no strength. The t-burn. I can't even feel the
amante anymore."

"Take a t-shot!"

"I can't. It could kill me."

"Kill you? And what's your miserable swing life worth? What?
You're not a *man*, Dana Anad."

He knows it is the pain of separation making her crazy and cruel.
Still. "No," he says, struck to his soul. "I'm not a man. And you're not
a woman, either. Not really. Are you."

"No," she says bitterly. Tears pool across her cheeks. "I am
damma."

Pride spurs Dana now. From his bound wrists he flips MU's portable jack at the old wachter's control console. The frontal claw of the
portable neatly snatches the old wachter's maincable.

"Override." Dana voice-activates MU, splicing the command directly into the old wachter's motherboard.

"Eh?" The old wachter pulls up, startled. The wire rat chuckles
maliciously at Dana. "Cain't override. This be security one. Cain't
override, not n'even fer ye, bud."

"All right. But don't take us back to the skin. Take us to the
docks. To the starbarges."

"T'well, t'well. To de docks, den." The old wachter swivels, then
lurches back toward the roiling fog of Porthandle. The wire rat squeals
and plunges through a crack into the old wachter's abdomen.

"One more thing," says Dana. "Who restored your main cable?
Who sent you after us?"

"Porthandle ain't a fit place fer man nor beast, eh, bud-oh?" The
old wachter chuckled to itself. "No sirree, not man nor beast."

•   •   •

As Dana had requested, MU traced Edstuart and the offspring through a corrupt vascular monitor in employ of the Nexus eastside district. Edstuart had resorted to immigration racketeers well known to Nexus revenue agents. The racketeers had taken them across town, changing transports in an obvious fashion, to a cheap hotel in the slum known as Atro City.

There, amid fugitives of a thousand worlds, Edstuart and the offspring Sha!n hid.

Dana kicked in the flimsy door, burst into the sour room. "Edstuart of Triad?" he said. "Tatiana's offspring Sha!n? By this injunction of the Interworld Court, and my citizen's power of arrest under Nexus law, I demand you come with me."

The Triadian turned.

Not the brutish playboy Dana imagined. Not the embittered ex-partner Tatiana described.

Edstuart was a frightened man. As elegant as Tatiana, with slim lavender limbs and graceful wings, Edstuart was, Dana realized with a hopeless stab of jealousy, the perfect mate for Tatiana.

"Please, sir," said Edstuart, trembling.

From a rumpled cot in the corner, the tiny Triadian Dana had seen only in Tatiana's holoid blinked up at him, even more endearing than the holoid had been able to convey. The youngster whispered, "Hadda?" and Edstuart said, "Shush, shush," and Sha!n yawned ingenuously, revealing two long canine teeth that arched from tiny upper gums.

With the gleam-edge of razors. Curved like crescent moons. The offspring's teeth flung shimmers of ivory light into Dana's bewildered eyes.

"We cannot go with you, sir," said Edstuart.

"But she wants to see Sha!n. She wants to see you, too. Do you hate her so much?"

"Hate her?" Edstuart laughed. "Tatiana? Who could hate her? She's magnificent! Haven't you found her so?"

"Yes," said Dana and turned away, burning with unexpected shame.

Could he tell this Triadian an androgyne was in love with his wife? In love. What did in love mean to a swing? It meant Dana wanted her more than he'd ever wanted anyone. It meant Tatiana shared her body and her amante and accepted Dana as a man even though she knew he was swing.

"Then why?" said Dana. "Why run away like this?"

The strange, beautiful offspring watched him curiously.

Edstuart bit his fist. "Don't you know? Ah, I see. No, of course not. She wouldn't tell you. She's a true damma. Keeps her secrets to herself." Edstuart bit his fist again so hard that he drew blood from the delicate lavender skin. He grimaced at the sight of it. "Well, sir. I don't hate her. I've loved her. I suppose I love her still. But I can't take Sha!n back to her. Not now. You see, she can't help herself. You don't know what she will do to him."

"Tatiana? *Do* to her own offspring?"

"Yes . . . yes. It's . . . more terrible than I can say."

And all her protestations, *my little one, I want my little one back.* Her entreaties sounded discordant in Dana's memory.

The offspring cooed, extending a tiny hand toward cockroaches scuttling down the wall.

"So I hope you will put away your injunction, sir," said Edstuart. "Say you never found us. Say we were already gone."

Sickened, Dana edged out the door. "What will you do now? Where will you go?"

"I don't know." Edstuart laughed ruefully. "We left in a bit of a hurry. I didn't take much."

Feeling ludicrous, Dana threw down a couple of Nexus bills he had in his pocket. "I suppose I should tell you. Prefect Tule is here."

"Prefect Tule!" Edstuart paled. He darted to the window, seized the shade, yanked it shut.

"Know him?"

"You—you're not working with him, are you, sir?"

"Working with him! Holy suns, no."

"He didn't follow you here?"

"I sincerely hope not."

"You're sure? You're sure? You were careful?"

"Very careful. He told me he's a police officer. Is that true?"

"Yes, yes." Edstuart sat down on the cot, folded Sha!n in his arms, stroked the offspring's downy hair. "And it is true that I am a criminal, sir. I cannot accept your charity, though I thank you."

Dana picked up the bills, tucked them into Edstuart's hand. "What possibly could be your crime?" he asked. "If she abuses . . . ?" He could not finish.

"I have failed the vows of Solemn Deux. I shunned the great Mystery. Ran from the duty of Triad. I love them both . . . too much. Whatever else has happened, Tatiana has never run away. She has never shirked the law of Holy Triad. Ah!" Edstuart brushed tears from his cheeks. The offspring began to whimper. "If Prefect Tule is here, then the time for Holy Triad is near. Please go, sir, and may grace go with you."

"Dana! Baby, wait!"

The familiar whiskey-and-smoke voice stopped him when he should have hurried on through the filth-choked alleys of Atro City.

"If you're following me, Lenni," said Dana, "cut it out right now."

"Following you, babe." In tweeds, with a pipe and a brass-knobbed cane, salt-and-pepper goatee. "I love Atro City on a free afternoon, what a surprise," said Lenni. "Say, Dan, you look like you've just seen a ghost. Come here. Sit a minute with me."

Lenni propelled him to a comparatively clean door stoop, made Dana sit, opened Dana's collar.

Dana sighed. "Thanks, Len."

"Well, baby. You don't look so good."

"And you look great. I don't know how you do it, Len."

"Oh, hell. You do it great yourself, babe. Don't kid me."

"No. Swinging isn't real. It's never real for me. Don't you see?"

"Yeah, I do see, Dan. I see you've swung stud for weeks now. Weeks and weeks."

"What's it to you . . . ?"

"It's not good for you, babe. With your allergies? Suns, you should know better. Getting burned? Want a v-shot? Give me your arm, I've got a fix."

"No. Hey, Len, you're not following me, are you?"

A troupe of chrome-clad gravity dancers who used Arkanian microboosters to defy the local g-force stopped before them and commenced a rollicking kick-and-float routine.

Lenni tossed coins into the scarlet helmet that bobbed before them.

"You worry me, babe. You're getting too wrapped up. You're working too hard."

"Because I'm getting into a bad tangle, Len," persisted Dana. "You get in the way, you could get hurt. And I don't want that."

A gravity dancer pranced up an invisible, one-story stairwell and executed a perfect swan dive off the invisible edge, swooping up from the concrete within millimeters of impact.

Lenni tossed her a bill, then scowled at the troupe, who all somersaulted away, cheering and hooting. "It's your little madame butterfly, isn't it, Dan?"

"Yes."

"Yeah. You really do worry me, babe. So I looked up some statistics on this world of hers at Trade the other day. Want to hear?"

"You're going to tell me anyway, so get on with it."

"Don't be so stubborn, baby. I'm trying to help. You listen to me. Triad's big; equatorial radius of nearly seventy-five thousand klics. The twelve billion natives aren't pressed for space like two dozen other worlds I could mention. Very healthy planetary profile. They've still got frontiers, habitable areas not yet cultivated. The population enjoys a growth rate of 105 percent. They want to increase that rate, with so much available niche. Boost the citizenry."

"Sounds good to me."

"Sure. But the demographics puzzled me. Statistics show a young adult population of some seven billion. They should be paired off. But they're not. Oh, I don't mean permanent pair bonding. You don't have to have that with 105 growth. Although in a frontier society with a stable homebase infrastructure, you tend to see restrictive institutions regulating reproductive functions. Yeah, but we observe no generalized pair-bonding system on Triad. *At all.*"

"Wrong, Len," said Dana. "What about Tatiana and Edstuart?"

"I said generalized. The population at large is productive, industrious, specialized, inventive. And, to all appearances, neuter. Can you beat that! What a kick in the rear for the likes of you and me, eh, babe?"

"Lenni, I'm warning you . . ."

"Hey, so how to account for a population growth of 105 percent? How to account for your little madame butterfly? I'll tell you how. A small class of Triadians are charged with the reproductive function. I suspect this elite has specialized biological equipment. And *they* enter into highly regulated reproductive unions."

"Solemn Deux."

"That's it, babe. Oh, it's hush-hush. Members of the reproductive class are of vital importance to the species. But how do they do it? What do they do? Nobody's talking. High state secret, with religious rhetoric thrown in to keep outsiders mystified, if not entertained."

"Tatiana and Edstuart have an . . . offspring, Lenni," said Dana.

She herself never *had* referred to Sha!n as a *child*.

"Fine, all right! But that isn't even zero population growth, Dan." Lenni took on the insistent tone that Dana always disliked. "The government protects this elite. Honors them. Indulges them. Allows privileges. There are rumors. Drugs, orgies, aphrodisiacal spices, exotic food, intoxicating drink. Amante."

"Amante isn't an aphrodisiac, Lenni. It's an anesthetic."

"An anesthetic!" Lenni howled with laughter. "Baby, the stories I've heard. Amante?"

"An anesthetic lotion, Lenni," said Dana, flushing, kindled with the quick anger of finding out what should have been obvious, and from someone else. Tatiana's explanations tasted ashy. "Used for medicinal purposes," he persisted nonetheless. "To ease a certain pain the damma must endure."

"A certain pain! Dana . . . You've tried it?"

"Yes! As a matter of fact, I have."

Lenni scrutinized him. "You didn't even know what amante really is, do you? Dan, she really has gotten to you, hasn't she?"

"It's not your business, Len."

"Yeah, it's my business. I love you, Dan. You and your fucking *real*. She's not what you think, don't you see? She's, oh hell, Dan, she's a *queen bee*, dedicated to propagation of her species. There's no dropping out. I'm talking strict behavior modification, babe. She wears a cybernetic centipede, doesn't she? She's a lifer, baby."

"Is that why you took all this trouble, Lenni?" Dana jumped up off the doorstoop. "To prove I'm a fool?"

"To prove you can't think of her as a *woman*," said Lenni, rising unsteadily. "Queen bees, they rip the guts out of their lovers. She's something else, Dana. Something you can't conceive of even in a swing's notion of sexual roles. Something you can't apply your concepts of family law to. Something you can't *love*."

"I don't want to hear this, Lenni. Of course she's got an obligation to her offspring and her people. She's always been frank about that. But don't tell me I can't love her. It *is* real, what's between us. Tatiana's a great lady. A damma."

Dana stalked away.

"Yeah, damma!" Lenni yelled after him. "Closest translation: mother with child!"

327

•   •   •

Pale limbs on red satin she shed across the bed. Wings arching up, beating, lifting her in amorous hover and swoop. Tender fingers guided the needle for Dana. She stroked his burgeoning genderization as though she'd invented Man herself.

"Excuse me, Dana Anad," said MU. "But this is the last t-shot you're going to be able to handle."

Tatiana laughed. She took the flask of amante from between her breasts, uncapped it, scooped a dewdrop.

Honey and haze flowed down over Dana again. He could think of nothing else but her again.

"Excuse *me*, Dana Anad," said MU. "The last t-shot for quite some time. You're going to *burn*."

Dana struggled against the pleasure. He sat up, seized Tatiana's hand. Examined her fingertips, rippled the sapphire spikes of the cybernetic centipede, whose head wriggled deeper into her palm. He cut his finger on the centipede's silvery, razor-edged neckridge. A drop of his blood slid down the crescent moon.

"My Tatiana," said Dana. He drew a deep breath. "Amante isn't just an anesthetic, is it? And you found out I was swing before you came to me, didn't you? So you knew I had pain. Pain; worse than that, I was vulnerable. Precarious. Yeah, a sophisticated being would know that about swings, and you're nothing if not sophisticated. And your being here with me now. A pleasant interlude before you go back to Edstuart? I hope it's been pleasant. Because you can never divorce him. You can never leave Solemn Deux." He threw her hand down. "What I don't understand is why you had to make me love you. I could have found Edstuart and the offspring for you anyway. The credit would have been enough. Why have you done this to me? Why?"

Sorrowfully, she arose from the bed, then glanced at him with glittering murex eyes. "You mean you've found them?"

"Naturally. MU is the best. Is it because you didn't know what I'd do when Edstuart told me about you, if you hadn't secured my loyalty?" Dana wiped amante off the wounds in his arm. "So. Am I addicted to this crap? Just what is amante, Tatiana? You tell me."

"You're not addicted," she said hastily. "You're not Triadian. What did that bastard Eddie tell you?"

"That you could do something terrible to Sha!n. Abuse the offspring, I don't know what else. Did you know there's a rumor Triadians butcher and eat their progeny? And that's why Edstuart is running from you, even though it means he's broken the vows of your precious Solemn Deux."

"Abuse! Butcher my Sha!n? Oh, that Eddie is such a coward. Oh, I would never do such a thing. Sha!n is the precious one, the *point* of the Triad. Don't be a fool, Dana! And don't look at me like that. Your ghastly rumor is pathetic. I would never harm Sha!n, you must believe me."

"Believe you? You have me code your injunction incorrectly in front of an Interworld Court judge. Prefect Tule says you've deceived me. Lenni, too. Your deux-partner is terrified of you. You've done nothing to make me believe you. You've done nothing but make love to me, damma of Triad. But that's your function, isn't it? Temple whore?"

"Ah. Then I need not try to convince you that I really do care for you, counselor of Nexus."

"That's right."

But he did want her to try.

"Fine." She shrugged. She pulled on a dress of black silk. "And . . ." The sideways glance. "You . . . have spoken with Prefect Tule?"

"Oh, you know him, too? Are you also a criminal on Triad?"

"Yes. I suppose I am. I've come too close to revealing the Mystery of the Triad, dear counselor. By coming to you. Well, and when did you see him?"

"At Interworld Court, before the hearing."

"Why didn't you tell me?"

"Our introduction was not exactly amicable. He demanded I drop the case. Leave you alone, abandon you. And I . . . I didn't want to do that. Thought I was defending your interworld rights to neutral counsel."

"I see, I see. Then truly the time for Holy Triad is near."

She grew suddenly distracted, withdrawn, pale. Despite his anger with her, Dana came to her side and held her.

"Edstuart said that, too; the time is near. Tatiana. What is the Holy Triad?"

"The Holy Triad is my duty as damma. Only I can initiate it. Oh, I'm sorry if I've wronged you, my Dana. That bungler, Prefect Tule." Her face twisted with contempt. Her voice was harsh. "Tule failed me. He was supposed to enforce our custody agreement. He is the Keeper, you see. He should never have let Eddie get this far. I deny blame for resorting to outsiders." She turned to Dana with the shimmering look that always pierced him. "But not you, Dana. You've never failed me. You must not fail me now."

"Tatiana, I don't know what you want me to do."

"Then listen, I will tell you. You know how to contact Eddie?"

"Yes."

"Contact him now. Let me speak to him. Maybe we can come to terms."

MU placed the connection, came back with the response at once. "They've gone."

"Of course!" cried Tatiana. "He knows about the Prefect? Oh, of course he will flee. We've got to go, we've got to find them. Please! They're leaving Nexus, I know it. How could they get away without notice of the Nexus brain?"

Dana said, "They'll go to Porthandle."

Porthandle crashes around Dana like a planetary sea. Sleet beats down. A thousand stratospheric voices shout, pressure exploding against pressure. Then abrupt, eerie silence, until the world gasps for breath again.

The old wachter basks in the stir Tatiana has created. Maybe it deserves some glory. It brought them to the right place.

Lashed to the launch pad, the great silver whale of the starbarge awaits departure. Oscillating green and purple lights ring the loading dock. Grizzled dockworkers stare. Indentured laborers make lewd noises. News reporters crowd around them, flashing recorders.

The old wachter beams. The hero who has captured the Triadian, an illegal alien once she attempted unauthorized exit from Nexus through the skin.

"In a bronchiole?" exclaim the reporters, furrowing their faces. "During *open port?*"

But after all, bronchioles have been used for quick exits before. It is not such a scandal as the hoopla would warrant. Except for Tatiana, the beautiful winged lady. Triadian damma. Butcher of her progeny, rumor says.

And then Dana sees the one who has followed them, who has harassed them both all this time. Patting the old wachter's backplate, chucking the wire rat under its scruffy chin. Gesticulating, raising havoc.

Lenni. Isn't it just like Lenni? In a dockworker's jumpsuit, almost frail in stasis, with a pale, delicate earnest face. Talking it up with the reporters. Saying who knows *what* about Tatiana.

Damn you, Lenni, Dana wants to shout. But the shout sticks in his throat. The sour lump on his gum slithers down into his tonsils. His throat can barely sustain a swallow now.

You're going to burn, MU said.

Exhausted, defeated, Dana doesn't know if he can stand himself for another minute, much less another tomorrow, and all because of her: Tatiana.

Tatiana.

She kneels in misery. Her chest rattles as though her lungs are crumbling. Sweat slicks the lavender curves of her cheekbones, forming rivulets down her neck. The cybernetic centipede ripples wildly around her finger, sapphire fur clacking. Its bloody head rears and wallows in the palm of her hand. The crescent moon of its neckridge slashes at her wrists. Only her wings still arch magnificently about her tiny crumpled body.

The pain of separation. How could Dana have doubted her?

Lenni was wrong. Whatever else it does, amante *is* an anesthetic. For the unspeakable pain of the damma of Triad, yes, intended for that. But whatever else she felt or did not feel for him, Tatiana pitied *his* pain.

The shimmering, slanting eyes glance up at Dana, full of that piercing look he thought he knew. Then dart away, toward some distant vision.

Prefect Tule.

The monstrous Triadian stands before the starbarge dock, brandishing the gleaming crescent moon of his knife. The arrogance of him, the flagrant disregard for interworld law. The terror he strikes in these frail, elegant people, his *own* people, whom he bears so little resemblance to.

Dana despises him.

"Tatiana," Prefect Tule intones. "The Time is at hand. We cannot wait to veil the Mystery from these outsiders' eyes. You must do it now. You must initiate the Triad."

Tatiana gasps. Then, amazingly, stands up, stands tall. An unknown strength visibly tightens her. She tosses back her sweat and tears.

"How dare you address me so," she says regally.

"Pardon, Damma. But your duty."

"I remind you of *your* duty, Prefect. Do it, and leave these outsider people alone. Dana," she says. "Tell the wachter to release me."

MU's portable jack does its work. The initial override command finally splices as the old wachter rattles on with the gathering crowd.

The steelyn cords fall away.

She rubs the circulation back into her arms, finds her celadon flask, pounds out the last drops, slathers amante over her throat and breasts.

Then she takes Dana's shoulders.

"Dana Anad," she says. "In my pain before, I spoke nonsense. I meant nothing. Do you forgive me?"

He has no answer.

"Please forgive," she says, assisting him out of his own steelyn bonds. "No, you're not a man. Not a man or a woman, but always my Dana. Find your balance and harmony, my love. Between good and evil lies objectivity. Between light and dark rises dawn. Between male and female stands Dana, the loyal one, the Lover. When everything else changes, the one who will love me forever. *This* is real, *this* is truth. Yes?"

Dana sees Edstuart and the offspring at the far side of the dock, huddled together.

"But my Dana," says Tatiana. "There is another kind of love. Mother love."

Edstuart is rubbing the offspring's head, murmuring baby talk. He looks up, sees Dana, and from across the distance, Dana looks into his eyes. In those eyes once filled with bafflement and sorrow, Dana sees terror. Brittle, bright terror.

"Don't go," says Dana, filled with dread. He takes Tatiana's hand.

But Sha!n sees her.

"Damma!" A weird shriek issues from the tiny, gleaming mouth.

Dana tries to restrain her, but she breaks away.

She runs to the offspring, takes Sha!n up into her arms. Their wings buzz joyfully around them, forming a chatoyant halo.

Tatiana rips her black bodice down, gives her breast to the offspring.

Sha!n suckles.

At the taste of her, its eyes bulge and its babyish cheeks turn hard and it sinks its long curved teeth into her. The crescent moons slash, ripping, tearing her chest open.

The time for Holy Triad.

332

Dana runs to her.

Prefect Tule kicks Dana aside, advances on Edstuart. Edstuart kneels, trembling like a leaf. At the sight and smell of Sha!n's assault, his skin begins to crack, harden, split open like a molting dragonfly. The Prefect swings the crescent knife down Edstuart's back, hastening, officially initiating that which has already begun.

Edstuart is in trance, body split and oozing, but stumbling toward the pair. He embraces the bloodied couple, then tenderly, inexorably, bites Sha!n's head off. Thick purple gushes from the tiny quivering neck. Tatiana, still moving somehow, reaches around Edstuart's waist, grips one stiff flap of his split back, pulls it free of his spine.

The three bodies entwine, disintegrate, merge.

Unite.

The gore speedily coagulates, transmutes, forming a blood-slick, veined globe of rippling flesh, over which a thick, gelatinous white skin begins to grow at once.

"The Holy Triad!" cries Prefect Tule, unable to conceal his own grotesque awe. "The World Egg!"

Dana crumples.

"Dana, baby." Lenni comes and holds him. "Listen to me. They're only larvae, swarm-born."

"Outsider!" Prefect Tule yells at Lenni. "Do not denigrate what you do not understand. They are the Chosen of Triad. They sacrifice their puny privileged lives to the World Egg. From this a million new citizens will spring. It's glorious!"

"Please listen, babe," says Lenni, stroking Dana's face. "There are biological analogies in terran bees, ants and termites, certain flies. The fertile ones, the reproductive elite of the swarm, produce the offspring that, when ripened, acts as the catalyst. When the time is right, the mother host yields royal nectar. The catalytic agent is stimulated, consumes the mother host, and the male partner both completes the synthesis and contributes his nutrients. Their union produces *that*. It's a pupa, containing genetic material for another swarm. Without the pupa, and the few who must create it, their entire race would die."

"Outsiders!" Prefect Tule charges at them, swinging the crescent knife. "See how you try to interfere! Look at your repugnance! You should not have seen the great Mystery. No outsider has ever seen the Holy Triad. This is Sacrilege! You all must die."

But rising up with a swagger and a sneer, Lenni confronts the

333

bloody edge of the remorseless steelyn moon. "Leave us alone, you ugly bastard. Your Damma commanded you."

The Prefect halts. The knife dives back into its sheath. "You are correct," he concedes at once. A Prefect. Fulfilling his duty as a Triadian. "But get away from here, outsiders. You have seen enough. This is a matter for the Keeper of the Triad now."

The World Egg rolls fitfully. Odd extrusions thrust here and there through the moist, pale skin.

Prefect Tule prepares a hexagonal box, spitting wax from his monstrous mouth. Next he fills the box with deep purple jelly spurted from an organ in his lower torso. With his huge long forearms, he carefully, laboriously lifts the fitful World Egg and deposits it inside.

"What about Tatiana?" whispers Dana. He tears his eyes from the spectacle that shifted shapes before them. "What about . . . her? Her pain?"

"She has no more pain, outsider," says Prefect Tule. "She has fulfilled her destiny."

"Come on, Dana," says Lenni. "Come home with me now, baby."

Dana looks at Lenni, and he sees a face that is neither male nor female, but human. Always human. A face filled with sorrow and compassion and love. A beautiful face. He takes Lenni's hand, and together they walk down into the dark and holy night.

Alex Jeffers for the second time this issue, with a dark, elegant glimpse into the troubled future.

You don't notice them easily. When he comes into il Paradiso he's just another joachim, a little richer maybe, a better cut of clothing than what hangs around and below most of the seventeen pairs of eyes that swivel, inevitably, to watch him. He's no taller than most, say one-point-seven meters, lean and fit. The lights are kept dim here in Heaven, but he's fair, we can see that, and his features are pleasant. He walks in the door with the same swagger we all assume in this territory: the arrogance of the doubly oppressed. We know why he's here. We watch him.

He doesn't look around as he comes straight to the bar. There's not much to look at, but that's not why. He leans against the slab of polished granite, says, "Chablis, iced, with lime," without looking at Pieter. His voice is light, flexible, sardonic, foreign. I turn away, hunch over my glass. *Chablis, iced, with lime.* Born to pretension, I say to myself, last scion of the late regime. The wine won't be Californian nor more than a year old, but he needn't admit it, and we're free to take him at his own estimation: il conte, le comte, el conde. No doubt he wears a signet on one of the long hands tucked into his pockets.

Pieter brings the wine, sets it down. El conde flips a high-denomination plastic chip onto the bar. Pieter stares at the chip in horror, his hands flutter about. "I can't—" he says, "we haven't change, signore, we cannot accept plastic." It's been years since I've seen so much money in one piece, and it is simply an octagonal wafer of steel-blue plastic impressed with the image of their greatest culture hero on the upper side and (I remember) the eight linked stars of the

ALEX JEFFERS

Coalition on the reverse. The ninth star, of course, Earth's sun, is not depicted.

"You don't accept tips?" le comte asks calmly.

"But," says Pieter, "it's—"

"It would pay to drunken everyone here ten times over," I say, "and still leave a more than handsome gratuity."

"Well," he says.

"Anyone here—almost anyone in the city—I myself—would smilingly slit Pieter's throat for that."

He shrugs elegantly. "I carry nothing smaller."

"You come ill-prepared," I say, fingering a glass token of considerably lesser value from my breast pocket. "Here, Pieter. And bring me a chablis, iced, with lime."

Pieter takes the coin with relief, stares a moment longer at the plastic chip. With ten of those he could open his own bar. And own its building.

"Thank you, signore," il conte says.

"Por nada." I turn away. The game is subtle, and the stakes have been raised a thousandfold in one move. He cannot be so naive.

My previous contact glances at me across the room, from the gaming table where he sits. Amused, yet he wishes me luck. We are a brotherhood as strait and close-bound as any monastery full of Trappists. He turns his eye to likelier prospects: that joachim, say, or the sulky young gymnast I'd had my sights on.

Pieter slides the squat glass of chilled wine to me, takes the half-finished cielazzurro away. The plastic chip still lies on the bar, and il conte's glass stands untouched beside it. Drops of condensation cling to it like ducal gems. Sipping my drink, I decide that le comte is not so subtle as he wishes to appear. His eyes range around il Paradiso, weighing, gauging, reckoning. At least he knows why he came here.

"Your wealth is apparent, signore," I say. "You needn't display it so recklessly." I flick the coin with a fingertip. Pieter winces. I have considered pocketing it myself, but Pieter watches and though he will not accept it in payment he would easily and without guilt take it from me—so that it could be taken from him. "It's a powerful invitation."

The count turns to me. His hooded eyes are an indeterminate color. His cheekbones are very high, very broad, and very sharp. "Thank you again. I suppose I wasn't thinking."

"That is highly unsafe."

His eyes lower, his hand flashes out to retrieve the chip.

"You are new to the city?" I turn my stool to face him, uncross my legs, reach into my pocket. "Would you care for a smoke?" I offer the package.

He shakes his head. "New to the country." His eyes shift erratically, his upper lip twitches. His sparse pale eyebrows, I notice, extend outward from his eyes like wings, merging into his hairline, and a downy stubble has crept up his cheeks and threatens to overwhelm his eyes. His chin, though, is innocent of beard. His face flicks away again, to gaze out over the angels of il Paradiso.

I light my cigarette. Perhaps I'm not attractive. "You're from Europe?" I ask. I don't think so.

"Most recently." Still he won't look at me. "Warszawa."

"How is it over there?"

"It is the same everywhere, is it not?"

Yes. Economies are moribund. Societies lie dazed on the floor, chuttering drunkenly to themselves. Perhaps in the rain forest of the Amazon or the catastrophically isolated interior of Japan or Kazakhstan there may still be those who don't know and hence haven't collapsed into catatonia, but they never knew anything anyway, living in a sort of cultural autism. *They* came, all on a bright September eve, made their demonstrations of power, and struck terror into the hearts of our governments. High ministers and officials ate their deaths, revolutions broke out in the devastated areas of Australasia and the Mediterranean, a prophet rose up out of Patagonia's windy plain and led several millions of his followers to a quick and humane decease on the (metaphorical) sword of the infidel. Was it not clear that we required their governance? Yet still, all our dreams are in the bottom of a glass in Heaven. But we keep on. Twitching.

And now the little gymnast comes up to the bar, swaying his taut nalgas and flaunting his improbable basket. He wants a drink. He can't decide. Can the signores offer any suggestions? *Chablis, iced, with lime.* It could become a fad. He asks Pieter for a cuba enlazada. Pieter obliges with a grin. He can understand the gymnast: he was one himself not too long ago, and still favors their company over that of his regular patrons—putative corpses like myself and the count, Draculas to the gymnasts' Mina Harkers.

Le comte looks on the gymnast with approval. The gymnast looks on el conde with calculation. I look on both of them with an emotion too tedious to distinguish. I take a drag off my cigarette. The gymnast prances away, having decided il conte looks too *hungry*.

339

"My name is Christopher," il conte offers unexpectedly.

Indeed. "Richard." We are both dated. The gymnast would be named Luigi or Lars or Guillermo. "You aren't drinking," I add, sipping at my own. The ice has all melted.

"No." No excuses. I like that. He leans back against the bar, props his elbows on its edge. His hands still hide in deep pockets. The silky gray fabric of his shirt clings and settles suggestively on long-muscled arms, narrow chest. His black trousers are flatteringly tight, showing off an extreme length of leg. The fly buttons beg to be undone, if only to discover what besides his hands he hides there. He rides his hips out from the waist.

Pieter rattles glasses. Curfew is nigh. My previous contact and his joachim have already left. Lights flash aimlessly in the glass tops of the empty gaming tables. A juggler and our gymnast perform subtle attenuated acrobatics at a corner table. Heaven is closing down for the night. Who will make the inevitable gesture, close the circuit, strike the spark? I ask Pieter for another, a final drink.

When he brings it to me, il conte leans over the bar and asks Pieter, "Where can one go after curfew?"

Pieter simpers. "No place, signore," he says, "no place that would accept your money, except home to bed."

"Was that an invitation, Pieter?" I feel protective of the count.

"Not to you."

"You could go to The Bridge," I tell the count, "if you had glass, or went with someone who did."

"I have no glass," he says.

"I have."

"Is that an invitation, Ricardo?" Pieter asks.

"What is The Bridge?" asks the count.

"A haven for the downtrodden."

"A trap," says Pieter.

"Of primary interest is that it's open. And welcoming. Shall we go?"

"Very well." Le comte makes no motion to leave.

Pieter takes away my glass, and il conte's. He pours wine and ice cubes into the sink behind the bar. He wipes black hair off his forehead. "I have to close up," he says.

"But aren't you coming?" I ask him slyly.

"Not just now, no, thank you."

"Okay, goodnight then." I touch his nose with my index finger. "Sleep well, and not alone."

Pursing his lips at me, Pieter sighs. El conde and I head out. Past gaming tables and their hectic lights, past overflowing ashtrays and disconsolate empty glasses. Past black windows that let only the brightest of the city's lights shine through like dim haloed stars. Into the vestibule where I pull the enveloping chador from its hook and struggle the folds over my head and onto my shoulders. Le comte swathes himself in a deep-green velvet cloak and settles his mask onto his face. It represents a tortured saint, Sebastian perhaps: dark chestnut hair flowing off its high creased brow, rosey-red lips twisted in pious anguish, heavily lashed black eyes set deep below thin eyebrows.

My own mask volunteers less psychology: it is the plush, opaque, and sultry visage of a white cat: serene blue eyes and bristling whiskers. It doesn't suit me—but then, it's not meant to.

Suitably disguised, we take the elevator down to street level, through the lobby and out onto Montgomery. The air has a brisk autumnal chill to it. A heavy pall of fog stands overhead, masking the jaggedly truncated apex of the pyramid. Down the street banks of spotlights glance off the faceted ruddy north face of the Bank of America massif where our masters deliberate the present and future of humanity. So we are arrogant enough to presume. The upper third of the building is subtracted by fog.

We go south, toward California and the station. The count walks with a loose-limbed abandon; his arms stagger and his cloak waves like a banner. He is constantly staring. The street is empty, and clean. The rubble was cleared away long ago. No one walks the streets. It's almost curfew. Everyone has locked themselves up; lights on the upper floors blaze, but entryways are dark and closed and the streetlamps shut off. We cross Pine, and le comte gazes upward at the looming shaft of the BofA building. Snug within, the alien Governor of Earth may sleep at the center of her vast information web, or she may be far away, in Cairo or Djakarta, Budapest or La Paz. When she first took the Grand Tour, circling the globe from city to city in search of a congenial seat, she found it here, in this magnificent abandoned hulk. If you can't grant them anything else, you must admit the aliens have an eye for architecture. The count stares up in awe. I urge him onward. We come to the California Street station.

341

I go to the board and request a car. Il conte watches me intently. "Where are we going?"

"The city-side tower of the Golden Gate Bridge."

"Let me pay for the trip."

"As you wish."

He slips his card into the appropriate slot. I'm just as pleased not to be identified as using the Net this close to curfew. A bell pings. We go to the indicated door, step into the slick sanitary bubble, I punch the destination code, and off we go. The Net runs faster than I can remember it doing, before the aliens revived the infrastructure, but, still, it will take us ten or fifteen minutes, most of it underground and nothing to look at. Except each other.

I take off my mask, stretch my legs, wiggle my toes within their boots. "The Bridge," I say, "is cantilevered out over the water from the pylon. It's a private, restricted-membership entertainment facility, so it doesn't have to shut down at curfew."

His hands are still in his pockets. They must find some comfort there. "You have a membership?" he asks.

"Yes."

"It's inclined?"

"Yes. And tawdry. But open."

He turns his mask away, gazes at the tunnels sliding past.

"There'll be lots of us," I say. "You needn't stay with me." Hesitantly I lower my left hand onto his knee. The other hand smooths the upholstery. Sebastian's dark eyes turn to me. I can see nothing in their depths. "Who are you?"

"Christopher Sebastian, known as Kit. Thirty-six years old. Born London, Britain, April seven, two ought five one." His voice runs in a monotone; his false eyes fix me; he's giving me his résumé. Until a month ago he was sole owner and operator of a successful informat in Warsaw; he followed a few bad tips and was edged out by a consortium under the invaders' seal; now he's traveling without destination. As good a story as I've heard lately.

Another bell pings, and we're here.

My mask fits back over my head like a sleeve. The bubble opens, and we clamber out. This last city-side station of the Net is not well kept: paper and foil wrappers huddle like rats in windswept corners, the dark glass windows are crowded with a dense population of fingerprints, and the white concrete walls riot with graffiti: LET NOTHING ALIEN BE HUMAN TO YOU   JUGGLERS PLAY WITH BALLS   WHY ARE SO MANY GYMNASTS SUICIDES?   THEY SWING OUT AT THE BRIDGE. The door slides open and a sweep of cold wind brings fog and the smell of the Pacific. I slip my arm through el conde's elbow and we slip out.

LEAVE YOUR CULTURE AT THE DOOR a sign invites, and the maître d'— a supple gymnast in scarlet domino, sex barely cached—politely divests us of our robes and masks and chivvies us into the elevator.

In good light il conte's face is more arresting than simply attractive. His touch with cosmetics is masterful and understated: were it not for the peculiar cyanotic tinge to his skin, I'd suspect naturalism. I catch my staring reflection in his eyes, consider the utility of masks, and notice a dent in the otherwise smooth descent of his nose. He shrugs, and the lift settles to a stop.

The lower floor of The Bridge is analogous to a circus safety net— in that successful gymnasts are not to be found here. Although the room we come into is crowded: joachims and joannas of all descriptions and varieties, jockets and jugglers, and others less definable. Here is a small squadron of fake aliens decked out in fanciful helms of black lacquer, sweeping grayish cloaks, knee-high boots of garnet-red suede (how well the invaders understand spectacle! how poorly we imitate them!). There is a juggler in full dress: silks and satins and the floppy three-pronged cap of bells. Joannas like ancient faded flowers; joachims in sober business garb; mechanical jockets in gold and silver plate. We press through the crowd toward the bar; il conte averts his eyes from the aliens—bitter for his lost livelihood, I imagine, or embarrassed at their display: as if a troop of Jews were to masquerade as Nazi stormtroopers or an Afrikaaner to dye himself black.

So we reach the bar at last. This bartender I don't know: he is tall and blond, and a stripe of fluorescing blue paint bisects him vertically from hairline to pubis. "Chablis, iced, with lime," I order. "Two." A fragile magenta blossom of a joanna by my side sniggers. Her eyes are bright and unfocused. He's inhaling siddharthin as though it were water, and drowning in it. An ex-gymnast stands beside him, sipping cielazzurro, his hand twined in hers. I offer them a sardonic grin— suggesting that el conde and I are, perhaps, so far behind the times as to be up to the minute.

And of course when the glasses arrive le comte has disappeared. The lights shudder now, and across the room a dense cobalt-blue curtain of light winks out, revealing a stage where a trio of rhythmatics are ready to entertain us. I am not in a mood to be entertained. Where is the count? So I had told him he needn't stay with me—so what? I had hoped for loyalty. But I'm patient. I'll find him, and if he's a bit

343

defused by then, all the better. The rhythmatics begin their performance. The Bridge quakes and the lights twitch, little explosions of sound race around the room like comets. I'll go upstairs.

Upstairs is a different space altogether. The center of everything is the Red Room: a huge demispherical volume, its two inner walls and the floor carpeted with scarlet plush, and then the vast quarter-dome of redwood struts and ruby-tinted glass. Far away the lights on the truncated Marin-side tower and the lights of buildings shine like stationary fireflies. In daylight you can see one of the old cables sliding from high above you, down into the bleak water below. At night, if you press against the glass and look down, you can watch reflections of the light around you chopping on the waves below. But the views are likely to encourage depression, and you—and I—would rather join the party.

The clothed body is rare here. Most of us are going to or just coming from the Maze. The taut muscles of a gymnast's thigh slide against a joachim's buttocks. Joanna fondles joanna: joanna is still dressed and thus retains his identity, but her filmy frock is steam-sodden and clings to his narrow chest and narrower hips, while naked joanna's wig is askew. A particularly accomplished gymnast perched on a small raised stage mimes autofellatio. Arms and legs—chests hairless and hirsute—nalgas and necks—balls and jacks. But here a billowing dashiki and there an urban toreador in skin-tight rose rayon and gold braid; a lumpy joachim in immediately fashionable mid-twentieth suit-&-tie; a single false invader looking lost; and over there, stovepipe black trousers, gray shirt, hands in pockets: the count. His shoulders hunch up around his ears, yet he towers over the little black-haired juggler whose hands flip about like enthusiastic sparrows and whose oiled brown skin and gold jewelry create a nimbus of reflected glory.

No need to be direct, I decide. A gymnast slides by me. I press a cold-sweating glass against his back. He stops, shocked. "A favor, signore?" I ask.

He peers at me disdainfully. "A chance of it. What?"

"You see joachim over there? Hands in pockets? Would you take him this, say he forgot it downstairs?" I give the gymnast the glass: chablis, iced, with lime.

He takes it. "Can be done, signore."

"Grazie."

341

And now into the Maze. I find an unoccupied cubicle and feed it coins and my clothes, and more coins until it produces a chain of glass counters I can use as money, without needing pockets to carry it. The string braceleting my wrist, I select a towel, lock the cubicle, and head into the labyrinth. Corridors tiled in the rusty red of old blood. Naked men and men wrapped in towels. The air is warm and humid and carries the rich scents of sweat and sex. I carry my own glass and sip at it from time to time.

"Ricardo!" someone calls from behind me.

I turn, and it's Pieter hurrying out of breath down the corridor. "Well, this is a surprise," I say. "I thought you wouldn't be caught here?"

He comes to a stop with his arm around my waist. "I was lonely. Have you lost your friend?"

"Misplaced him for a moment. Nothing permanent."

"That's good. You make an attractive couple." Pieter is a romantic: he wants to see everyone with someone else, permanently. Unfortunately for his peace of mind, he's promiscuous by nature. Not that he's ever before shown any interest in me. His hand strays across my buttocks, and I look at him for the first time. He's taller than I, and more muscular; his walnut-stained skin is sown liberally with black hair. Hazel eyes hide behind lids painted the silver-gray of beech leaves; his hair is curly, loose, disheveled. Ordinarily I'd be more than interested, indeed I'm taken: but the fact remains that I am taken and would further rather not discolor his vision. We head down the corridor, bantering like old friends who needn't say anything to get their points across—only we're not friends, so little of what he says means anything to me and much of what I say must find no resonance in Pieter's mind.

And finally he leans against me and, with apparent dismay, whispers, "I've got a room around here somewhere."

"I think not . . . just now."

He sighs and squeezes me affectionately, and walks a little faster. I don't know whether to stay with him, follow, or strike out on my own.

For the moment, I'll stay with Pieter.

The corridors twist and turn and bi- and trifurcate seemingly without reason, although it's all planned, of course: it is after all a labyrinth. Pieter knows his way through it almost as well as I, and I know where we're going. Nevertheless, it's something of a shock when we round an angle—cleverly sound-muffled to increase the surprise— into a vast empty space full of water and men: the observation gallery that runs around the bottom of the pool. The insurance would be

345

ALEX JEFFERS

crippling were it not for the miracles of alien technology—think of it: a half-Olympic-size swimming pool suspended in the center of a building that is itself suspended some fifty meters above the water, and with a continuous glass-walled viewing gallery around the floor . . . think what just a little earthquake might do.

Cruisers all along the corridor. And within the aquarium like exotic fish a hundred naked men dancing weightless in clear water laced (one part in a million) with cielazzurro. They're so involved. It's a cruel game, actually. You're in the gallery gently deflecting the sighs and leers of other predators and through the glass you see a plume of bubbles and there, there, gliding slowly past, is just who you want (he waves to you, purses his lips, lets loose a shimmering bubble of a kiss) and . . . how do you get to him?

I loop my arm carelessly around Pieter's shoulders. "I feel like a swim."

"Not for me, thanks."

"See you later, then. Good hunting." I touch my fingertip companionably to his nose, and head for the stairs. They take me up and out. Figures of fog and flesh amble about the redwood deck. A railing protects one from falling overboard into the channel of the Golden Gate, and a low parapet indicates the pool edge. It's cold, and the fog is full of the ghosts of drowned sailors stinking of salt. I drape my towel over the railing where I'm not likely to find it again, balance my glass next to it. The water will be warm.

I slip over the edge. It *is* warm, just above blood temperature, superoxygenated, and heady: the cielazzurro. It's lit from below: the swimmers are black cutouts against a great brightness. I go down, submerged as in amniotic fluid. Water slides around my thighs like gentle hands. Pieter peers through the glass windows, beckons to me. I mouth kisses at him, coyly; he points down the corridor. Along the corridor to where an all too familiar dark figure declines against the wall and idly watches the dance. Here is a cruel reversal of the usual game. I cannot picture le comte swimming here. In a sybaritic underground grotto with a small number of aristocratic friends and adorable waterbabies, yes, or disporting himself in the lily-choked basin of a renaissance fountain, but not here, not here amongst the indiscriminate masses. No. He declines to notice me, intent on the high-pitched monologue of a frail passion-flower joanna.

Suddenly the charm of playing piranha is gone and I feel abysmally foolish. What am I thinking of, when all I'm thinking of is penetrating his reserve, forcing him to acknowledge and to desire me. This is it, this is the truth I must face: all I want tonight is him. I am obsessed.

I stroke up to the surface, avoiding gleaming bodies like electric eels. The water empties from my lungs, the pure air rushes in but brings no rush. The residue of cielazzurro in my blood only intensifies the ambient chill and makes the crawling fog feel like worms on my skin. At least I have discovered my own intentions. My towel is still where I left it; I dry myself, toss off the last centimeter of watered wine, and toss the glass over . . . a sacrifice to sea-foam Aphrodite.

I descend into the Maze in search of, not minotaurs, tricephalic dogs, nor the lords of the revels, but a beast as mythological and shy as the unicorn, as terrifying as the basilisk, as magnetic as the gorgon. I return to my cubicle. The bathing machine first strips me of grime, then burnishes my skin with fine oils, styles my hair and beard. I inspect the cosmetics it offers, but opt for shameless naturalism. The mirror admires me: no beauty, no, but a man of the world, self-assured, urbane, cultured, with the light of fanaticism in his eyes. I discard my previous clothing as nondescript, and allow the cubicle to outfit me. It offers as options: gymnast, juggler, joanna, joachim, generalissimo, jester, jefe, Job, Jokanaan, Judas, Jove. Choosing to impersonate a jongleur, I select plum-colored hose and peach velvet doublet set off by a scarlet codpiece of no mean dimension. I refuse the wide-brimmed, slashed and tasseled hat, the purely decorative lute, but accept the soft suede boots. The mirror admits I cut quite a figure.

And now the hunt.

I sally out to the Red Room. The crowd is thinning a bit in the late hours of the morning, but the action is if anything more intent. A single rhythmatic on a raised platform conducts concealed synthesizers with the industrial jewels on his many fingers, flexes his bright body, and sings—the dank lyrics contradicted by his clear, straining tenor and the glittery histrionics of the music. Some of us, in couples and triples and quadruples, dance. The bar's packed with elbows. I push my way through to order chablis, iced, with lime. I cannot see el conde.

With a clash of automated cymbals the rhythmatic ends his song. A funnel of black light falls on him. A gleaming gold jocket and a stodgy joachim who have been contentedly waltzing square off. The jocket pulls a ten-centimeter-long blade, slashes at the joachim's face. The older man shrieks and falls to the floor. Crowing, the jocket dances a tattoo around him. The black light lifts, the rhythmatic stum-

347

bles out, the jocket embraces him, steers him to the windows. Whispering, they stand there apart. The joachim pulls himself to his feet, staggers off toward the Maze. A red line bleeds across his left cheekbone. The house music comes back up.

I look back at jocket and rhythmatic: they are no longer alone. El conde perches with them like a great black vulture. Here's my chance.

I saunter across the floor. The count looks up—not recognizing me—and back. And at me again when I lay my hand on his arm. The blue on his skin is darker around jawbone and cheek. He says abstractedly, "Yes?"

"Shall we dance?"

"I'm sorry?"

"May I have the pleasure of a dance?"

His eyes tighten suddenly. "Of course, Richard, I'd be delighted."

I lead him out. Putting his arms around me with some delicacy, he presses against shoulder blade and the small of my back with two fingers of each hand. The music is sedative, with a slow, complex, repetitive bass. I hold him close, and with great slow dignity we circle and circle. He is uncannily graceful, but has no feel for the music. I lick my lips, look up at his face. His eyes are not there. I rest my head on his chest, run my fingers up and down his spine.

The number comes to an end. I clench my fingers into his buttocks. He stares down at me in gentle surprise. "Shall we go?" I ask.

"Go? Go where?"

"Somewhere else. Where we could be alone."

He might never have thought of it before. Can he be so naive? "Where can we go after curfew?"

I pull him gently from the center of the floor. "My apartment."

"Oh." He glances around, at all our multiformed splendor. "Very well, Richard." There is a thread of resignation in his voice which I will have to deal with later. Taking his arm (his hands are back nestling in their pockets), I lead him to the elevator. We collect our cloaks and masks, and walk out into the wind. The span of bridge from tower to shore is scarred, the tarmac buckled and pitted. The railings are still maintained, although the hundreds of layers of red paint have been flaking off for seventy years and the steel beneath is more red with rust than the paint ever was.

348

I order a Net car at the station. The count doesn't offer to pay. He is bemused, and I know better than to press my illusory advantage during the twelve-minute ride to Kezar Pavilion. He doesn't speak either as we climb the short distance from Golden Gate Park to the small Victorian on Frederick where I maintain my residence. Noname, my little Siamese, is waiting at the top of the stairs outside my door. She shies away from il conte, darts through the door, and hides in the big philodendron by the French door to the deck. I switch on the lights. Closing the door gently, I lock it. Name, the fat flame-colored Persian, comes out of the kitchen. He warily approaches, but two meters from le comte arches his back suddenly, spits, and flees.

"May I offer you a drink?"

He stares at me coldly. "You may," he says. "But I won't drink it."

"I didn't think you would." I move up to him; he pulls back. "I'll take your cape and mask."

He moves very quickly: his mask is in my hands, and I have had only a bare glimpse of his own hands before they return to refuge. I ease the cape from his shoulders.

He goes to look out the window. I light a cigarette. "You're awfully edgy."

"I did not plan this."

"No more did I. I'm enjoying it as it happens." I begin unlacing the front of the doublet.

He turns. "Those are not the clothes you were wearing." His eyes flick away from the extravagant claims of the red codpiece.

"I was hoping to make an impression."

He sits down suddenly. The rattan chair creaks. "Your pets do not like me."

"They like very few people. Noname doesn't even like me very much."

"Cats don't like me. Nor dogs. Their senses are clearer."

I pull off the doublet, drape it over a chair. I sit, facing him. "Does that mean something?"

"Yes."

"Are you going to undress?" He stares at me—as a mouse stares at a python? Or is it the other way around? "What are we going to do? What's your preference? I'm adaptable."

He says nothing.

I go into the bedroom, pull the spread back. He follows, but I don't turn. I unfasten the codpiece, peel down the hose. "I've been told the couch can be slept on with some success," I tell him. His cold hand touches the small of my back. He says, "I do not want that."

349

He retreats when I turn. I reach out to touch the tip of his nose (an habitual gesture), and it falls off. He covers his face with his hand.

I sit down on the bed. I understand now. Why he hides his hands. His hand has only three fingers. The thumb is too long. He lets his hand fall. Where the false nose-tip was his nostrils are long slits. It changes the cast of his face entirely.

"You're not human."

He unbuttons his shirt faster than I can watch, takes it off. His chest is very narrow. Fine golden fur completely covers his torso, ending unexpectedly and incongruously at his collar and a few centimeters above his wrists. The skin that glows through it is very faintly blue.

"You're one of them."

"Yes."

He's trembling hard. So am I. He unfastens the front of his trousers.

He sits at the end of the bed, removes shoes and socks. His feet are not wide enough to balance on.

"If I knew what I wanted," he says, not looking at me, "I would not be here."

He spreads his fingers out on his thighs. He looks at me with those eyes whose color I still can't place.

I have, I think, got a grip on myself now. "Presumably," I say, "there is something we can do together. Or you wouldn't have exposed yourself to the possibility."

He stares at me some more.

"Take off your trousers."

He stands, finishes unbuttoning his fly. Not coyness, no, but fear. The trousers slip down his long, oddly muscled legs. He sits down again.

Standing, I go to the window, look down at the street. It is impossible. Perhaps the most disconcerting aspect is that, for all, I find him attractive. He is elegantly put together—not, granted, to human standards of beauty or function, but nonetheless. I want him. I'm not sure *how* I want him, whether sex is still the issue, but to possess him, yes. Obsession is a kind word.

I glare at my reflection in the glass, and at his, dimmer, beside. It's his move.

I want to know what his fur would feel like against my skin. I want to know the taste of his mouth. I want to learn his tendons and muscles, their points of insertion, the angles and degrees of their pull and the strength of their tension. I want to comprehend the structure of his skeleton and the meanings and functions of his internal organs. I want, insofar as is possible, to *know* him, to know him so completely that he can be a surprise.

"What is your name?" I ask his reflection.

He looks at me. "Arael is the significant part of it."

"Well, Arael, what are we going to do with ourselves? Do you kiss?"

"I know how."

I go over to him. I sit beside him on the bed. I touch his shoulder. He is very cold. I lean over, place my lips on his. They are firm, hard with the teeth behind them. I push against them with my tongue. He turns his head a fraction. I grasp his shoulders, force him down on the bed. He doesn't struggle. His inner mouth is tart and tastes slightly of citrus. The surfaces of his teeth seem somehow rough, and there are fewer of them than in a man's mouth. His tongue pushes past mine into my mouth, recoils. His vertical nostrils flutter with breath. My fingers run down his arm, comb the soft fur. He moans, and pushes, and pulls. I gaze into his eyes.

His eyes are colorless as light. The pupils float in them like sunspots.

He pulls me down on top of him. His body feels hard and excessively boney: it's as though I'm making love to a staircase, all knobs and hard projections with a carpet-runner of fine dense fur. His mouth swallows mine. His hands clench into my buttocks. I do not know how to deal with such passion . . . except to give in to it and feed it with my own.

We wrestle across the bed, throwing blankets and spread onto the floor, an hysterical tangle of limbs and torsos; and it seems to me that I am fighting with him for my life and my integrity as a free human being. For he is the Invader: the physical manifestation of Earth's conquest.

He grunts heavily, closes his face for a moment, then stares at me through those clear, clear eyes.

Undone, I roll away from him across the bed and gaze at the wall. "What do you want?" I ask him.

Knowledge, I expect. Understanding. Contact. "Sex," he says bluntly.

"Is that it?"

"In effect." He throws an arm over me, grasps my jack in one of his narrow hands. Tugs and squeezes.

I don't know that I like this sudden personality shift. Dealing with il conte the unreachable was frustrating, yes, but fine food for obsessive infatuation. Arael the angel of lust presents a much more problematic thesis. His mouth with its strange teeth and agile tongue takes my jack. The ceiling is very white. I wonder where homosexuality stands in the aliens' sexual spectrum, and how perverse is this specific act: miscegenation? bestiality? or—considering that humanity is as a race less advanced than they—pedophilia?

I remember a boy of twelve who watched his father come out of the rolling surf, dark hair matted wet against chest and sturdy legs, the fabric of his trunks molded around sturdy jack and heavy balls; who watched his father under the outdoor shower peel off the clinging shorts and rub soap into lather in private hair. I don't know what my father thought of as he routinely masturbated in the shower; I don't believe he ever knew that I as routinely watched. We hid from each other always.

Arael is hairier than my hairy father, and seems much younger, but it is surely my father's back I finally caress and his mouth that nuzzles up my chest to meet my own. I have my father in my hands. His warm psychotropic breath fills my throat, bubbles through my lungs. His hands fold around my skin with the frail small gentleness of thunderclaps. His mouth on mine is as strong and unyielding as a snail's shell. His body, warm as slate, moves slowly slowly, soft as eggs. The beach under the towel beneath us is hard and unyielding; the towel itself is thick with sand. Grains cling to our slick skins. My father is damp with warm seawater and sweat, greasy with sweet oil. I can't open my eyes for the bright sunlight. Surf chatters. Children shriek. The summer before the storm I had just turned nineteen and was hiding out in Heaven. I worked four nights a week, eight to four—this was precurfew—pushing liquor and drugs at men as anxious to know me as I was to know them, but they were less afraid. I was afraid. I was afraid to meet a man I could desire as much as my father. Not that I didn't get my share of sex. I was a fair gymnast in my prime—and how many joachims needed more than my body.

And then the aliens came. With their seat of governance in the magnificent abandoned hulk of the Bank of America building only a few blocks from Heaven's outpost in the broken Transamerica Pyramid, I kept my job under the table and took a more reputable day position in an augury. The aliens were among us—although you didn't notice them easily. Masks became fashionable, indispensable, and finally mandatory. Curfew locked in at midnight. The homosexual underground was suddenly the only available hell after hours. It was well populated. Heaven thrived. I made some lucky guesses and a lot of money, but did not find my true love. And have not. But am still searching. And so have found myself back in my daddy's arms. Safe and sound.

He rocks and charms me, holds and transfixes me. Hands like warm crustaceans web me about. The soft stubble on cheeks and wrists must raise welts on my skin; the softer fur is like water. I am replete with his flesh.

He groans. His breath, rank with carnivorous instinct, washes over me. He bucks and tosses and moans and becomes. His eyes blaze. I bring him down onto my chest, into my arms, wrap my legs around his narrow back. I will carry him through his storm and to a safe haven.

He mutters deeply. I run my hands down his back. His face is hidden in the corner of my neck and shoulder; he speaks to the pillow in a language I cannot interpret. I pull my fingers down his side. He pushes his head farther into the pillow, his chin into my shoulder. How can I call him out? What can I say to him?—I love you, Daddy?

He lifts his head and his chest and the rest of him up and off me, rolls over onto his back. His hand lies on my belly like a benediction. I cover it with one of mine. He sighs, a deep tragic exhalation. I close my fist around his narrow hand. The fingers twitch, broken double-jointed twigs. The nailless thumb pokes at my palm. It is not my father's hand.

I curl into his side, stare at his shallow profile broken only by the bridge of his nonexistent nose. His lips are flat, pulled back and away from teeth. His chin juts sharp as a razor blade. This is my beloved: his profile is a skull's. His chest expands and contracts. There's so little flesh on him I can see each rib distinctly. His sunken belly, his prominent hips, the long slender bones of his legs. He stirs and settles. His flesh sifts down to cloak the sheets in dust. His bones creak and disengage as cartilage dissolves. My hand is full of fingers. This is my beloved.

"What do you want?" I ask.

"Comprehension. Trust. Affection." His teeth rattle. His bones shift and scrape. His fingers fall in percussive clatter from my hand to the floor. What can he do without his fingers? I get out of bed—carefully, so as not to disarrange him further—and search for them.

353

They glisten like shells on the hardwood floor amid the dust under the bed.

Two eyes glare at me from deep in the dust, fiery green and angry. Name growls around the finger bone in his teeth, backs away. Can Arael be reconstituted lacking one joint? I reach for Name. He scrabbles farther into the dust, which clings to his fur like iron shavings to a magnet. I grab at him; he scratches my hand and vanishes, feet thumping hard, into the living room.

And my mouth is full of dust and I've scattered little segments of bone about the floor and my own finger will infect, and all for my beloved. I go to the bathroom, rinse my mouth and face, wash my hands under hot water.

When I return there's movement in his chest, a pushing and pulling, a sensual kneading. Noname turns to stare at me from where she crouches in a citadel of ribs. She wraps her jaws around a rib, crunches it, then, as I approach, tears it from its appointed place and drags it away with her.

"Affection," he whispers, conspiratorial and snide, "love and understanding."

I kneel heavily at his side. The rocking of the mattress dislodges still more components, disrupts still more connections. I don't know what to do. He is lost to me—more lost than sleeping Briar Rose to her prince, than poisoned Snow White to Charming, than the Beast to Beauty or Osiris to Isis. Can this transformation be reversed by a kiss?

I lie down beside him (bones collide with the sound of a spastic marimba) and stare at the ceiling.

The cats come to me in my despair. Name reclines purring on my chest. Noname huddles into my armpit. I feel like weeping. The tears carve runnels into my cheeks, puddle the sheet. Name's purr is rhythmic, hypnotic as distant surf. The mattress bobs on the calm expanse of the lagoon. A splash. Hands reach out of the glittering water, grasp the side of the inflated raft. It rocks. He pulls himself up, balancing on the teetering edge. The raft collapses and I roll into the blood-warm liquid. Below the surface it's bright as noon. Three or four meters below me the lagoon floor is clean white sand, obstructed by boulders, laced with waving weed. A school of brilliant painted fish darts away. I slide over onto my back. A banner of bubbles rises, waves. A flashing web of blue and gold scales interprets the sky. The waterproofed red silk of the raft pushes through it, quicksilver globules of air caught in pockets. Legs thrash by it, then lift through the sky and disappear.

I stare around my new kingdom, dissatisfied. It is bright and shiny, the light of an extraordinary clarity, the water feels deliciously dense in my lungs. Yet something lacks. I can't see far enough. Distance dissolves into haze.

I'm drawn by the rocking red intrusion of the raft. Approaching it stealthily, I move with only the smallest flips of fingers and toes. A foot dangles over the side and into the real world: long, high-arched. I reach out, touch it. It kicks the surface into froth as it disappears.

I push my head through stiff resistance into air, cough my lungs clear.

He stares at me. "Right of conquest," he says.

"It's big enough to share," I say.

"The raft?"

"No, the lagoon." I tip the raft. He spills generously into my arms. We slide easily down. The water rocks around us like a bed. I kiss his chin. He winds his legs about mine. Bubbles of air trapped in body hair make him glisten like a spun-sugar confection. The sandy bottom rises to meet us. We recline there. A parrot-fish hovers above us for a moment.

A curtain of bubbles rises between us as I explore his chest. He smiles beatifically. The bubbles in his crotch are a nest of jewels; his jack rises from it arrogant as a hoarding dragon. His skin slick and soft as the water. My tongue a warm current in the harbor of his mouth. His hand a starfish on my thigh. An octopod, we move as one in senseless pursuit of sensation. He clasps me in. I pin myself deep inside. He grasps and moves me. We scuffle up sand as the strength of our exertions raises us into the liquid light. I reach into him, and reach in, and reach in. He surrounds me and I reach into his core—and am deflected, inevitably. The water boils. The sea floor erupts. Fish flash around us like fireworks. The lagoon thrusts us out into the air and up and in and out and down and down. And down.

An inaudible music sighs into closure. Arael's hands slide from my back. This person, this figure of a man in stovepipe trousers and gray shirt steps away from me. The fairy lights of the Red Room coruscate like the tears in one's eyes. His face is as closed as ever. He smiles distantly. "Thank you, Richard," says le comte, "for the dance."

I reach after him—he's gone. Someone somewhere changes the music crystal; the lights rise; a modulated, transformed whale song quavers through the brilliant air. I look around. I go to the bar. The brawny bartender, split down the center by a line of fluorescence that

355

skews the gaze of his transparent eyes, grins at me, cocksure and amiable.

I'm about to order—chablis, iced, with lime. A finger plays my vertebrae. Pieter leans over my shoulder, says to the bartender, "Two cielazzurros, straight up." He leans against my ear. "And then we'll go home."

We are a conquered people, but there're places you don't expect to see them. They are unfailingly polite and would never, for example, enter a private area without permission. They know their place as well as they know ours. So it is all the more shocking: they're all around.

Pieter holds my drink for me. His eyes are familiar, large, hazel— and not there.

They're all around, but you don't notice them easily.

Carolyn Gilman's science fiction stories have been appearing since 1987 in such places as Full Spectrum, Fantasy & Science Fiction, *and the* Writers of the Future *anthologies. But she has also written several popular books on frontier and American Indian history and has worked as a museum curator and an editor of scholarly books. Her background in those fields seems apparent in this moving, quietly told tale of faith and fanaticism along the new frontier in the stars.*

"Final arguments before the vote?" the town clerk asked.

Two hundred people—almost the whole population of Shiloh Colony—were packed into the chapel. The air was hot and breathless; insects buzzed loud in the swamp outside. Unnamed species careened around the yellow gas lights above the colonists' heads.

The room fell silent as Gideon Jones rose. He felt sweaty and drained from having argued the unpopular side all night. Now he needed to say something that vibrated with the same depth of conviction he felt. He glanced at the blackboard where someone had written, "Resolved: that all residents of Shiloh Colony shall be members of the Faith." It gave him the indignation to speak.

"Friends, this resolution would banish free speech from our community." ("Me!" he wanted to shout. "It would banish me!" But they knew that.) "A diversity of ideas is healthy. Milton once said, 'I cannot praise a fugitive and cloistered virtue, unexercised and unbreathed, that never sallies out to see her adversary.' Whatever you think of dissenters, be tolerant and your own ideas, if true, will become stronger."

He sank back onto the floor, and Rachel Esperanza rose. She had spoken as long and as hard as Gideon, but she still looked electrically charged. Not one hair of her glossy black bob was out of place, and her shirt still looked white against her toast-brown skin.

"I am not a learned person like Mr. Jones," she said. "I cannot quote you great writers."

Gideon winced. She had neatly made him into an elitist.

BURNING BUSH

CAROLYN
GILMAN

She went on. "Do you remember why we left our Earth? Mankind had nearly murdered the mother planet that gave him birth. As a spiritual being, he was almost dead. Centuries of rationalism had blinded him to the Spirit that bound him in harmony to his world and the higher forms of consciousness. When we saw that life-denying science setting out to conquer yet another world, we said, 'No! It will not happen again!' "

Her voice thrilled with conviction, then was suddenly gentle. "Friends, our community has a mission. Our own planet we poisoned, and that crime will be on our consciences forever. But this one we still can cherish. We are here to plant a seed of spirituality. Do not let it die. It is too important."

Gideon dug his big, rough hands into his unruly tangle of hair. The town clerk was passing out the ballots. He took one without much hope. The neighbors he had counted on were avoiding his eye. He wrote "NO" in big block letters and folded the ballot again and again till it was a hard little lump.

The clerk rose to read the results. "We have 137 votes in favor, 14 against. The resolution is passed."

People were rising all around him, but Gideon sat staring at his knees. His back ached. His legs were stiff from sitting on the floor, but he didn't want to get up. A pair of feet stopped in front of him, and he looked up to see George Mendes watching him from dark, grave eyes.

"We weren't voting against you, Gideon," Mendes said softly. "We were voting *for* you, too. This might be a good thing, if you think about it. You need to make a decision."

His intentions were good. Gideon hoisted himself up and put a hand on the man's shoulder, then headed for the door. An animated clump of people was gathered around Rachel Esperanza. Gideon slowed, thinking of saying something conciliatory; but when she looked at him he forgot his intentions. It was like coming near a buzzing transformer; his hair began to prickle. He knew then that she hated him—not his ideas, *him.*

The screen door banged shut behind him, and a cool evening breeze met his face, carrying the faintly ammoniac smell of the swamp. He trudged loose-limbed across the empty mud square, trying to keep from thinking.

Shiloh Colony had changed since he had first arrived, a free-lance technician on contract to set up a methane plant. Then, the village had been a collection of aluminum shanties in the wide, desolate swamp. Now, after eighteen months, it was a circle of orange brick houses, all facing inward toward the domed chapel. By day the houses still looked shabby, half finished; by night they seemed to huddle in a circle for mutual defense. It was night now. Out beyond the buildings the swamp burned with flagrant color. Whorls of luminous gas danced over steaming pools; above, the incandescent clouds flickered with red sheet lightning that never thundered, and never stopped. Uneasy at the sight, Gideon quickened his pace.

He had intended to head to the room above the school where he had been staying since his contract expired; but he turned aside when he saw that Frederick Mabbott, the village doctor, had his electric generator on. Gideon's big work boots clumped loudly on Mabbott's porch steps. He felt relief when he stepped into the brightness of the electric lights, leaving the swamp-glow outside.

Mabbott was nowhere to be seen, so Gideon went to the kitchen and took a bottle of beer from the refrigerator. He wandered through the small clinic and into Mabbott's workshop. There, in the flickering light of a video screen, he found the doctor staring intently at a stop-action tape of the swamp.

Mabbott glanced up as Gideon entered. "I think I've got something this time," he said, his voice high and tense. His bald head was shiny. On the screen, a clump of tube-grass waved like snakes. Mabbott stroked his trim white beard with pudgy, nervous fingers.

"I almost caught one on camera this time," he said. His face was even pinker than usual.

Gideon sank into a chair, stretching out his long legs. He stared at the orange mud on his boots. Mud was everywhere in Shiloh. It crept into houses, onto freshly painted walls, into closets of shined shoes. Everyone called it "the ecology."

Mabbott punched a button, and the image froze. "There it is," he said triumphantly. "See it? Behind the tube-grass. The first evidence of alien intelligence on this planet."

Gideon couldn't see anything where Mabbott was pointing. He looked around the room, cluttered with the incomprehensible detritus of Mabbott's hobby—no, his obsession. He believed in aliens as deeply as the rest of the community believed in the Spirit. The swamp around Shiloh was peppered with his remote cameras and detector boxes: little votive offerings to his faith that man was not alone.

"See?" Mabbott said. "That shadow there. It looks quadripedal, about six inches high, trying to sneak up on the camera." When Gideon didn't react, Mabbott scowled at him. "Is that all you can do? Here I'm making First Contact, you just sit and guzzle my beer." He replayed the scene once more.

"I still can't see anything," Gideon said.

"All right, so it's subtle," Mabbott glowered. "But there *are* life-forms out there. Our mystical neighbors believe it already."

Gideon stared at his beer. "I've got some bad news for you, Fred. They voted to kick us out."

For once, Mabbott was speechless. He glanced around his workshop, then at his screen. He looked panicky. "They can't make *me* leave! I'm their only doctor."

"They discussed that. They decided to promote wellness by cultivating spirit, mind, and body together."

"Rubbish! They'll get scurvy and anemia. They need us. And more like us: agronomists, hydrologists, architects."

"I tried to tell them that. You should have been there."

Mabbott scowled suspiciously. "So they let you speak? What did you do, quote Locke and John Stuart Mill?"

Gideon shifted uncomfortably. He wished he weren't so transparent.

"Damn!" Mabbott brought his fist down on the table, making a collection of microchips and old tea bags jump. "They can't do this! They have such a good start here. Shiloh's the best chance this planet has at a real experimental community. They have all the right ideas: self-sufficiency, voluntary simplicity, participatory democracy. And now they add intolerance. It doesn't make sense."

"They're not a political community," Gideon said. "They're a religious one." He went over to the small window and lifted the metal blind. Pulsing veins stood out in the bloodshot sky. He turned away. "We could always join the Faith."

Mabbott gave an explosive snort. "I've got a picture of me pretending to believe in their dippy macrobiotic mysticism."

Gideon was silent. Mabbott watched him, frowning. "You're not serious, are you?"

"I don't know. This is my *home*, Fred."

Mabbott scratched his beard thoughtfully. "Let me give you some advice. They know you're a godless technocrat. Don't try to outwit them. You have some enemies here, even though you don't know it."

I know of one, Gideon thought. Rachel Esperanza. But why?

When he left Mabbott's house, Gideon stood for a moment on

the porch, not sure which way to turn. Across the circle of houses, the chapel lights still burned. A rhythmic singing drummed through the air.

He felt typecast in his role as town skeptic. The fact was, he liked Shiloh. He cared if it survived. For a while, he had even dared to think it could be the place where he fitted, a home.

But he'd been wrong. He was a stranger here, like everywhere else, always standing on the outside looking in. Now, he would probably drift on, the way he always had. From time to time he would pause to press his nose against the panes of other people's windows, unable to find the key to let him in. And that would be his life.

He clumped down Mabbott's steps. Without his asking them, his feet turned toward the bright, crowded chapel. But halfway there he stopped. What would happen if he walked in? He imagined the music faltering and all eyes turning to watch him, the intruding stranger.

Shaking his unkempt head, he retreated toward his empty room.

Inside the Shiloh chapel, a wildfire faith was burning.

Rachel Esperanza lifted her clenched fists as if in ecstasy, but all she felt was a hungry, unconfessable longing.

The Spirit was palpably there; the air quivered as a hundred souls breathed it in. The lamps burned its presence.

The Spirit was taking them, Rachel saw. This was the flashpoint. The power flowed into the congregation, kindled, and roared.

She looked past her fists to the ceiling. All I have done tonight I have done for You, she cried without words. Enter into me now. Let this be the time. I am ready.

But her senses were treacherously clear. She felt the carpet under her knees, the acrid sting of gas smoke in her nose. She was herself, only herself.

The old anger surged up in her; ashamed, she tried to pray it down. All around her people swayed in the inner currents, possessed. Rachel alone knelt untouched, a stone in a tempest. The Spirit to whom she had given everything, for whom she had done everything, had once again taken all others and passed her by.

What more must I do? she pleaded. But there was no answer. There never had been. The Spirit was around her, outside her, it filled the chapel; everywhere but in her.

363

· · · ·

In the morning light the swamp looked like a still, green prairie stretching to the horizon. The patch of dry ground where Shiloh stood rose like an island above the endless not-water, not-land.

Looking out from her kitchen window, Rachel Esperanza could think of the scene as unspoiled, bucolic, like rural Nicaragua when she was a child. From this distance, she could blot from her mind the writhing tube-grass and the fleshy wormroots that wriggled unpleasantly underfoot. She could feel in harmony with the scene.

Two doors away, Dr. Mabbott was loading crates of electronics into a muddy hovercraft. She smiled grimly and turned back to slicing a green pepper from her garden. We are cutting the apron strings, she thought. Let the old techno-imperialism rule elsewhere on the planet; Shiloh would be free. Free of the soulless, industrial ideology that had impoverished her ancestors and despoiled her homeland. Here there would be no exploitation—only faith, reverence, and harmony.

But she could not shut out the smell of the swamp. It seeped into her mind like a low-level anxiety. She tried to like it, to think of it as natural, but couldn't. Humans were still strangers on this world, after all. This was not their ecosystem.

There was a tap on the kitchen door. Mandy Burke was peering in. The expression on her round, rosy face showed that something was going on. Mandy was always first to know. Shiloh would never need a newspaper while she was around.

Rachel opened the door and asked her in. Mandy shook her head. "No, I can't stay, I've got to get home." She always said that, then usually stood talking for half an hour on the doorstep.

"Did they get the methane collector working?" Rachel asked.

"No. The gas will be out for the rest of the day."

Rachel sighed. Such breakdowns were all too frequent. But she could tell that was not Mandy's news. "What is it?" she asked.

"We are going to have a baptism tomorrow," Mandy said, her voice low. "When the outsiders are gone."

A tingle crept up the back of Rachel's neck. Shiloh's residents did not practice the plain Christian baptism, but something far more demanding and dangerous: the fire baptism. It was outlawed in the city. That anyone survived the rite was a miracle. But that was the point.

"Who will it be?" Rachel whispered.

"Christina Mendes."

"Does her father know?"

"He gave his blessing."

Rachel searched Mandy's face, wondering how much she knew. The secret gnawed at Rachel's mind. Last night a delegation had come to ask if she wanted to test her own faith in the baptism. She had refused. She had been afraid.

"Christina has faith," Rachel said. "She will be all right." But the words felt bitter. Of course Christina had faith. She was just a girl. She'd never known injustice or failure. Let her struggle through the years without reward, without once feeling the personal touch of the Spirit inside her, and *still* keep her faith: then Rachel would believe she was fit.

When Mandy left, Rachel went back to the sink with an angry discontent. At last she snatched a jacket from her closet and left to see what the problem with the methane collector was.

The village was laid out according to a sacred geometry, keyed to the sun and stars. The inner circle of houses was surrounded by paddies where the colonists had beaten back the native tube-grass to raise rice and bamboo in the orange mud, careful to keep the nonindigenous plants from spreading into the larger ecosystem. The methane wells lay beyond the fields, tapping the vast renewable resource of the swamp. Pipes threaded from them to the domed storage tanks just below Shiloh's hill. As Rachel walked toward the tanks, she could see three men standing by the compressor, staring at some dials.

"What's the matter?" she asked.

The men seemed to have talked themselves out. At last Len Yates answered. He was a big Kansan who looked so like a farmer that everyone asked him to fix things; Rachel knew for a fact he was hopeless with machines. "We can't keep the pressure steady," he said.

There was a long pause. "I think we need a new pump," another man said.

"What's the treasury like, Rachel? Can we order one?"

Rachel sighed. This was always happening. "When are we going to start depending on ourselves?" she asked. "We're always going outside for more technology, more expertise."

Len folded his arms uncomfortably. "Yeah. Maybe we should just ask Gideon. He could probably build us a pump with thumbtacks and string."

She tried to sound patient. "Gideon's not going to be around. We have to figure this out ourselves."

Len stared at her. "Haven't you heard? Gideon's staying. He's asked to join the Faith."

365

An old, snarled knot of anger constricted inside Rachel. She had thought it exorcised the night the nonbelievers had been expelled; but now it was back, bitter and familiar.

"They're not taking him seriously, are they?" she asked sharply.

"Sure they are. There's a panel talking to him now in the chapel."

There were four pairs of shoes on the chapel doorstep. Rachel left her own beside them and entered silently across the soft carpet into the main room. Prayer cushions were stacked around the walls, but the center was empty for asanas and sacred dancing. At the far end, where a traditional altar would have been, a stone-lined pit still held the ashes from the last fire-walking ceremony. The plaster wall behind it was yellow from the heat.

Low voices came from a screened-off alcove on one side. When she entered she found four people sitting on cushions in a circle. Gideon Jones was first to see her. Apprehension crossed his face, and he moved as if to stand up. He checked himself when the others did not stir.

Rachel picked up a cushion. Without a word, the others moved to let her into the circle.

No one spoke at first. Gideon fidgeted uncomfortably. Everything about him looked too big: big ears, big nose, big mouth, big hands and feet. He slumped, his spine an unhealthy curve under his T-shirt. Rachel sat absolutely straight, every chakra in line.

At last Gideon spoke. "I'll admit there's a lot I have to learn. I guess I don't know anything about your doctrines."

Rachel waited for someone to correct him, but no one spoke. "Scientists and college professors have doctrines," she said shortly. "We don't."

"What do you mean?" he asked, glancing at her without meeting her eyes. "You must believe in something."

"We don't teach others what to believe. We experience it. Our way of life is our way of worship."

He looked around the circle. "But if I choose to join—"

"No one chooses to become one of us. They are chosen."

"Who by?"

"If you don't know, then you haven't been chosen."

George Mendes was sitting on Rachel's right. His drooping mustache gave him an unhappy look. "Gideon doesn't claim he's been chosen, Rachel. He just feels called to live with us till he knows."

This seemed to encourage Gideon. "I can't very well be chosen till I learn how," he said.

He spoke as if it were a college degree. Take the courses, earn the diploma. The long years of trying and failing flashed through her mind, the years that had forced her to stake out ever-smaller ambitions, smaller hopes. And this man who had never tried spoke as if it would be easy.

"Do you think you can be chosen just by learning some rules?" she said. "You could live like a saint, you could have enough desire in you to make the continents move, and still you would not be chosen unless the Spirit entered you."

He looked at the others, trying to lure them to contradict her. "Is this true?"

Rachel's anger and self-disgust mixed like volatile gases. "Of course, you could always lie, and say you had been chosen. But remember, our ways are dangerous to follow without faith."

Gideon glanced at the fire pit. He looked unsettled. Rachel knew then that she could win. He had fear in him.

"I know your type, Gideon Jones." It felt good to finally say it out loud. "You have no reverence in you. You have only contempt for people who believe the world holds things that can't be proved in a laboratory."

Gideon leaned forward, finally looking at her face. He spoke with an effort, as if it were as hard for him to express sincerity as for her to express hate. "I don't know what I've done to make you think that, Rachel. I love this community. I want to contribute to it. Give me a chance!"

Mendes spoke quietly. "I'm willing to give you a chance, Gideon. You haven't been chosen yet, but there is hope for you."

The other two nodded, looking at Rachel. Only three votes were needed to sponsor a new member; but they rarely went ahead against a strong objection.

"I cannot believe this man is ready," Rachel said. "He has no faith, no humility. He has no real desire."

Gideon gave an inarticulate sound of protest.

"Perhaps we should hold hands for a while," one of the others suggested.

"No, I want to settle this," Gideon said. He had risen to his knees so that he loomed over her. She knew it for a confrontive, patriarchal

367

reaction. "Rachel, what do I have to do to convince you I'm sincere? Tell me."

She sat composedly, refusing to be physically dominated. "Are you really willing to take a risk for the sake of the Faith?"

"Yes."

"Then tomorrow we are going to celebrate the fire baptism. Give your body to the fire, trusting the Spirit to save you, and I will believe you."

He sat back, shocked. Rachel felt a giddy triumph. She had pegged him right; intellectual courage and physical cowardice. He would never do it.

"Rachel!" Mendes was looking at her in dismay. "We can't ask him to do that. It's far beyond most of us."

Rachel looked to Gideon. His face was stiff. "No, it's all right," he said. "If that's what will convince her, that's what I will do."

"We can't allow it!"

"If he wants to do it," Rachel said coolly, "we can't stop him. Gideon, do you truly want to?"

She expected him to back out, but he had a reckless, combative look. "Yes," he said, "that's my choice."

He would not last. She knew the others would offer him plenty of opportunity to back down. And if not, once he saw what was involved, his courage would fail.

She rose. "Then I'll see you at the celebration tomorrow. I hope your sincerity is as great as you say. For your sake."

In his bedroom, Gideon tugged on the white robe they had given him, knowing he would look like a fool. The robe was too small for his big frame, and his work boots stuck out conspicuously. He laughed at the sight of himself in the stainless steel cookie sheet that was his only mirror. For a moment, humor dispelled his dread.

Outside, it was twilight, almost time for the ceremony. As he ambled across the muddy circle, he was acutely aware of glances cast in his direction by others converging on the chapel. He walked out of his way to pass by Mabbott's house. The doctor was supposed to have left that morning, but the hovercraft had broken down. It was now ready to go, and Mabbott was loading his last bits of luggage.

"You look ridiculous," Mabbott said. He slammed a suitcase angrily under a seat.

"Good luck, Fred," Gideon said.

"You're the one who will need it. They're going to see through you, you know."

It was useless to contradict him. Mabbott hadn't believed in Gideon's sincerity any more than Rachel Esperanza had.

"I gather they're having an auto-da-fé tonight." Mabbott glowered toward the chapel. "Take care they don't try to burn any heretics."

Gideon shifted uncomfortably. He hadn't told Mabbott what he had agreed to do. He held out his hand. "Well, good-bye, Fred."

Mabbott didn't look up. "Good-bye. You have my address in case you get fed up with cosmic consciousness."

Gideon turned away. There was no longer any excuse for avoiding the chapel.

He had hoped to finally participate in a service; but when he entered, two church members led him to the same screened alcove where he had sat the day before. Christina Mendes was already there, dressed in a white robe like the one Gideon wore—but snowy clean, where Gideon's had already picked up an orange ring of mud. She sat cross-legged on a cushion, eyes closed. "We'll give you time to prepare yourself," one of his guides whispered.

Gideon sat with his back to the wall, trying to act calm. For a long time the church was silent, as if a group meditation were going on. He watched the girl opposite him; she was motionless as a Botticelli angel, golden hair flowing down over her shoulders. The light from the small window above him faded. Scarlet glints from the evening sky flickered in her hair.

At last he heard a rhythmic thumping from beyond the screen, as of a dance or exercise. Voices began to sound out in ecstatic, jumbled phrases. Something in their timbre unnerved him. They sounded strung tight, like a piano wire about to break.

Two worshipers moved the screen aside and Gideon saw into the chapel. The room was hazy with gas light. The faces turned toward him seemed incandescent. He felt a strange thrill of tension.

From the alcove opposite Gideon's, two men entered with a steaming caldron suspended on shoulder poles between them. On the edge of the ashy fire pit they set it down, then hooked it to a metal winch line hanging from a wheel mounted in the beamed ceiling. With a ratchet clatter they began raising it. As it swayed unsteadily up, one of the men carelessly let a wooden carrying pole pass close to the caldron's surface. With a bright flash, the pole ignited. The man hurried to extinguish it. There was a murmur from the congregation. Whatever the caldron held, it was more than naturally hot.

Christina was standing, eyes bright and glassy. She moved past Gideon on bare feet toward the fire pit. At the edge, her father took her hand and helped her step across onto a small metal platform in the center of the pit, directly underneath the hanging caldron. The men hurried away. For a moment she stood in a motionless tableau, glowing hair cascading down, the bucket of deadly heat poised above her head.

She gave a signal, and a wire tightened. The caldron tipped. With a hiss, a glowing liquid poured onto her head. As it struck her, it exploded into a white fireball. Huge billows of smoke boiled to the ceiling. The overheated air rippled.

Gideon's knuckles were pressed painfully to his teeth. Even from a distance, the heat made his eyes water. The girl's form had disappeared in a fiery pillar. There seemed not a chance she could survive.

The caldron was empty. The fire subsided into the pit below. A strange, tangy smell filled the church. And there, where Gideon had expected to see a charred cinder, stood a girl, eyes closed, a slight, wondering smile on her face. There were gasps as she opened her eyes, then broke her pose to step down from the platform. Her face was flushed, the ends of her hair and the hem of her dress singed—but otherwise she was miraculously untouched.

Wild cheering swept the chapel. Gideon found himself on his feet, applauding with all his heart, taken from himself by wonder.

George Mendes stood by the fire pit. "Is there anyone else who wishes to test their faith?"

Gideon felt paralyzed. He searched the downturned faces. Would they blame him for losing his nerve?

In all the room, only one person was looking at him. Rachel Esperanza's black eyes were like drills aimed at his soul.

A hand from behind gave him a sharp push between the shoulder blades. He stumbled forward, catching himself practically on the edge of the fire pit. He turned back angrily; but there was no one behind him.

"Gideon?" Mendes was staring at him, troubled. "Are you still determined?"

370

Gideon's mind felt off balance. He could sense Rachel's eyes. He heard himself saying, "Yes. I want to go forward."

A tiny, rational part of his mind cried out; but it was overwhelmed by a rush of combative confidence. Some sleight of hand was clearly involved in the spectacle; it couldn't be as dangerous as it looked. They would have to tell him the trick. Then, once he had stepped through the fire, he would never be an outsider again.

Mendes drew him aside as the men prepared for a second ceremony. "Gideon, think clearly about this. It is dangerous. The fire is very real."

"But there is a way to survive," Gideon said.

"Yes. Listen carefully. The fire is not really liquid, but a heavy gas. It will not cling to you or even touch you if you stay perfectly still."

"Where do you get it?" Gideon whispered.

"Never mind. It is very hot. Close your eyes when the caldron tips. Do not breathe it in. It is poisonous. Above all, *do not move!* You will be burned alive if you do."

The room fell utterly silent as the two men emerged from the alcove, a second caldron of fire slung between them. Gideon could see the contents bubbling like angry lava. It had the color of the burning clouds, the smell of the swamp. It was Shiloh's night, distilled and purified. For an instant, he thought he saw shapes moving in the seething fire.

The men hitched the caldron to the cable and winched it up. Gideon watched it rise, swaying like a hypnotizing pendulum. Mendes was looking at him as if his conscience hurt. "Please think hard, Gideon. Don't do this if you're not sure. There are children watching."

But Gideon's mind felt crystal clear. He was buoyed up by a manic confidence. As he stepped across onto the metal platform, he saw that the steel was scorched and blue. He turned to face the audience, aware of the heated pot hanging over his head. Mendes, with a last, reluctant look, moved away.

In that last moment he saw every single face before him in a flash of surpassing clarity. A small girl clutching her mother, ready to hide her eyes. A woman with one hand pressed to her mouth. A bearded elder, face drawn in anxiety and dread. And Rachel Esperanza. But her eyes were no longer diamond bits; they were full of horror. With that sight the real Gideon, the rational Gideon, returned in a rush. *My God, what am I doing?* he thought in panic. His hand jerked, and above him the caldron tipped.

It hit him on the head, hot enough to blister skin off like old paint. He gasped for air and the heat was inside him, flaming down his throat like a blowtorch.

371

Brightness scorched his eyes. Shapes moved in the gas canopy that covered him like a star's corona, burning him, blinding him.

He tried to scream, but his vocal chords were aflame. He tried to raise his hands to shield himself. He was falling like a meteorite, searing the air, falling into night.

The curtains in Rachel Esperanza's bedroom were thick, but they could not keep the night from her mind.

Outside, she knew the sky whirled with mocking colors. Inside, she was locked up with all she stood to lose.

There would be investigations and lawsuits. Now the outside world had its excuse to pounce on Shiloh, to rationalize and regulate. The colony's accomplishments would soon be forfeit. And all because of her stubborn rage against that poor, foolish Gideon Jones.

She sat up on her bed, tense as the memory came back. She had never seen the flames roar so hot, or climb so high. When he fell the people rushed forward, but no one could touch him, for his body glowed like an ingot. And yet when the fire left him he was, barely, alive.

It had burned him capriciously. The palms of his hands, spots on his chest and throat. But worst were his eyes. The lashes and brows were singed and smoking; and when they raised his lids the corneas were opaque. He had been unconscious ever since.

Why had he done it? Rachel's fingers flexed, itching to slap sense into him. She had never intended him to go into the fire. And yet in that final moment when she alone could have stopped him, she had not been able to do it. She had stood and watched him burned alive because she could not say she accepted him without it.

There was a soft tap on the bedroom door. Rachel rallied her energy to answer.

It was Christina. "I think he's rousing," she said.

Rachel followed the girl through the kitchen to the spare bedroom. Rachel had insisted they bring Gideon to her house. Christina and her father had come over to help. Under her smock, the girl still wore the white robe of baptism.

When she entered, Rachel tensed to see an IV rigged up and a blood analyzer on the dresser. Frederick Mabbott's attempt to leave had ended in a second broken-down hovercraft; as soon as he had heard of the accident, he had come over, bringing his medicine of plastic and steel with him. She would have ordered the machines out of her house, but George Mendes had asked her not to.

"It's like a lightning strike, as much as it's like anything," Mabbott was saying to Mendes. "Once we get him rehydrated, we'll see. The EEG seems all right, but we'll need a CAT scan to make sure. The eyes are hopeless. I don't see much alternative but transplant."

No, you wouldn't, Rachel thought fiercely. If the part's broken, replace it like a worn-out gear. Never mind the organic wholeness of the human.

She turned to look at Gideon, and her heart clenched, for his eyes were open. Her skin crawled at the sight. They were like milky opals. For an instant she saw a flash of color deep inside them; then the light changed and it was gone.

At her indrawn breath, the men turned. Mabbott moved to the bedside. "Gideon?" he said. "It's Fred. Can you hear me?"

"Fred?" Gideon's voice was breathy and hoarse.

"How do you feel? Any pain?"

Gideon's head turned, searching. "Where are you?"

"Here. You can't see me."

Mabbott touched his arm. Gideon started and looked down. "That's amazing," he said. "What is this place?"

Rachel came forward. "It's my house, Gideon. Rachel Esperanza. I . . ." She wanted desperately to say she was sorry. But Mabbott was watching her with a grim skepticism. She fell silent.

Gideon shook his shaggy head, then raised a bandaged hand to his temple, as if to still it from spinning. "No," he said gently. "I'm somewhere else. I don't know where, but it's beautiful." He reached out as if to grasp something from the air; his forehead wrinkled in puzzlement.

Christina came forward with a glass of water. Gideon sat up with a smile that made his awkward face seem radiant. "Christina! You were beautiful tonight! You know, I thought I saw you—" He stopped, staring into space.

But Mabbott was frowning, studying him. "Gideon, can you see her?"

"Yes, she's very bright," he said. "I can't make out the rest of you as well." He held out a hand, and Christina took it carefully. "There's something wrong, isn't there?" he asked.

"Yes," she said.

"But it's not me. It's him. It. The thing in the flames."

"What's he talking about?" Mabbott asked. Christina slowly shook her head, her eyes on Gideon's face.

Rachel felt the back of her neck prickle. Surely his words were only the random firings of a damaged brain. They meant nothing.

Mabbott motioned Rachel and Mendes to the door. Out in the kitchen, he planted his feet like a bulldog and said, "We have to get him to a hospital. It's clear there's neurological trauma. I can't treat it here."

Rachel thought of the invasive, dehumanizing medicine he meant, and something in her revolted. Gideon's burns were *hers*, her own cruel gift to him. It was her right to atone for them. "He stays here," she said.

She could see the pressure of flouted arrogance behind Mabbott's eyes. Any moment he would explode. But George Mendes spoke in a plain, soft voice: "I think Rachel may be right. There is a spiritual dimension to this problem. That is best dealt with here."

The doctor's eyes narrowed. "Is there something you haven't told me?"

"No," Mendes replied. "It's just . . ." He glanced toward the bedroom, and Rachel saw the trouble in his eyes. "I think he was not hallucinating; he was actually *seeing* something the rest of us could not."

The words released a surge of jealous yearning Rachel had been trying to keep back. Could the world be so unfair? Had she given him the gift she had longed for?

Beside her, Mabbott's look of suspicion deepened. "What exactly *is* this substance that burned him?" he asked.

"We don't really know," Mendes said. "It comes from the swamp."

"Can I get a sample to study?"

Mendes hesitated. "Are you staying in Shiloh?"

"Is that the bargain? If I keep my mouth shut and don't call in the ambulance, you'll let me stay and study this phenomenon?"

Mendes glanced at Rachel. She nodded. Mabbott would do less harm here than telling tales to the authorities.

"All right," Mabbott said. "I'll give it eight days, till the next communication satellite passes over. If Gideon's no better by then, I'll call for help."

* * *

When everyone had gone, Gideon sat up and unplugged the IV. He felt oddly alert, and curiosity at what he saw consumed him. For a while he just sat watching the whorls of fire curl through the air. Iridescent currents were everywhere. He tried to touch them, but they merely drifted on, glowing but not illuminating the room, making his groping hand look vague and unreal.

His other senses told him he rested in a bed in Rachel Esperanza's house. But the world he had always taken for real—the world of bed-clothes and furniture and walls—looked shadowy, a barrier between him and the vivid world of colors. That other world hung just beyond his reach, like a word on the tip of his tongue, something he couldn't quite remember. But when he tried to concentrate on it, to make sense of the pattern, it slipped away.

He had to know more. He swung his feet out of bed, surprised to see them bandaged like his hands, yet feeling no pain. He opened the shutter to look out.

It was night, but the world outside was a noiseless explosion of light. He stared, awestruck at the bright beauty he had never had the senses to see before. This was not the motionless and passive land-scape he was used to, but a moving, living terrain, dancing, thinking—

As soon as the idea occurred to him, a shiver raced outward from where he stood, vibrating through the pattern. When the kaleidoscope focused again, he knew something sentient was out there, and it had seen him.

Panic stabbed through him. He slammed the shutters, pulled the curtains, then turned—to find his bed still wreathed in drifting colors, just like the ones outside.

It was only then it came home to him—he couldn't get away. This wasn't a night's worth of entertainment; it was his life, forever. Desperately he wanted to declare time out, to say "All right, that's enough, fellows," and have everyone laugh and stop pulling this joke on him, this joke that wasn't really funny anymore.

Rachel was standing beside him, roused by the slam of the shut-ters. "I thought something was out there," he said sheepishly, knowing it would sound crazy.

She didn't laugh. There was a tight-lipped intensity about her. "Of course something was out there," she said. "The Spirit is out there. It is in here, too."

The thought terrified him. There was no place to hide.

A deep red light emanated from her; somehow he knew it was the color of envious longing. "What do you want?" he asked.

"I only want you to go where the Spirit leads," she said. But he could tell it was not the truth.

The next morning, the burns began to hurt in earnest. As the day passed, the scorch marks crept up his arms and legs, blistering skin that had been whole. He lay panting and parched from a high fever, unable to find a position that didn't chafe.

But the outward pain wasn't the worst part. The fire had spread inside him, too, and it was slowly burning away his past. Panicky, Gideon started mooring himself to favorite memories, clinging as long as he could; but before an hour was up, each one would be gone. He could feel his likes and dislikes fading. His personality was growing thin, like smoke.

He didn't dare take the painkillers Mabbott offered him, for fear they would make him groggy, and he would wake to find himself no longer there.

That evening, as Rachel was helping him drink some fruit juice, she said, "The community is holding a prayer meeting for you. Is there anything you want me to say to them?"

Gideon felt a terrible urgency. "Yes!" He clutched her arm. "There's something important."

"Go on."

But it was gone as soon as Gideon tried to think it.

"Let me go there," he said. "I'll think of it, I know."

In the end he got his way. His feet were too swollen to fit in shoes, so Rachel got him some cloth slippers. Leaning on her shoulder, he hobbled out into the twilit village.

The air was still. A thin thread of music came from the chapel, an old Christian hymn tune from deep in the human past. Gideon stopped, aware of the vast, listening swamp around them. For a moment, the song pierced through the fire that swathed him, and the hymn words welled up from a deep reservoir of memory, poignant and familiar. There was a taste like wood smoke in the air—pine wood, campfire smoke from his childhood.

The instant he entered the chapel, he sensed a presence there—not alien now, but familiar. He stood, oblivious of the others, oblivious even of himself. There was a deep well of clear water inside him. A current of air took him by the hand and he followed it, diving down into the crystalline darkness. He became nothing. He was a thought in another brain, a ray of insubstantial light. Out of him erupted such an intense rush of joy that his knees buckled under the load and he flung up his arms, partly to welcome, partly to fend it off.

There was a tumult of voices behind him. He realized he was kneeling near the fire pit. The bandages on his hands itched; he began tearing them off. Someone seized his arm to prevent him, but it was too late. He felt a touch on his heated palm. There was no burn there anymore.

"Listen," he said to the person nearest him. He had to get the words out before he forgot. "This is the message. We are not conscious beings—not yet. We have the potential. I know the way to find it—either slowly, through evolution, or fast, through the fire. The fire can help us. It can burn away our selves and free us. It's not an alien in the fire. It's not different from us. It is our own true being."

It was gone. Gideon began to laugh, the nervous aftermath of the implosion of emotion that had nearly shattered him. He felt weak and shaky, but very pleased with himself.

Hands were reaching out to help him up, to lead him away. He didn't need them. A ripple of air grasped him by the shoulders and steered him firmly from the chapel.

Rachel poured more chicory coffee into George Mendes's cup. He scarcely seemed to notice. He sat at her kitchen table fingering his cup, deep lines running into his dark brows and mustache. Rachel had never seen him look so disturbed.

Mabbott entered the kitchen, closing the bedroom door behind him. "He'll sleep now," he said. He sank down at the table, frowning as he watched Rachel pour. "He's still got a high fever. Other than that, he seems to be in perfect shape."

"No burns?"

"Not a sign of them. Except the eyes. They're the same."

"Then it *was* a miracle," Rachel said. Her voice sounded flat.

Mabbott cradled his cup in pudgy fingers. "This whole thing scares me."

It occurred to Rachel that she and Mendes, the people of faith, ought to be able to reassure Mabbott. A miracle should have made them more sure, not less.

And yet it had not been like any other faith healing she had witnessed. Gideon, who had scarcely been able to walk, had lifted his weight from her shoulder and moved forward, all the light in the room condensing around him. For an instant, his body became only a bright hole in the air, a blinding conduit to elsewhere. In that light, the familiar chapel seemed like a place she had never been before, and herself like a person she had never known.

"I had suspicions before," Mabbott said. "Now I'm virtually certain. Gideon has gotten linked to an Entity we know nothing about. He is the conduit. The question is, what message are we supposed to get? Is it a warning or a friendly hello?"

"I think you're partly right," Mendes said slowly. "I think there is an Entity, and Gideon is linked to it. Call it aliens if you want. I call it by an older name."

A flicker of concern crossed Mabbott's face. "You're talking about demonic possession?"

"There is divine possession, too. If that's what this is, it's a great and terrible gift."

They fell silent. Rachel, too, had the gnawing intuition that something ancient and unknowable was at work. She felt as if the walls of her house were thin as paper and the circle of houses tiny in the waste. What force have I invoked? she wondered. Shiloh is too small to contain such things. Too much alone.

"We need to experiment," Mabbott said at last, unnecessarily loud. "We need to find out what we're dealing with. I propose we take Gideon for a CAT scan and observe whether the effect disappears away from the swamp. If so, we'll know they're using him as a transmitter."

Mendes's face had a set, immovable look. "This has happened here for a reason. The Spirit has become aware of *us*, of Shiloh. We don't understand the message yet, but we need to hear it out all the way."

Mabbott began to bluster. "So you'll deny science the right to know—"

"To know what? The psychologists will say it's a sickness. The anthropologists will say it's a belief. The biologists won't think it's real in the first place. Face it, doctor; they won't believe either of us. We're alone in this."

Mabbott stared morosely at his coffee.

"It's strange," Mendes said. "I used to feel cheated living in these times, because there were no longer any saints in the world. Now I'm afraid God has given us one."

When they had gone, Rachel went into her bedroom and took from her closet a small cardboard shrine. It had been her mother's going-away gift. Back then, she had scorned it as a remnant of the superstitious faith of her childhood. Now, she unfolded it and sat staring at the printed crucifix, finding comfort in its ancientness, its humanity.

She wanted desperately to pray. *Don't do this*, she wanted to beg the figure on the cross. *It's too cruel. He never wanted you, and I did.* But the Spirit had never listened to her before; why should it now?

In the next week, Rachel realized that while the outward scars might be gone, Gideon's ordeal was far from over.

He still seemed restless with pain. He took to wandering around Rachel's house, looking for something. As Rachel worked silently, he asked again and again what she was saying. "I can't hear you!" he insisted. "You're trying to tell me something, but I just can't hear!"

At last Rachel began to wonder if there *were* something she wanted to say. As the days passed, her guilt and envy made a slow metamorphosis. Gideon, who had been her victim and her penance, became something more: a *person*. In the slow afternoons, when she sat reading to him, he seemed familiar as an old friend, and she could imagine a future filled with such peaceful companionship.

But at night he spent hours by the window, watching the sky with his uncanny eyes. One night, she came softly into his bedroom and stood at his side, trying to see what he saw, as if through him she could grasp what had always eluded her.

"What is it you see?" she asked at last.

He paused. "I thought it was a presence at first, a presence that took up the world. But now I think it's just me. The real me."

"What is the real you like?"

"I don't know yet."

"And is there a false you?"

"Of course. Everything I have been. It's not bad, it's just fuel. Fuel for the fire." He looked up, his face half in shadow. His voice was suddenly human again. "I can't do it for you, Rachel. You have to do it yourself."

She flinched to know he had seen through her. But she said, "How?"

"Through the fire. I'm sorry. If I knew another way, I'd tell you."   379

Fear had her by the throat. She stared out into the night, trying to force herself to feel kinship with what lay out there. The Spirit is the same here as on Earth, she told herself. It is the same everywhere. But the flaming clouds stayed alien, and she shivered at their smell.

The next day she returned at sunset from some errands to find her house empty. Quickly she walked over to Mabbott's. The doctor was alone in his workshop, staring at rows of numbers on his computer screen. Rachel had to knock to draw his attention.

He looked up, eyes pouched and gleaming. "Do you see this?" he demanded. "I had the data all along. This swamp is an electrochemical soup, and there are reactions all the time—patterned reactions. Swamp gas, that's what I should have been looking at. The whole damn thing is alive."

"Where is Gideon?" Rachel said.

"He's gone?" Mabbott asked sharply, then quickly started shutting down his machines to help her search.

They met Mandy Burke crossing the square, and as usual she knew something. "Len saw him going toward his old flat," she said.

Rachel and Mabbott climbed the rickety outside stairs together. The room they entered still looked lived in: unmade bed, dishes in the strainer, and books strewn everywhere. Rachel stopped in amazement when she saw that one whole wall was lined with them—real books, Earth books, with a musty paper smell. She wondered how he had gotten them to Shiloh.

Gideon was there, standing tall and ramshackle before the bookcase, staring at the spines. A patch of golden sunset light picked out the faded cloth, the gilt letters. There was a reverence in his pose that made questions seem impertinent.

Quietly, Mabbott moved forward to stand beside him. Rachel realized that they shared a kind of brotherhood in this place.

Gideon took a book down and ran his fingers across the embossed letters on its cover: Bertrand Russell, they said. He opened it to scan a page. But his face changed, and he closed it with a soft whack. "I don't know what it means anymore," he whispered.

A flash of pain crossed Mabbott's face, as if he had just heard of the death of a friend.

"I was looking for something," Gideon said. "I thought it might be here. But there is nothing here. Nothing."

Carefully he placed the book back on the shelf, then turned to the door. He passed Rachel as if he didn't see her.

Mabbott was staring after him. "We're losing him," he said.

"I know," Rachel answered softly.

"It's not worth it, not for all the knowledge in the world. Damn it, he's my *friend*."

Rachel turned away so he couldn't see her face, or guess the pang his words gave her.

When Rachel got home, she found Gideon sitting on the porch, staring fixedly ahead of him. She sat down beside him.

"They weren't just books," he said at last. "They were friends. They were the only ones who never let me down." He turned his strange, opaque eyes on her, and she saw how lost he was. "You know what I'm afraid of?" he said. "I'm afraid I'll finally get wherever I'm going, and I'll be alone. Totally alone."

Rachel wanted to take his hand and say, "I'll be with you." But it would have been a lie.

That night, Rachel looked in to see if he were asleep. She went quietly to his bedside, half fearing to see signs of an unknowable presence. But all she saw on Gideon's sleeping face was exhaustion.

On a sudden inner bidding she bent over and let her lips touch his forehead, then drew away guiltily. But he didn't stir; he would never know.

She no longer cared about the mystery that had taken hold of him. She cared about *him*, the person. Her caring was growing with every day. And yet she could feel him slipping away, dissolving like sugar on the tongue. He was becoming alien just when she was learning to be human.

The swamp burned unusually bright for several nights. For Gideon the display was mesmerizing. At dusk, as everyone was closing their curtains, he went to sit on the hillside to see the landscape come alive. And every night he knew the fire would come back to burn more of him away.

One evening, Gideon realized he almost understood the patterns of light. They were beckoning him. If he raised his hand, they responded in intricate moiré patterns.

An air current tugged at him. It was a lead, and he needed urgently to follow it. He closed his eyes and let the air take him.

He moved like a blown leaf, trusting the air not to let him stumble. When he felt cold water seeping into his boots, surprise made him open his eyes. The thread of wind gave out. He was standing in an empty, open spot far out in the swamp, under a vast arch of sky. The sun had gone down, but the sky was still light. All was silent until some bubbles broke the surface of a pool nearby.

At sight of the desolation, his old self cried out in fear. He wasn't ready to be alone here. Not yet. The horizon looked the same everywhere, but he knew instinctively where Shiloh lay. He turned back.

The air was immediately alive with insects. The ground that had seemed so easy to traverse was now a mass of clutching, wormlike roots. He sank ankle-deep in orange mud with every sucking step. He was soon exhausted and cold.

Night had fallen by the time he saw a man's shape outlined against the glowing mist, and heard his name called hoarsely. When he came up, he saw it was George Mendes. There was fear in the man's normally sensible face.

"Gideon!" he said. "I saw you running into the swamp, and followed. Where did you go?"

"Nowhere. I had to come back."

There was a bright, silent flash near them as a wisp of mist ignited. Mendes recoiled.

"We'd better get out of here," Gideon said. "Take my hand."

All around, the night was uncannily bright. The underbellies of the clouds seemed to be sagging low.

Gideon could see the lights of Shiloh in the distance when he realized they were being followed. He slowed to look back, but Mendes said in a cracked voice, "No, Gideon! Go on!"

Something in his voice made Gideon obey. Their shadows splayed out before them as they leaped forward. Mendes was ahead now, dragging Gideon by the hand. Gideon could feel heat on his back, a pressing fever-heat. He wanted to stop.

The hill of Shiloh was just ahead. Mendes pulled him up like a dead weight. Someone shouted, and there were people around them, frightened faces, nervous words. At last Gideon turned to see what they had been fleeing.

In a ring all around Shiloh the swamp was aflame. Not the cool luminous flame of mist, but a fierce, white-hot wall without a break. The village was surrounded.

"Is it coming nearer?" someone shouted.

"No, it's stopped now," came the answer.

Gideon felt a terrible certainty that the ring of flame had to do with him. His future lay out there, beyond that blazing boundary. He realized he was shaking when a still hand touched his arm. He looked down to see Rachel beside him.

"What is it?" she asked.

"I don't want to go through it again," he said.

"Go through what?"

"The fire."

"You don't have to. No one wants you to. Come home, Gideon. The fire's not coming any closer."

He wanted to believe her. But as he turned to follow her he felt he was hauling along heavy, dead shreds of himself, like an old skin that couldn't slough off.

Mabbott called the city for help the next day.

The fire had left a charred circle through the rice paddies and bamboo fields around Shiloh. For meters in every direction the plants were cooked. And the people who talked to George Mendes came away looking grave. Not even Mandy Burke would repeat his story.

It was two days before the helicopter arrived, and each night the ring of fire returned, tightening around the village. In the end it was not an ambulance that came, but a huge evacuation helicopter. When it settled down outside the chapel, a line of people assembled, carrying backpacks and suitcases, to be ferried back to safety.

Gideon watched from Rachel's porch. It was all wrong, all backwards. He didn't want them to be afraid.

Mabbott was leading a man and woman in flight suits toward him. They were obviously not from Shiloh; their clothes had never seen mud. Gideon willed them not to see him. They mounted the steps and walked past him into the house.

He was still watching that afternoon when they loaded the helicopter and started to take off. The rotors had barely gotten to full speed before the engine gave a piercing whine and died. The pilot got out to look for the trouble, but Gideon knew it would be useless.

The daylight no longer hid things from him. The mud glowed like lava, and the houses were translucent. The village was a blanket hung in front of a fire; the light showed through the gaps in the weave. Every object was bursting with rays of divine essence, hidden till now under a shroud of matter.

When twilight came, the people gathered in the chapel, seeking safety in song. But Gideon still stood on Rachel's doorstep, half en-

383

tranced, half terrified. Out across the swamp wisps of fire gathered. Soon they would surround the village.

"Come to the chapel, Gideon." Rachel stood beside him.

He had never yet joined them in worship. He wanted to. Rachel had gone down the steps, and was waiting for him to follow. He took a step forward. Rainbows swirled in the air around him, and he stopped. How could he join them now? He was scarcely human.

"Gideon?" Rachel was staring at him.

A fierce pang of loneliness gripped him. He realized there were tears on his cheeks. He brushed them away, and saw they glowed in the dark.

It was useless, this pretending to be human. There was no solution, except to give up the part of him that still cared.

He turned to the swamp. Rachel cried out his name, but it didn't really mean him anymore.

It was like tearing through clinging brambles; parts of his personality kept catching on him, and he had to pull free. But no, it wasn't really the brambles that clung to him, but him that clung to the brambles. He had to let go.

When he saw the wall of fire ahead, its reflection dancing in the water under it, the sharp memory of pain brought him to a halt.

"Gideon!"

He looked back. She had fetched the people from the chapel; they stood in a crowd at the edge of Shiloh's hill, watching.

The part of him that was still human was shaking in terror. "Will someone come with me?" he asked.

No one moved.

Rachel stood there, out in front of them all. He held out a hand to her. "Hold my hand, Rachel. Please."

She hesitated, then started forward, then stopped.

It seemed as if she was immensely far from him, too far for mere arms and hands to reach.

He turned. The fire was freedom. Freedom from himself, and therefore from all loneliness.

From where the crowd stood on the hillside, his figure was silhouetted against the wall of bright fire. When he stepped in, the flames shot up to the clouds, bright as a welding torch. The people turned away, shading their faces from the heat, their shadows painted on the grass. Suddenly there was darkness and they turned back, blinking the afterglow away. The wall of fire was gone. The field where it had been was empty.

The next day when the helicopter was ready to leave, Rachel was first in line. She had with her only the belongings she could carry; she didn't want to bring back memories.

George Mendes shook her hand before she boarded. "You can always come back," he said. "We will be here."

Rachel shook her head. "I'm not ready to be a saint. I have to try out being a person first."

As she sat inside, waiting for the takeoff, she could feel the emptiness inside her. Last night, there had been an instant when she could have brought Gideon back from the edge of the fire, or walked with him into it. She could have had either the Spirit or true humanity. She had chosen neither.

As the helicopter rose into the air, she looked down on the circle of Shiloh and felt like a total stranger.

It's a theme as old as H. G. Wells's War of the Worlds: *what will happen to us when the aliens come?* But there's no theme in science fiction so old that a fresh new treatment can't invigorate it, as Lou Fisher deftly shows within the space of four thousand words here.

His stories have been in Galaxy, Terrors, Shadows, Aboriginal SF, *and other magazines and anthologies. His most recent novel is* The Blue Ice Pilot, *published in 1986.*

METAL TEETH

LOU
FISHER

One night Freddy followed me all the way across Tinker Street to Loryanne's little loft, but I told him he couldn't come up. Insulted, pouty, he sat on the porch steps, and hours later when I stumbled down, he was still there, waiting, like a doormat that's been kicked aside. " 'Bout time, pal," he said. He sure was dreamy: sprawled across the steps, shoes unlaced, hair blown around, and probably feeling as if he had as many eyes as the aliens.

After I sat him up, we shared another vial. A sip for him, a sip for me, and so on. He asked, "Hey, was this a big night?" and I had to make up some lurid details. Loryanne did this. I did that. Some of it of course was true.

"That Loryanne," I said.

Listening, Freddy leaned first against me and then against the porch post. "If you could run away with Loryanne"—he gave me a bleary wink—"to a place where the aliens couldn't find you . . ."

"No," I said.

"Hey, why not?"

"They'd find us."

"You think?"

I nodded. "That's what Docto-Darr says." I knelt down and in a few fumbling minutes retied Freddy's shoelaces, not perfectly but at least together. When I straightened, I could see that the sky was brightening; yes, beyond Freddy's narrow face and through the thick grove of trees, the sky was brightening, and, hooray, we'd made it to another dawn in the little village of Woodstock. Not that the morning mattered. If any of the old farts were waiting for me to open the luncheonette, well, it was just a bad and useless habit. "Anyway," I went on, "how would we know where to go? We could run right into a reduction."

"Yeah." Freddy rolled his eyes. "Yeah, pal. Imagine."

"And Loryanne," I added, "she'd rather stay here and draw. She likes the way the light hits the loft in the middle of the afternoon."

"You think?"

Again I nodded. Freddy nodded, too, with his neck and rounded shoulders and all. He opened his eyes a little wider and tried to take a deep breath, and when he couldn't, he coughed, just once, and leaned away from me to grope for another vial. "Enough for now," I said, pulling him to his feet. We helped each other off the porch. Then, as the sun rose, we swayed down Tinker Street, side by side, talking, laughing, groaning, hitting each other on the arms . . . friends. Well, big deal, you might say—but I haven't had many friends. Not many who stayed around. When I first arrived in Woodstock, I was asked, as I wandered kind of alone and lost down that same section of Tinker Street, to join Amnesty International. Hmmm, I said, can you help me find my father? and they said no.

So for a friend, I have Freddy.

Oh, I suppose I'm just as bad as he is when it comes to taking dope. The only difference is, he has more time for it. Like the nights when I'm at Loryanne's.

How ugly are the aliens?

Depends who you are, and no one agrees. The old farts say the aliens don't look any worse than some of the rock bands of their generation.

Maybe it even depends *where* you are. Who knows how you take to them in your part of the country.

But Freddy, he goes crazy just looking at their eyes. Those chunks of crystal, clear and icy, wedged and wicked, are embedded above what we think are flesh-and-bone cheeks, and spaced—now, this is what gets Freddy—all the way around the head. Since alien heads, like ours, come in different sizes, each alien has as many eyes as needed to complete the circle. Not that it's easy to take a count. You know, even if you run around an alien, you can never see more than a few eyes at a time. Freddy says the range is from seven to twelve, but he can't guarantee it.

"You stand in back of that guy," Freddy said on one Examination Day, "and I'll stand in front."

But as I walked around behind the alien, he watched me from eye to eye and then gazed at me with the three that remained. "The possible consequences of this involvement are second nature," he said, in a way that made me hustle back to where I'd been, right next to Freddy.

The possible consequences . . . All right, the aliens have gone from initial grunts to attempts at language. But what do they say? Even Docto-Darr, who's the main alien rep and their TV spokesperson, seems no more coherent than those who just carry the laserods.

"Let's try it again," Freddy said.

"Not me."

"Well, hey, you stay here and I'll go around."

I shrugged, but he didn't go. Deep down, he's as leery as I am. Maybe one day, though, we'll send Loryanne.

She and some of the girls in Woodstock always check out the aliens' sleek silver pants, looking for bulges, and wondering. And once when we were at the Green picking up our quota of nutritive pills, Loryanne tried to snatch the glove off an alien's hand, to see what the fingers were like. She didn't succeed, mainly because of a laserod that got pointed into the valley between her breasts.

"What would you do," I asked her as we hurried away, "if one of them came after you?"

"You mean, for my body?"

"Yeah."

"Well, I'd have to let him," she said.

"You'd *have to*?"

"Sure." She tilted her head and for a moment looked up at the clouds. She had one of those perfect chins, like you see on cheerleaders or English teachers, and because she was a little on the plump side, her cheeks were full, pink; her whole face glowed as she considered the prospects. "Sure," she said.

There was a twinge in my neck. I rubbed it. "Suppose you got pregnant?"

"With an alien?"

"Yeah."

"Oh, wow!" she said. Then she paused to chew on her tongue. "A big baby, though. Probably rip me apart."

I agreed with that.

389

The aliens are bigger than almost anybody I know, and their ships are like Pentagon buildings in the sky. Every day we see the ships streaming in, coming from wherever they come from, more and more, sometimes low enough to spray crazy shadows right where we stand. One of the old farts, a gray-haired guy named Winters, says that even though the aliens are big and tall, they don't really need such gigantic ships. The ships are just an efficient means of packaging. The same way, he says, that thousands of vials of dope come in a single carton. You can see, Winters goes on, how the aliens now manage to fit pretty well in our Blazers and Cadillacs and helicopters.

The dogs in town do not bark at the aliens.

Personally, I am only repulsed by their metal teeth. The fact that these teeth would have to be manufactured makes me wonder what, on their own world, they were born with, and what they were born to consume. The metal teeth must have been a planned improvement, but an improvement over what? Frankly, when I first saw the aliens, I worried that between their metal teeth and their so-called program of reduction, we, the earthfolks, were going to be their food supply. But, no, mainly they eat trees.

In the beginning Docto-Darr asked where the dope came from and who was paying for it. All right, I can't be sure that's what he asked—"Is inactivity a free matter of life?"—but one interpretation is as good as another.

The discussion took place during Docto-Darr's first trip to Woodstock. That particular afternoon we were lined up at the curb as if for a parade, though they were watching us as much as we were watching them. Freddy, who was standing next to me at the time, thought he understood Docto-Darr and answered boldly, "Hey, dope just grows." I had to remind Freddy that it doesn't grow in vials. Someone else suggested that the dope was still original stock from Vietnam. Docto-Darr laughed at that and said, "How much experience is experience?" At least it seemed like a laugh. On them, you can't really tell a grin from a nine-eyed frown, a smile from a gnashing of metal teeth. Nor can you figure out what exactly any alien is trying to tell you. The way most of them talk, they would have been wiser to stick to their grunts, I would think.

As soon as Docto-Darr passed by, Loryanne reached across Freddy and tugged at my sleeve. "Jesus—from *Nam*." Her eyes widened, then narrowed, and her fingernails went through the sleeve to my arm. "Did you hear that? Your father was in Nam, you said. Funny if he used this same batch of dope."

390

"You think?" asked Freddy, to her, then to me.

I shook my head. "No, they had to smoke it, or sniff it, or something. Back then."

And who knows if my father was really in Vietnam. No one could keep track of him: not the government, not his family, not the downtown bar where he ran a tab. My mother got a divorce on grounds of desertion, but then she died. And me?—well, at seventeen, I was in Icelandic waters on a Greenpeace ship.

As for the dope, best I can figure it's kind of a Woodstock heritage, another habit of the old farts who always used dope here in secret and never named the sources. Last week we heard a rumor that the aliens were manufacturing the stuff at the former IBM plant in Kingston, and sending it up here in a panel truck with graffiti bleeding through the blue overpaint, and, yes, I've seen that truck. But so much for rumors. We checked it out, Freddy and me. We walked down to Kingston—took us all day—and what we saw at nightfall was the whole complex of twenty-some buildings surrounded by barbed wire and under control of the aliens. But they were making weapons there. Stacks of laserods. Truckloads of laserods. Anyone who thinks that aliens would forgo even one laserod in order to make dope, well, they just don't know aliens.

To make sure, I stopped the blue panel truck one day and asked the old fart who was driving what exactly he was about, and he said, "In the course of doing this three or four times a week, I have developed an attitude of secrecy, and my fees, in general, are low. Quite low." Obviously, he was trying to talk like an alien, as if that would get him off the hook. But I scrunched up his shirt collar in my fist and asked him directly where he got the dope, or else, and finally when his face turned red he blurted out, "At a pier in New York City."

Ah, yes.

I got off the Greenpeace ship at a pier in New York City, and then hitched my way up to Woodstock. At that time I was fixed with the idea of becoming a poet, an artist, even a musician. As it turned out, what I did was work full-time with Freddy at the luncheonette. Until the aliens came.

We called it a luncheonette, but the boss and I opened up at seven o'clock in the morning and the doors didn't close until eight or so at night, which meant we served breakfast and dinner, too, though dinner, as you might expect, was just the organic lunch at higher prices.

391

Freddy and I worked any and all hours. For us, the luncheonette was more a hangout than a job. For the old farts, too, who would sit strung along the counter and complain about how cheap the tourists were, while in the whole morning they themselves would buy only a single donut apiece and never fail to hold out their cups for coffee refills. The money, the profits, came mainly from tourists. Nicely dressed, they came into town to browse the shops, to buy a drawing from Loryanne, even to sign up for writing workshops or guitar lessons.

Some tourists, like the weekenders from Manhattan, would stop in the luncheonette to ask where the famous rock concert was held, and we had to tell them, well, that wasn't really in Woodstock, that was on a farm far out of town.

"Hey," Freddy would say to their disappointed faces, "we're hippies here just the same."

They'd give him, you know, that look. And I would come over from maybe waiting on a booth or washing glasses at the sink.

"Listen, my dad was there," I would lie. "And did he have a time. Rocked all night. *All* night. In the rain. Let me tell you about the bandstand that sunk in the mud." If we were lucky, we'd get the tourists to sit down and look at a menu.

For several days after the aliens landed, the luncheonette remained open for business. The boss thought maybe we'd stay open, didn't see why not, everything seemed peaceable, and maybe we'd add to the menu an alien special, like metal-teeth stew. But by the middle of the second week, we had closed, closed for good, and so had all the other restaurants in town, as well as the souvenir shops, the library, the veterinary clinic, the art galleries, the bookstores, and the movie theater. Of course, the movie theater had been on its last legs anyway.

At least once a day Freddy would stand in front of the closed luncheonette.

"Damn," he'd say if I came by.

I'd put my hand on his shoulder. "I thought you were happy about not working."

"Hey, I am. Hell, yes."

Still, I'd have to stand with him for a while, looking in the windows, seeing the stopped clock on the far wall, the row of empty seats, the reflection of light off the coffee urn. Stand there and look . . . think, too. Sooner or later Freddy would clench his teeth and throw up his hands, and then at last we'd leave. Sometimes, from there, we'd go over to the Green and talk to old fart Winters, about aliens.

. . .

The problem with the aliens is that they want to be in charge. Landed in just about every major city, but really poured onto Washington, and there it was on TV: the wheel-shaped ships, the tall aliens who towered over the President and Secretary of State, and the U.S. Army kind of laid back on its heels. In fact, at no point that day did the army attempt to test their guns against laserods. Not after they saw some potent examples, like the instant disintegration of the entire White House.

Even on a small TV, that was impressive.

Next thing we knew Docto-Darr rolled into New York State, with parades and speeches and closings and special monthly Examination Days. We heard thirdhand through supposed eyewitnesses that there were pockets of resistance. The students at Cornell—well, as we now say, the *poor* students at Cornell. Some earthfolks, you know, are pretty combative when it comes to giving up their rights. Others, like Freddy, say, what the hell, let the aliens have everything, they're doing a better job, aren't they? Free dope. Nutritive pills. No work. Sure, you can say that when you're not the ones being reduced. But who is, is anyone? The aliens just call their program *reduction*. Oh, they *try* to explain, like one of them on Examination Day said, "It is the difference between collusion and maintenance," and on TV Docto-Darr refers to "a strand of reduction . . . the need takes the cure." Go figure that out. All I know is that earthfolks have to contribute, or volunteer, or line up, and I hope they don't call on me soon. Docto-Darr informs us, over and over, that we shouldn't take it personally— "Not you as person, as human, just multiple for us." And, personally, I don't. Of course, I'm high most of the time and that's all I ask. Leave me high and leave me out of the reduction.

The same for Freddy and Loryanne.

A lot of the old farts get so damned excited when they hear of another city reduced, as if they can prove anything really happened. Disintegration, they claim—a laser sweep. Even the *bones*. Well, sure, believe what you want. If a reduction happened close by, like Kingston or Poughkeepsie, we could probably send someone to take a look and report back, but so far we've only got word of mouth to go on, and always about someplace farther west or way down south. The closest was Buffalo.

"Where's that?" asked Loryanne, in bed with me.

I said, "Near Cleveland."

393

Her blue-gray eyes studied me dazedly.

I told her, "That way," and pointed over my shoulder.

She didn't look in that direction. Not for the rest of the night.

On TV and radio, Docto-Darr never discusses specific events. If you listen to him carefully, you still don't know. There is something more general, more worldly, I think, about his announcements; about making room for millions or billions of aliens.

How much room will they need?

But Freddy says, "Hey, we don't have to work anymore. We get fed full and doped up." He says that's okay. Some of the old farts see it differently, but wouldn't you know it, they're the ones who are always grabbing most of the dope for themselves.

The old farts like to sit around in the library. The books are gone but the shelves are there, a handy place now to stash their belongings. Still there, too, are the chairs and tables, and good southeast light from the windows. What they talk about in the library is videotaped, of course, which is the only way the aliens will let them get together, but even off on their own, what would they say, that bunch of old farts. Sure, if you run into any of them individually, as I did with Winters, he's likely to whisper something subversive. "We can hide out in the Catskills," he told me one day on his way to the library. It wasn't an idea I could appreciate, because even in such low mountains you can get cold and wet and hungry for pizza. Please, Winters, I thought, don't ask me to live off the land. "Rabbit," he said, "and deer." And, no, don't ask me to shoot animals—wasn't I on a Greenpeace ship, and didn't we *ram* those relentless whalers. Where would I get a gun, anyway? According to Winters, armed remnants of the U.S. Army are supposed to be holed up, plotting something, in the old government-made caverns near Boulder, Colorado. Maybe so. Maybe not. I mean, if they're that far underground, who can tell? And okay, say it's true—they're still more likely, I think, to suffocate than uprise.

On another day when I was just walking down the street, Winters grabbed my elbow and came up breathing in my ear: "They're not letting anyone in or out of Manhattan!" As if I'd care. I'm the last guy to want to go into the city, or to have a visit here from, say, a stockbroker. What we have in common with Manhattan is that when it comes to getting doped up, they're our biggest competitor. So who needs them?

Some of the old farts sneak off to Bearsville right before Examination Day and sneak back afterward. When I hear them claim to be unrecorded, I wonder, though. Aren't the aliens aware that that can be done? I believe you're better off playing it straight, not calling special attention to yourself, standing *in front* of the aliens, and, if asked, you never heard of Bearsville.

But I have to admit, if it weren't for Winters and his old fart friends, we wouldn't get much news of what the aliens are up to, and we would probably never think about subversion or flight. Sometimes, something inside tells me we should pay a little more attention. Climb the fence at the old IBM plant. Get our hands on a crate of laserods. How do you suppose a laserod works—is there a trigger? Or maybe we could find someplace to go, just Loryanne and Freddy and me. That wouldn't be a conspiracy, would it? If just we three slipped away? But when I ask Freddy he says, "We'd have to go too far. They got Albany, they got New York City, they got Philadelphia. And Buffalo's just gone, you know what I mean? Besides, pal, the worst part—hey, listen, you leave here, you leave the dope." So I have to nod and agree. True. No work. No taxes. No escape. I don't know about the old farts, but the rest of us are more interested in just staying high and passing the day.

Except Loryanne. She has been drawing the aliens in charcoal and has them posted all over her loft and in a thick fourteen-by-twenty-inch portfolio.

Every so often I ask her to marry me, and she says no.

"Come off it," she says.

But I get to feeling that I owe her a commitment. After the year on the Greenpeace ship I was so removed from any sexual action that all I did the first few months I knew Loryanne was serve her coffee in the luncheonette. "What do you say, Lory—warm it up for you?" But she came around every day, early and late. Soon she stopped bringing the sketch pad. Then she began wearing scoop-necked blouses and leaning in across the counter, and things like that.

"We could get married," I said, up in her loft for the very first time and out of breath on top of her.

Loryanne looked at me, well, as if I were crazy.

"You *want* to?"

"Uh-huh."

"How much?"

I rolled over on the bed so that I was looking up at the ceiling. "Not much," I said. "How about you?"

Loryanne clicked her tongue.

"Artists don't get married," she told me. "Offends the muse, you know."

On Examination Day the aliens ask no questions about marital status. From that, I assume we do not need their permission. We could live in her loft. I could put up with the smells of paint and turpentine and fixative. Maybe pose for her when the aliens weren't around. So I go on asking Loryanne to marry me, not every time I see her, not every night I'm there, but now and then when I feel too much in debt; though frankly it would worry me more than anything if she ever said yes.

To tell you the truth, she gives it to a couple of the old farts, too, and I'm sure she even has her eye, impossibly, on some of the aliens.

We have Examination Day once a month, but aren't the dates always different? And I seem to remember that the first two were held on Fridays, then the ones after that on other days, even a Sunday, so you can see there is no kind of routine unless the schedule is according to some alien calendar. You would think, now that they're here, they would need to use a calendar based on the rotation of Earth, based on the distance to our sun, but evidently, even among aliens, ties to the past are important. Anyway, it was Docto-Darr in person who started off the examinations, though he doesn't bother much with us any more now that he's the big-deal state rep. In fact, the alien examiners seem to change every time, the only similarity being that there are twenty-two of them, twenty of whom are armed with those laserods.

The other two have clipboards in their gloved hands. We line up, and they ask questions.

"Last living month, were you there?"

"What income dollars by any much?"

"Has loose dope in hand?"

"Pills or meals what?"

"How scanned Docto-Darr with network?"

We line up and answer, truthfully, untruthfully, it seems not to matter. I once said my meal consisted of turkey and Morse Code, and they didn't even blink. All they do is, they make little scratches on the clipboard with an odd little scratcher, but I doubt that any of our answers are actually being retained. So where does all this get them? Personally, I think the exam is a show—put up, put on—so that we know they are right here, that they are watching us, keeping track of us, letting their presence be known.

Comes Examination Day, we really get doped up. The higher we are, the better the aliens seem to like us. If that's the case, us guys in Woodstock, old farts included, could turn out to be survivors. Stay high, then. Dig in, wait for a turn of events . . . But no, on this month's Examination Day, the old fart Winters knocks the clipboard out of an alien's hand; and as it hits the ground, Winters and three of his cheering old fart friends vanish before our eyes.

Examination Day continues, hardly interrupted.

But right the morning after, Freddy looks at the shut-down luncheonette and says, "Hey, let's walk to Colorado." And I'm for it, I guess, so I go over to tell Loryanne.